子連れ狼

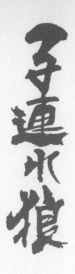

LONE WOLF AND CUB

子連れ狼

story
KAZUO KOIKE

art
GOSEKI KOJIMA

DARK HORSE COMICS

translation
DANA LEWIS

lettering & retouch
DIGITAL CHAMELEON

cover artwork
FRANK MILLER with **LYNN VARLEY**

publisher
MIKE RICHARDSON

editor
MIKE HANSEN

assistant editor
TIM ERVIN-GORE

consulting editor
TOREN SMITH for **STUDIO PROTEUS**

book design
DARIN FABRICK

art director
MARK COX

Published by Dark Horse Comics, Inc., in association
with MegaHouse and Koike Shoin Publishing Company., Ltd.

Dark Horse Comics, Inc.
10956 SE Main Street, Milwaukie, OR 97222
www.darkhorse.com

First edition: May 2001
ISBN: 1-56971-510-6

1 3 5 7 9 10 8 6 4 2

Printed in Canada

Lone Wolf and Cub Vol. 9: Echo of the Assassin

To find a comics shop in your area, call the
Comic Shop Locator Service toll-free at 1-888-266-4226

ECHO OF THE ASSASSIN

子連れ狼

By KAZUO KOIKE
& GOSEKI KOJIMA

VOLUME

9

A NOTE TO READERS

Lone Wolf and Cub is famous for its carefully researched re-creation of Edo-Period Japan. To preserve the flavor of the work, we have chosen to retain many Edo-Period terms that have no direct equivalents in English. Japanese is written in a mix of Chinese ideograms and a syllabic writing system, resulting in numerous synonyms. In the glossary, you may encounter words with multiple meanings. These are words written with Chinese ideograms that are pronounced the same but carry different meanings. A Japanese reader seeing the different ideograms would know instantly which meaning it is, but these synonyms can cause confusion when Japanese is spelled out in our alphabet. *O-yurushi o* (please forgive us)!

LONE WOLF AND CUB

TABLE OF CONTENTS

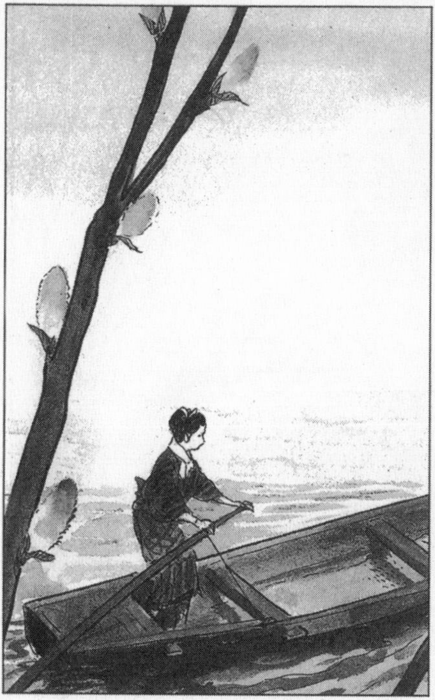

the forty-fifth

Wife of the Heart

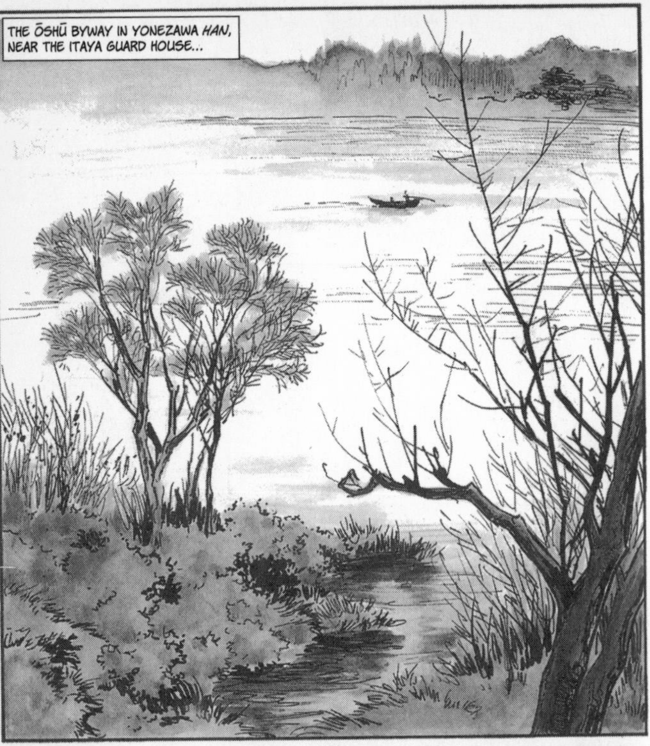
THE ŌSHŪ BYWAY IN YONEZAWA *HAN*, NEAR THE ITAYA GUARD HOUSE...
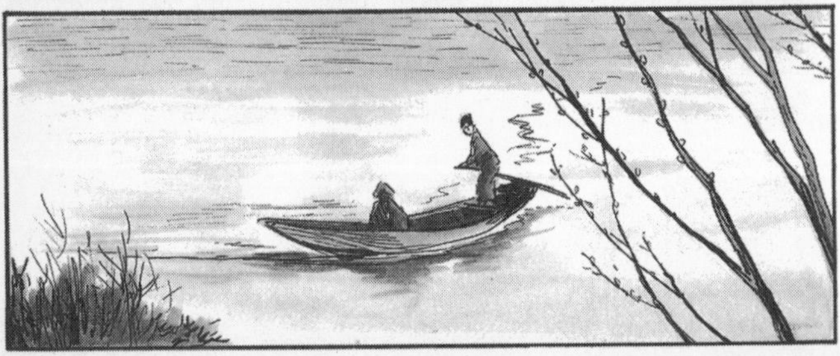

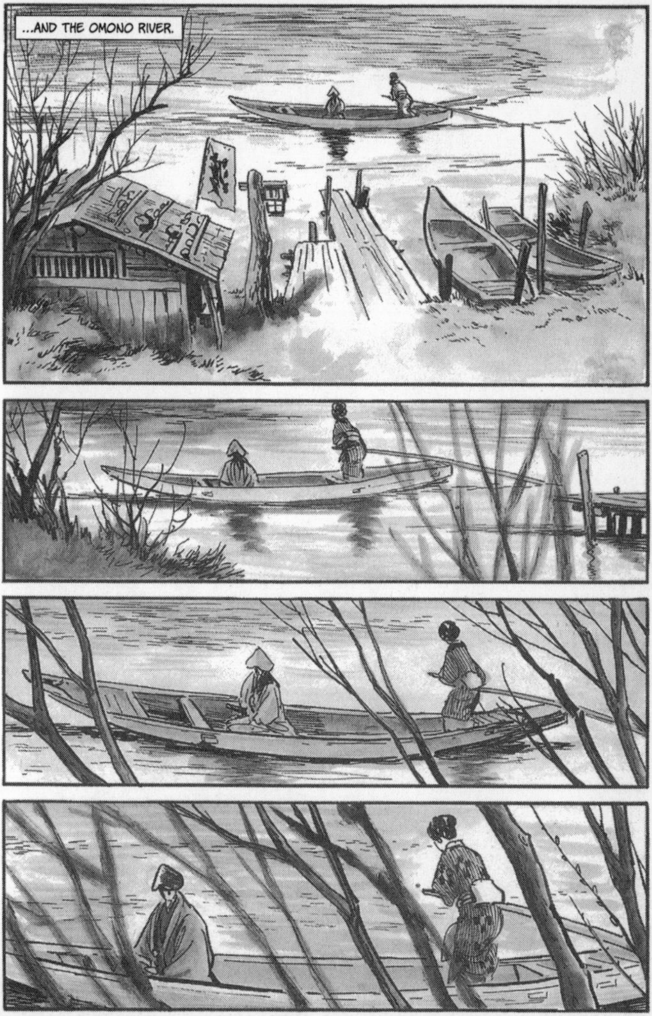
...AND THE OMONO RIVER.

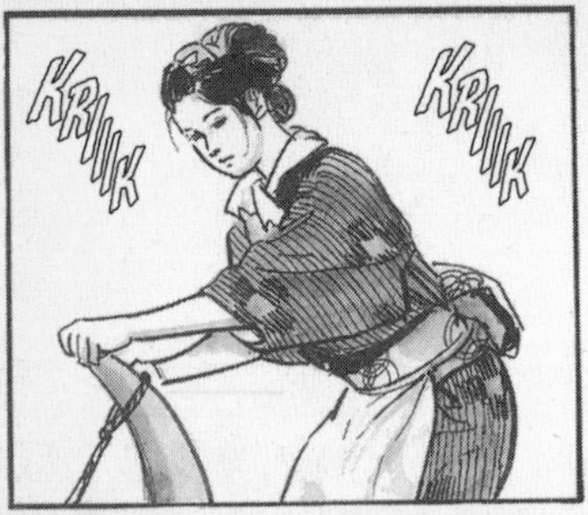
KRIIIK
KRIIIK
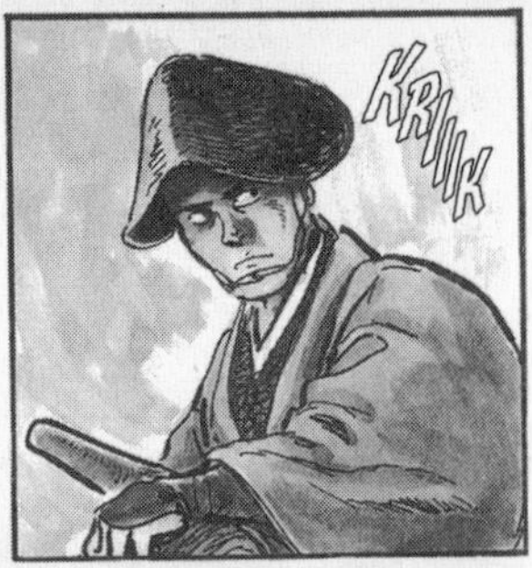
KRIIIK
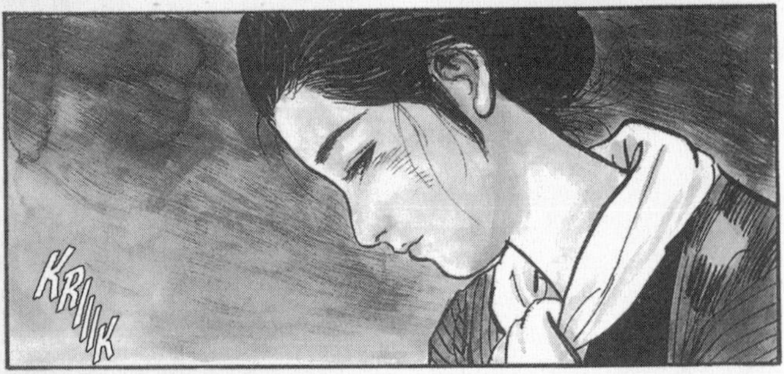
KRIIIK
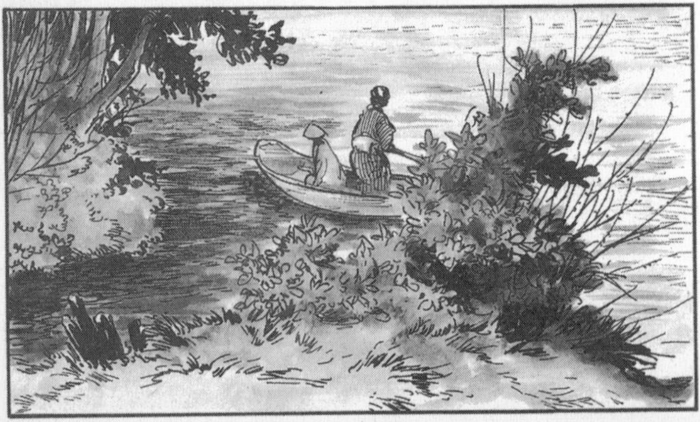

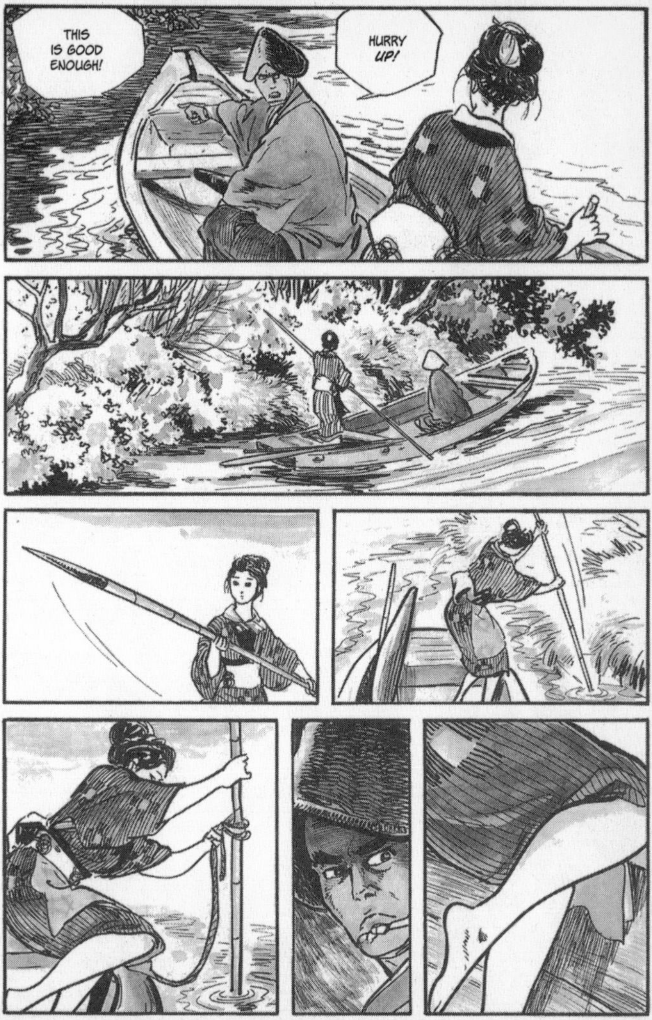
THIS IS GOOD ENOUGH!
HURRY *UP!*

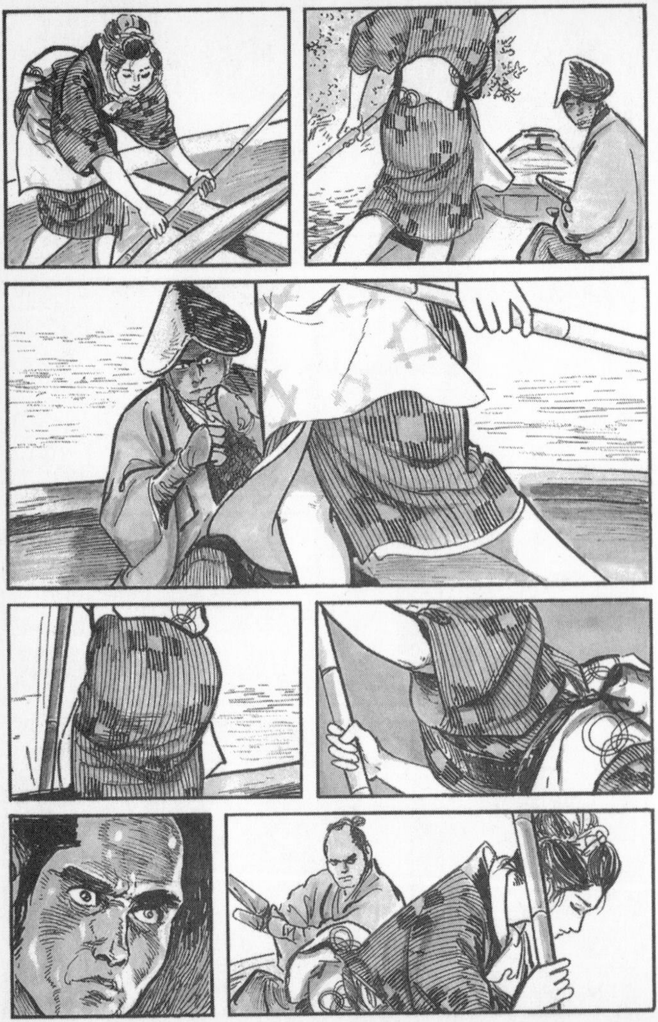

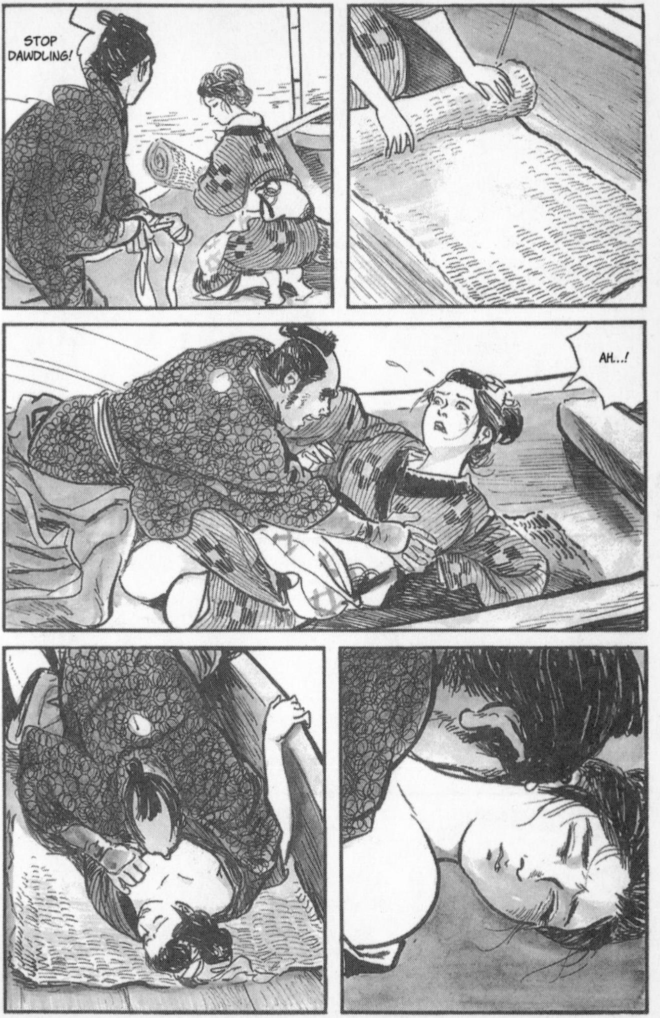
STOP DAWDLING!
AH...!

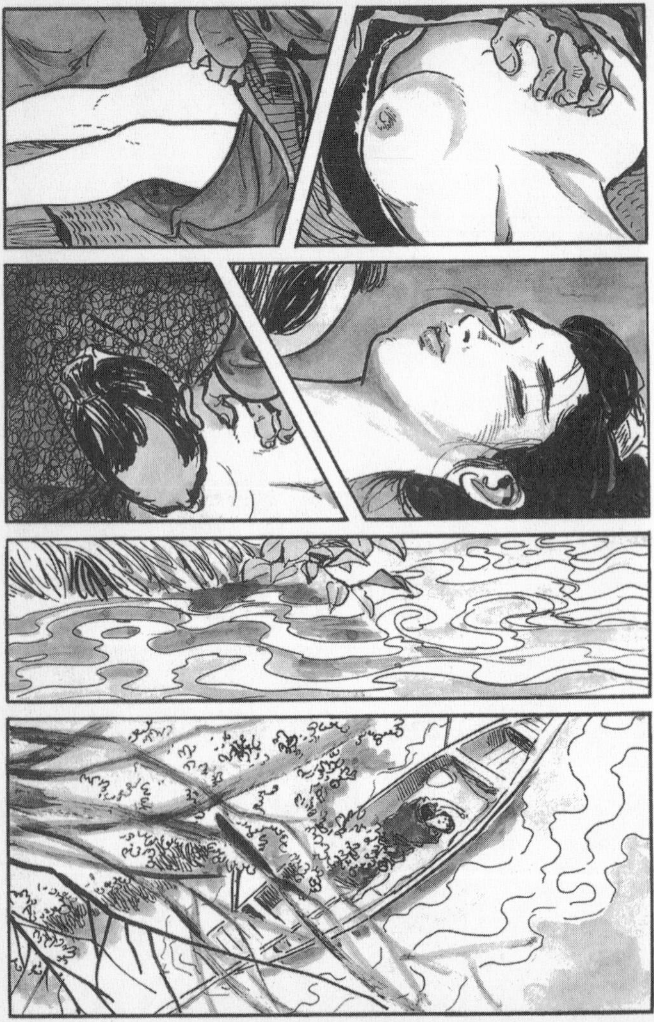

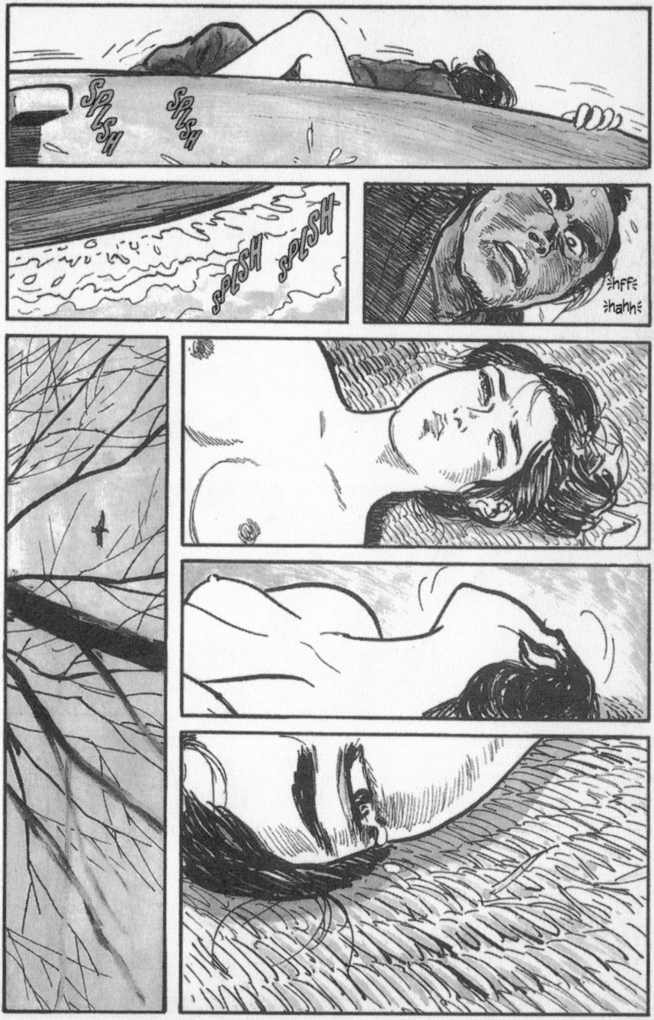
SPLSH
SPLSH
SPLSH
SPLSH
hff
hahh

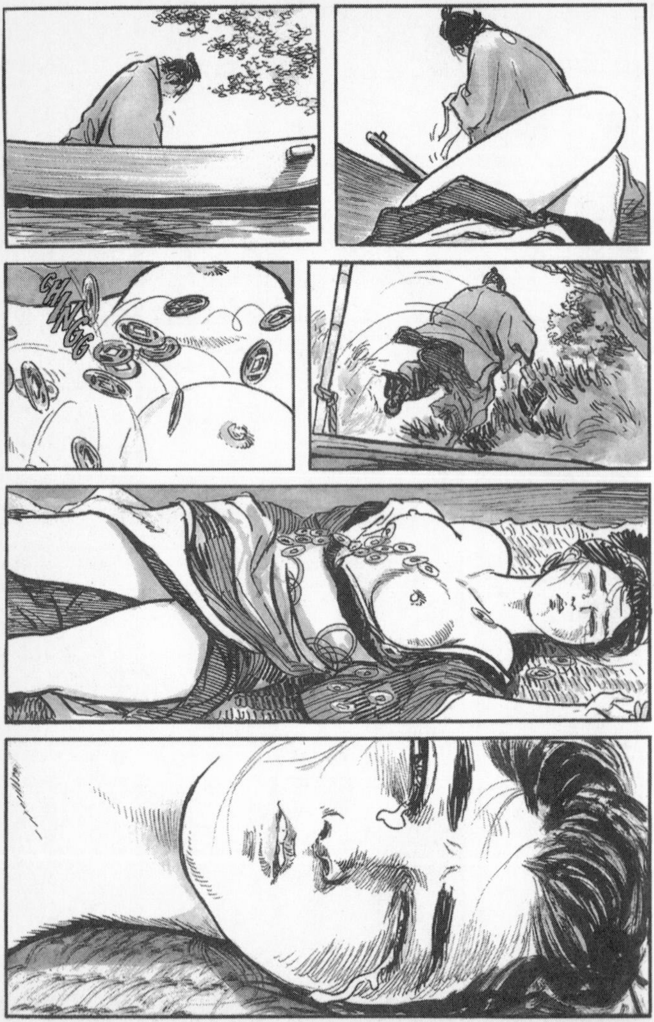
CHINGG

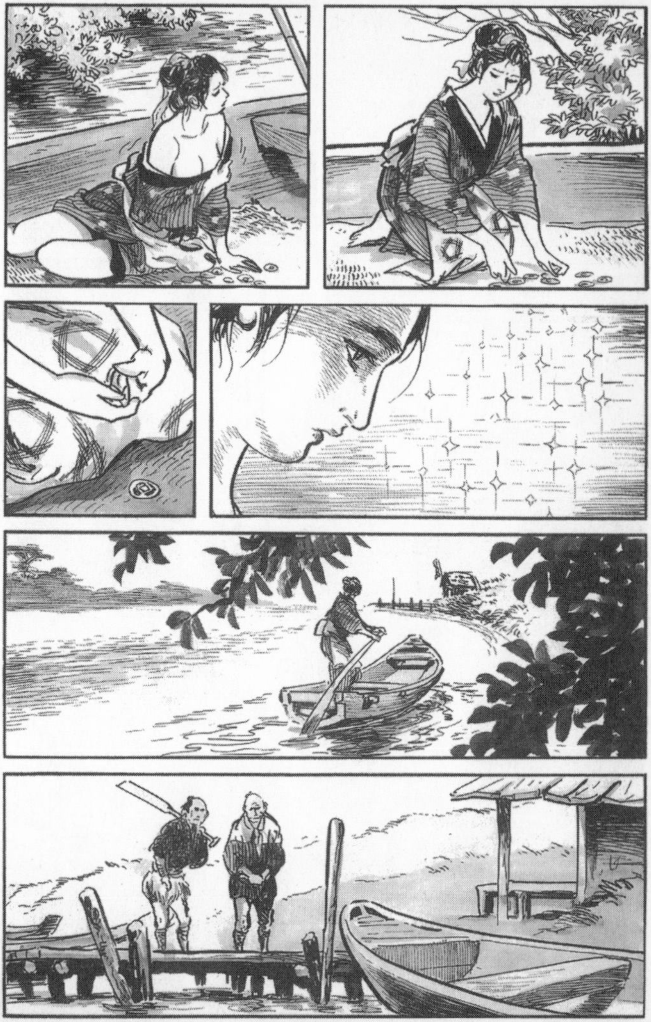

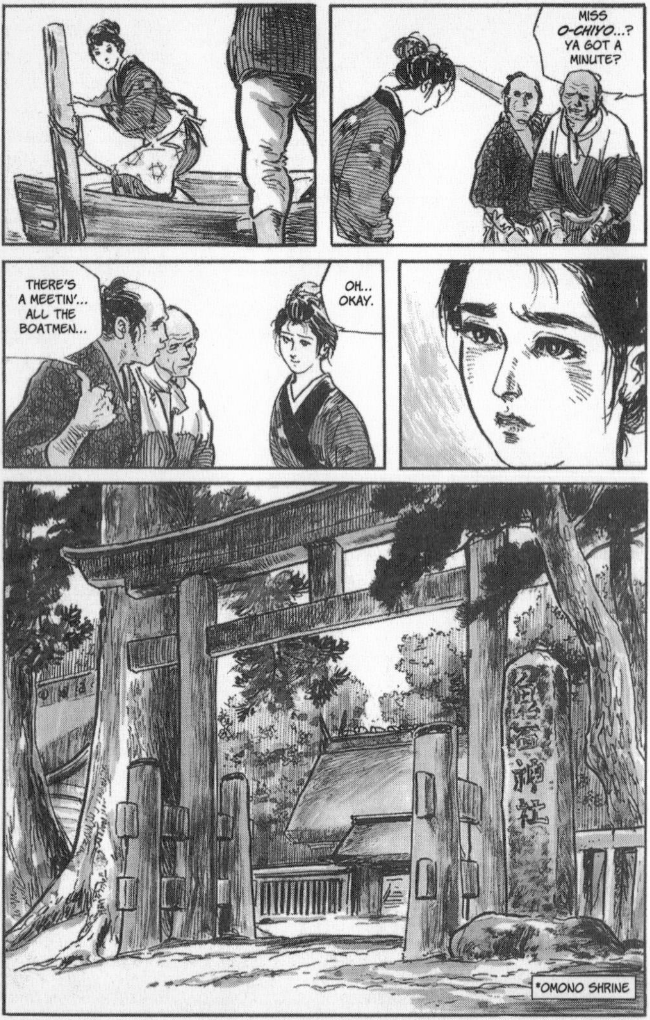
MISS O-CHIYO...? YA GOT A MINUTE?
THERE'S A MEETIN'... ALL THE BOATMEN...
OH... OKAY.
*OMONO SHRINE

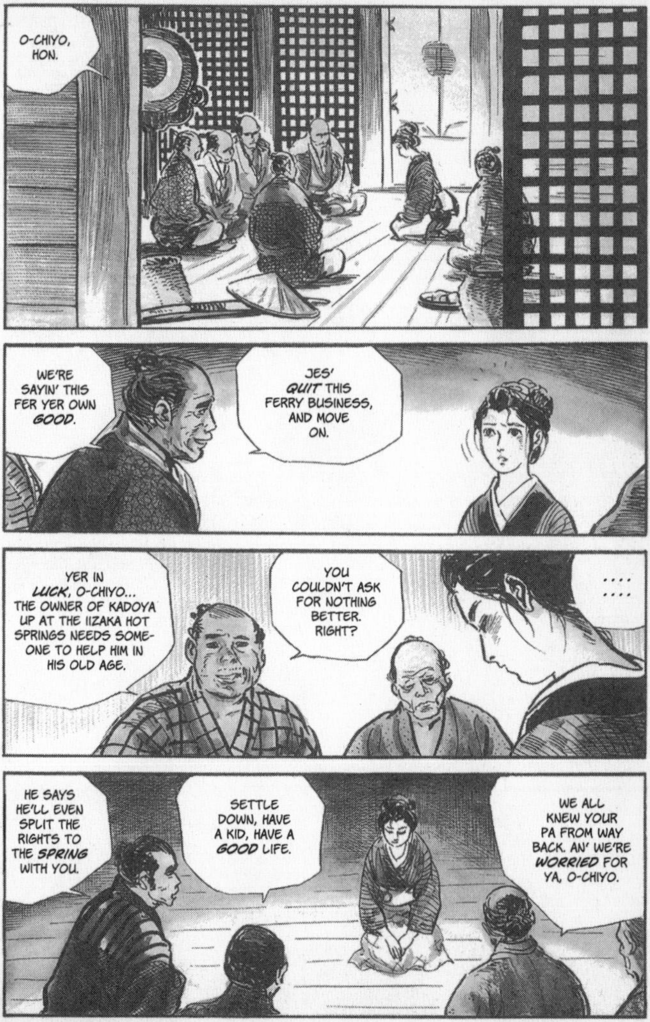
O-CHIYO, HON.
WE'RE SAYIN' THIS FER YER OWN GOOD.
JES' QUIT THIS FERRY BUSINESS, AND MOVE ON.
YER IN LUCK, O-CHIYO... THE OWNER OF KADOYA UP AT THE IIZAKA HOT SPRINGS NEEDS SOME-ONE TO HELP HIM IN HIS OLD AGE.
YOU COULDN'T ASK FOR NOTHING BETTER. RIGHT?
....
HE SAYS HE'LL EVEN SPLIT THE RIGHTS TO THE SPRING WITH YOU.
SETTLE DOWN, HAVE A KID, HAVE A GOOD LIFE.
WE ALL KNEW YOUR PA FROM WAY BACK. AN' WE'RE WORRIED FOR YA, O-CHIYO.

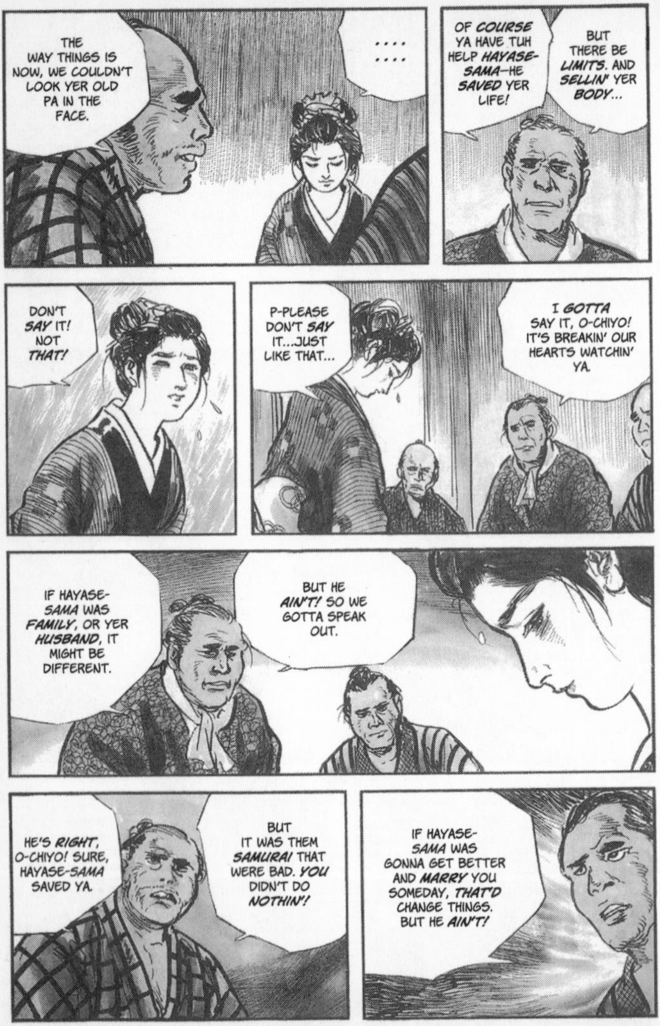
THE WAY THINGS IS NOW, WE COULDN'T LOOK YER OLD PA IN THE FACE.
....
....
OF COURSE YA HAVE TUH HELP HAYASE-SAMA—HE SAVED YER LIFE!
BUT THERE BE LIMITS. AND SELLIN' YER BODY...
DON'T SAY IT! NOT THAT!
P-PLEASE DON'T SAY IT...JUST LIKE THAT...
I GOTTA SAY IT, O-CHIYO! IT'S BREAKIN' OUR HEARTS WATCHIN' YA.
IF HAYASE-SAMA WAS FAMILY, OR YER HUSBAND, IT MIGHT BE DIFFERENT.
BUT HE AIN'T! SO WE GOTTA SPEAK OUT.
HE'S RIGHT, O-CHIYO! SURE, HAYASE-SAMA SAVED YA.
BUT IT WAS THEM SAMURAI THAT WERE BAD. YOU DIDN'T DO NOTHIN'!
IF HAYASE-SAMA WAS GONNA GET BETTER AND MARRY YOU SOMEDAY, THAT'D CHANGE THINGS. BUT HE AIN'T!

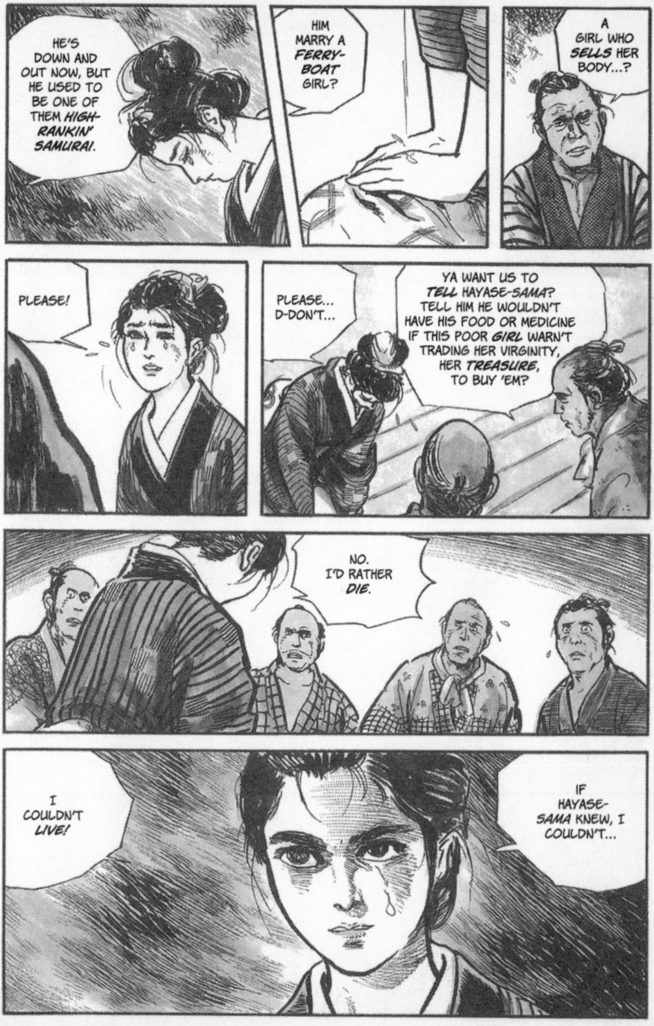
HE'S DOWN AND OUT NOW, BUT HE USED TO BE ONE OF THEM HIGH-RANKIN' SAMURAI.
HIM MARRY A FERRY-BOAT GIRL?
A GIRL WHO SELLS HER BODY...?
PLEASE!
PLEASE... D-DON'T...
YA WANT US TO TELL HAYASE-SAMA? TELL HIM HE WOULDN'T HAVE HIS FOOD OR MEDICINE IF THIS POOR GIRL WARN'T TRADING HER VIRGINITY, HER TREASURE, TO BUY 'EM?
NO. I'D RATHER DIE.
I COULDN'T LIVE!
IF HAYASE-SAMA KNEW, I COULDN'T...

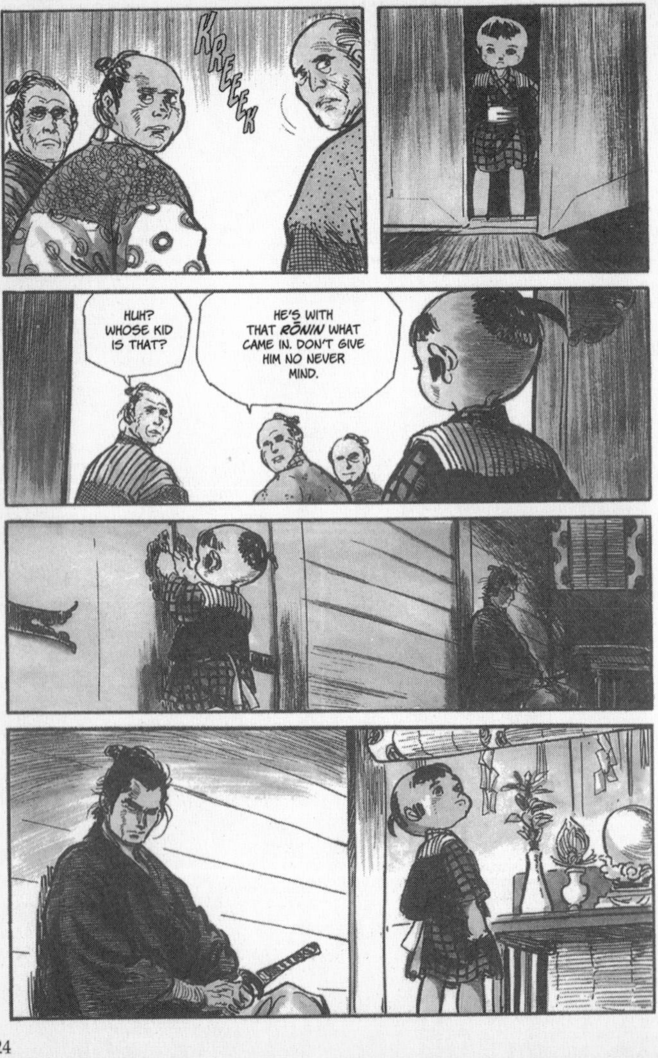
KREEEK
HUH? WHOSE KID IS THAT?
HE'S WITH THAT *RŌNIN* WHAT CAME IN. DON'T GIVE HIM NO NEVER MIND.

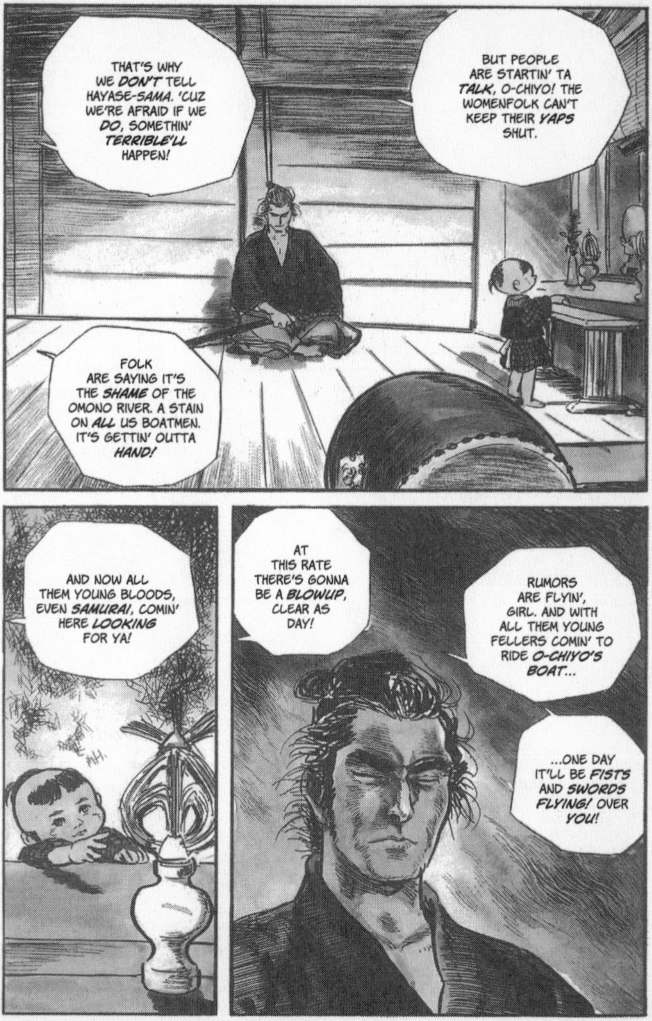
THAT'S WHY WE DON'T TELL HAYASE-SAMA. 'CUZ WE'RE AFRAID IF WE DO, SOMETHIN' TERRIBLE'LL HAPPEN!
BUT PEOPLE ARE STARTIN' TA TALK, O-CHIYO! THE WOMENFOLK CAN'T KEEP THEIR YAPS SHUT.
FOLK ARE SAYING IT'S THE SHAME OF THE OMONO RIVER. A STAIN ON ALL US BOATMEN. IT'S GETTIN' OUTTA HAND!
AND NOW ALL THEM YOUNG BLOODS, EVEN SAMURAI, COMIN' HERE LOOKING FOR YA!
AT THIS RATE THERE'S GONNA BE A BLOWUP, CLEAR AS DAY!
RUMORS ARE FLYIN', GIRL. AND WITH ALL THEM YOUNG FELLERS COMIN' TO RIDE O-CHIYO'S BOAT...
...ONE DAY IT'LL BE FISTS AND SWORDS FLYING! OVER YOU!

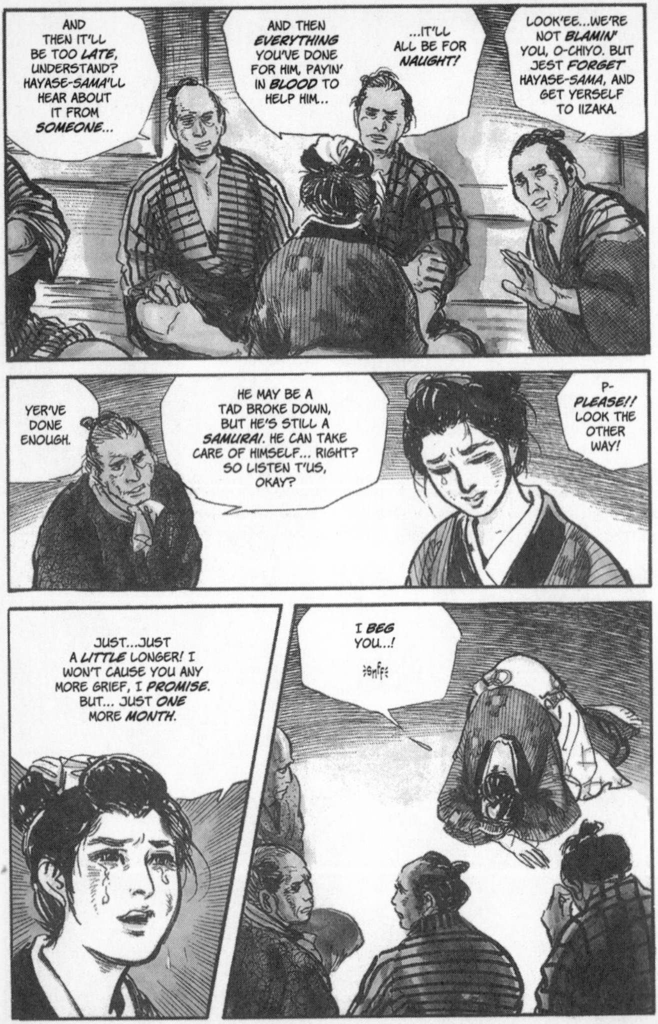
AND THEN IT'LL BE TOO LATE, UNDERSTAND? HAYASE-SAMA'LL HEAR ABOUT IT FROM SOMEONE...
AND THEN EVERYTHING YOU'VE DONE FOR HIM, PAYIN' IN BLOOD TO HELP HIM...
...IT'LL ALL BE FOR NAUGHT!
LOOK'EE...WE'RE NOT BLAMIN' YOU, O-CHIYO. BUT JEST FORGET HAYASE-SAMA, AND GET YERSELF TO IIZAKA.
YER'VE DONE ENOUGH.
HE MAY BE A TAD BROKE DOWN, BUT HE'S STILL A SAMURAI. HE CAN TAKE CARE OF HIMSELF... RIGHT? SO LISTEN T'US, OKAY?
P-PLEASE!! LOOK THE OTHER WAY!
JUST...JUST A LITTLE LONGER! I WON'T CAUSE YOU ANY MORE GRIEF, I PROMISE. BUT... JUST ONE MORE MONTH.
I BEG YOU...!
SNFF

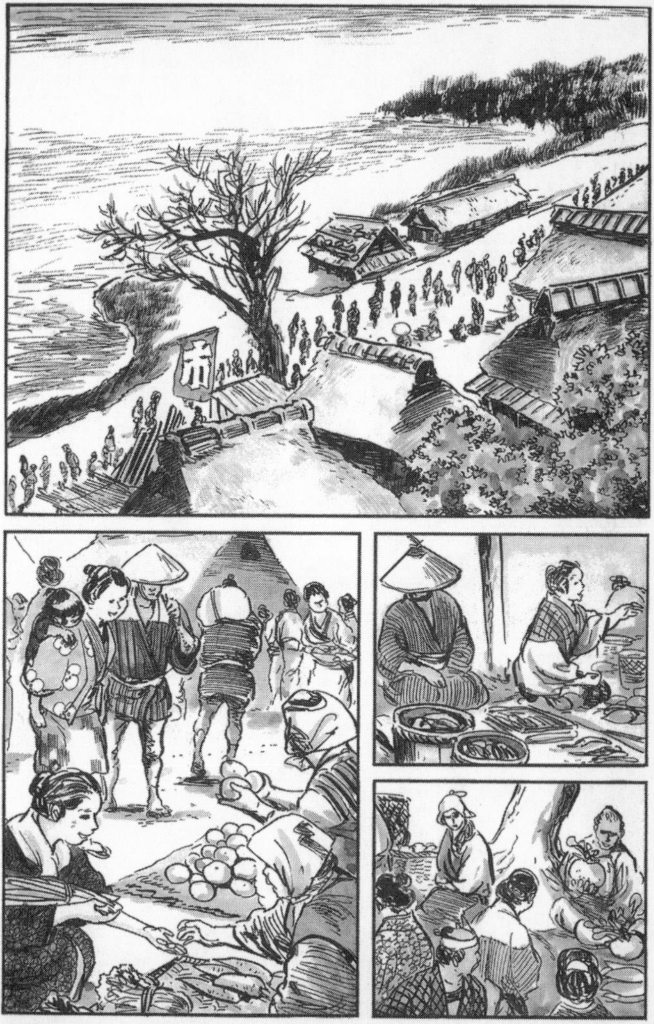
市

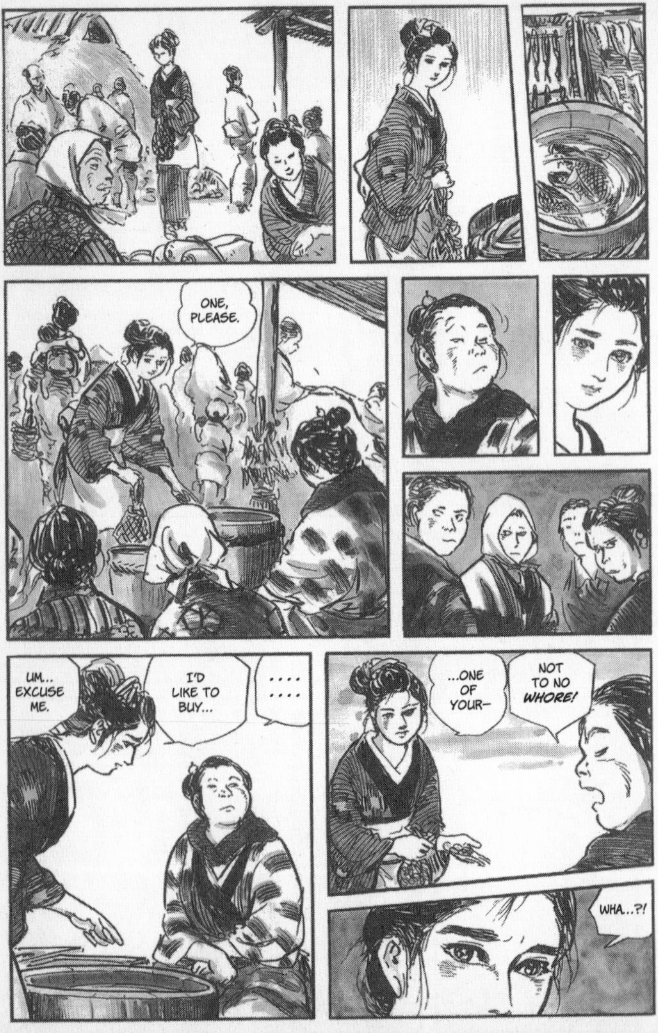
ONE, PLEASE.
UM... EXCUSE ME.
I'D LIKE TO BUY...
....
....
...ONE OF YOUR—
NOT TO NO WHORE!
WHA...?!

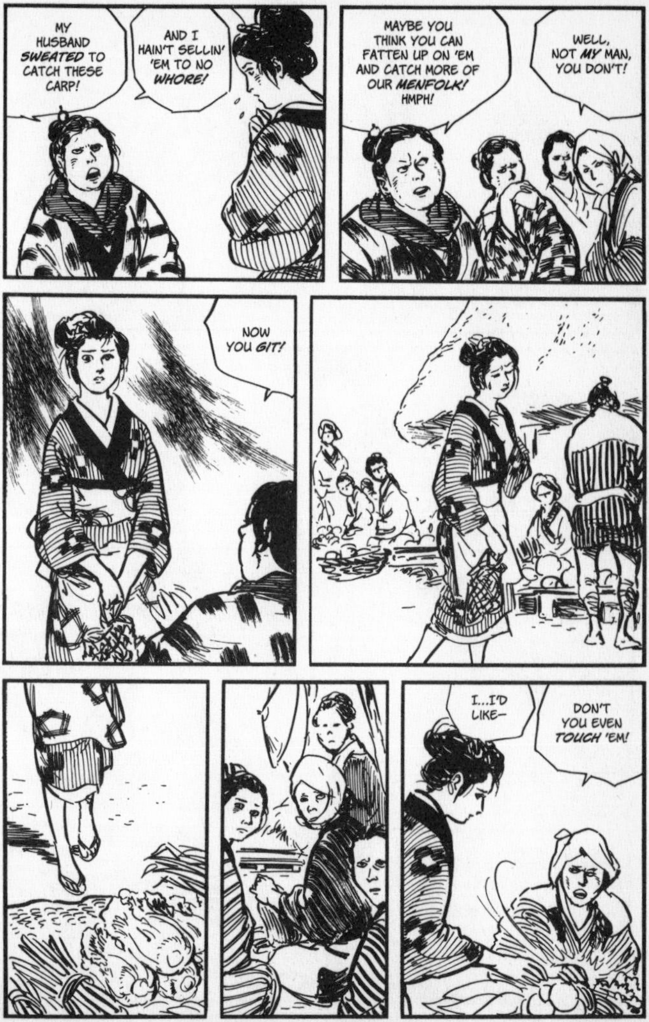
MY HUSBAND SWEATED TO CATCH THESE CARP!
AND I HAIN'T SELLIN' 'EM TO NO WHORE!
MAYBE YOU THINK YOU CAN FATTEN UP ON 'EM AND CATCH MORE OF OUR MENFOLK! HMPH!
WELL, NOT MY MAN, YOU DON'T!
NOW YOU GIT!
I...I'D LIKE–
DON'T YOU EVEN TOUCH 'EM!

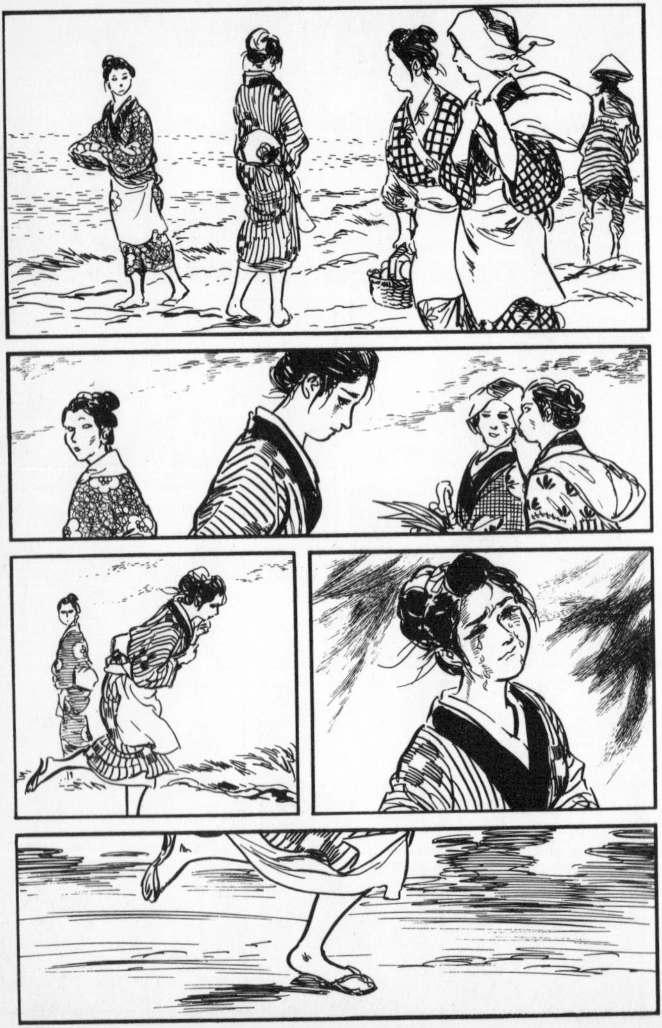

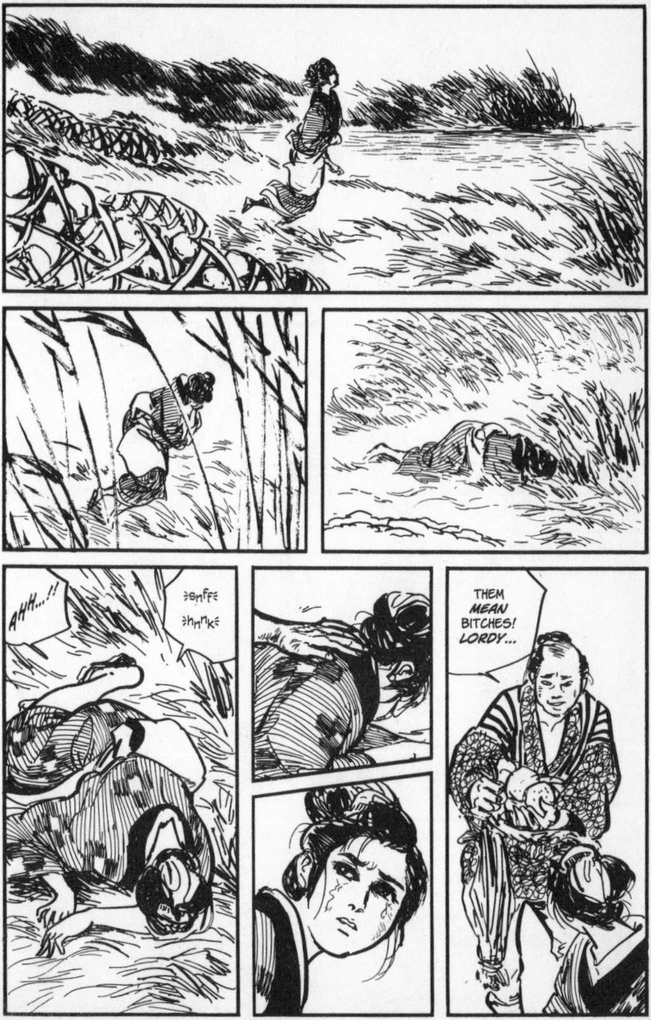
AHH...!!
≶snff≶
≶hnnk≶
THEM MEAN BITCHES! LORDY...

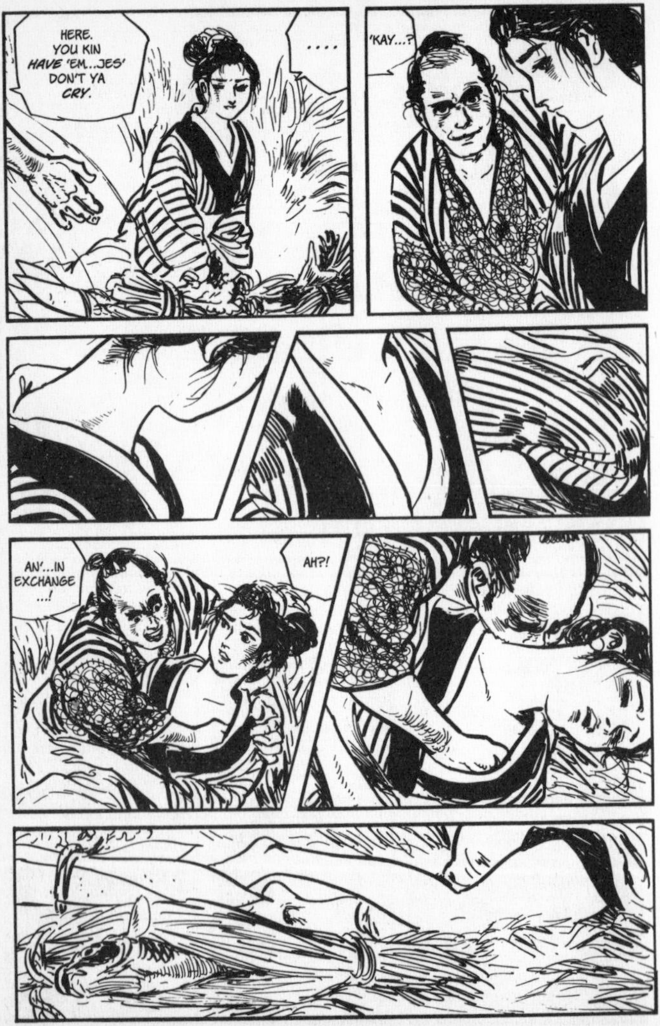
HERE. YOU KIN *HAVE* 'EM...JES' DON'T YA *CRY*.
....
'KAY...?
AN'...IN EXCHANGE ...!
AH?!

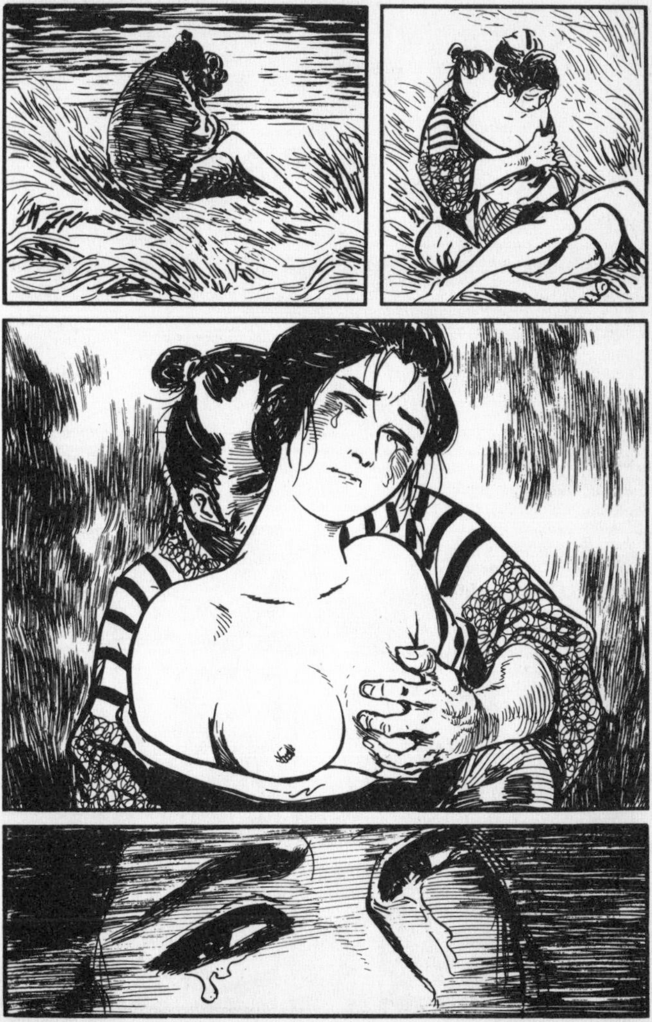

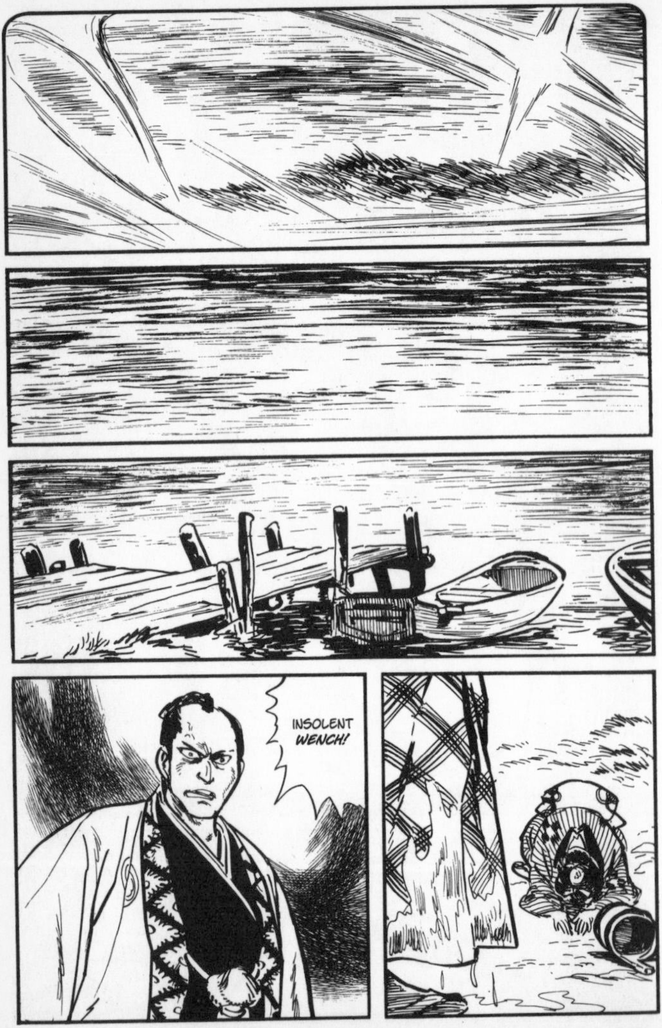
INSOLENT
WENCH!

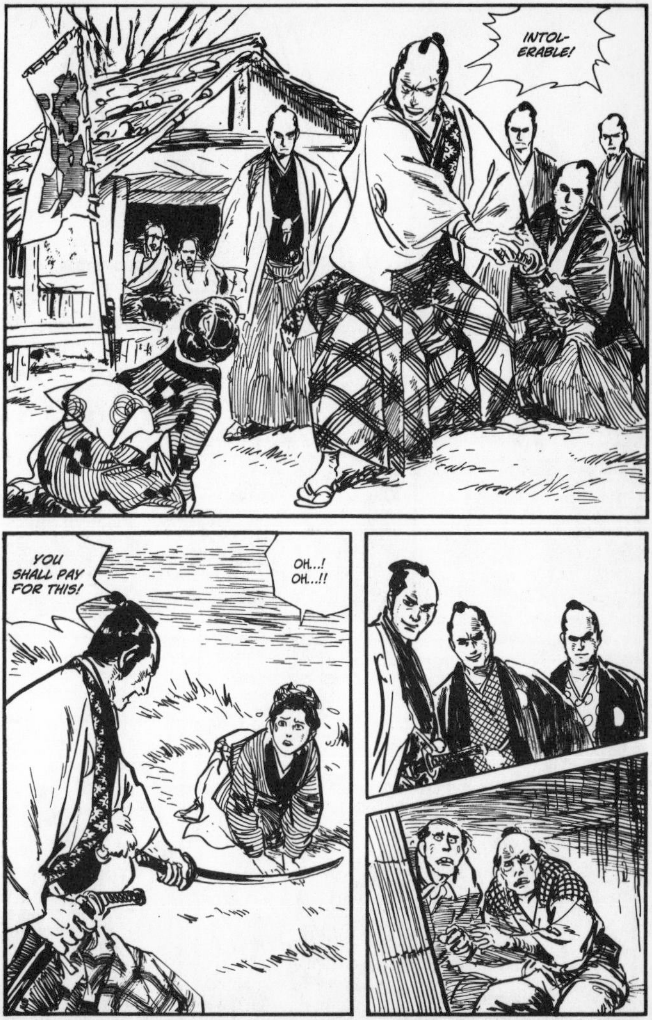
INTOL-
ERABLE!
YOU
SHALL PAY
FOR THIS!
OH...!
OH...!!

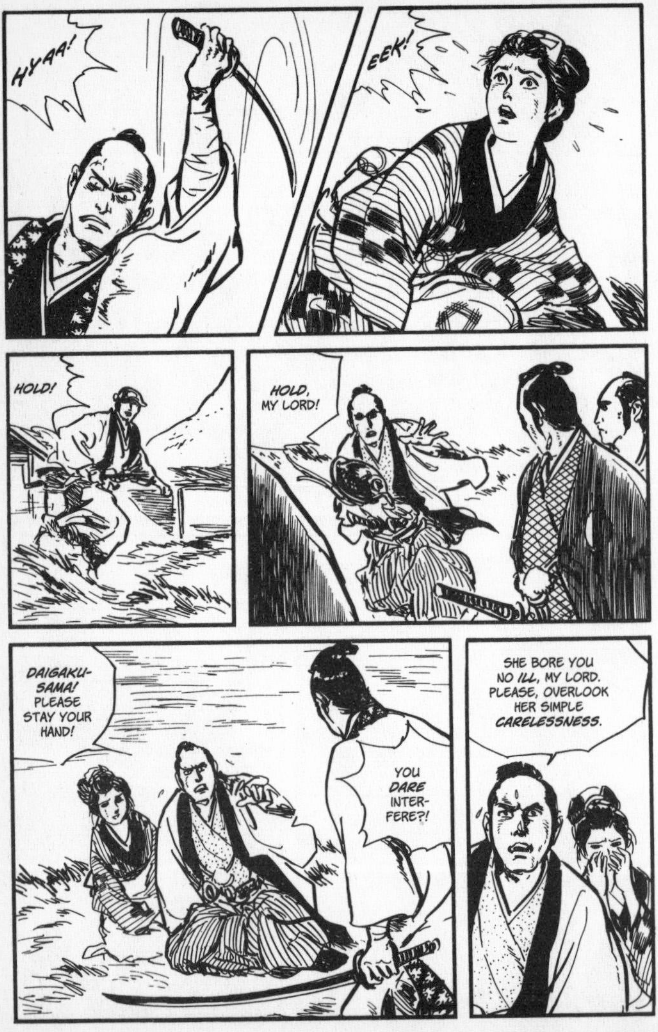
HYAA!
EEK!
HOLD!
HOLD, MY LORD!
DAIGAKU-SAMA! PLEASE STAY YOUR HAND!
YOU DARE INTER-FERE?!
SHE BORE YOU NO ILL, MY LORD. PLEASE, OVERLOOK HER SIMPLE CARELESSNESS.

NEVER! NOW MOVE!

MY LORD! IF SHE HAS *ERRED*, IT REFLECTS UPON *MYSELF* AND THE *ITAYA GUARD HOUSE* I COMMAND—IT IS *I* WHO SHOULD BE PUNISHED!

HUH! WELL *SAID*, HAYASE.

HEH HEH HEH... IF SHE'S SO WORTH PROTECTING...

...THEN YOU MUST BE WILLING TO TAKE HER PLACE, YES?!

I AM!

HOW INTERESTING! VERY WELL—*STRIP HIM!*

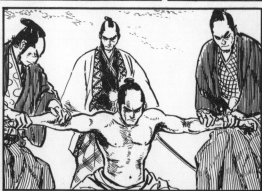

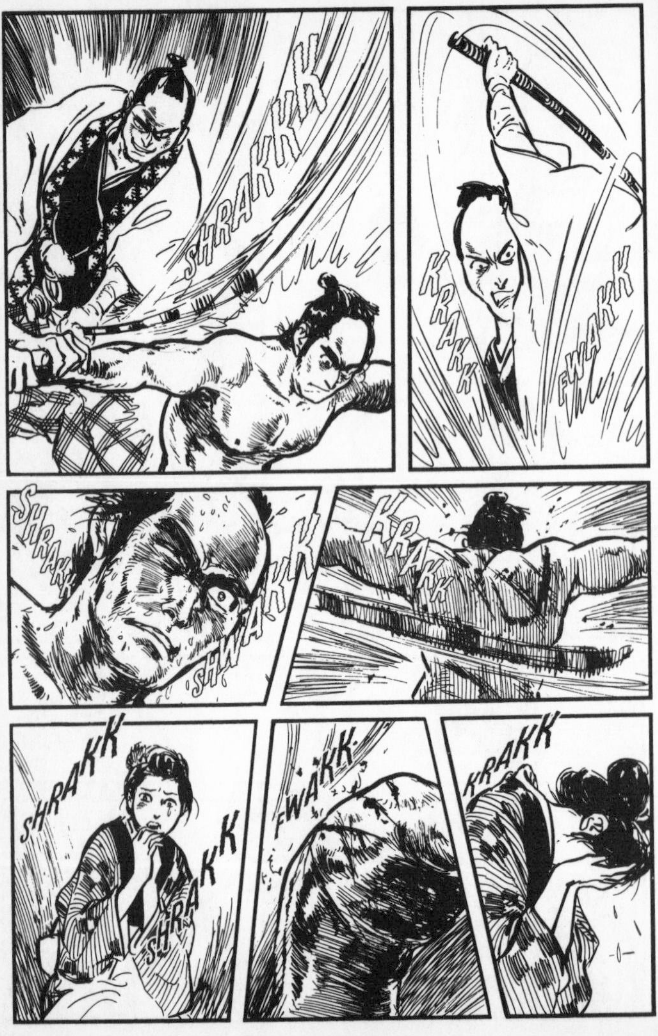
SHRAKKK
KRAKK
FWAKK
SHRAKK
SHWAKK
KRAKK
SHRAKK
SHRAKK
FWAKK
KRAKK

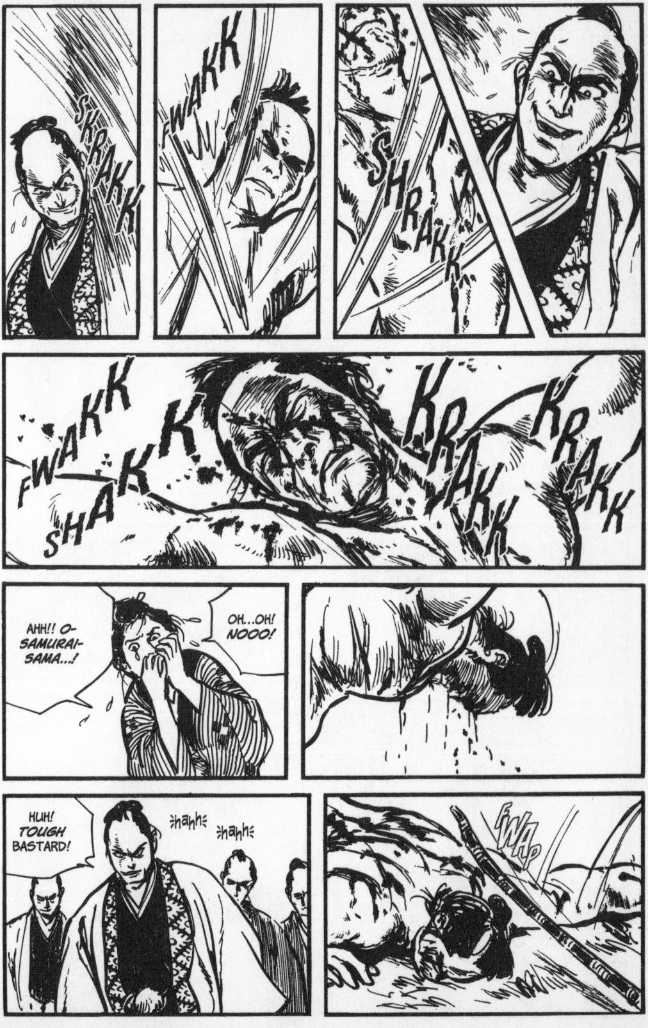

SHRAKK
FWAKK
SHRAKK
FWAKK
SHAKK
KRAKK
KRAKK
AHH!! O-SAMURAI-SAMA...!
OH...OH! NOOO!
HUH! TOUGH BASTARD!
hahh
hahh
FWAP

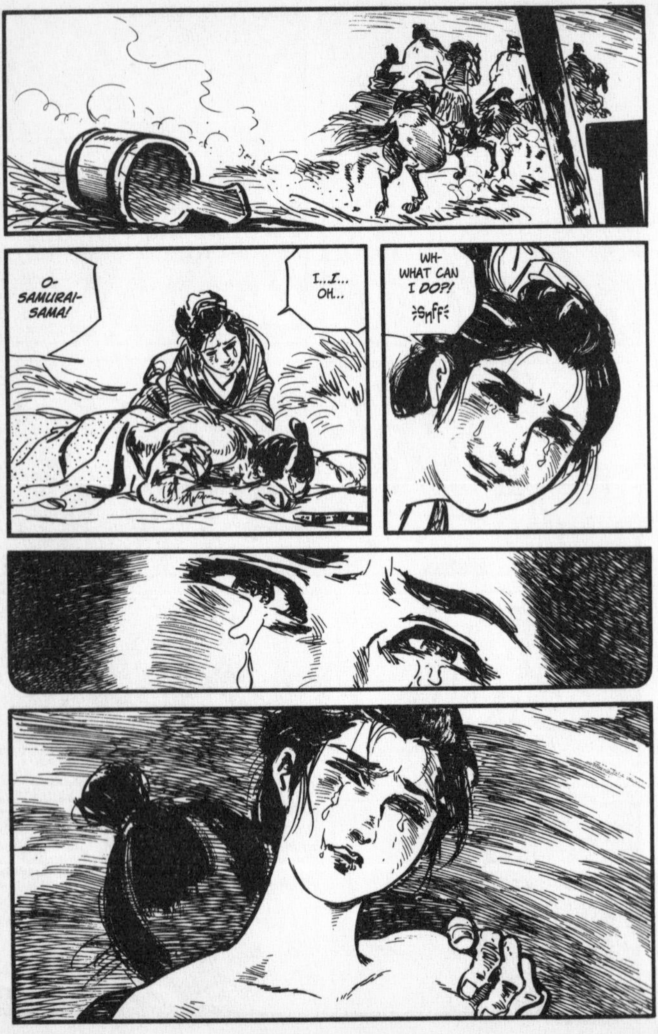
O-SAMURAI-SAMA!
I...I... OH...
WH-WHAT CAN I DO?!
SNFF

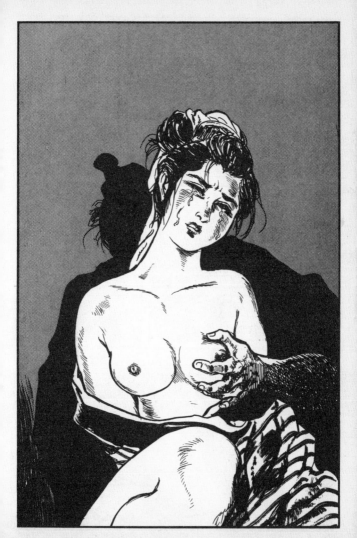

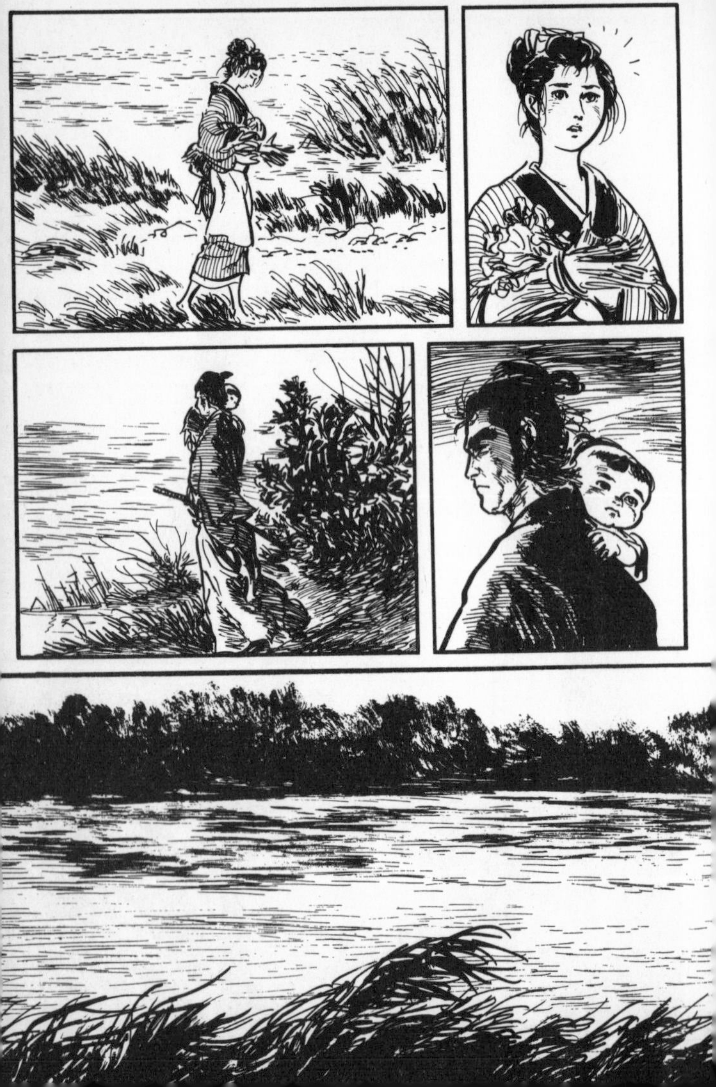

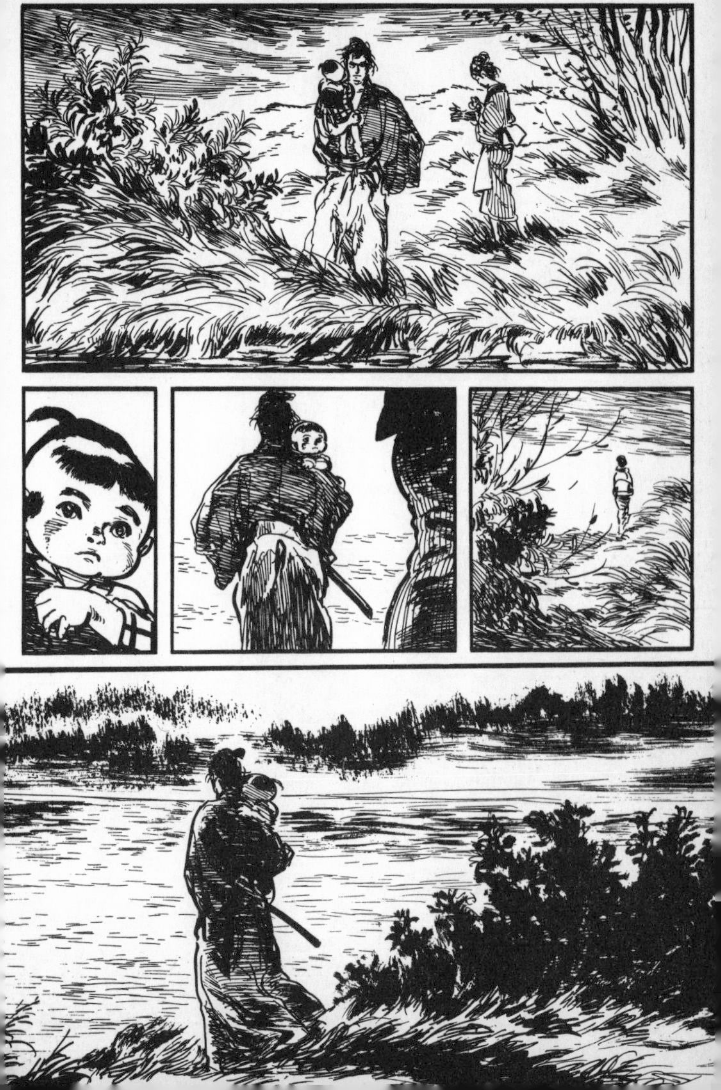

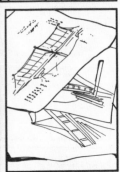

DONE! AT LAST!!

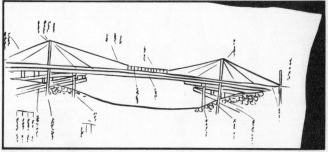

OH..?

ARE YOU *STILL* AT WORK?!

IF YOU DON'T GET YOUR REST...

DON'T *WORRY!* NOW THAT SPRING'S HERE, MY WHOLE *BODY* FEELS LIGHTER.

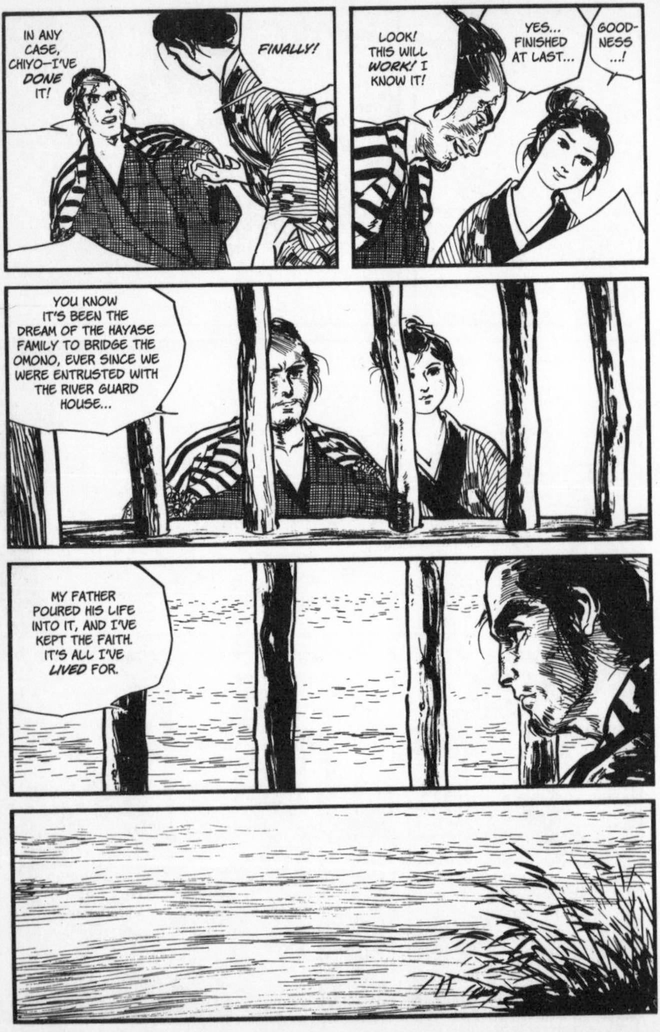
IN ANY CASE, CHIYO—I'VE *DONE* IT!
FINALLY!
LOOK! THIS WILL *WORK!* I KNOW IT!
YES... FINISHED AT LAST...
GOOD-NESS ...!
YOU KNOW IT'S BEEN THE DREAM OF THE HAYASE FAMILY TO BRIDGE THE OMONO, EVER SINCE WE WERE ENTRUSTED WITH THE RIVER GUARD HOUSE...
MY FATHER POURED HIS LIFE INTO IT, AND I'VE KEPT THE FAITH. IT'S ALL I'VE *LIVED* FOR.

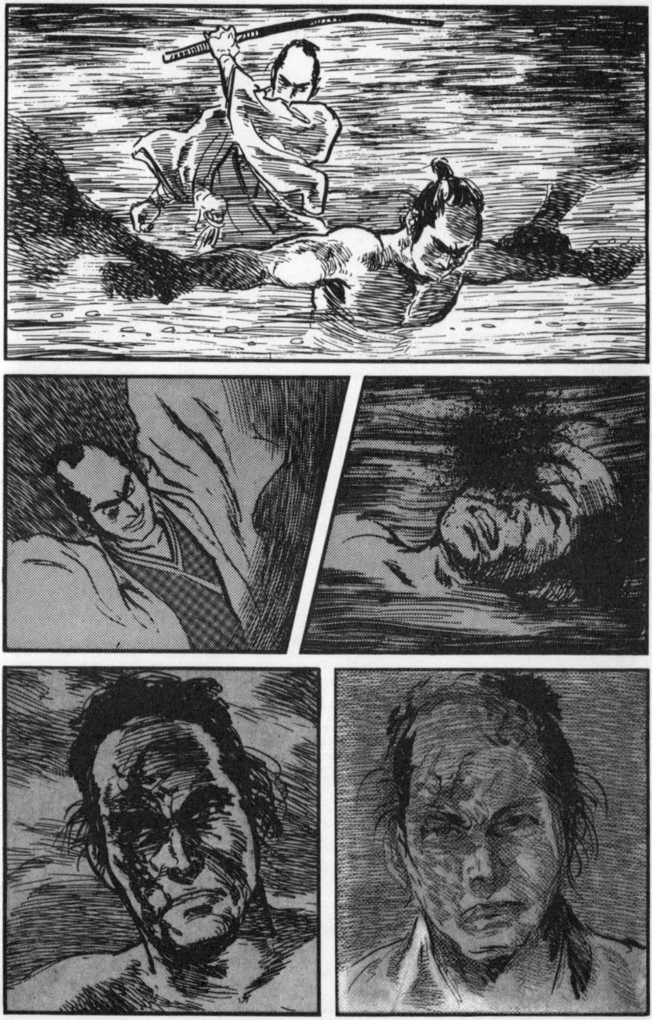

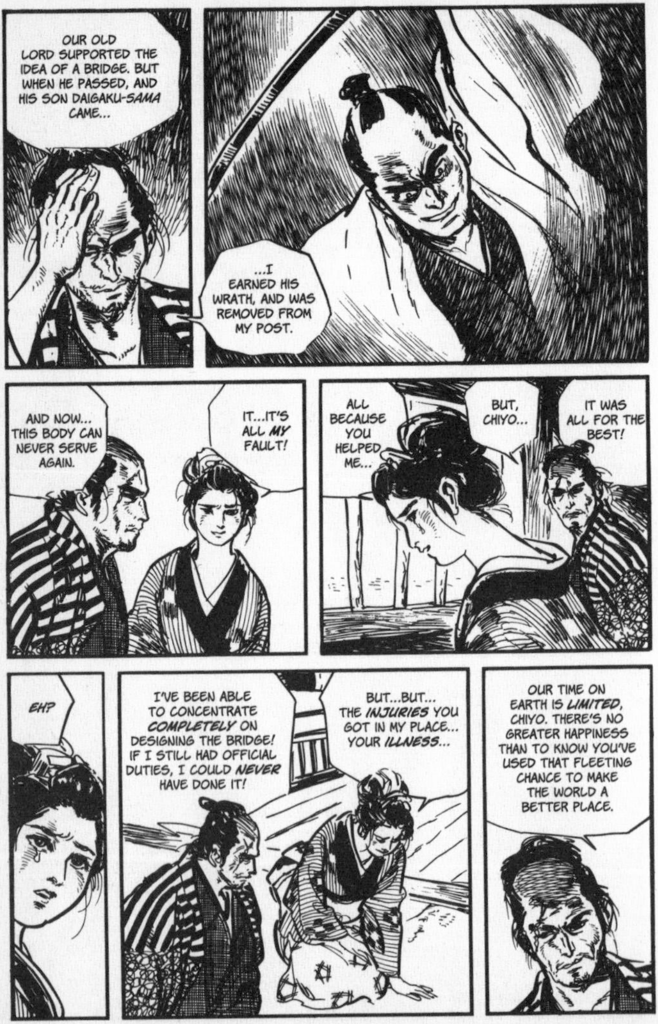
OUR OLD LORD SUPPORTED THE IDEA OF A BRIDGE. BUT WHEN HE PASSED, AND HIS SON DAIGAKU-*SAMA* CAME...
...I EARNED HIS WRATH, AND WAS REMOVED FROM MY POST.
AND NOW... THIS BODY CAN NEVER SERVE AGAIN.
IT...IT'S ALL *MY* FAULT!
ALL BECAUSE YOU HELPED ME...
BUT, CHIYO...
IT WAS ALL FOR THE BEST!
EH?
I'VE BEEN ABLE TO CONCENTRATE *COMPLETELY* ON DESIGNING THE BRIDGE! IF I STILL HAD OFFICIAL DUTIES, I COULD *NEVER* HAVE DONE IT!
BUT...BUT... THE *INJURIES* YOU GOT IN MY PLACE... YOUR *ILLNESS*...
OUR TIME ON EARTH IS *LIMITED*, CHIYO. THERE'S NO GREATER HAPPINESS THAN TO KNOW YOU'VE USED THAT FLEETING CHANCE TO MAKE THE WORLD A BETTER PLACE.

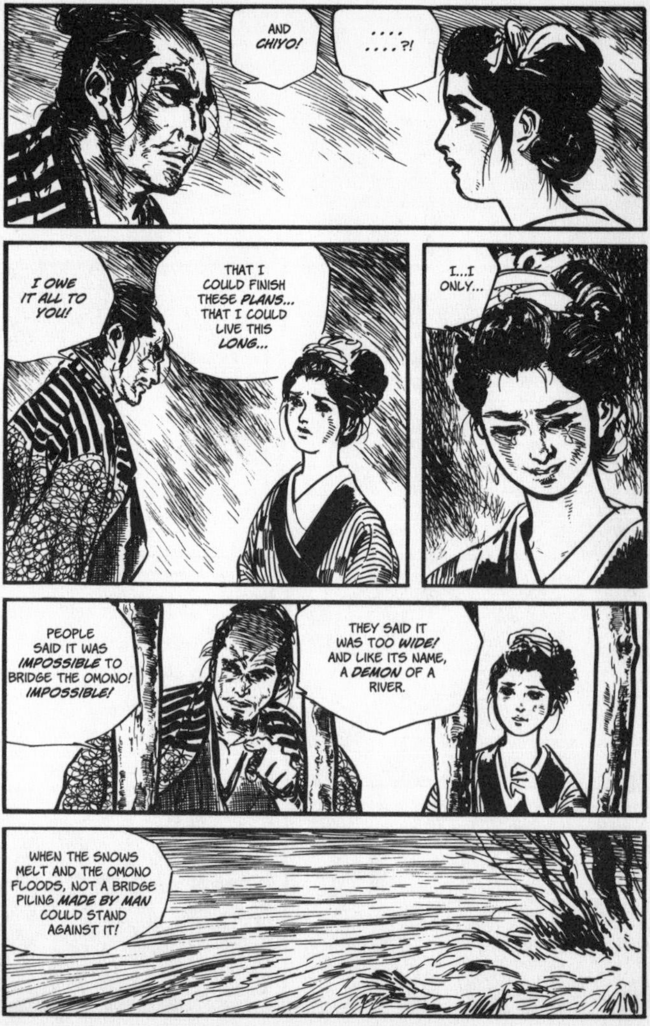
AND CHIYO!
. . . .
. . . . ?!
I OWE IT ALL TO YOU!
THAT I COULD FINISH THESE PLANS... THAT I COULD LIVE THIS LONG...
I...I ONLY...
PEOPLE SAID IT WAS IMPOSSIBLE TO BRIDGE THE OMONO! IMPOSSIBLE!
THEY SAID IT WAS TOO WIDE! AND LIKE ITS NAME, A DEMON OF A RIVER.
WHEN THE SNOWS MELT AND THE OMONO FLOODS, NOT A BRIDGE PILING MADE BY MAN COULD STAND AGAINST IT!

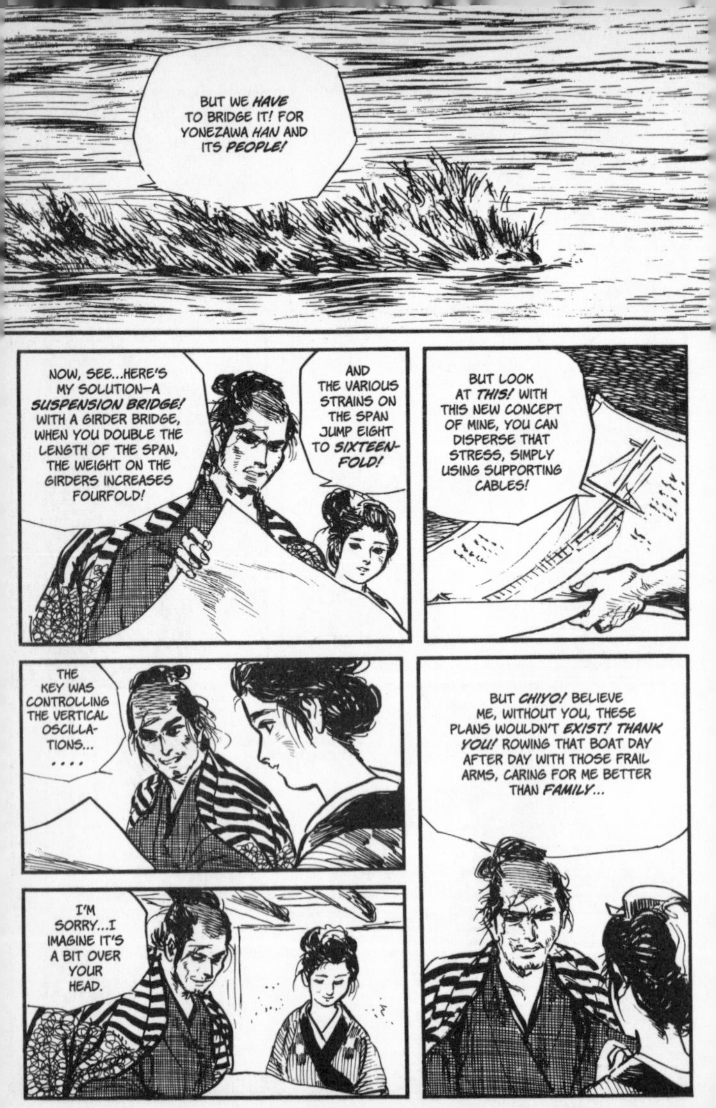
BUT WE *HAVE* TO BRIDGE IT! FOR YONEZAWA *HAN* AND ITS *PEOPLE!*
NOW, SEE...HERE'S MY SOLUTION—A *SUSPENSION BRIDGE!* WITH A GIRDER BRIDGE, WHEN YOU DOUBLE THE LENGTH OF THE SPAN, THE WEIGHT ON THE GIRDERS INCREASES FOURFOLD!
AND THE VARIOUS STRAINS ON THE SPAN JUMP EIGHT TO *SIXTEEN-FOLD!*
BUT LOOK AT *THIS!* WITH THIS NEW CONCEPT OF MINE, YOU CAN DISPERSE THAT STRESS, SIMPLY USING SUPPORTING CABLES!
THE KEY WAS CONTROLLING THE VERTICAL OSCILLA-TIONS...
....
I'M SORRY...I IMAGINE IT'S A BIT OVER YOUR HEAD.
BUT *CHIYO!* BELIEVE ME, WITHOUT YOU, THESE PLANS WOULDN'T *EXIST! THANK YOU!* ROWING THAT BOAT DAY AFTER DAY WITH THOSE FRAIL ARMS, CARING FOR ME BETTER THAN *FAMILY*...

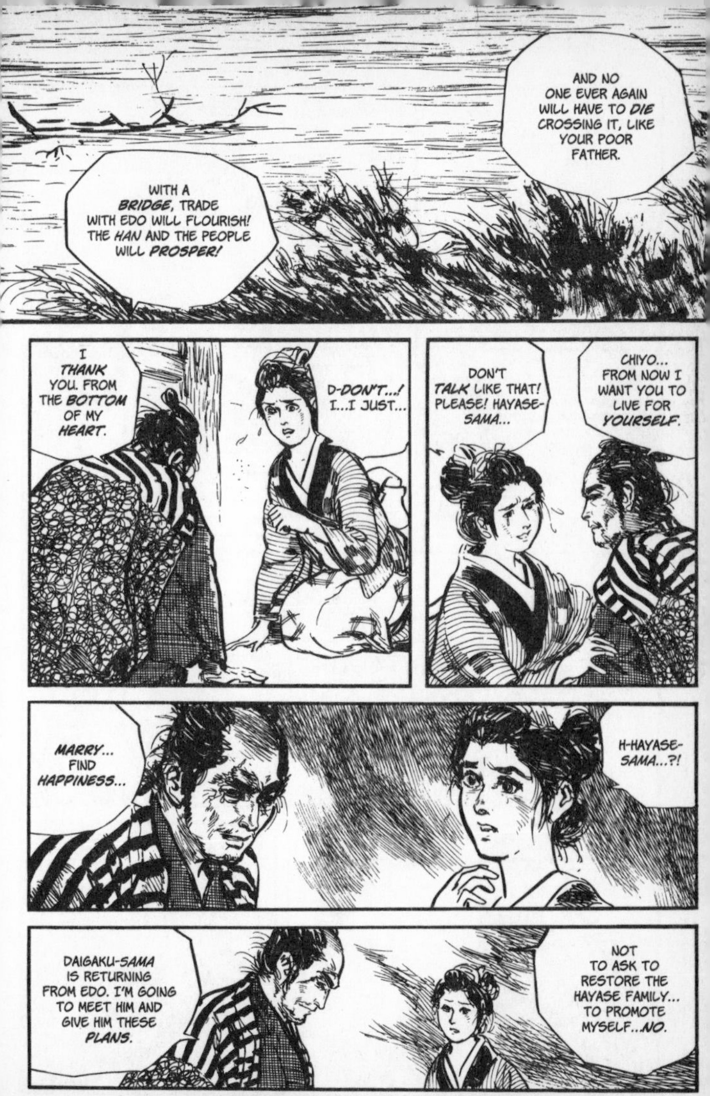
WITH A *BRIDGE*, TRADE WITH EDO WILL FLOURISH! THE *HAN* AND THE PEOPLE WILL *PROSPER!*
AND NO ONE EVER AGAIN WILL HAVE TO *DIE* CROSSING IT, LIKE YOUR POOR FATHER.
I *THANK* YOU. FROM THE *BOTTOM* OF MY *HEART*.
D-*DON'T*...! I...I JUST...
DON'T *TALK* LIKE THAT! PLEASE! HAYASE-*SAMA*...
CHIYO... FROM NOW I WANT YOU TO LIVE FOR *YOURSELF*.
MARRY... FIND *HAPPINESS*...
H-HAYASE-*SAMA*...?!
DAIGAKU-*SAMA* IS RETURNING FROM EDO. I'M GOING TO MEET HIM AND GIVE HIM THESE *PLANS*.
NOT TO ASK TO RESTORE THE HAYASE FAMILY... TO PROMOTE MYSELF...*NO*.

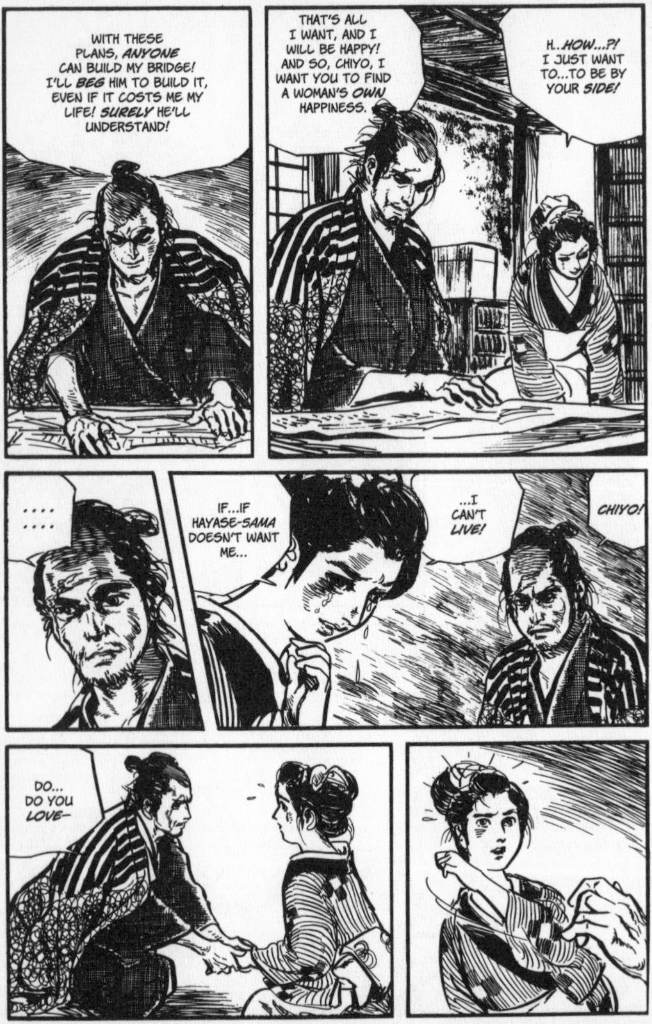

WITH THESE PLANS, ANYONE CAN BUILD MY BRIDGE! I'LL BEG HIM TO BUILD IT, EVEN IF IT COSTS ME MY LIFE! SURELY HE'LL UNDERSTAND!
THAT'S ALL I WANT, AND I WILL BE HAPPY! AND SO, CHIYO, I WANT YOU TO FIND A WOMAN'S OWN HAPPINESS.
H..HOW...?! I JUST WANT TO...TO BE BY YOUR SIDE!
....
....
IF...IF HAYASE-SAMA DOESN'T WANT ME...
...I CAN'T LIVE!
CHIYO!
DO... DO YOU LOVE-

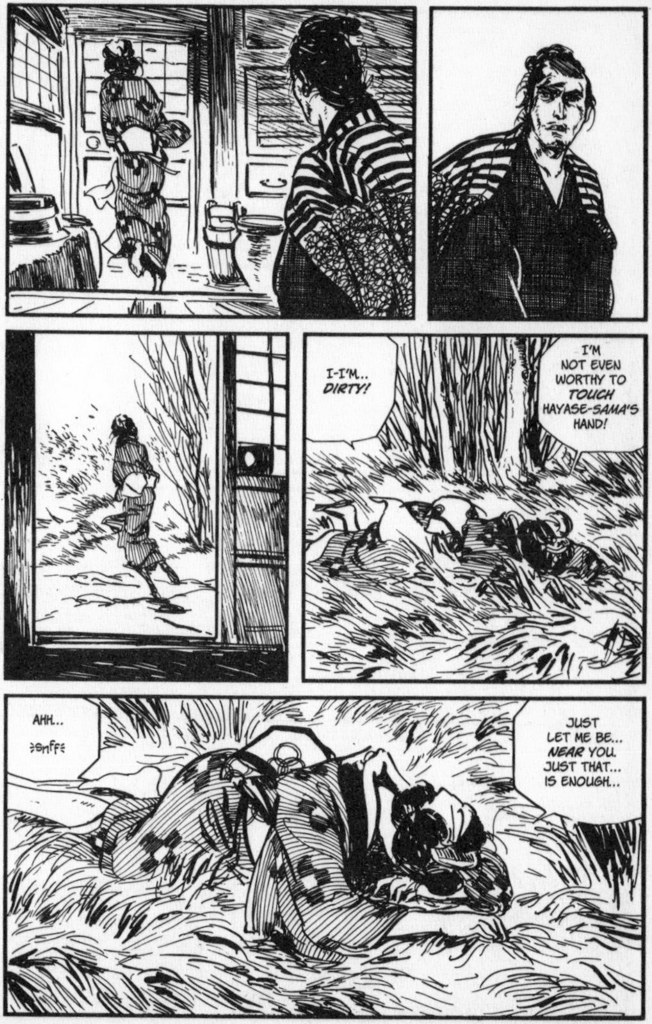
I-I'M... DIRTY!
I'M NOT EVEN WORTHY TO TOUCH HAYASE-SAMA'S HAND!
AHH...
snff
JUST LET ME BE... NEAR YOU. JUST THAT... IS ENOUGH...

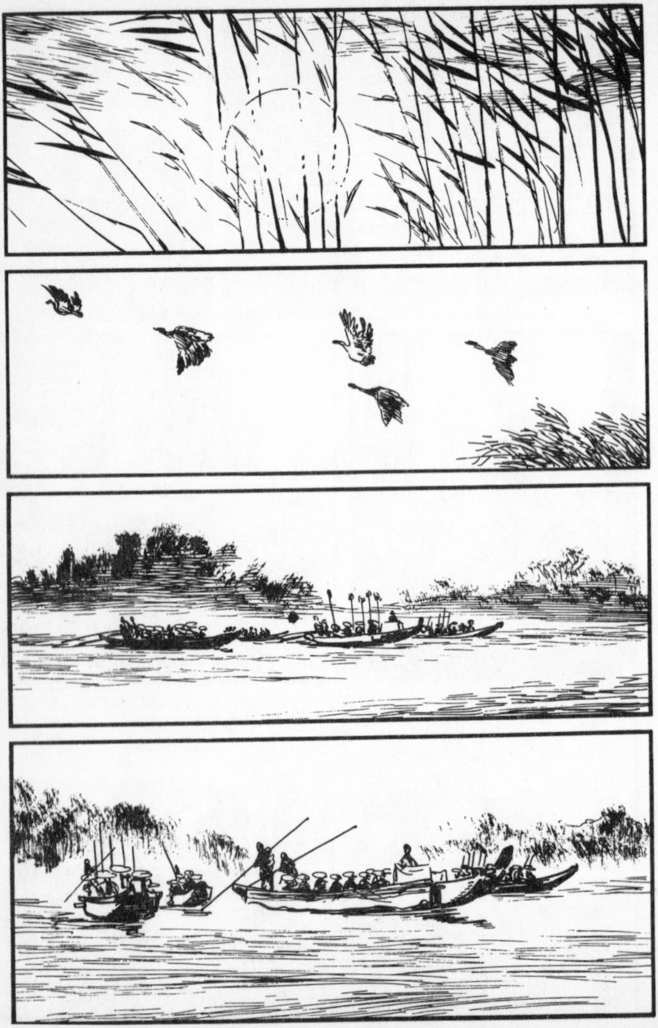

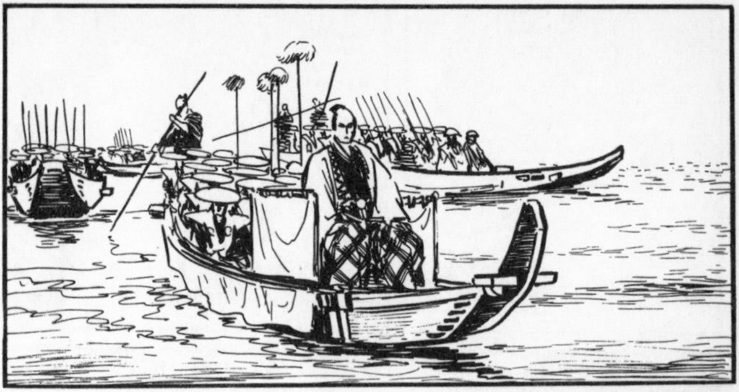
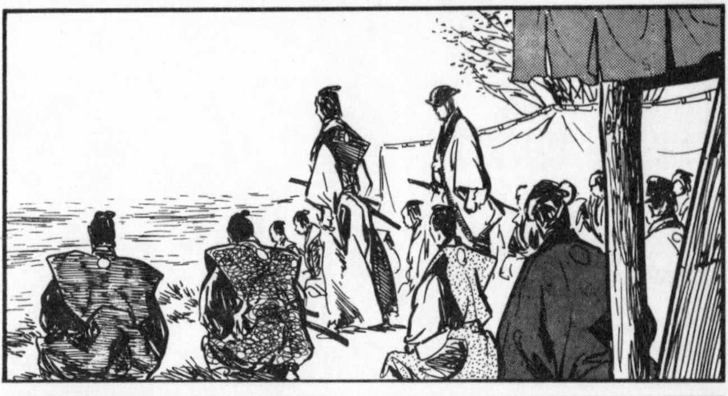
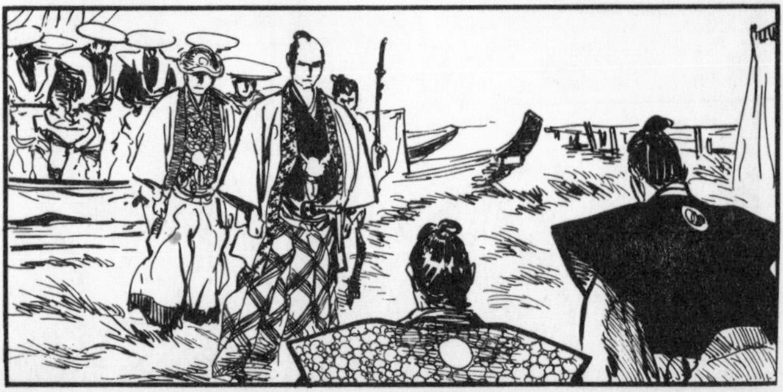

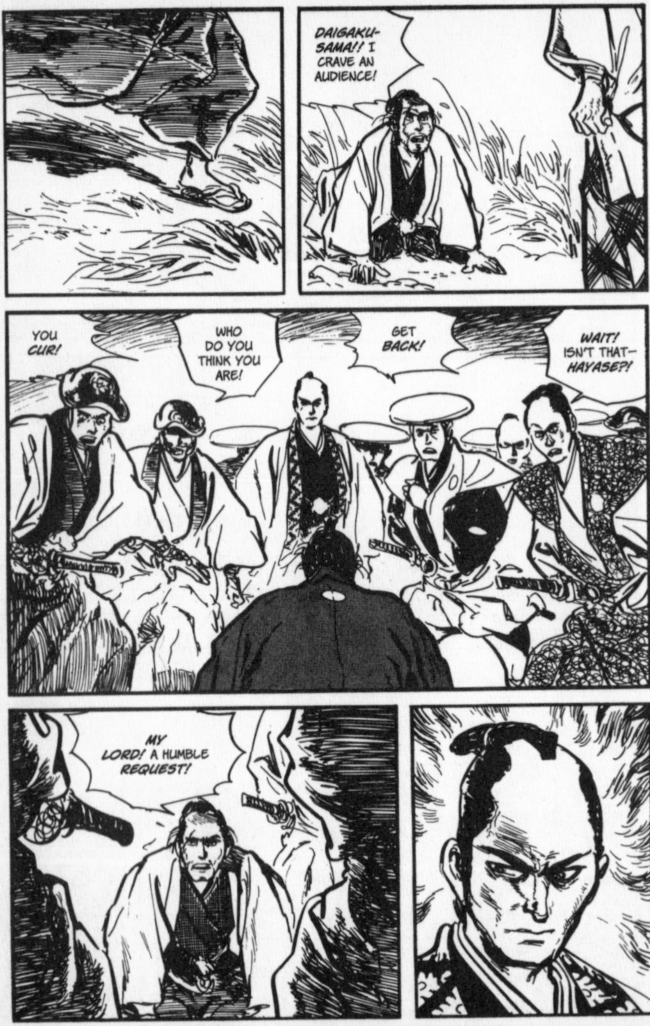
DAIGAKU-SAMA!! I CRAVE AN AUDIENCE!
YOU CUR!
WHO DO YOU THINK YOU ARE!
GET BACK!
WAIT! ISN'T THAT-HAYASE?!
MY LORD! A HUMBLE REQUEST!

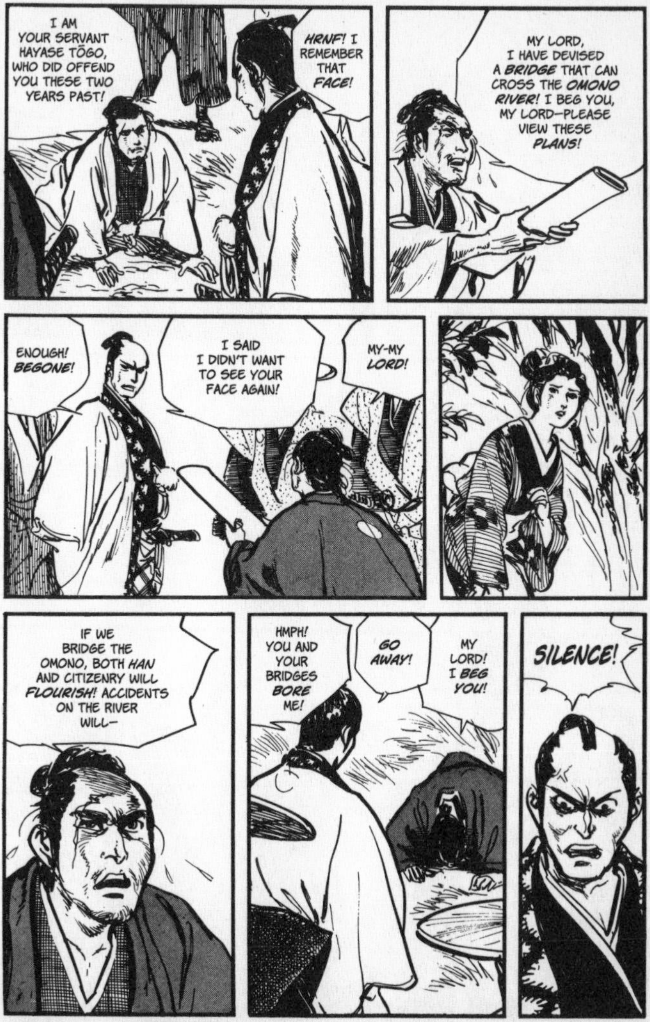
I AM YOUR SERVANT HAYASE TŌGO, WHO DID OFFEND YOU THESE TWO YEARS PAST!
HRNF! I REMEMBER THAT FACE!
MY LORD, I HAVE DEVISED A BRIDGE THAT CAN CROSS THE OMONO RIVER! I BEG YOU, MY LORD—PLEASE VIEW THESE PLANS!
ENOUGH! BEGONE!
I SAID I DIDN'T WANT TO SEE YOUR FACE AGAIN!
MY-MY LORD!
IF WE BRIDGE THE OMONO, BOTH HAN AND CITIZENRY WILL FLOURISH! ACCIDENTS ON THE RIVER WILL–
HMPH! YOU AND YOUR BRIDGES BORE ME!
GO AWAY!
MY LORD! I BEG YOU!
SILENCE!

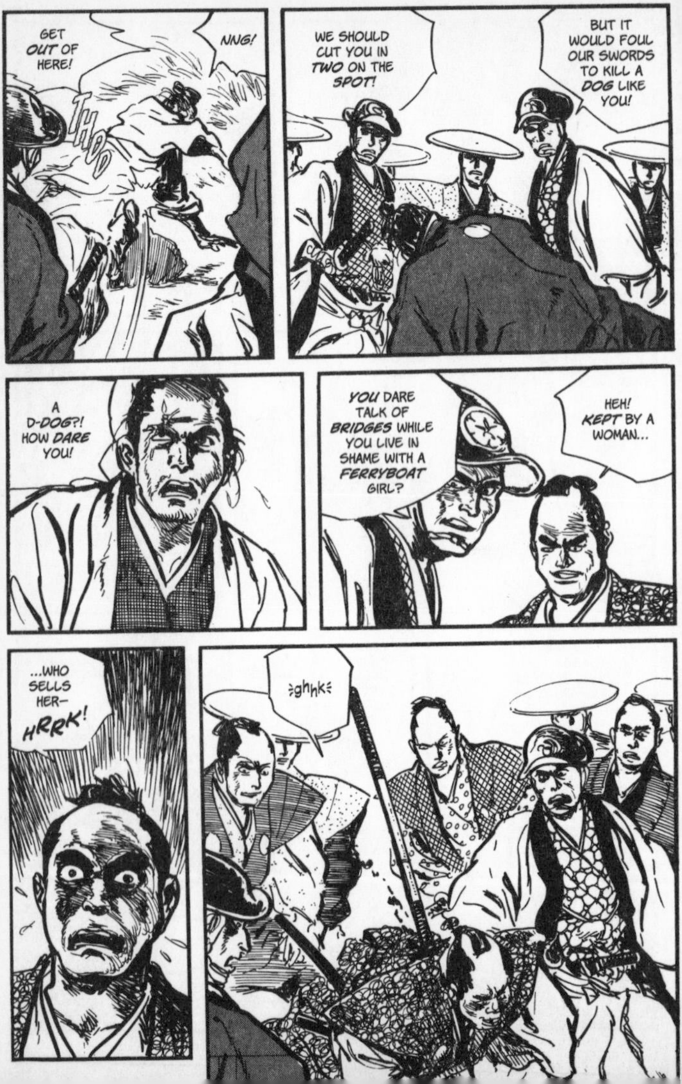
GET OUT OF HERE!
THOD
NNG!
WE SHOULD CUT YOU IN TWO ON THE SPOT!
BUT IT WOULD FOUL OUR SWORDS TO KILL A DOG LIKE YOU!
A D-DOG?! HOW DARE YOU!
YOU DARE TALK OF BRIDGES WHILE YOU LIVE IN SHAME WITH A FERRYBOAT GIRL?
HEH! KEPT BY A WOMAN...
...WHO SELLS HER-
HRRK!
ghhk

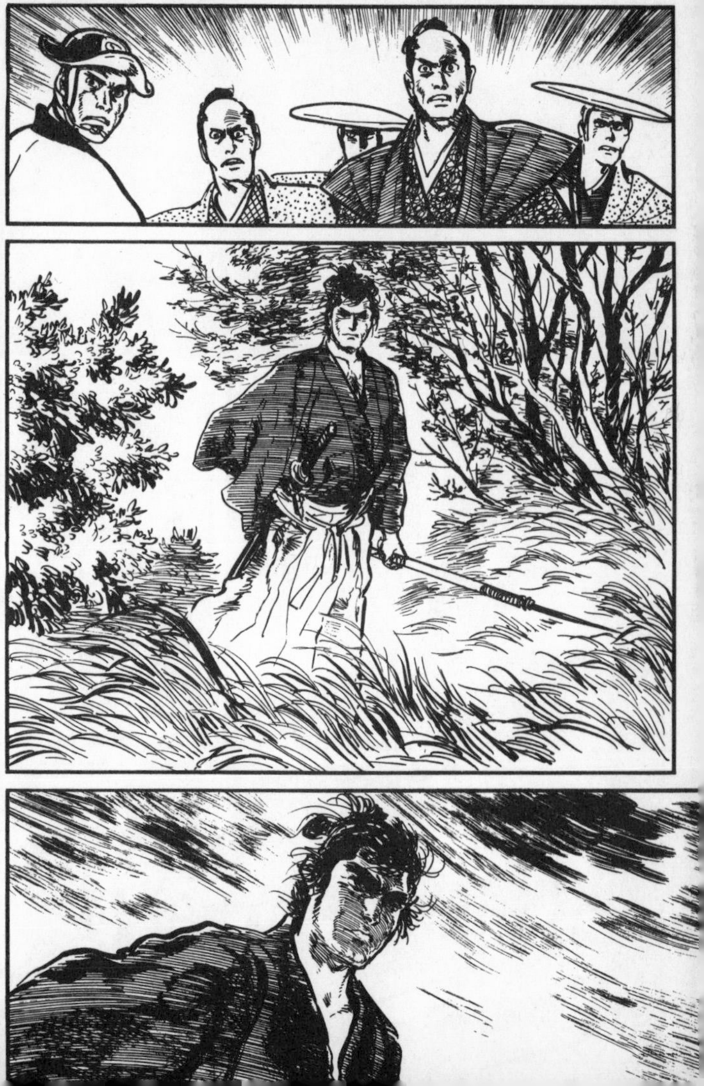

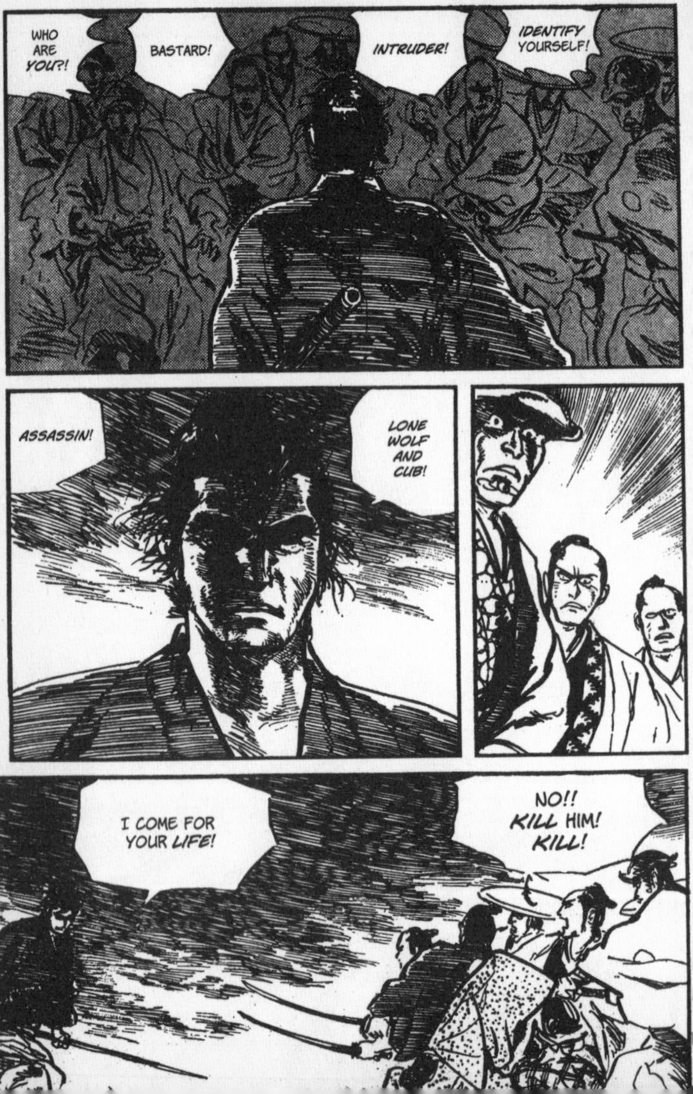
WHO ARE YOU?!
BASTARD!
INTRUDER!
IDENTIFY YOURSELF!
ASSASSIN!
LONE WOLF AND CUB!
I COME FOR YOUR LIFE!
NO!! KILL HIM! KILL!

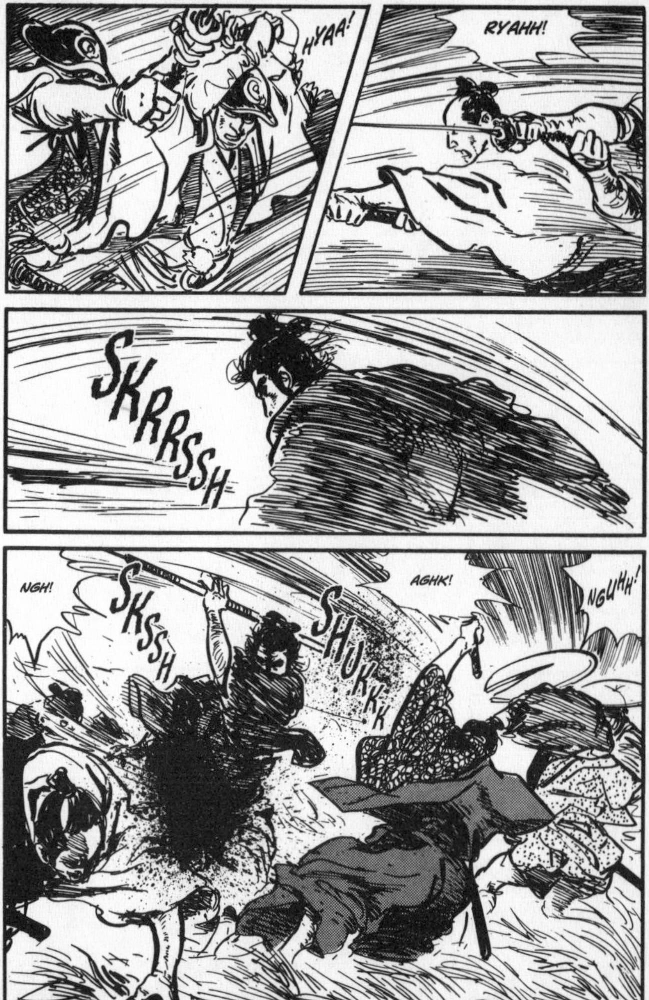
HYAA!
RYAHH!
SKRRSSSH
NGH!
SKSSH
SHUKKK
AGHK!
NGUHH!

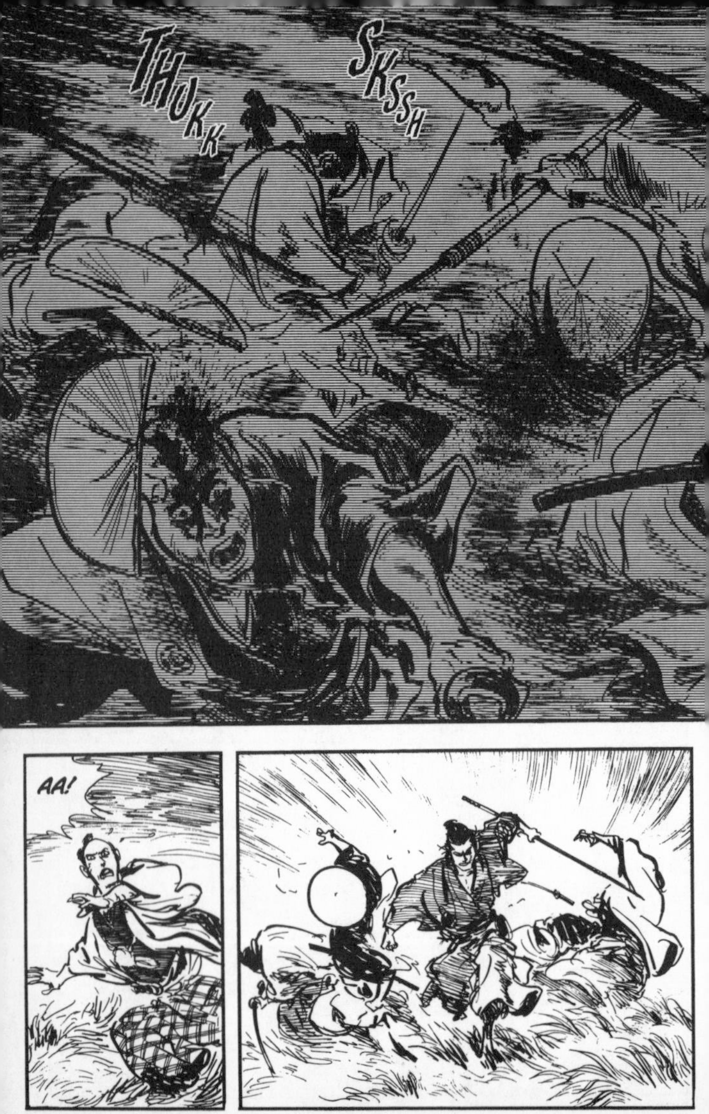
THUKK
SKSSH
AA!

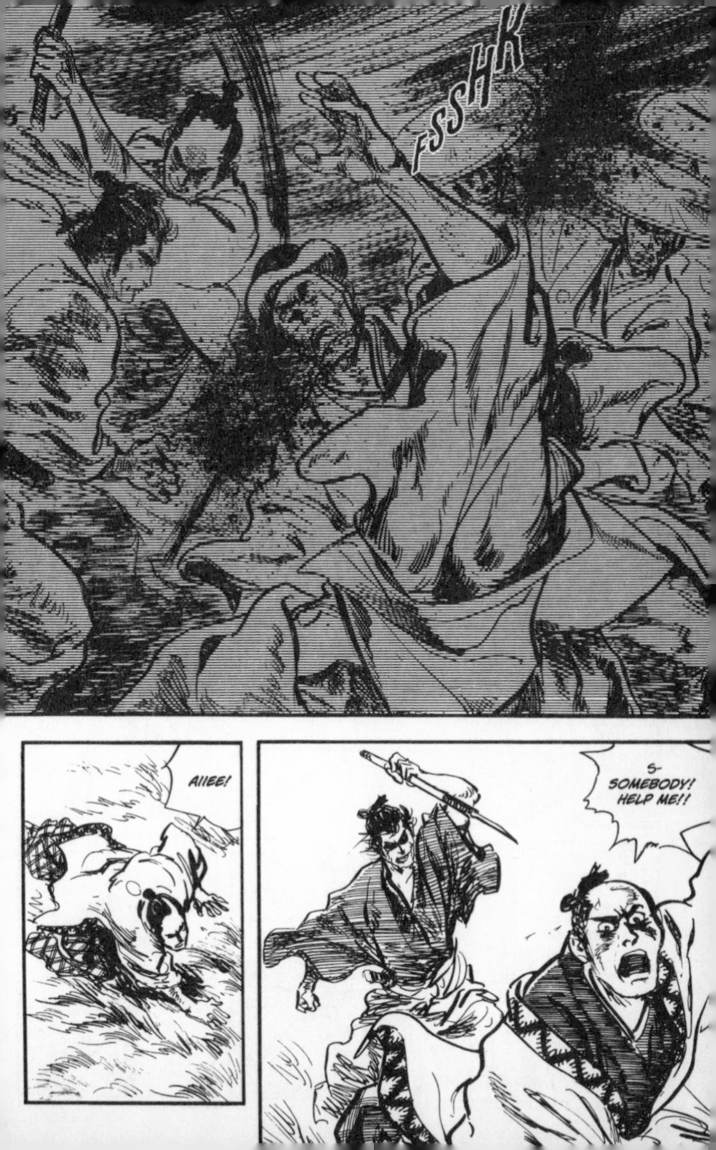
FSSHK
AIIEE!
S-
SOMEBODY!
HELP ME!!

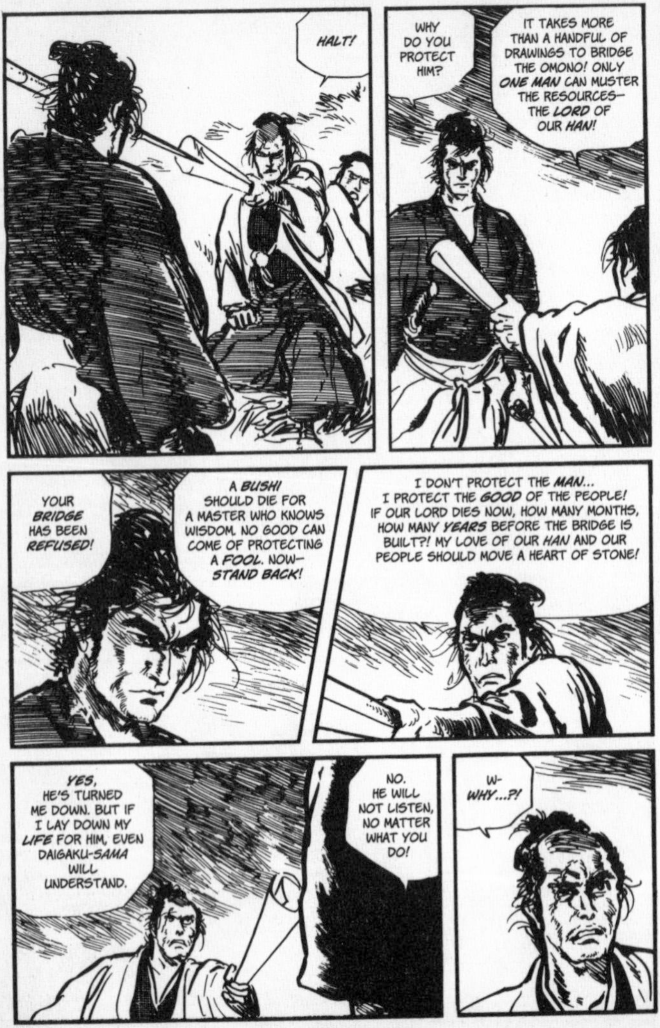
HALT!
WHY DO YOU PROTECT HIM?
IT TAKES MORE THAN A HANDFUL OF DRAWINGS TO BRIDGE THE OMONO! ONLY ONE MAN CAN MUSTER THE RESOURCES— THE LORD OF OUR HAN!
YOUR BRIDGE HAS BEEN REFUSED!
A BUSHI SHOULD DIE FOR A MASTER WHO KNOWS WISDOM. NO GOOD CAN COME OF PROTECTING A FOOL. NOW— STAND BACK!
I DON'T PROTECT THE MAN... I PROTECT THE GOOD OF THE PEOPLE! IF OUR LORD DIES NOW, HOW MANY MONTHS, HOW MANY YEARS BEFORE THE BRIDGE IS BUILT?! MY LOVE OF OUR HAN AND OUR PEOPLE SHOULD MOVE A HEART OF STONE!
YES, HE'S TURNED ME DOWN. BUT IF I LAY DOWN MY LIFE FOR HIM, EVEN DAIGAKU-SAMA WILL UNDERSTAND.
NO. HE WILL NOT LISTEN, NO MATTER WHAT YOU DO!
W- WHY...?!

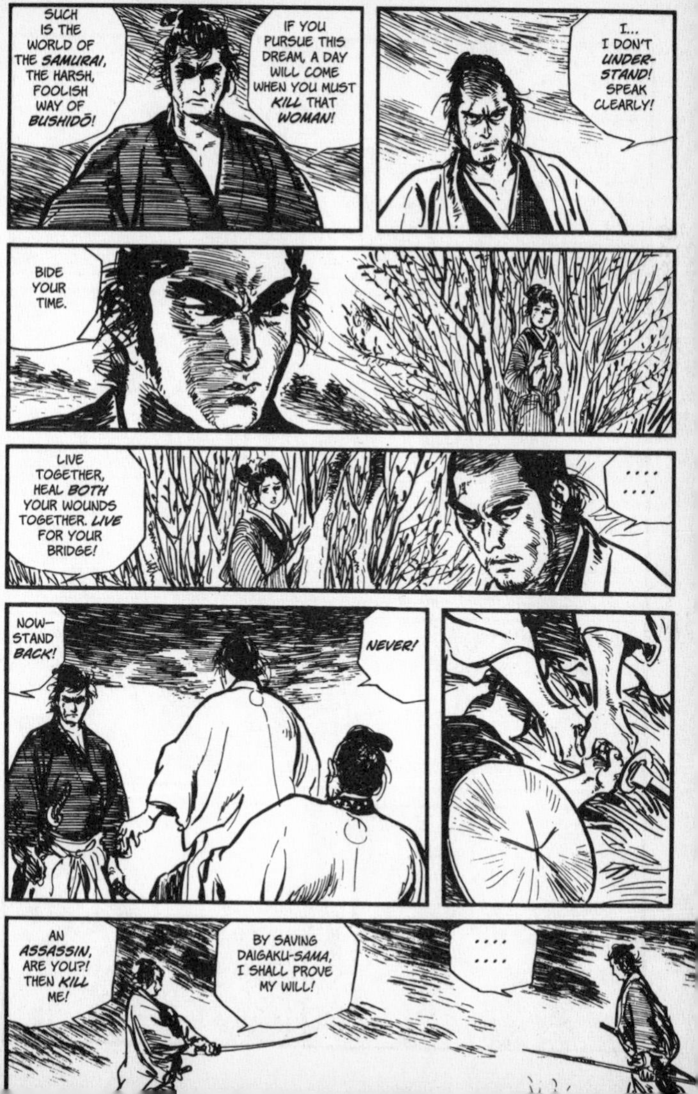
SUCH IS THE WORLD OF THE *SAMURAI*, THE HARSH, FOOLISH WAY OF *BUSHIDŌ*!
IF YOU PURSUE THIS DREAM, A DAY WILL COME WHEN YOU MUST *KILL* THAT *WOMAN*!
I... I DON'T *UNDERSTAND*! SPEAK CLEARLY!
BIDE YOUR TIME.
LIVE TOGETHER, HEAL *BOTH* YOUR WOUNDS TOGETHER. *LIVE* FOR YOUR BRIDGE!
....
....
NOW— STAND *BACK*!
NEVER!
AN *ASSASSIN*, ARE YOU?! THEN *KILL* ME!
BY SAVING DAIGAKU-*SAMA*, I SHALL PROVE MY WILL!
....
....

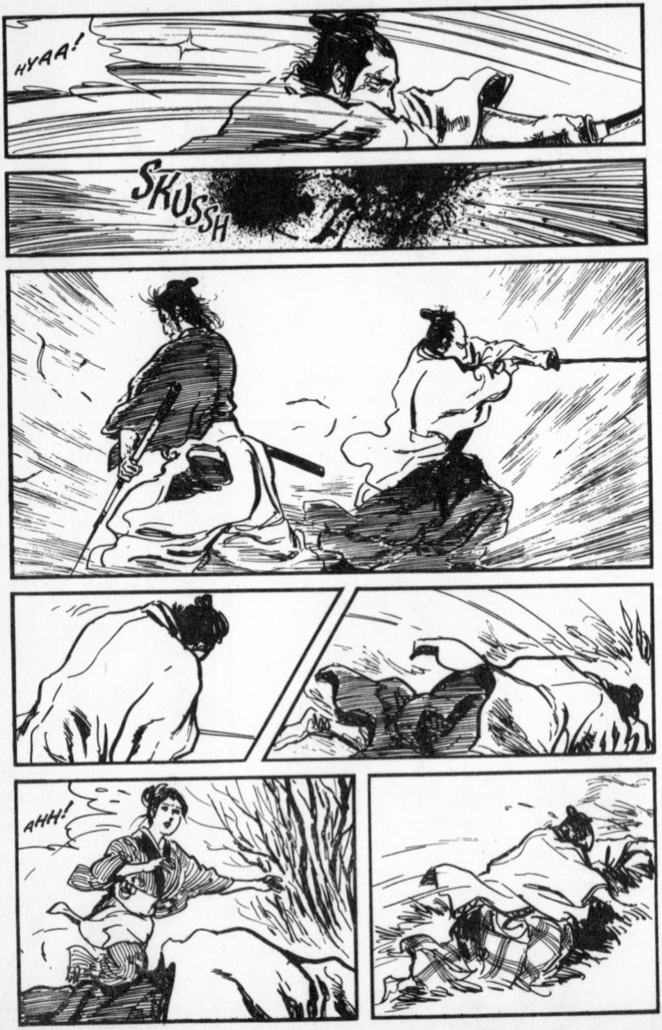
HYAA!
SKUSSH
AHH!

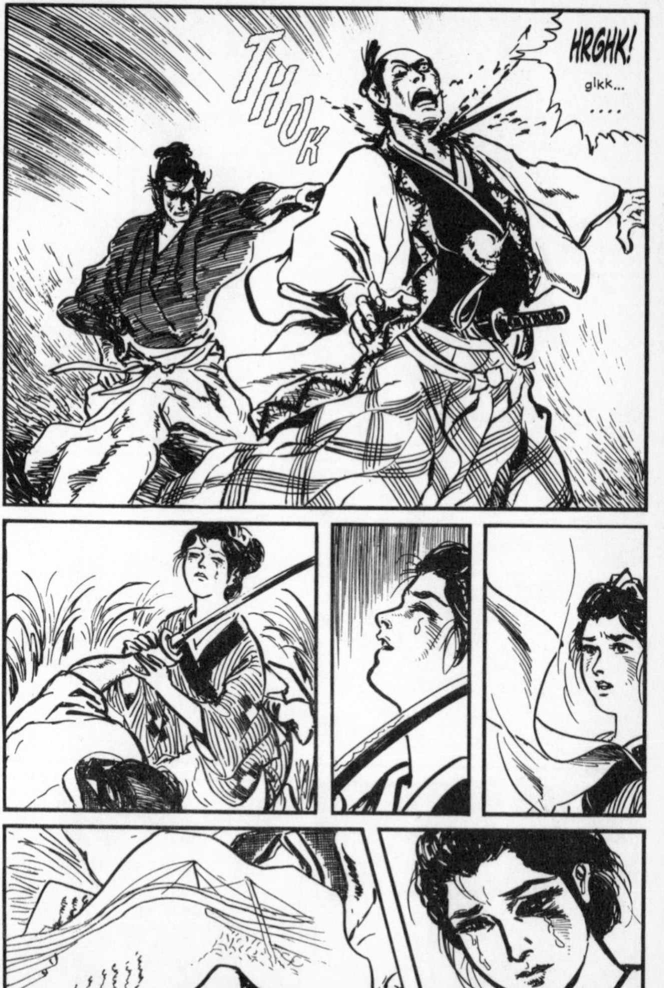
THUK
HRGHK!
glkk...
....

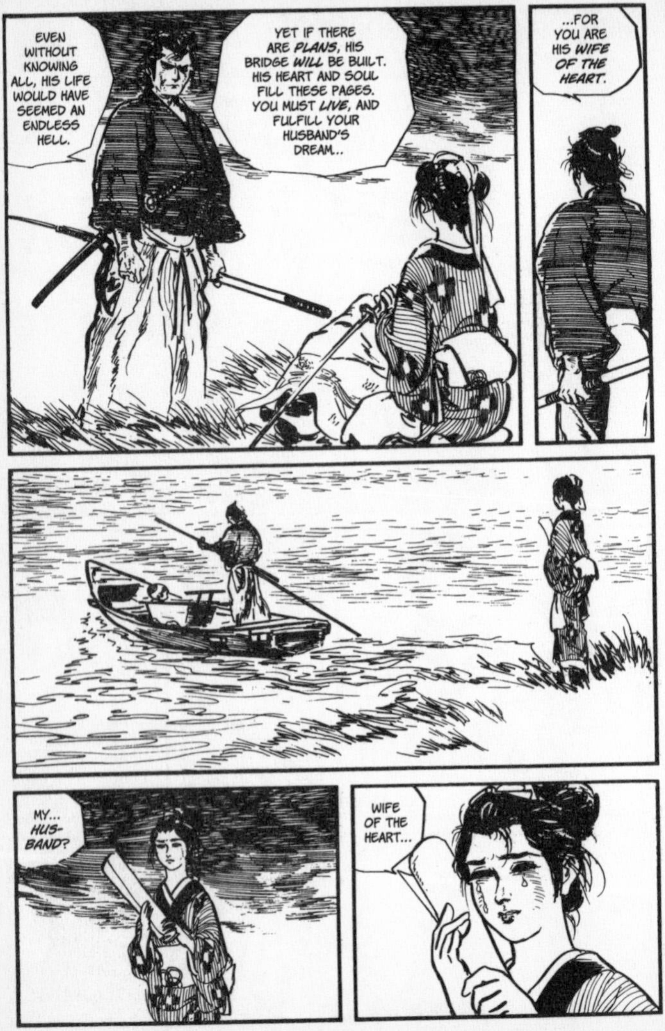
EVEN WITHOUT KNOWING ALL, HIS LIFE WOULD HAVE SEEMED AN ENDLESS HELL.
YET IF THERE ARE *PLANS*, HIS BRIDGE *WILL* BE BUILT. HIS HEART AND SOUL FILL THESE PAGES. YOU MUST *LIVE*, AND FULFILL YOUR HUSBAND'S DREAM..
...FOR YOU ARE HIS *WIFE OF THE HEART*.
MY... *HUS-BAND?*
WIFE OF THE HEART...

the forty-sixth

Wandering Samurai

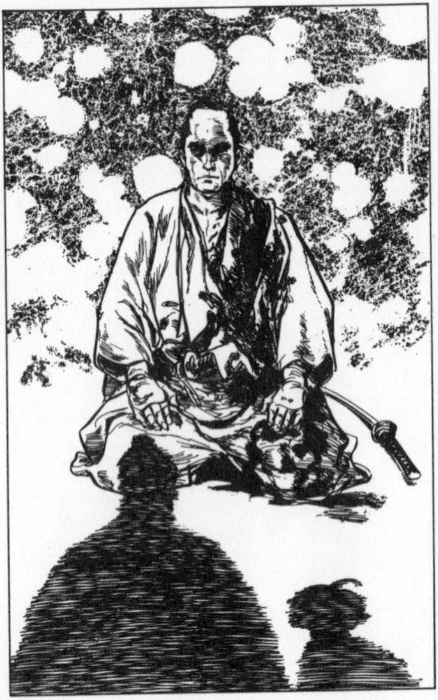

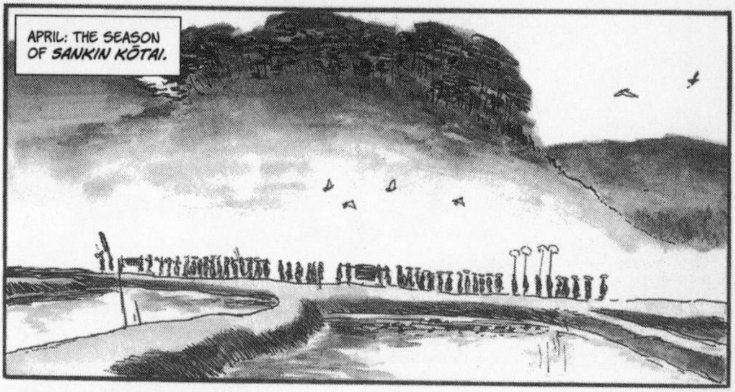
APRIL: THE SEASON OF *SANKIN KŌTAI*.

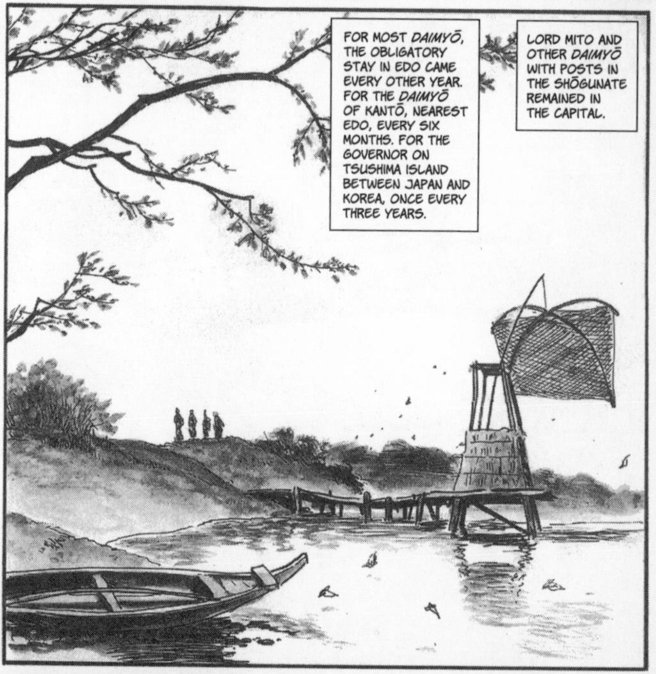
FOR MOST *DAIMYŌ*, THE OBLIGATORY STAY IN EDO CAME EVERY OTHER YEAR. FOR THE *DAIMYŌ* OF KANTŌ, NEAREST EDO, EVERY SIX MONTHS. FOR THE GOVERNOR ON TSUSHIMA ISLAND BETWEEN JAPAN AND KOREA, ONCE EVERY THREE YEARS.
LORD MITO AND OTHER *DAIMYŌ* WITH POSTS IN THE SHŌGUNATE REMAINED IN THE CAPITAL.

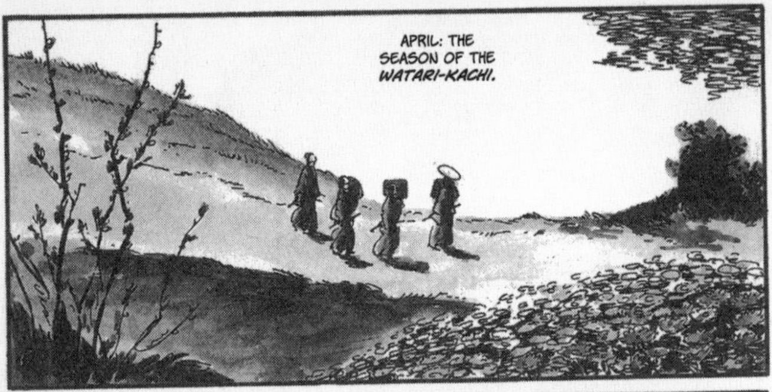
APRIL: THE SEASON OF THE WATARI-KACHI.

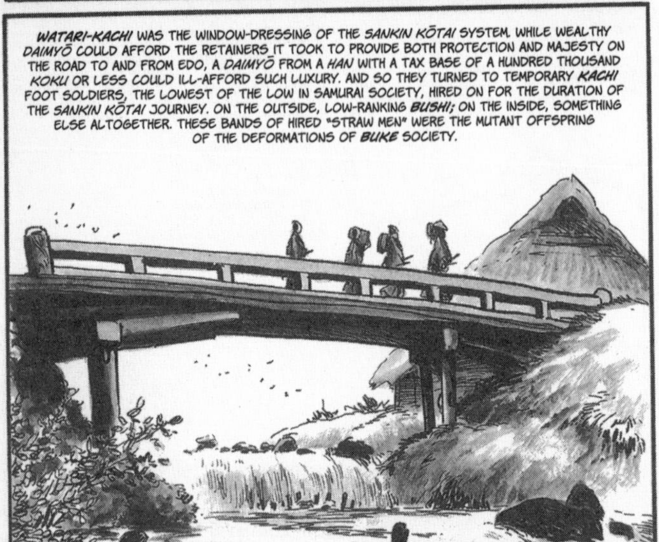
WATARI-KACHI WAS THE WINDOW-DRESSING OF THE SANKIN KŌTAI SYSTEM. WHILE WEALTHY DAIMYŌ COULD AFFORD THE RETAINERS IT TOOK TO PROVIDE BOTH PROTECTION AND MAJESTY ON THE ROAD TO AND FROM EDO, A DAIMYŌ FROM A HAN WITH A TAX BASE OF A HUNDRED THOUSAND KOKU OR LESS COULD ILL-AFFORD SUCH LUXURY. AND SO THEY TURNED TO TEMPORARY KACHI FOOT SOLDIERS, THE LOWEST OF THE LOW IN SAMURAI SOCIETY, HIRED ON FOR THE DURATION OF THE SANKIN KŌTAI JOURNEY. ON THE OUTSIDE, LOW-RANKING BUSHI; ON THE INSIDE, SOMETHING ELSE ALTOGETHER. THESE BANDS OF HIRED "STRAW MEN" WERE THE MUTANT OFFSPRING OF THE DEFORMATIONS OF BUKE SOCIETY.

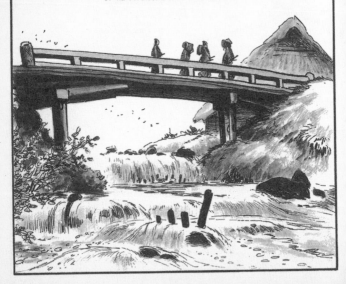

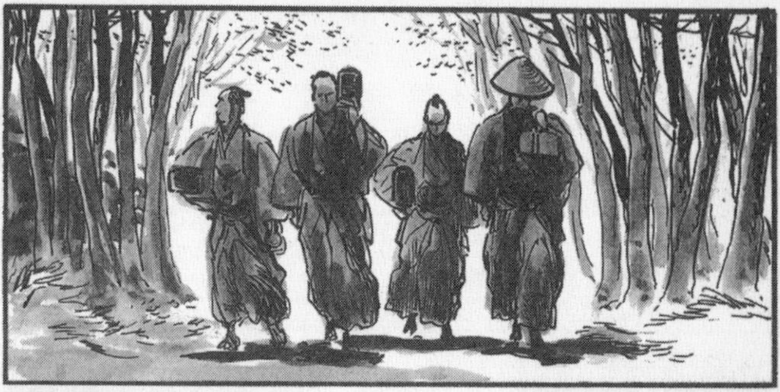

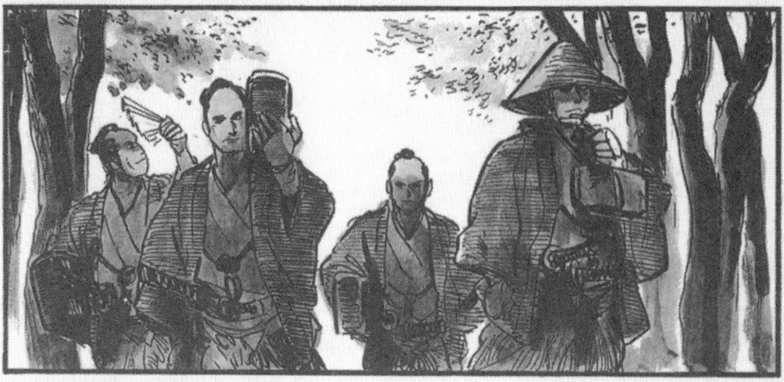

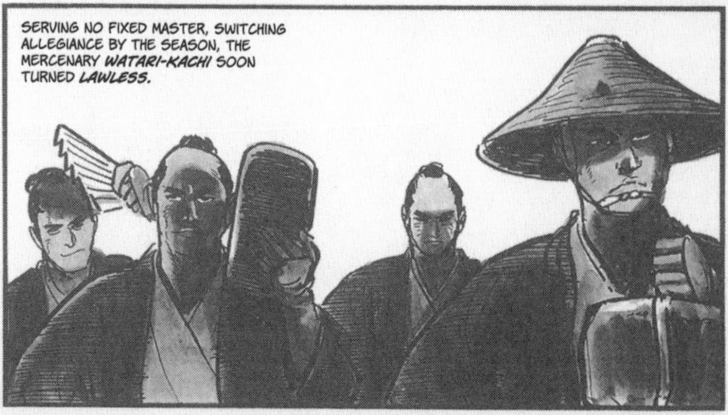
SERVING NO FIXED MASTER, SWITCHING ALLEGIANCE BY THE SEASON, THE MERCENARY WATARI-KACHI SOON TURNED LAWLESS.

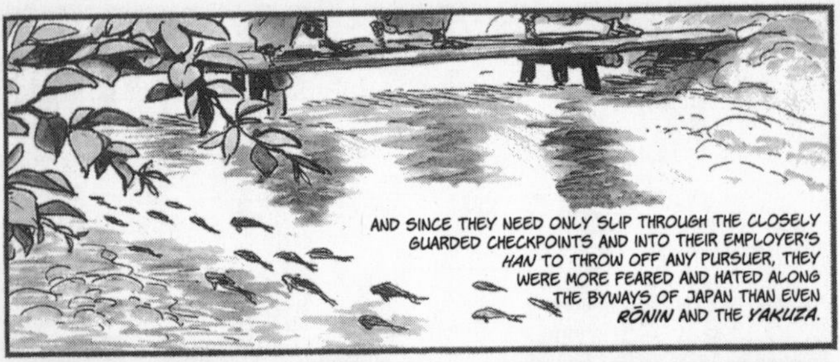
AND SINCE THEY NEED ONLY SLIP THROUGH THE CLOSELY GUARDED CHECKPOINTS AND INTO THEIR EMPLOYER'S *HAN* TO THROW OFF ANY PURSUER, THEY WERE MORE FEARED AND HATED ALONG THE BYWAYS OF JAPAN THAN EVEN *RŌNIN* AND THE *YAKUZA*.
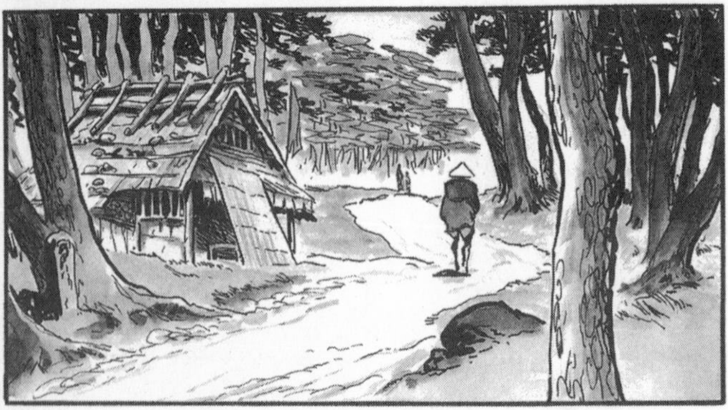
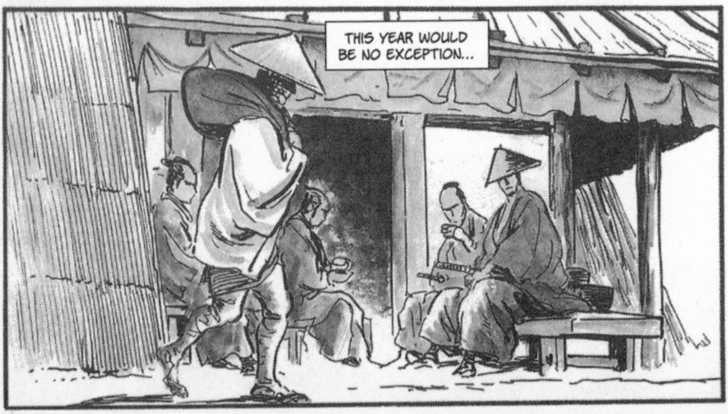
THIS YEAR WOULD BE NO EXCEPTION...

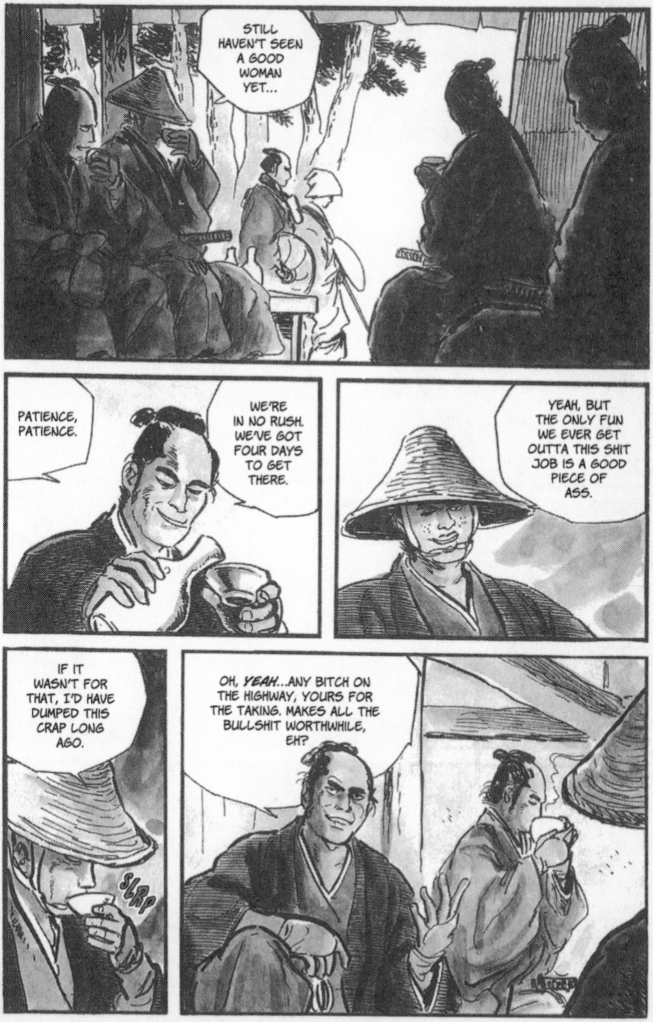

STILL HAVEN'T SEEN A GOOD WOMAN YET...
PATIENCE, PATIENCE.
WE'RE IN NO RUSH. WE'VE GOT FOUR DAYS TO GET THERE.
YEAH, BUT THE ONLY FUN WE EVER GET OUTTA THIS SHIT JOB IS A GOOD PIECE OF ASS.
IF IT WASN'T FOR THAT, I'D HAVE DUMPED THIS CRAP LONG AGO.
SLRP
OH, *YEAH*...ANY BITCH ON THE HIGHWAY, YOURS FOR THE TAKING. MAKES ALL THE BULLSHIT WORTHWHILE, EH?

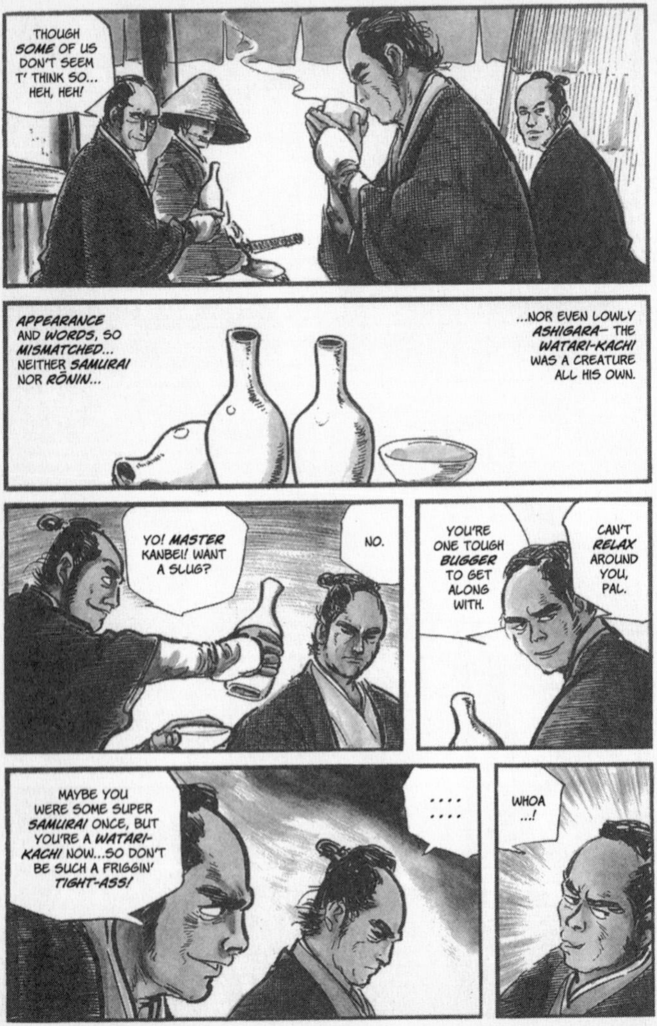

THOUGH SOME OF US DON'T SEEM T' THINK SO... HEH, HEH!
APPEARANCE AND WORDS, SO MISMATCHED... NEITHER SAMURAI NOR RŌNIN...
...NOR EVEN LOWLY ASHIGARA– THE WATARI-KACHI WAS A CREATURE ALL HIS OWN.
YO! MASTER KANBEI! WANT A SLUG?
NO.
YOU'RE ONE TOUGH BUGGER TO GET ALONG WITH.
CAN'T RELAX AROUND YOU, PAL.
MAYBE YOU WERE SOME SUPER SAMURAI ONCE, BUT YOU'RE A WATARI-KACHI NOW...SO DON'T BE SUCH A FRIGGIN' TIGHT-ASS!
....
....
WHOA ...!

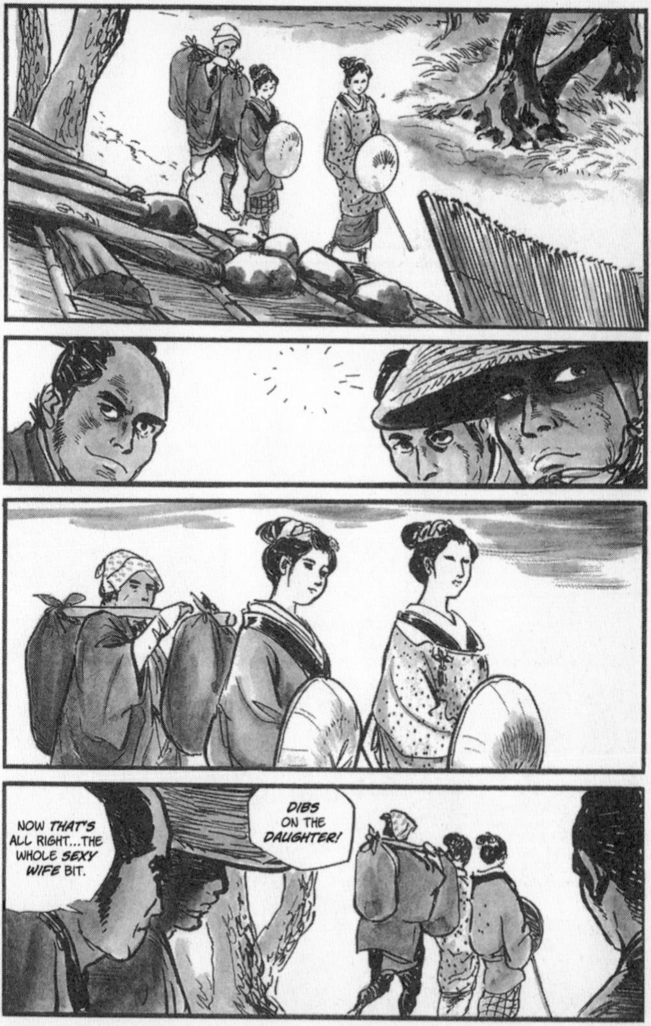
NOW THAT'S ALL RIGHT... THE WHOLE SEXY WIFE BIT.
DIBS ON THE DAUGHTER!

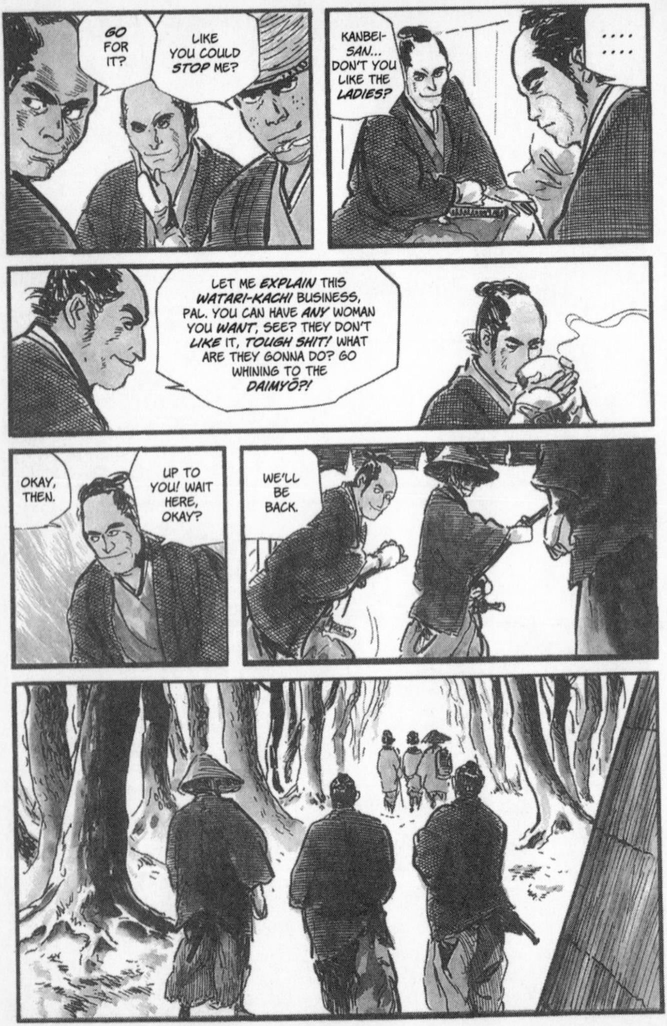
GO FOR IT?
LIKE YOU COULD STOP ME?
KANBEI-SAN... DON'T YOU LIKE THE LADIES?
....
....
LET ME EXPLAIN THIS WATARI-KACHI BUSINESS, PAL. YOU CAN HAVE ANY WOMAN YOU WANT, SEE? THEY DON'T LIKE IT, TOUGH SHIT! WHAT ARE THEY GONNA DO? GO WHINING TO THE DAIMYŌ?!
OKAY, THEN.
UP TO YOU! WAIT HERE, OKAY?
WE'LL BE BACK.

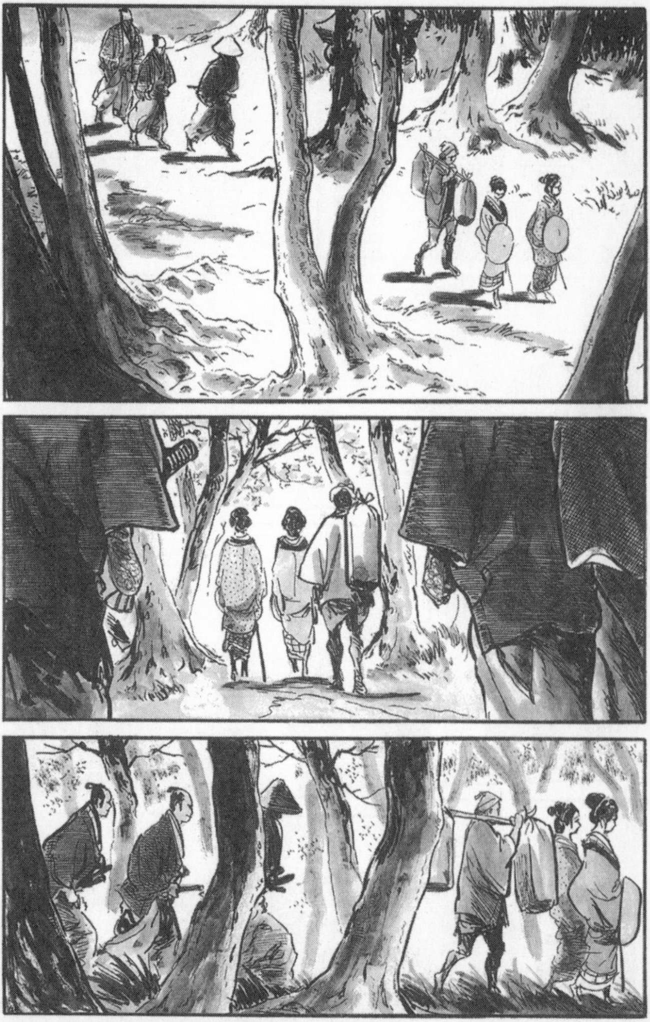

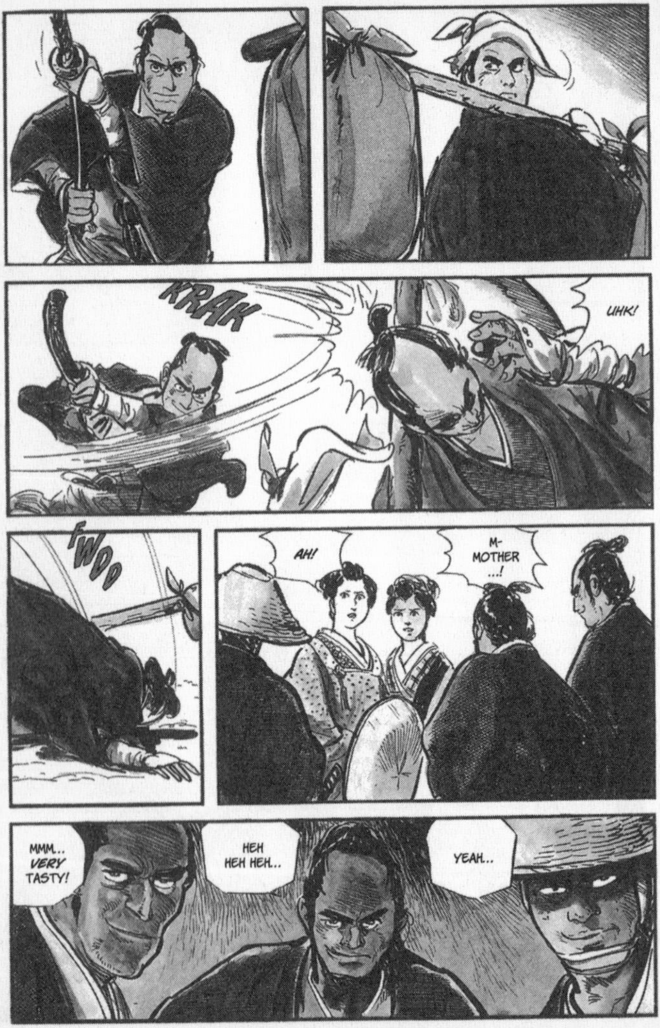
KRAK
UHK!
FWOO
AH!
M-
MOTHER
...!
MMM...
VERY
TASTY!
HEH
HEH HEH...
YEAH...

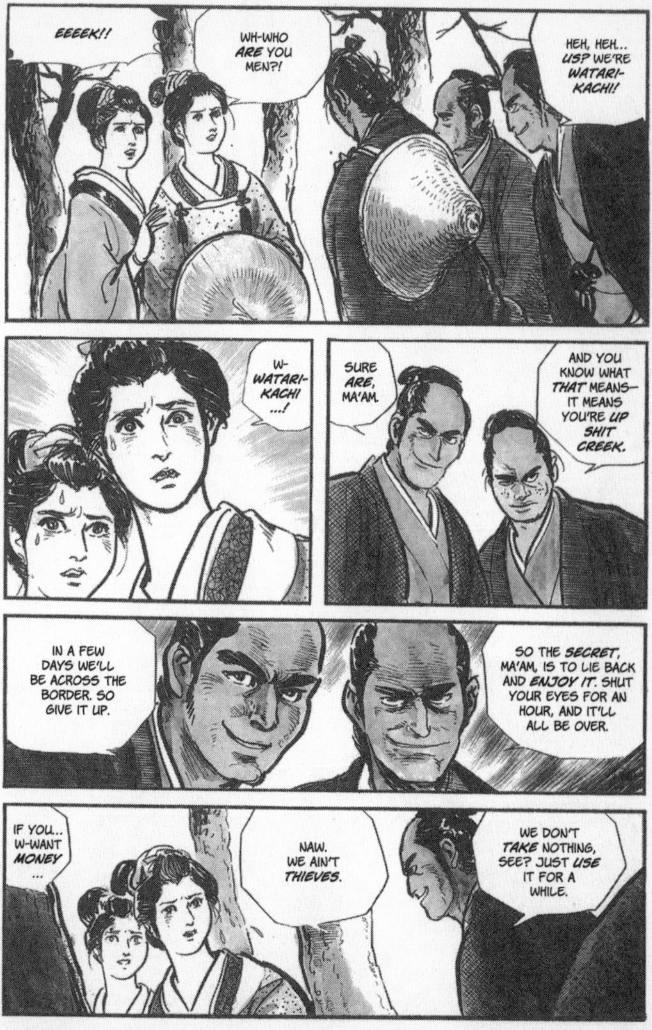

EEEEK!!
WH-WHO *ARE* YOU MEN?!
HEH, HEH... *US?* WE'RE *WATARI-KACHI!*
W-*WATARI-KACHI* ...!
SURE *ARE,* MA'AM.
AND YOU KNOW WHAT *THAT* MEANS— IT MEANS YOU'RE *UP SHIT CREEK.*
IN A FEW DAYS WE'LL BE ACROSS THE BORDER. SO GIVE IT UP.
SO THE *SECRET,* MA'AM, IS TO LIE BACK AND *ENJOY IT.* SHUT YOUR EYES FOR AN HOUR, AND IT'LL ALL BE OVER.
IF YOU... W-WANT *MONEY* ...
NAW. WE AIN'T *THIEVES.*
WE DON'T *TAKE* NOTHING, SEE? JUST *USE* IT FOR A WHILE.

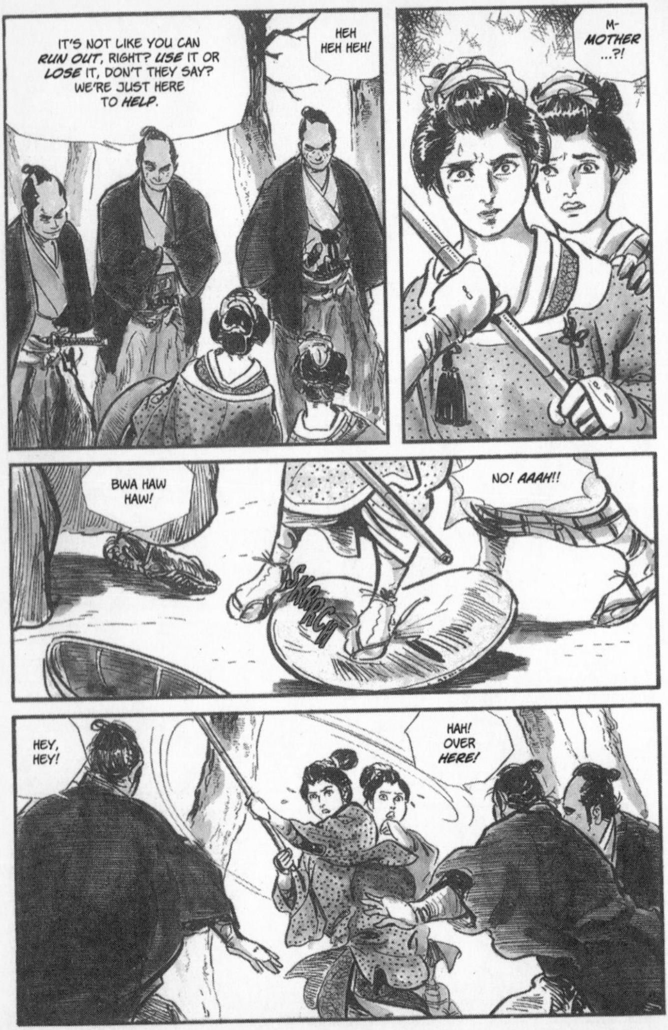
IT'S NOT LIKE YOU CAN RUN OUT, RIGHT? USE IT OR LOSE IT, DON'T THEY SAY? WE'RE JUST HERE TO HELP.
HEH HEH HEH!
M- MOTHER ...?!
BWA HAW HAW!
SKRCH
NO! AAAH!!
HEY, HEY!
HAH! OVER HERE!

GOT-CHA!
OH!
AHHH!
EEEK!! H-HELP!!
OH, NO YA DON'T!
EEEEK!!
WHOA!
S... SOMEBODY!!
HELP US!!

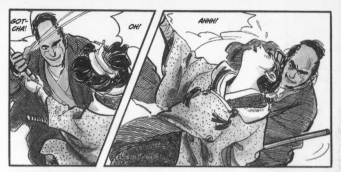

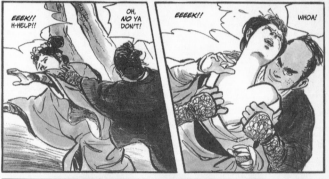

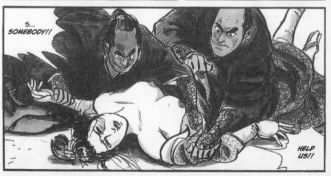

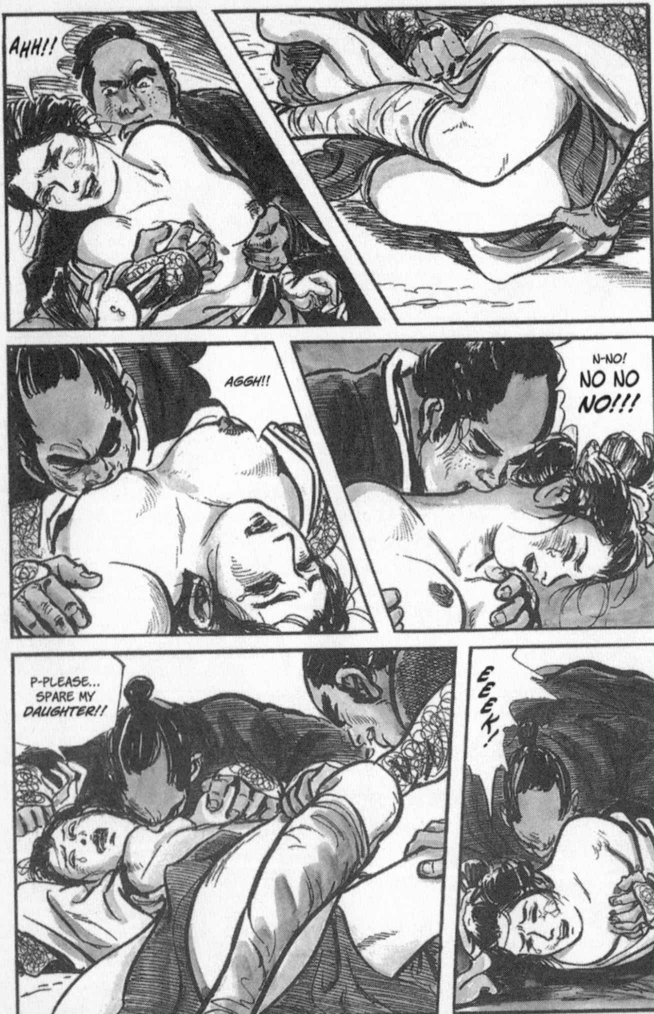
AHH!!
AGGH!!
N-NO! NO NO NO!!!
P-PLEASE... SPARE MY DAUGHTER!!
EEEK!

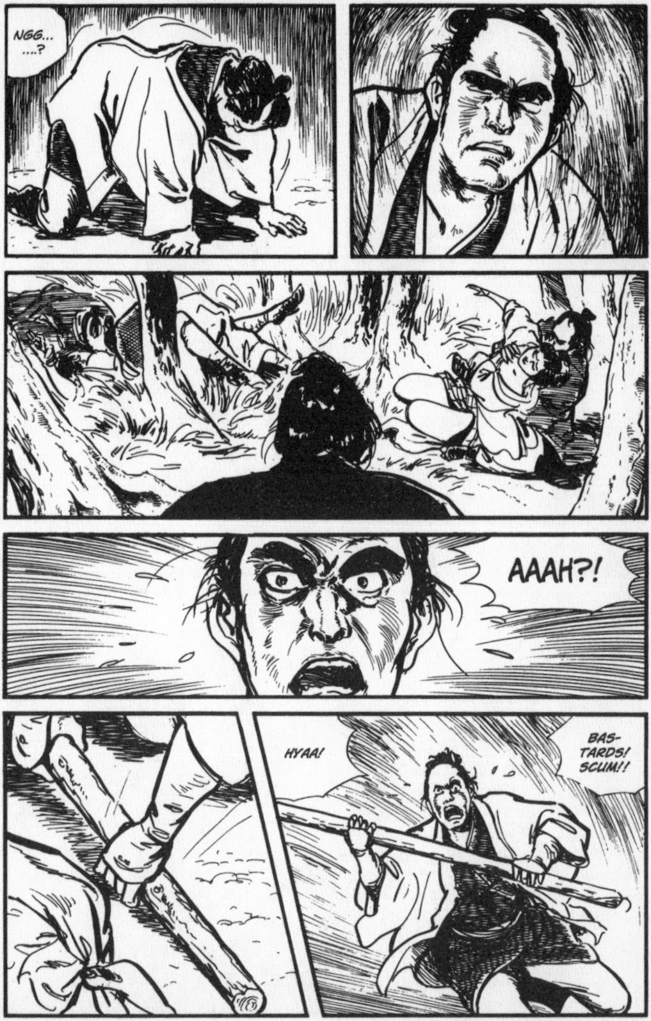
NGG... ....?
AAAH?!
HYAA!
BAS-TARDS! SCUM!!

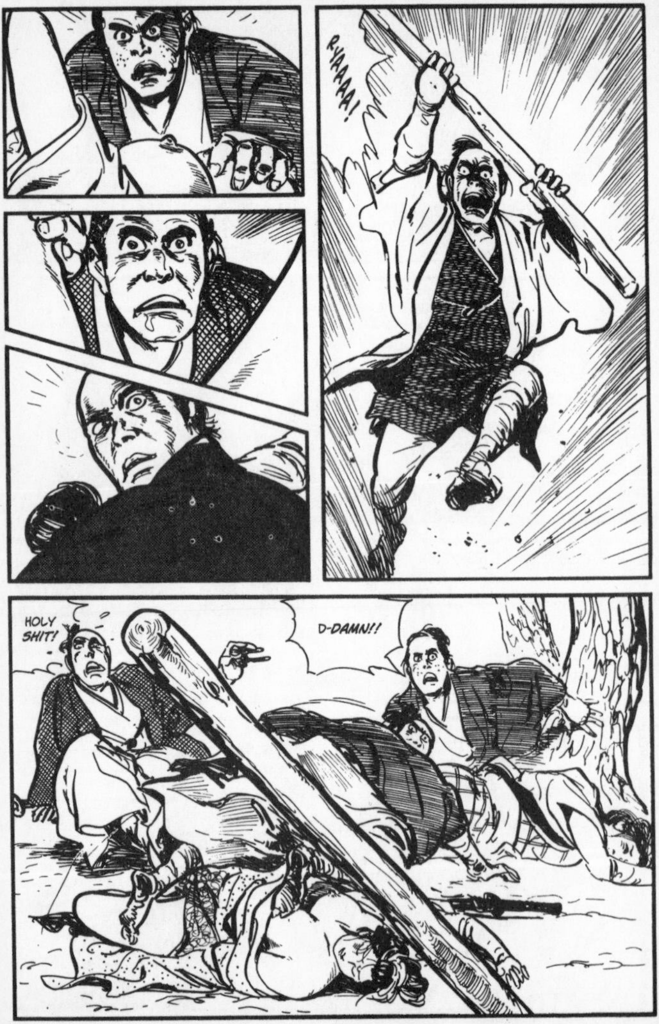

R-YAAAA!
HOLY SHIT!
D-DAMN!!

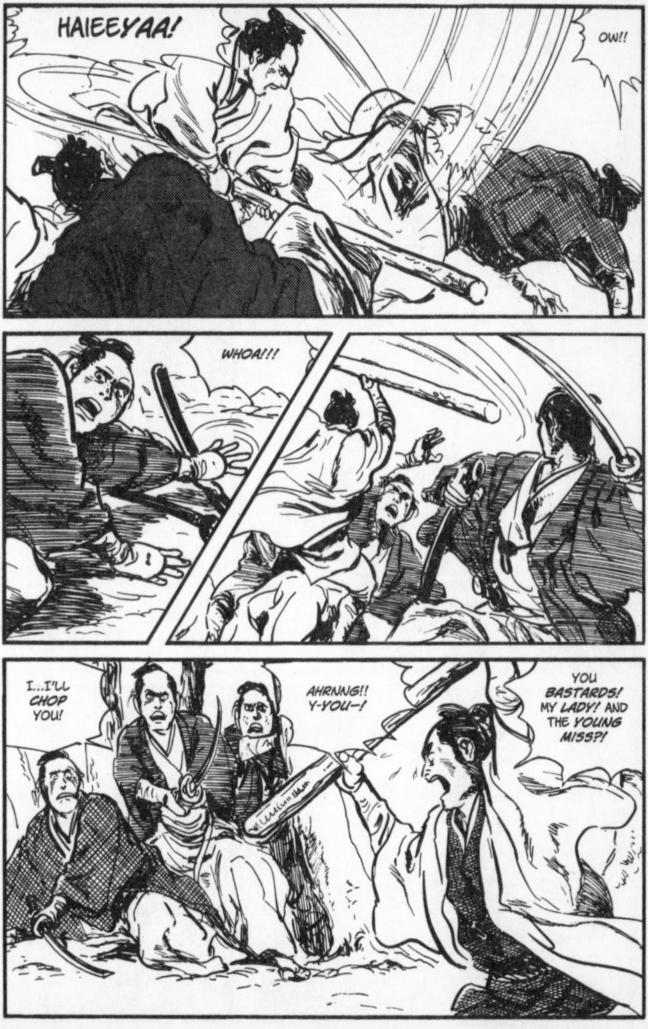
HAIEEYAA!
OW!!
WHOA!!!
I...I'LL CHOP YOU!
AHRNNG!! Y-YOU-!
YOU BASTARDS! MY LADY! AND THE YOUNG MISS?!

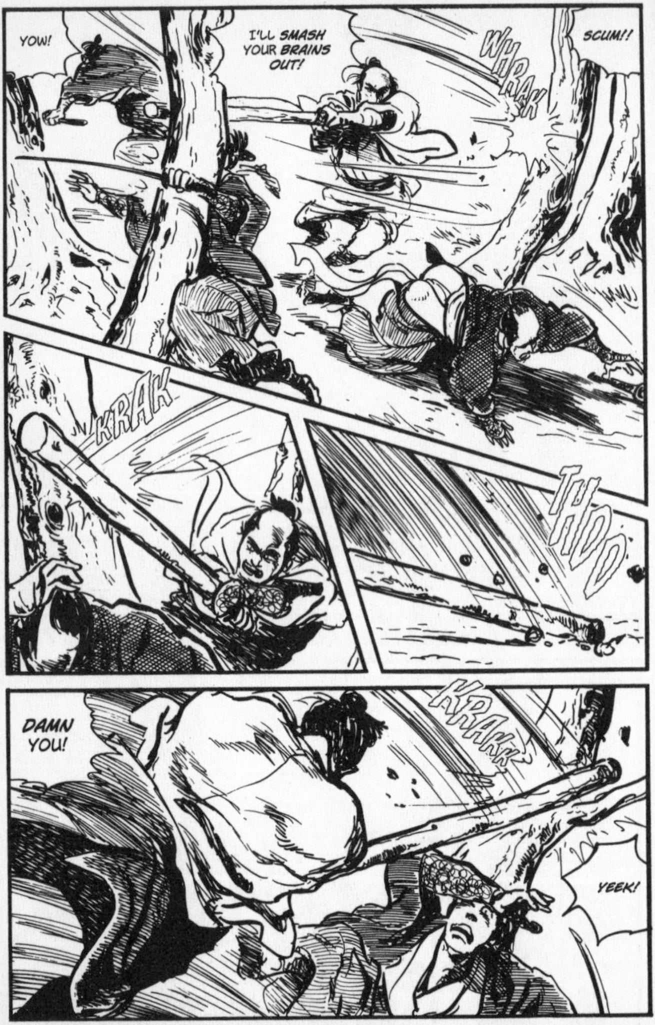
YOW!
I'LL SMASH YOUR BRAINS OUT!
WHRAK
SCUM!!
KRAK
THOO
DAMN YOU!
KRAKK
YEEK!

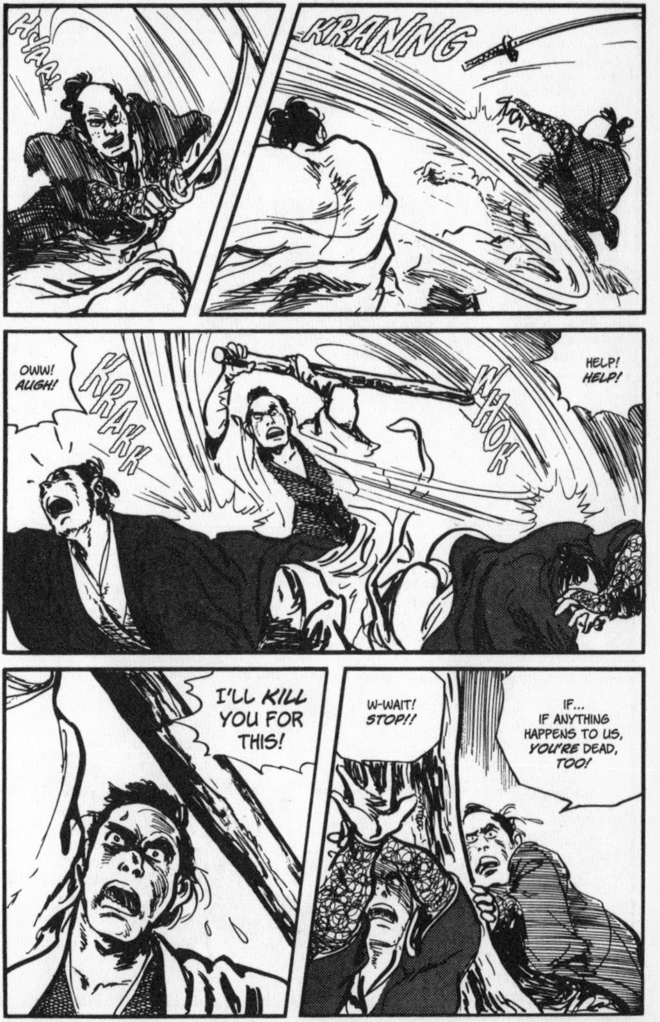
HYAA!
KRANNG
OWW! AUGH!
KRAKK
WHOK
HELP! HELP!
I'LL KILL YOU FOR THIS!
W-WAIT! STOP!!
IF... IF ANYTHING HAPPENS TO US, YOU'RE DEAD, TOO!

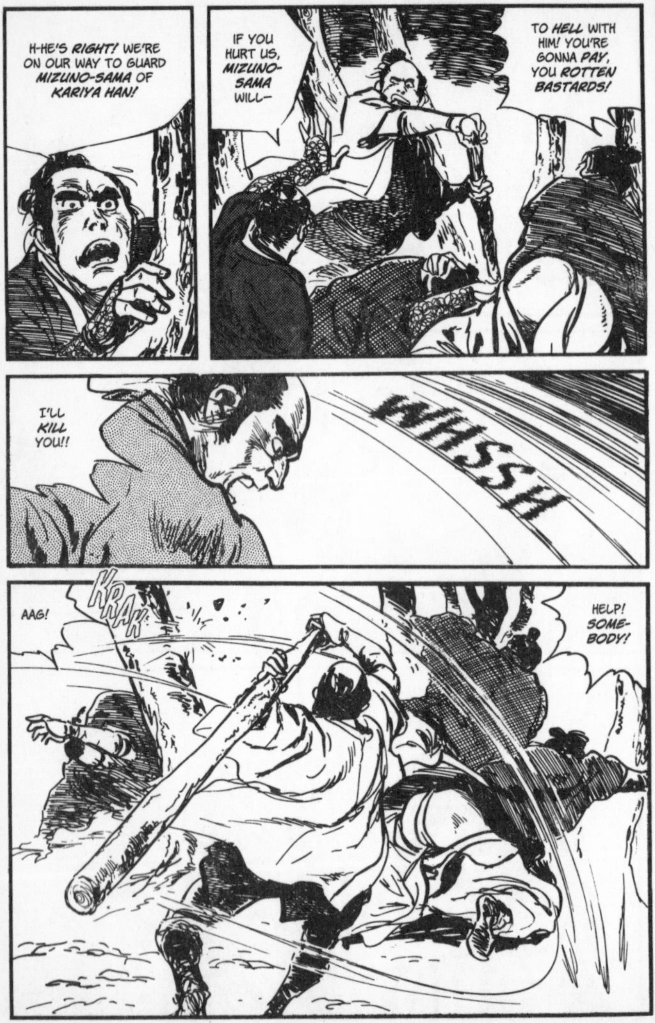
H-HE'S RIGHT! WE'RE ON OUR WAY TO GUARD MIZUNO-SAMA OF KARIYA HAN!
IF YOU HURT US, MIZUNO-SAMA WILL–
TO HELL WITH HIM! YOU'RE GONNA PAY, YOU ROTTEN BASTARDS!
I'LL KILL YOU!!
WHISSH
KRAK
AAG!
HELP! SOMEBODY!

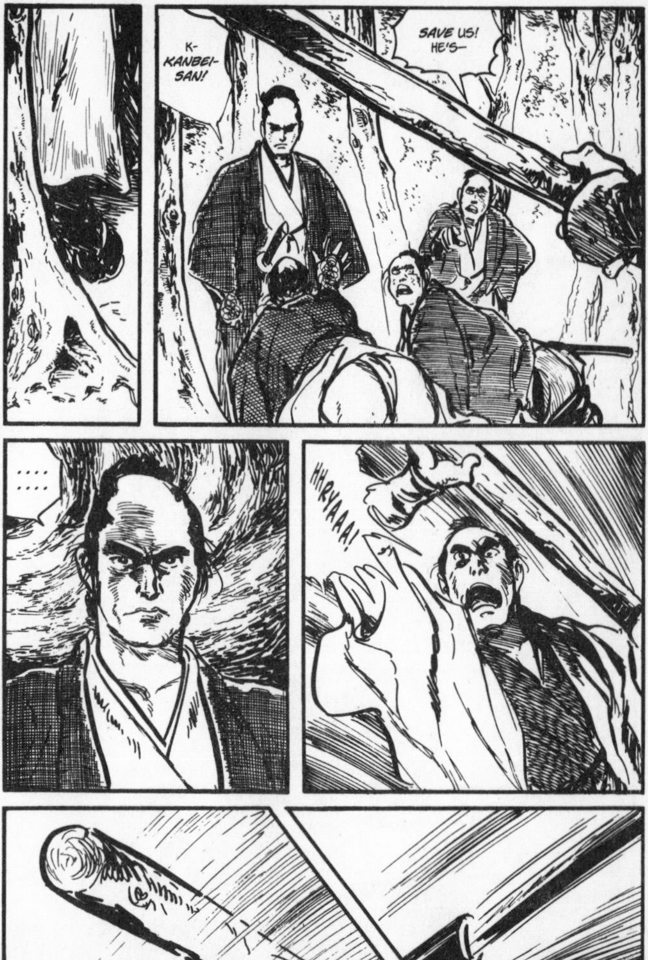
K-
KANBEI-
SAN!
SAVE US!
HE'S—
....
....
HHRYAAA!

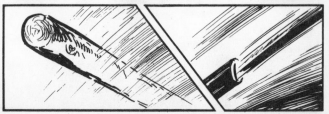

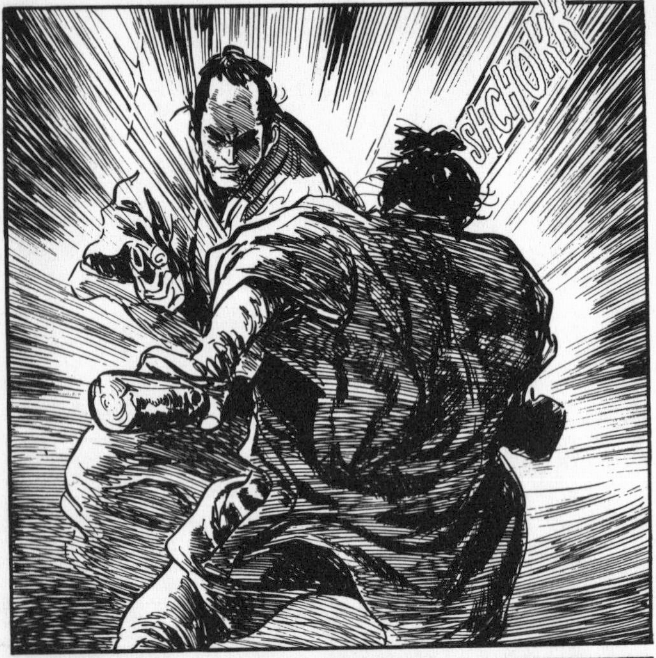
SHCHOKK
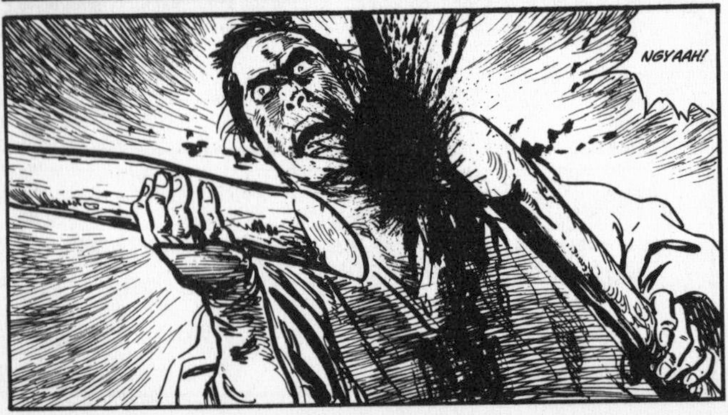
NGYAAH!

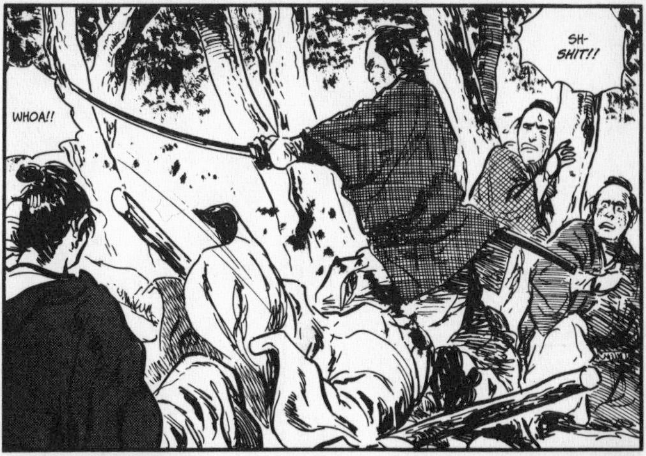
WHOA!!
SH-
SHIT!!

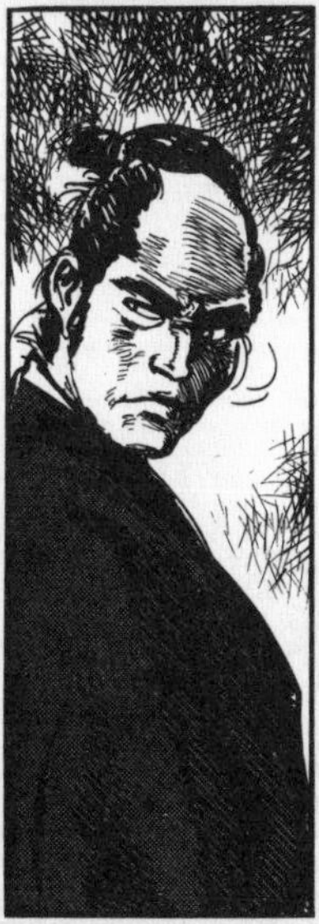
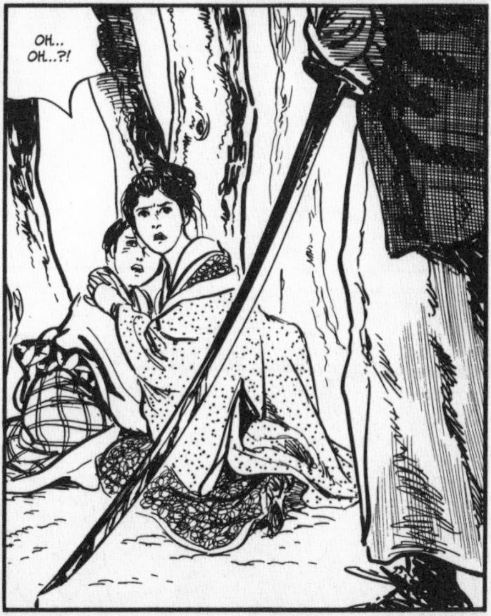
OH..
OH..?!

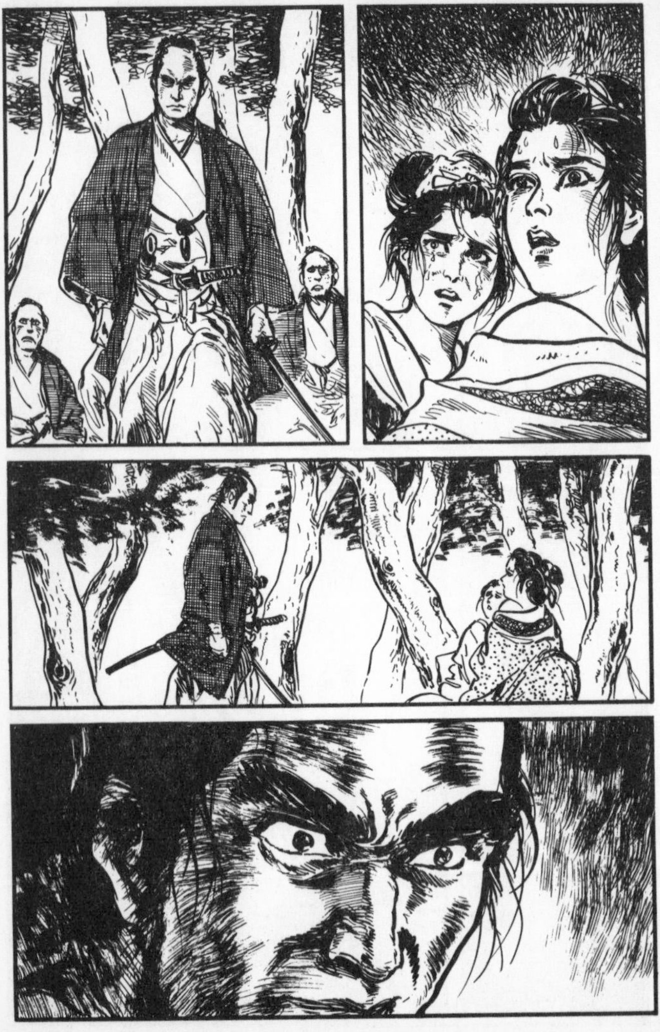

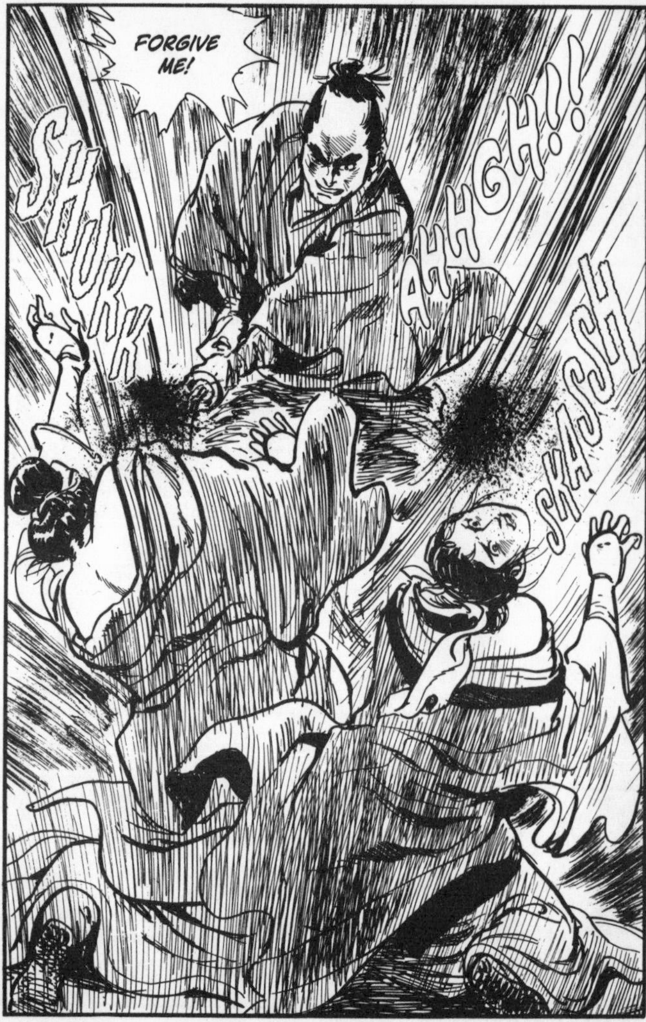
FORGIVE ME!
SHUKK
AHHGH!!!
SKASSH

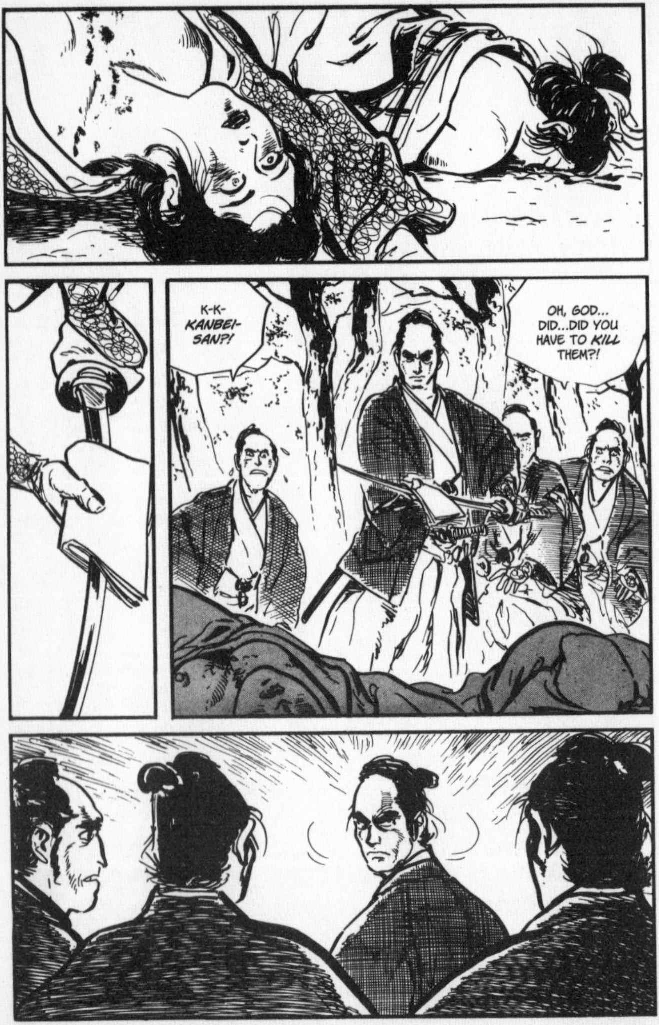
K-K-KANBEI-SAN?!
OH, GOD... DID...DID YOU HAVE TO KILL THEM?!

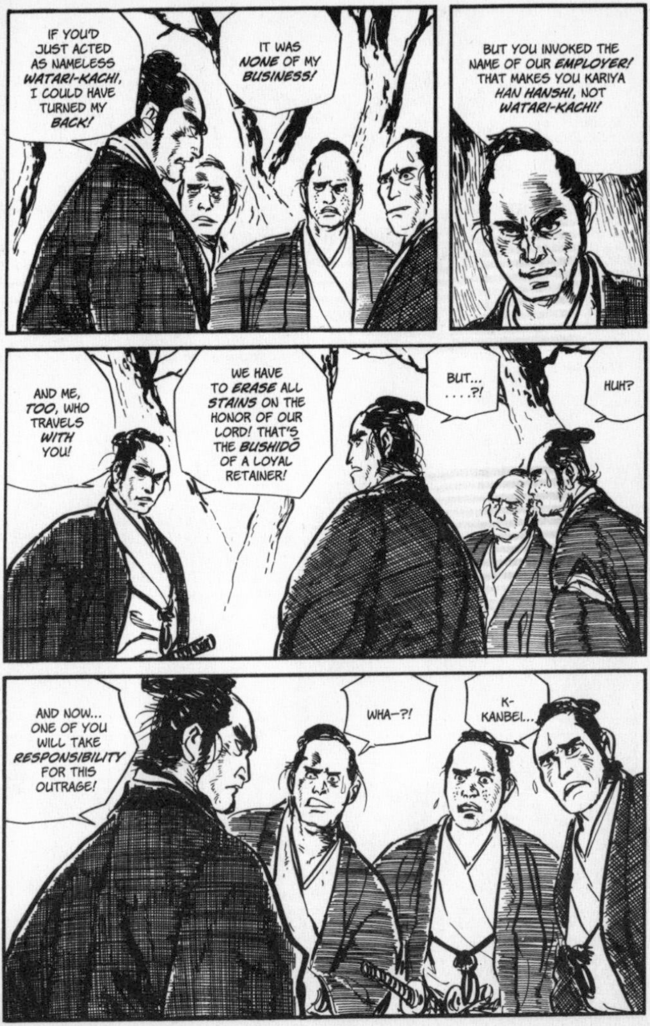
IF YOU'D JUST ACTED AS NAMELESS WATARI-KACHI, I COULD HAVE TURNED MY BACK!
IT WAS NONE OF MY BUSINESS!
BUT YOU INVOKED THE NAME OF OUR EMPLOYER! THAT MAKES YOU KARIYA HAN HANSHI, NOT WATARI-KACHI!
AND ME, TOO, WHO TRAVELS WITH YOU!
WE HAVE TO ERASE ALL STAINS ON THE HONOR OF OUR LORD! THAT'S THE BUSHIDŌ OF A LOYAL RETAINER!
BUT... ....?!
HUH?
AND NOW... ONE OF YOU WILL TAKE RESPONSIBILITY FOR THIS OUTRAGE!
WHA-?!
K-KANBEI...

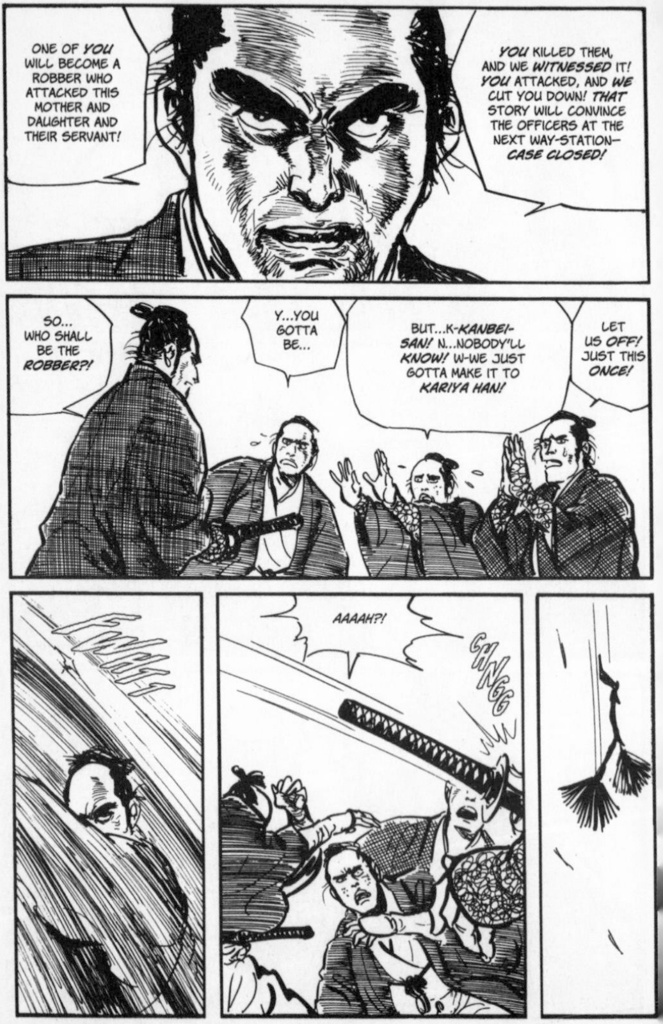
ONE OF *YOU* WILL BECOME A ROBBER WHO ATTACKED THIS MOTHER AND DAUGHTER AND THEIR SERVANT!
YOU KILLED THEM, AND WE *WITNESSED* IT! *YOU* ATTACKED, AND *WE* CUT YOU DOWN! *THAT* STORY WILL CONVINCE THE OFFICERS AT THE NEXT WAY-STATION— *CASE CLOSED!*
SO... WHO SHALL BE THE *ROBBER?!*
Y...YOU GOTTA BE...
BUT...K-*KANBEI-SAN!* N...NOBODY'LL *KNOW!* W-WE JUST GOTTA MAKE IT TO *KARIYA HAN!*
LET US *OFF!* JUST THIS *ONCE!*
AAAAH?!
CHNGG

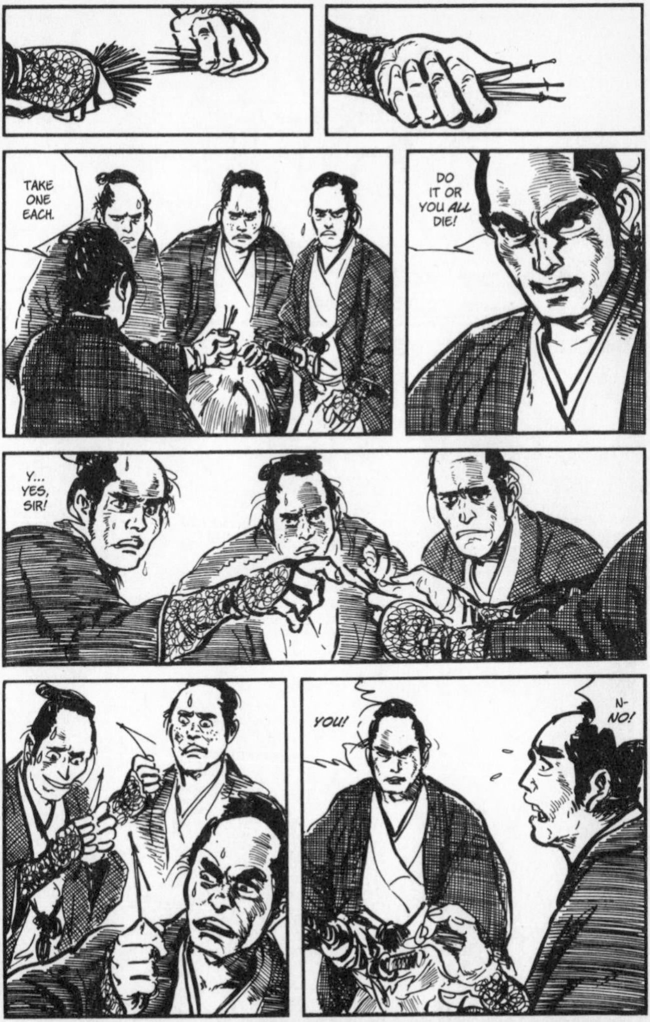
TAKE ONE EACH.
DO IT OR YOU ALL DIE!
Y... YES, SIR!
YOU!
N- NO!

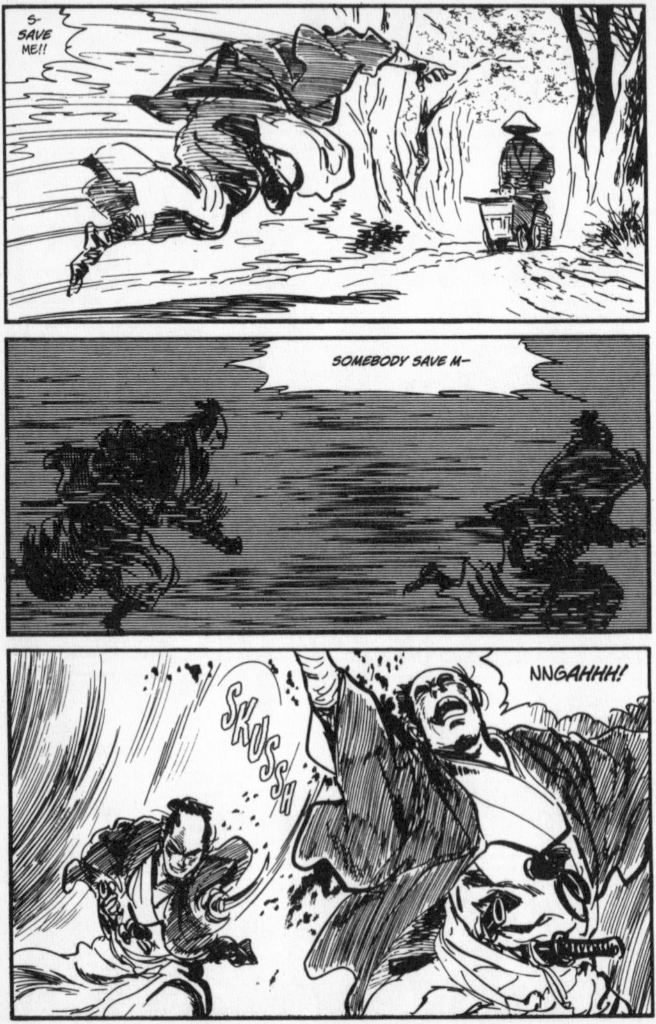
S-
SAVE
ME!!
SOMEBODY SAVE M–
SKUSSH
NNGAHHH!

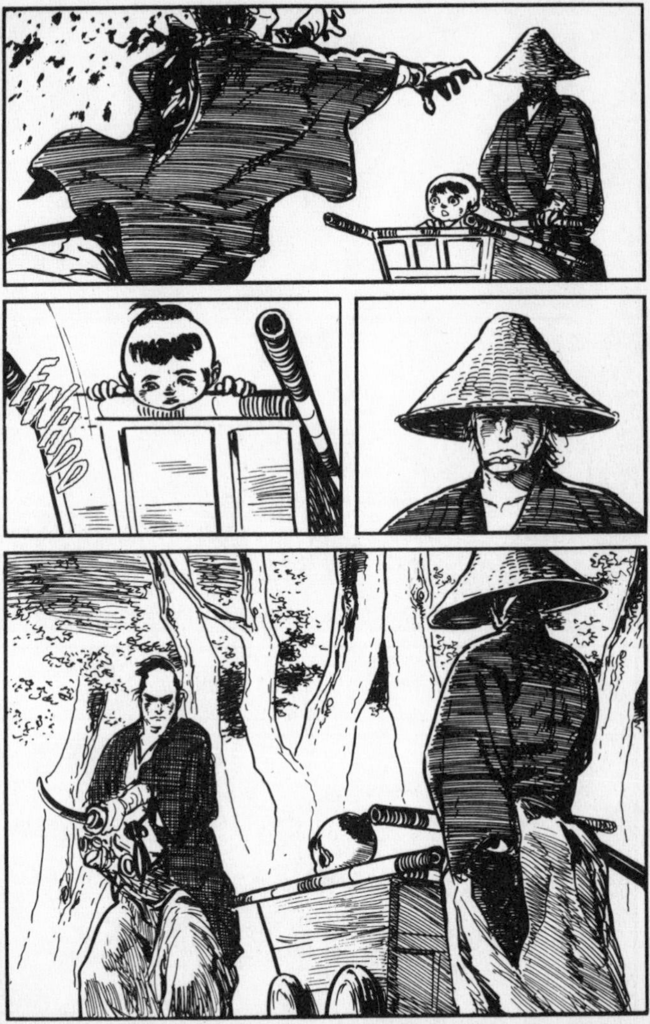
FWHOO

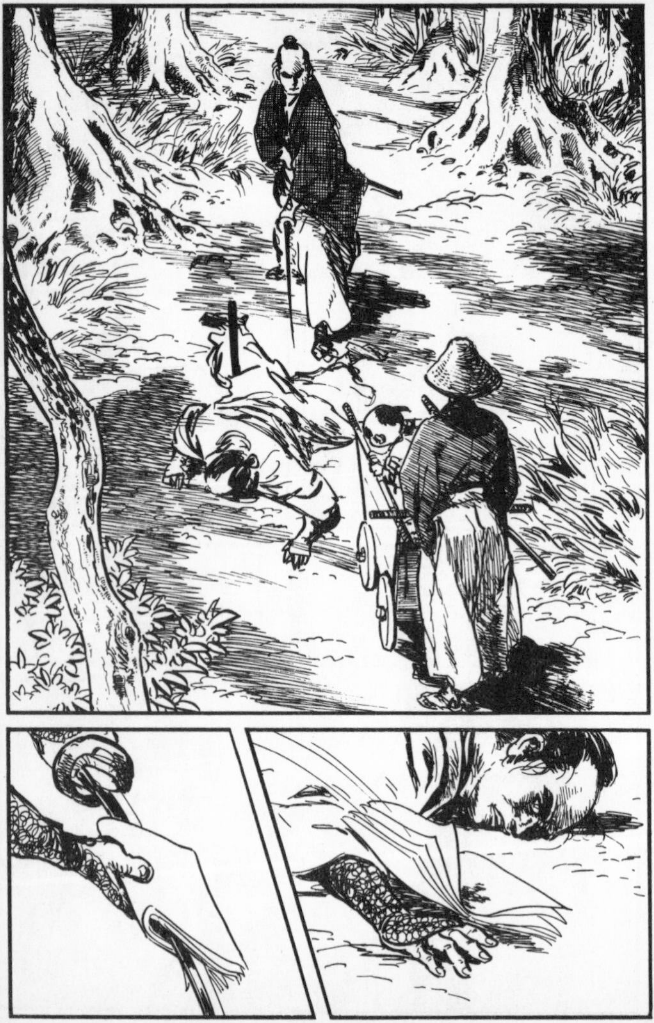

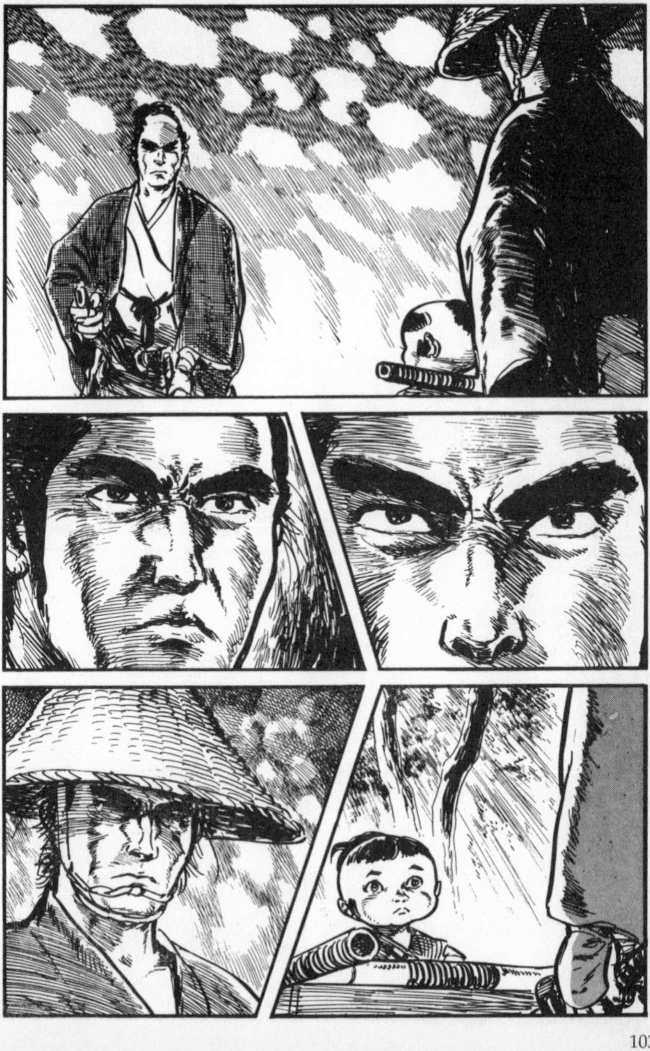

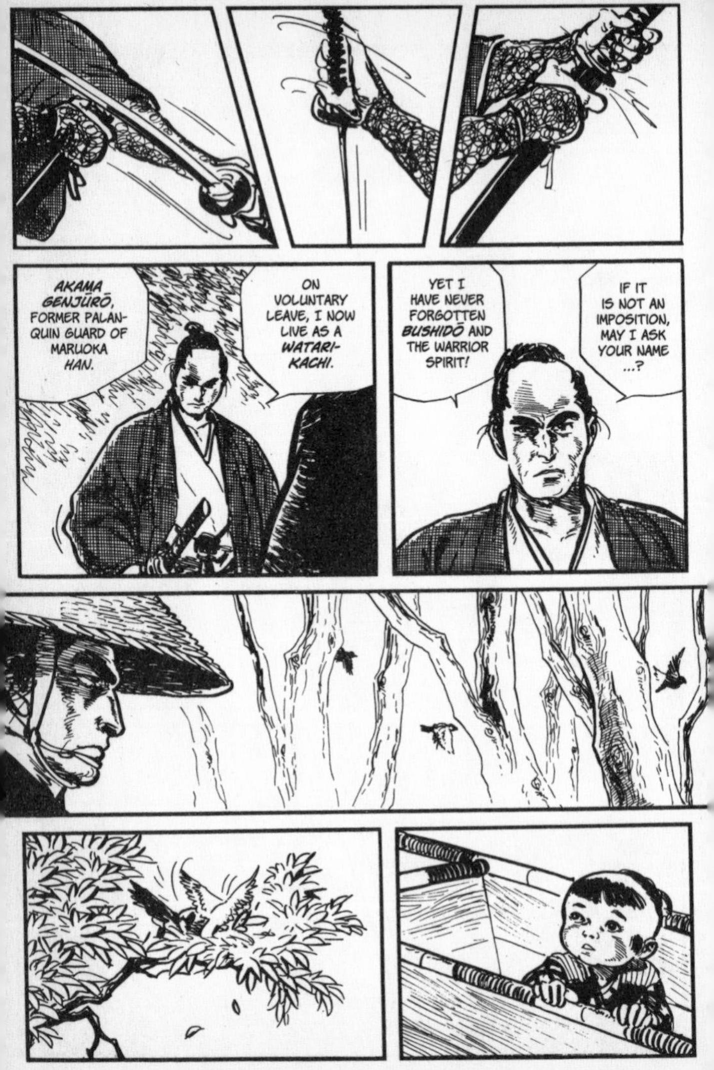
AKAMA GENJŪRŌ, FORMER PALANQUIN GUARD OF MARUOKA HAN.
ON VOLUNTARY LEAVE, I NOW LIVE AS A WATARI-KACHI.
YET I HAVE NEVER FORGOTTEN BUSHIDŌ AND THE WARRIOR SPIRIT!
IF IT IS NOT AN IMPOSITION, MAY I ASK YOUR NAME ...?

FORMER *KŌGI KAI-SHAKUNIN*, ŌGAMI ITTŌ.

I *KNEW* IT WAS SO! IN YEARS PAST, I HAVE SEEN YOU FROM AFAR, SIR, WHILE LEADING MY LORD'S HORSE IN EDO CASTLE!

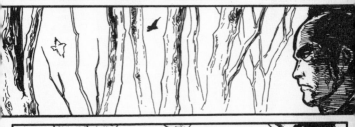

AND I HAVE HEARD OF *AKAMA GENJŪRŌ* ...

...A MASTER OF *KAGE-RYŪ* IN THE MARUOKA HAN PALANQUIN GUARD.

YOU *FLATTER* ME, SIR...AND NOW I FEAR I HAVE OFFENDED YOUR EYES. PLEASE UNDERSTAND THAT CIRCUMSTANCES LEFT ME NO CHOICE.

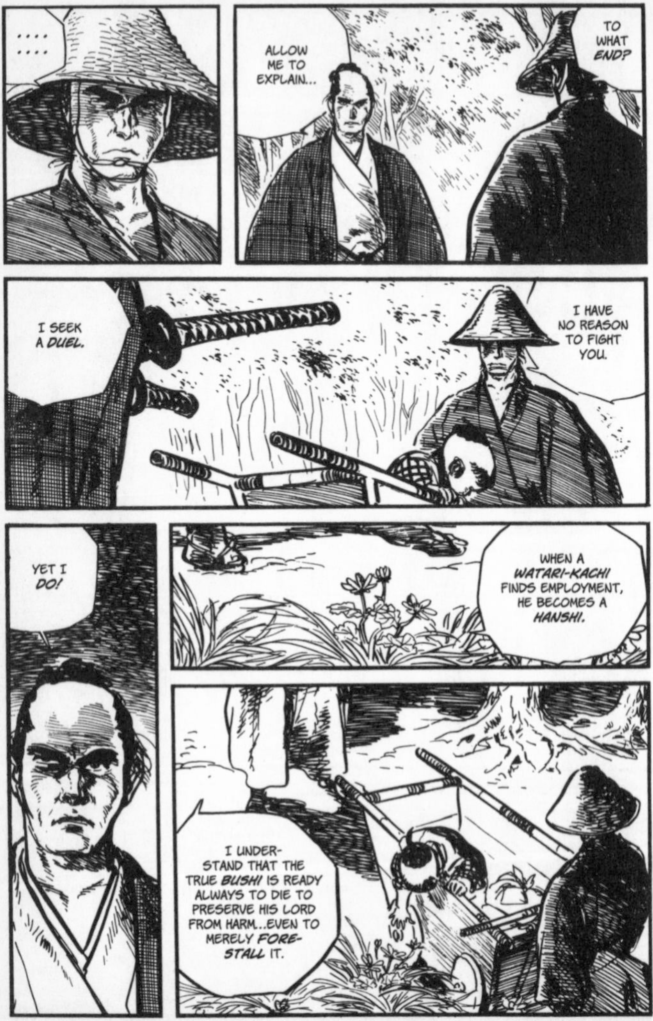
....
....
ALLOW ME TO EXPLAIN...
TO WHAT END?
I SEEK A DUEL.
I HAVE NO REASON TO FIGHT YOU.
YET I DO!
WHEN A WATARI-KACHI FINDS EMPLOYMENT, HE BECOMES A HANSHI.
I UNDER-STAND THAT THE TRUE BUSHI IS READY ALWAYS TO DIE TO PRESERVE HIS LORD FROM HARM...EVEN TO MERELY FORE-STALL IT.

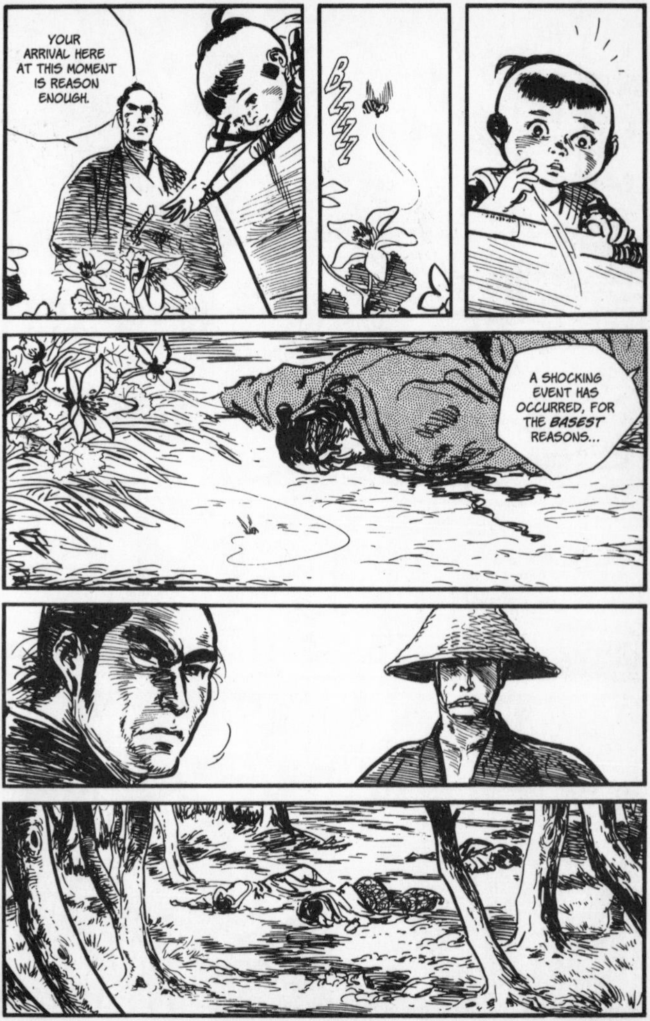
YOUR ARRIVAL HERE AT THIS MOMENT IS REASON ENOUGH.
BZZZZ
A SHOCKING EVENT HAS OCCURRED, FOR THE *BASEST* REASONS...

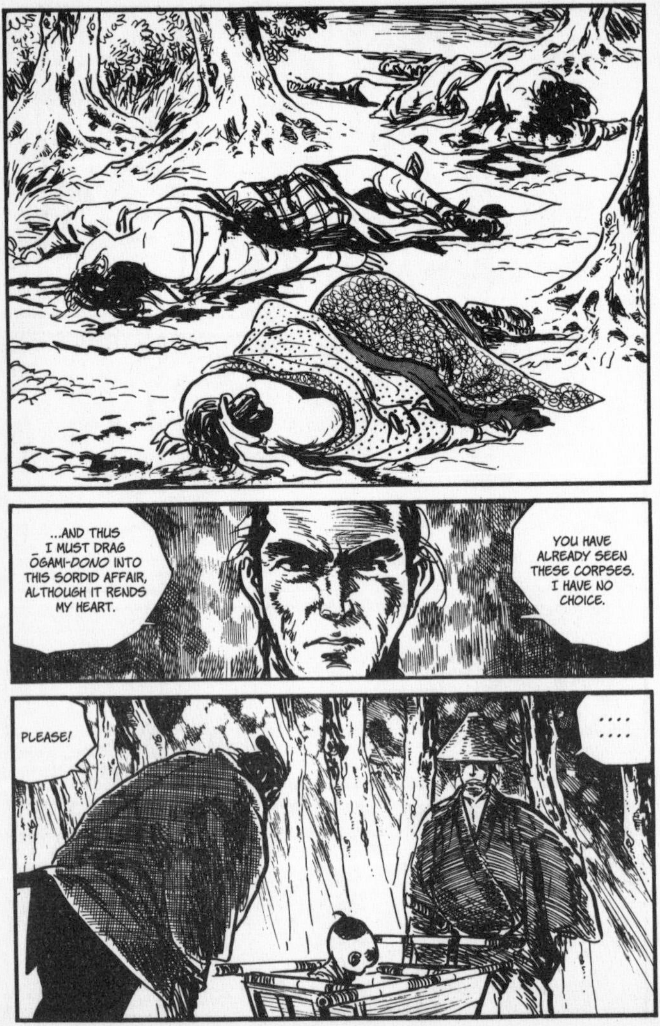
...AND THUS I MUST DRAG ŌGAMI-*DONO* INTO THIS SORDID AFFAIR, ALTHOUGH IT RENDS MY HEART.
YOU HAVE ALREADY SEEN THESE CORPSES. I HAVE NO CHOICE.
PLEASE!
....
....

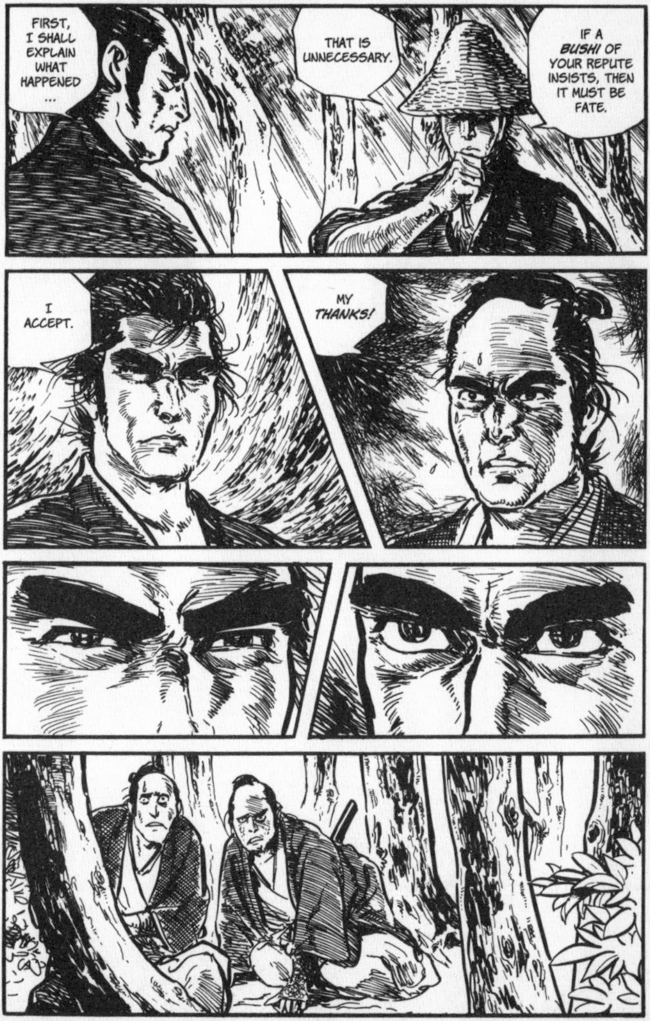

FIRST, I SHALL EXPLAIN WHAT HAPPENED ...
THAT IS UNNECESSARY.
IF A *BUSHI* OF YOUR REPUTE INSISTS, THEN IT MUST BE FATE.
I ACCEPT.
MY *THANKS!*

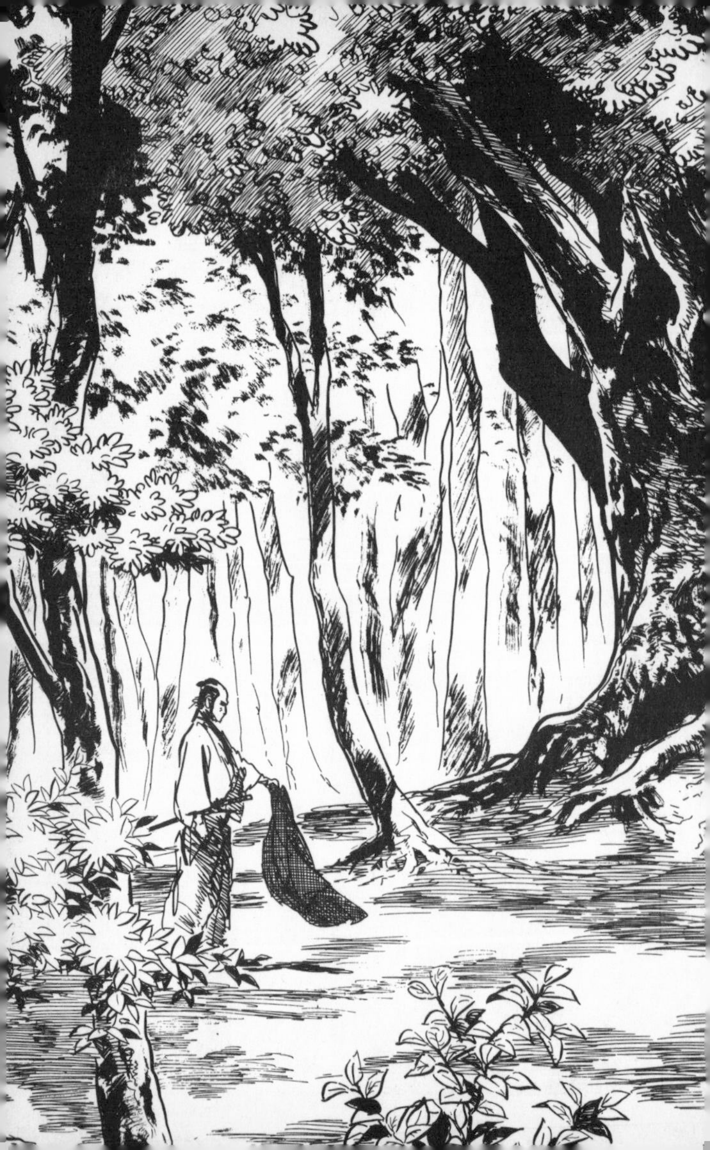

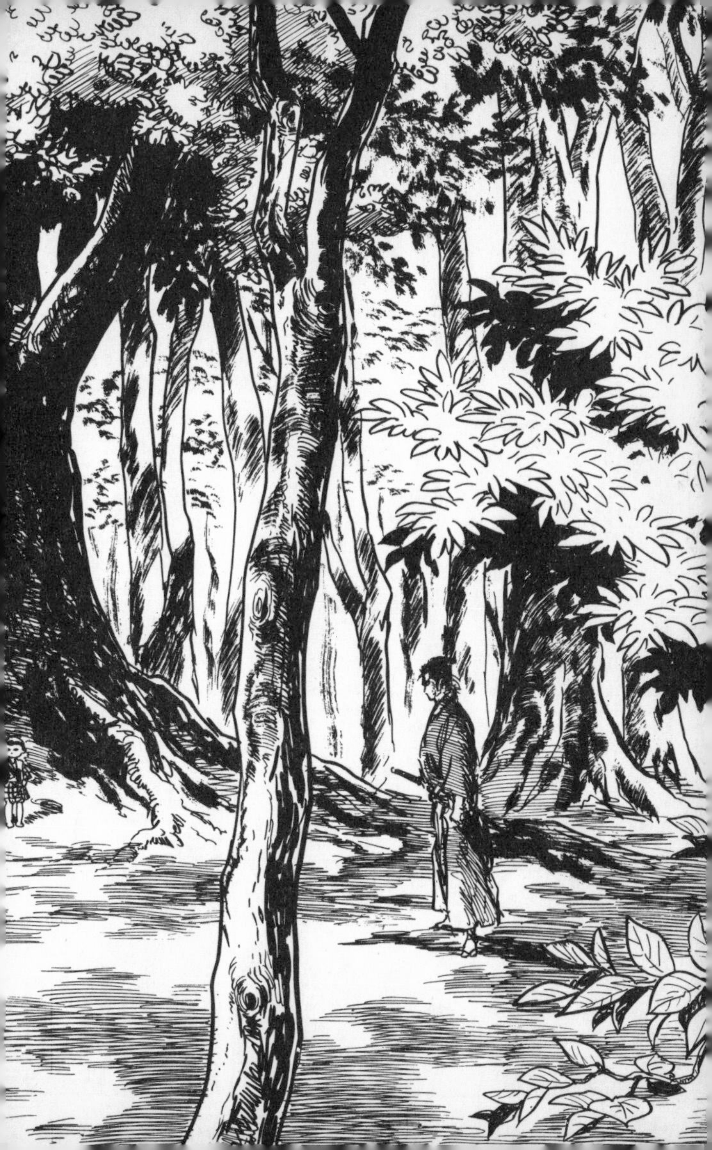

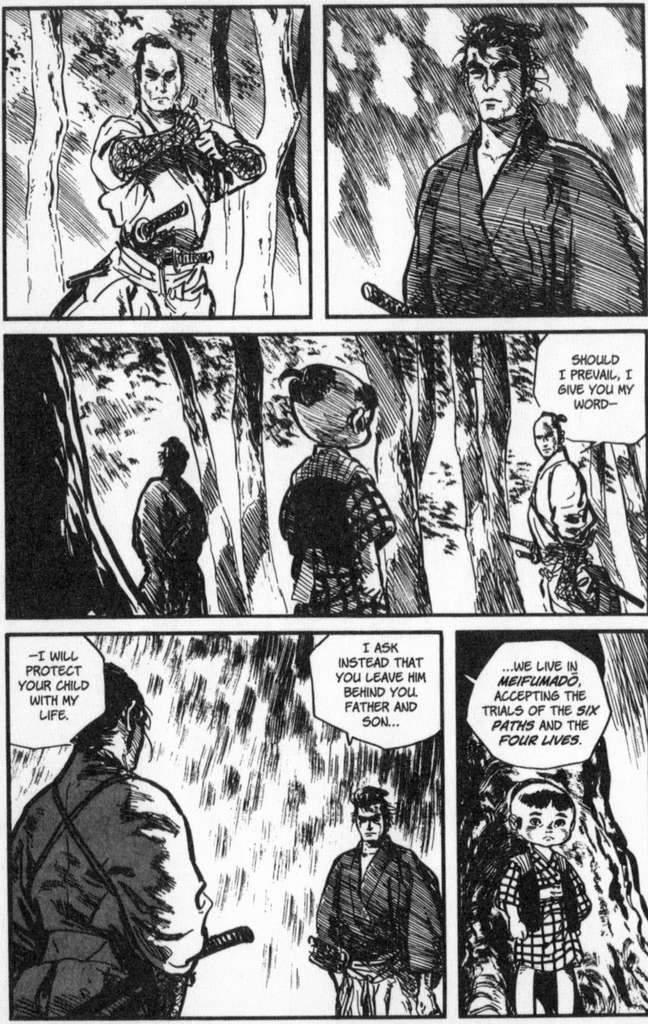
SHOULD I PREVAIL, I GIVE YOU MY WORD—
—I WILL PROTECT YOUR CHILD WITH MY LIFE.
I ASK INSTEAD THAT YOU LEAVE HIM BEHIND YOU. FATHER AND SON...
...WE LIVE IN *MEIFUMADŌ*, ACCEPTING THE TRIALS OF THE *SIX PATHS* AND THE *FOUR LIVES*.

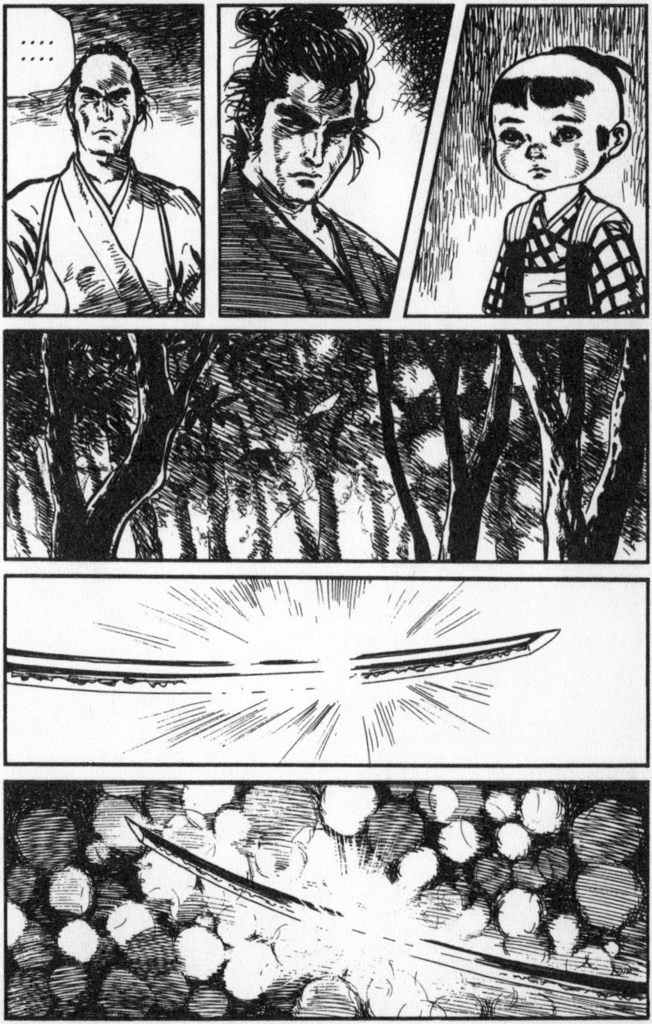
....
....

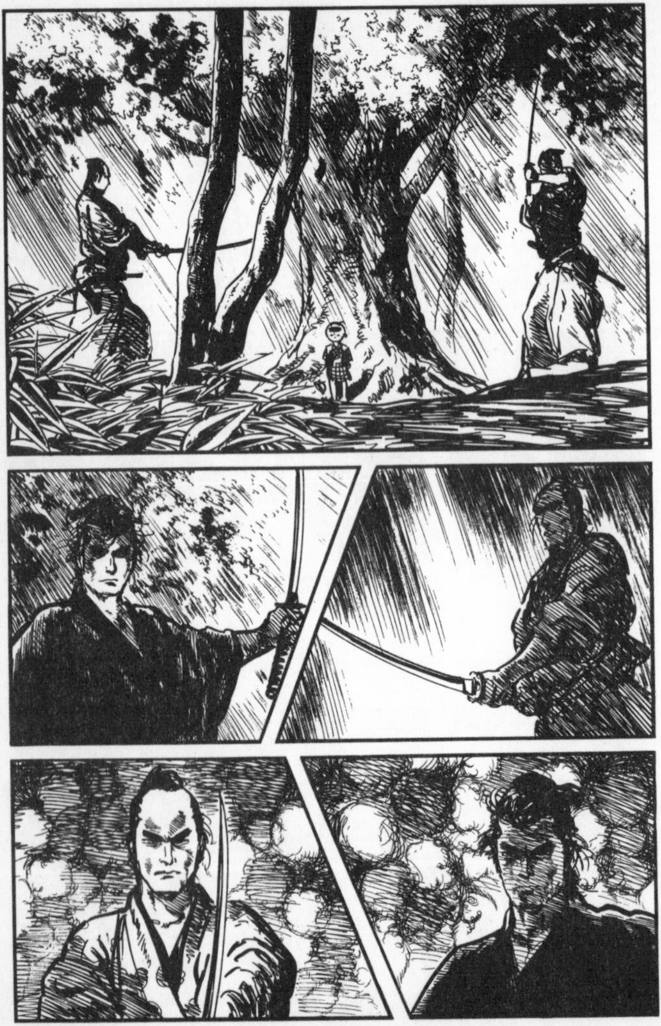

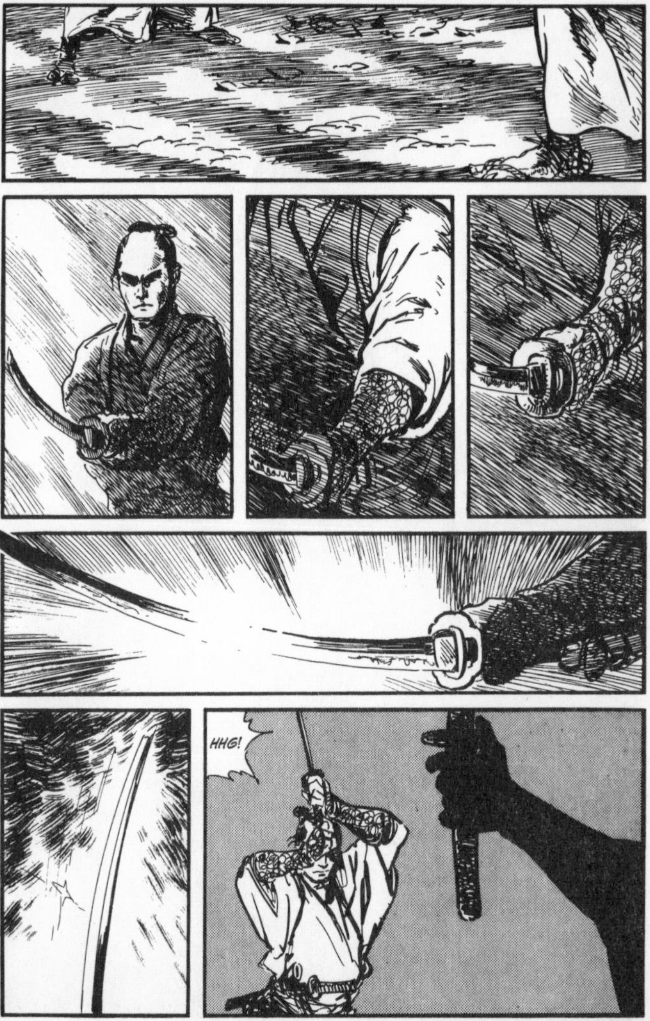
HHG!

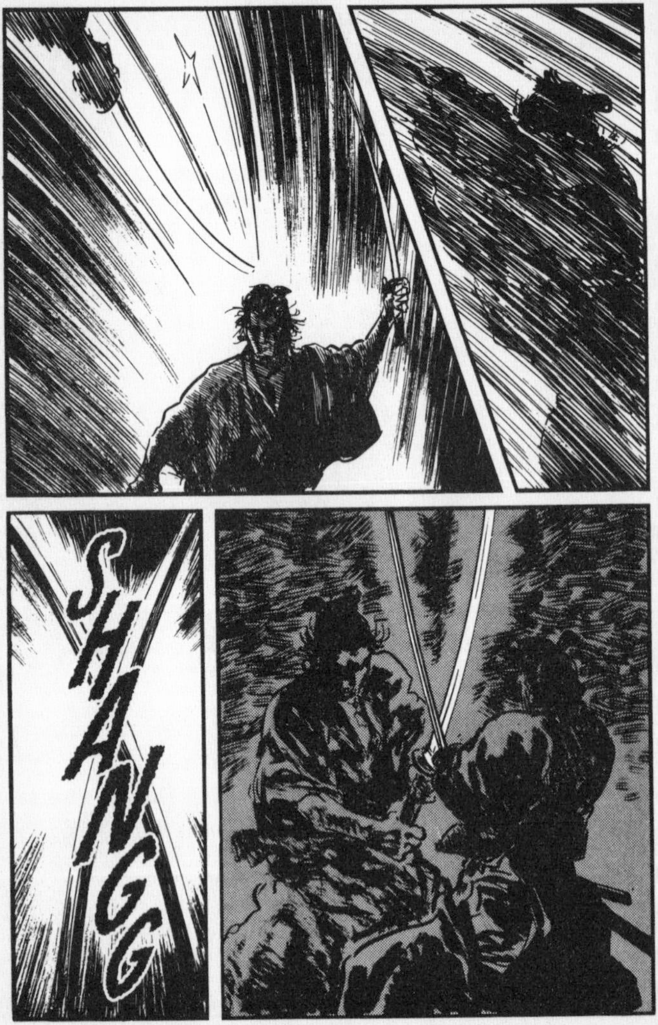
SHANGG

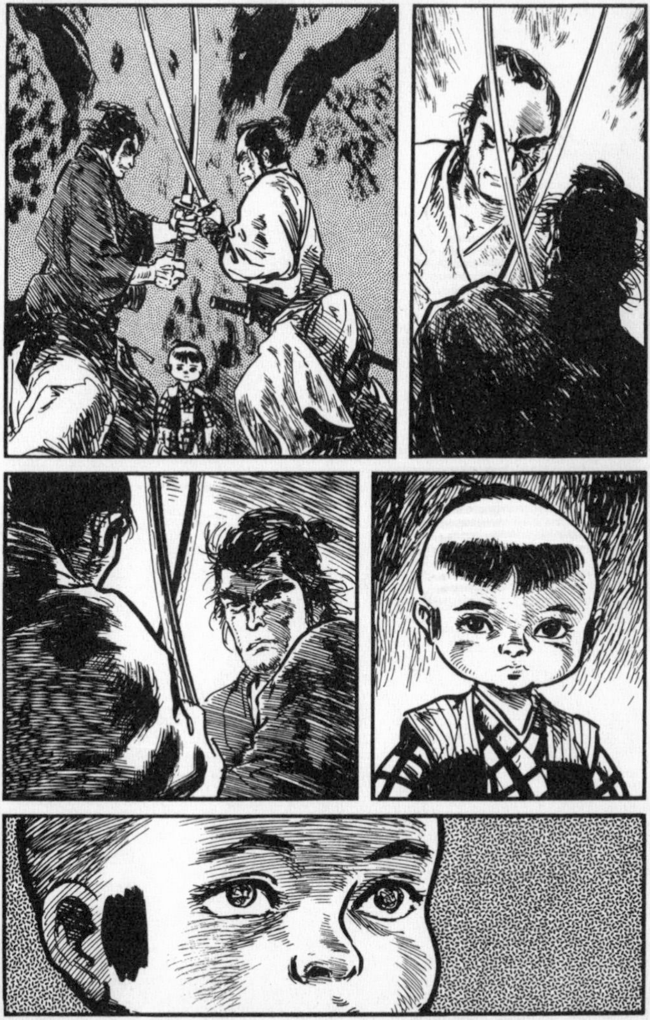

KSHUNGG

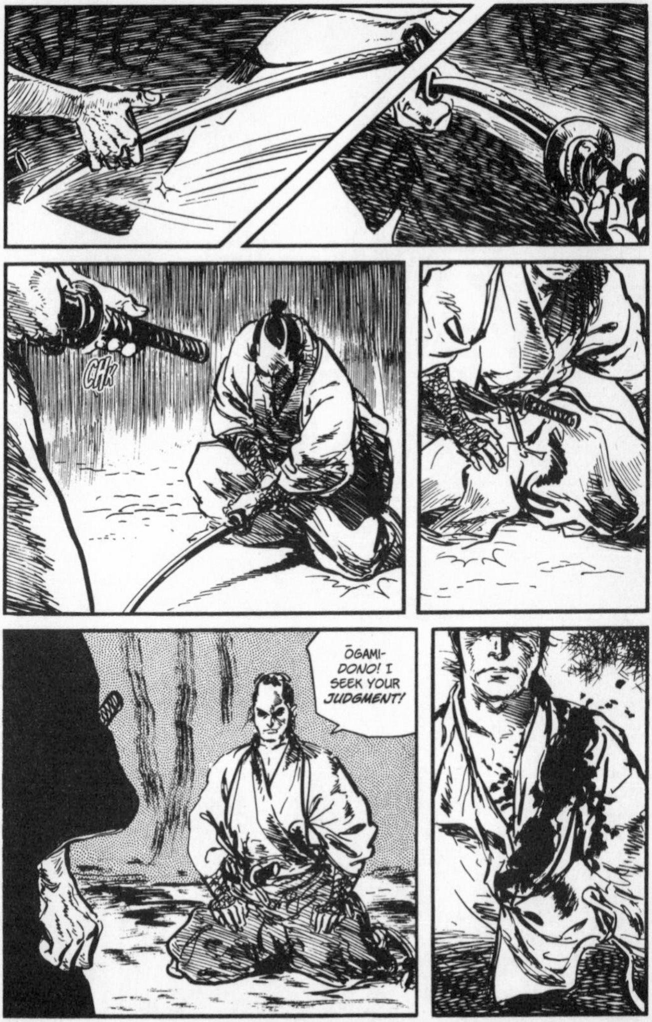
CHK
ŌGAMI-DONO! I SEEK YOUR JUDGMENT!

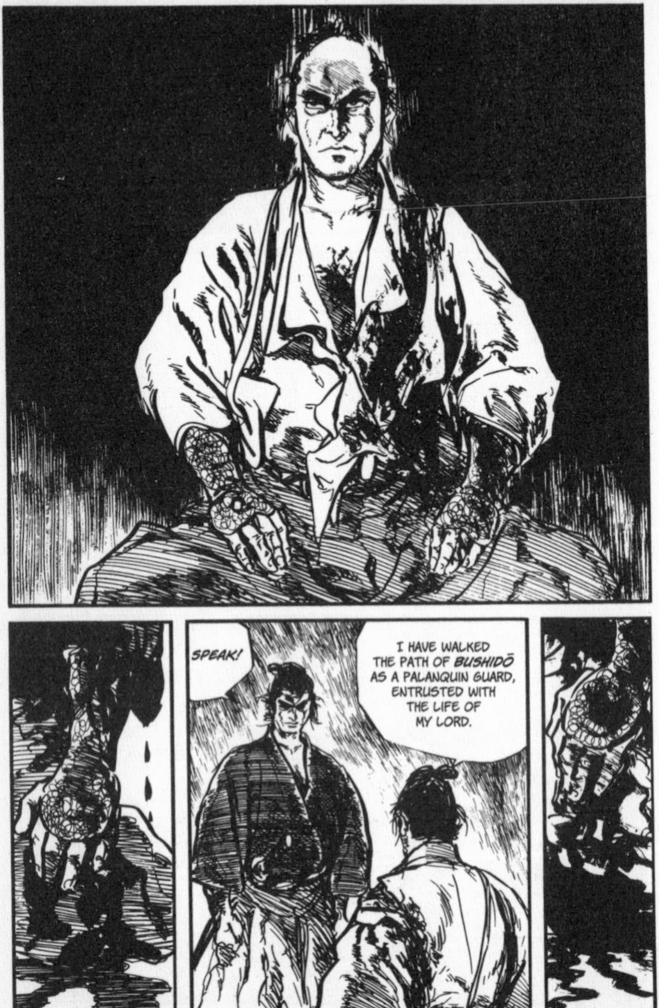
SPEAK!
I HAVE WALKED THE PATH OF *BUSHIDŌ* AS A PALANQUIN GUARD, ENTRUSTED WITH THE LIFE OF MY LORD.

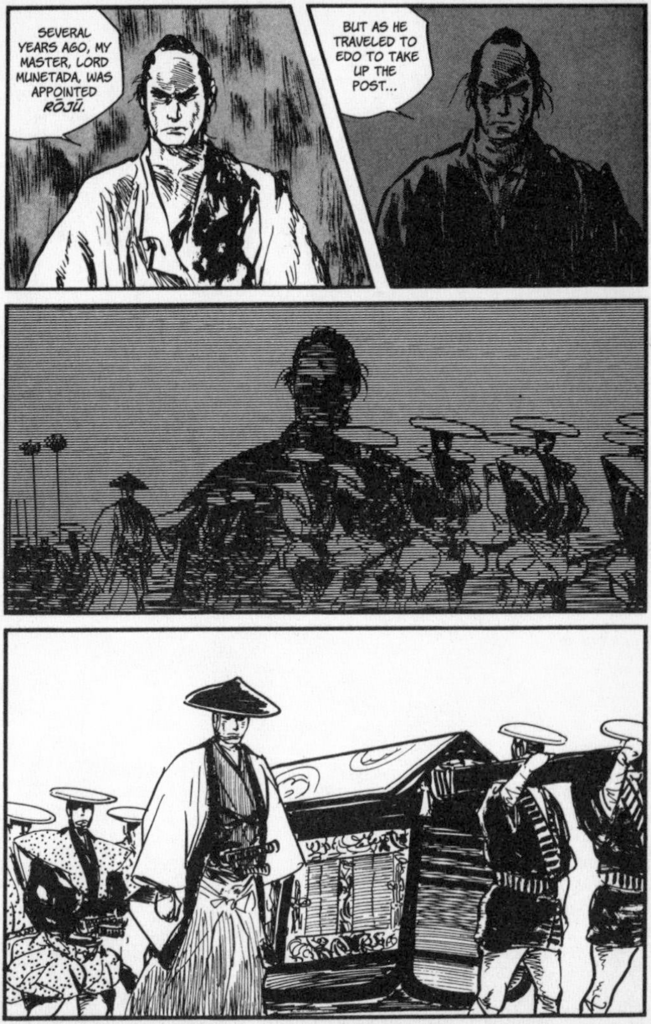
SEVERAL YEARS AGO, MY MASTER, LORD MUNETADA, WAS APPOINTED RŌJŪ.
BUT AS HE TRAVELED TO EDO TO TAKE UP THE POST...

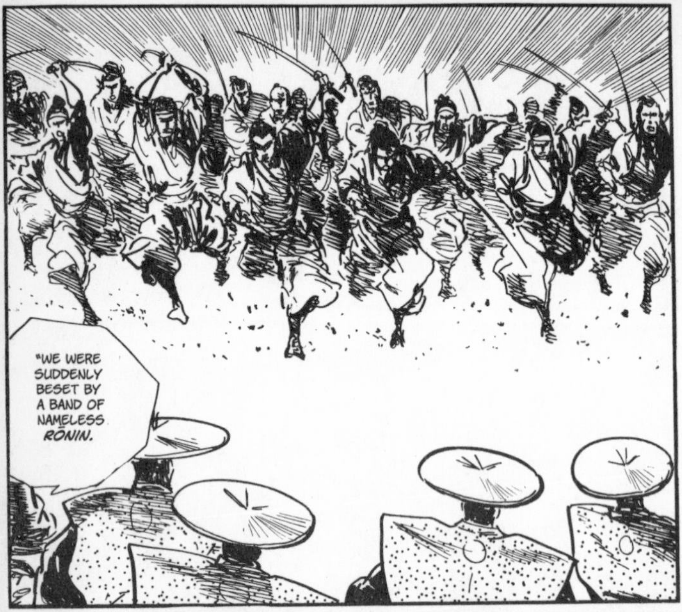
"WE WERE SUDDENLY BESET BY A BAND OF NAMELESS *RŌNIN*.

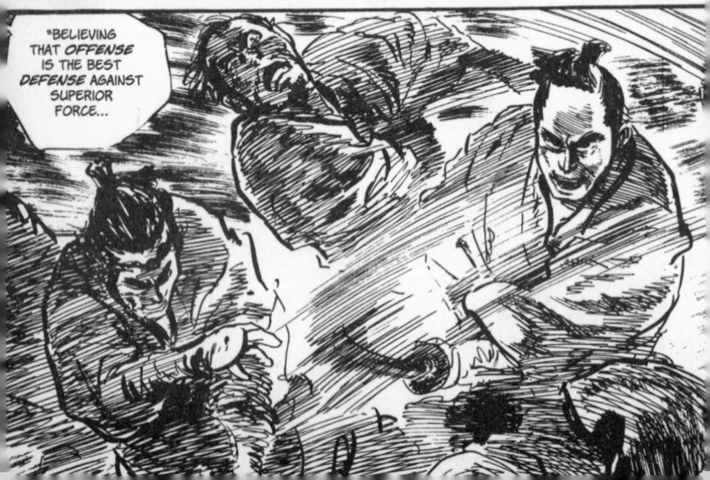
"BELIEVING THAT *OFFENSE* IS THE BEST *DEFENSE* AGAINST SUPERIOR FORCE...

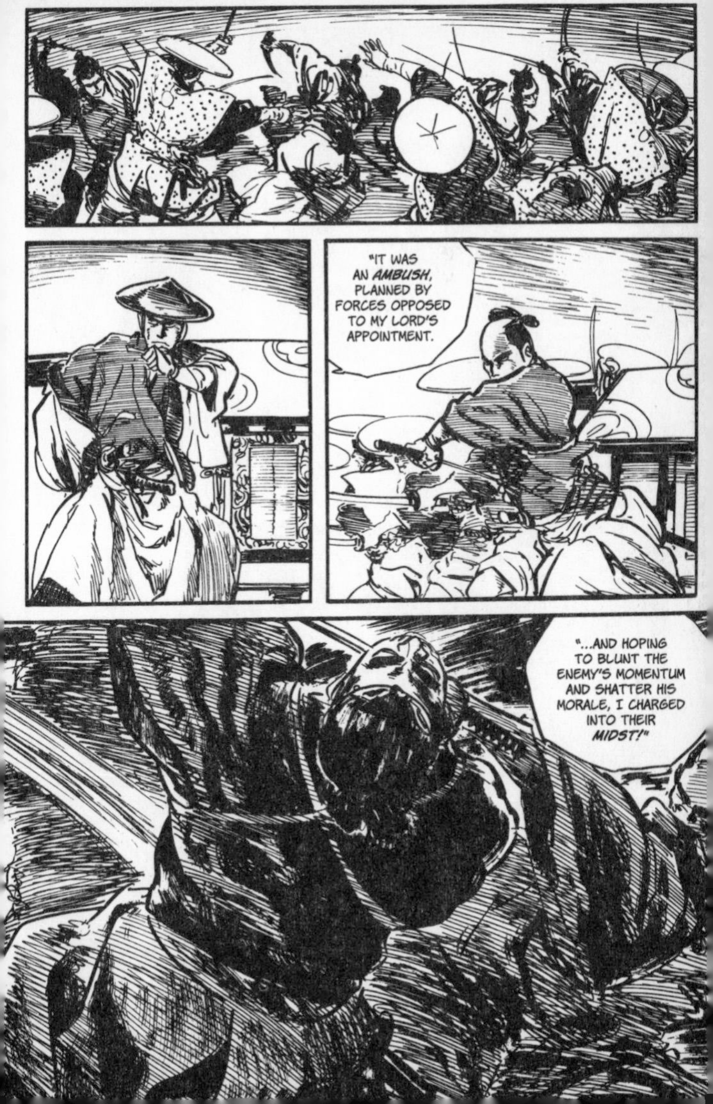
"IT WAS AN *AMBUSH*, PLANNED BY FORCES OPPOSED TO MY LORD'S APPOINTMENT.
"...AND HOPING TO BLUNT THE ENEMY'S MOMENTUM AND SHATTER HIS MORALE, I CHARGED INTO THEIR *MIDST!*"

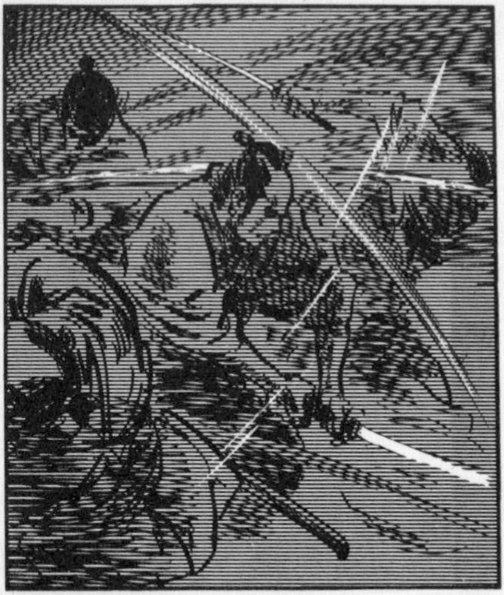
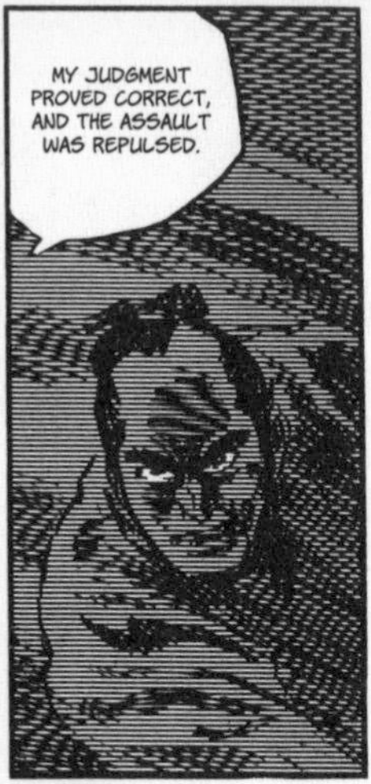
MY JUDGMENT PROVED CORRECT, AND THE ASSAULT WAS REPULSED.
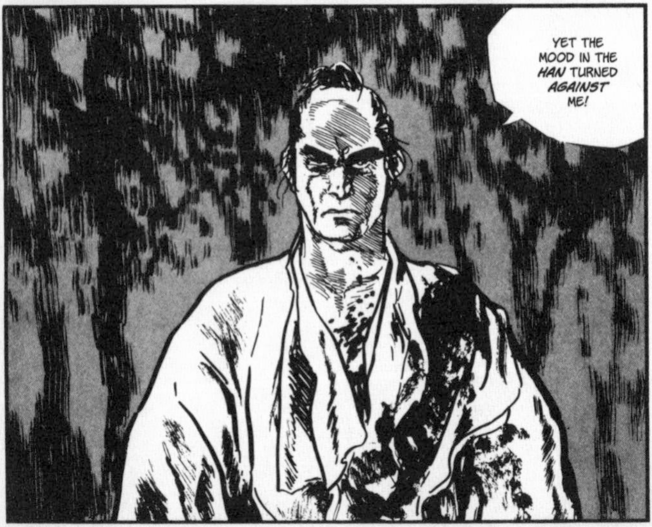
YET THE MOOD IN THE *HAN* TURNED *AGAINST* ME!

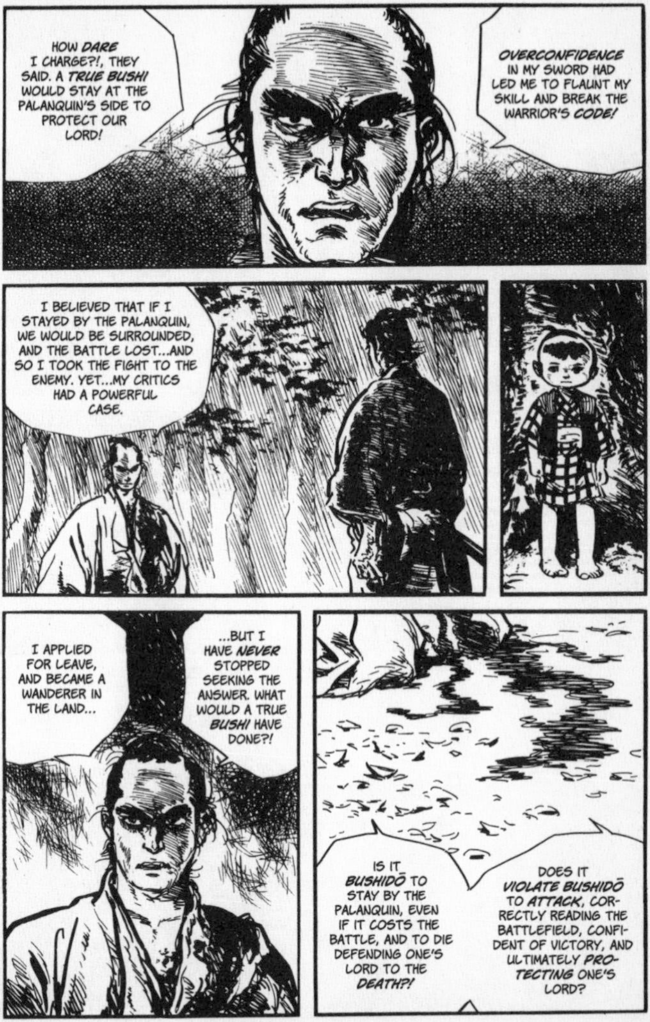
HOW DARE I CHARGE?!, THEY SAID. A TRUE BUSHI WOULD STAY AT THE PALANQUIN'S SIDE TO PROTECT OUR LORD!
OVERCONFIDENCE IN MY SWORD HAD LED ME TO FLAUNT MY SKILL AND BREAK THE WARRIOR'S CODE!
I BELIEVED THAT IF I STAYED BY THE PALANQUIN, WE WOULD BE SURROUNDED, AND THE BATTLE LOST...AND SO I TOOK THE FIGHT TO THE ENEMY. YET...MY CRITICS HAD A POWERFUL CASE.
I APPLIED FOR LEAVE, AND BECAME A WANDERER IN THE LAND...
...BUT I HAVE NEVER STOPPED SEEKING THE ANSWER. WHAT WOULD A TRUE BUSHI HAVE DONE?!
IS IT BUSHIDŌ TO STAY BY THE PALANQUIN, EVEN IF IT COSTS THE BATTLE, AND TO DIE DEFENDING ONE'S LORD TO THE DEATH?!
DOES IT VIOLATE BUSHIDŌ TO ATTACK, CORRECTLY READING THE BATTLEFIELD, CONFIDENT OF VICTORY, AND ULTIMATELY PROTECTING ONE'S LORD?

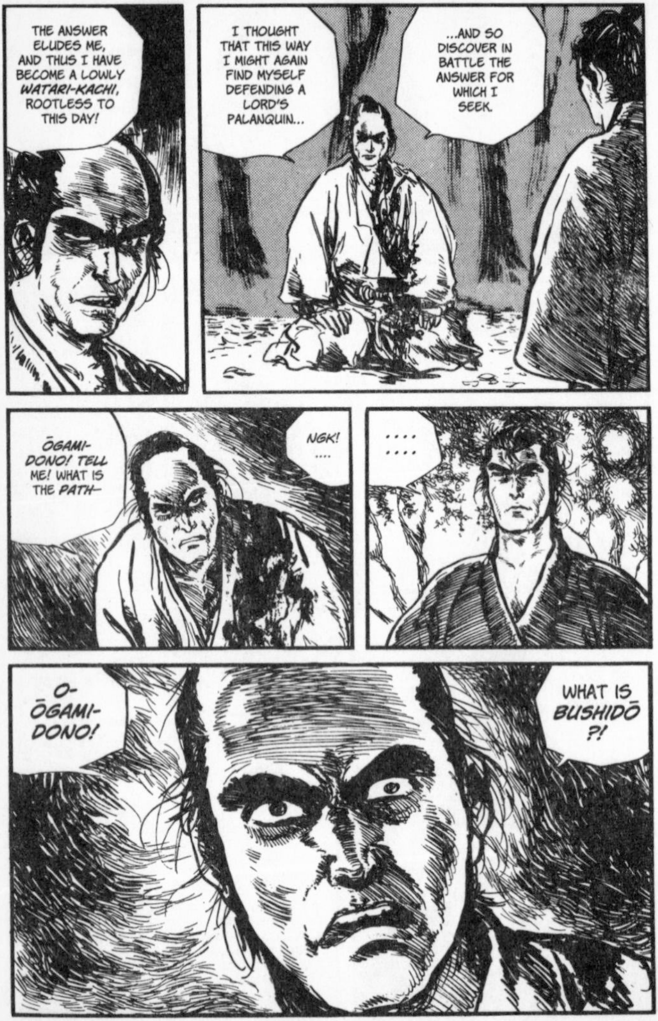

THE ANSWER ELUDES ME, AND THUS I HAVE BECOME A LOWLY *WATARI-KACHI*, ROOTLESS TO THIS DAY!
I THOUGHT THAT THIS WAY I MIGHT AGAIN FIND MYSELF DEFENDING A LORD'S PALANQUIN...
...AND SO DISCOVER IN BATTLE THE ANSWER FOR WHICH I SEEK.
ŌGAMI-DONO! TELL ME! WHAT IS THE *PATH*—
NGK! ....
....
O- ŌGAMI-DONO!
WHAT IS *BUSHIDŌ* ?!

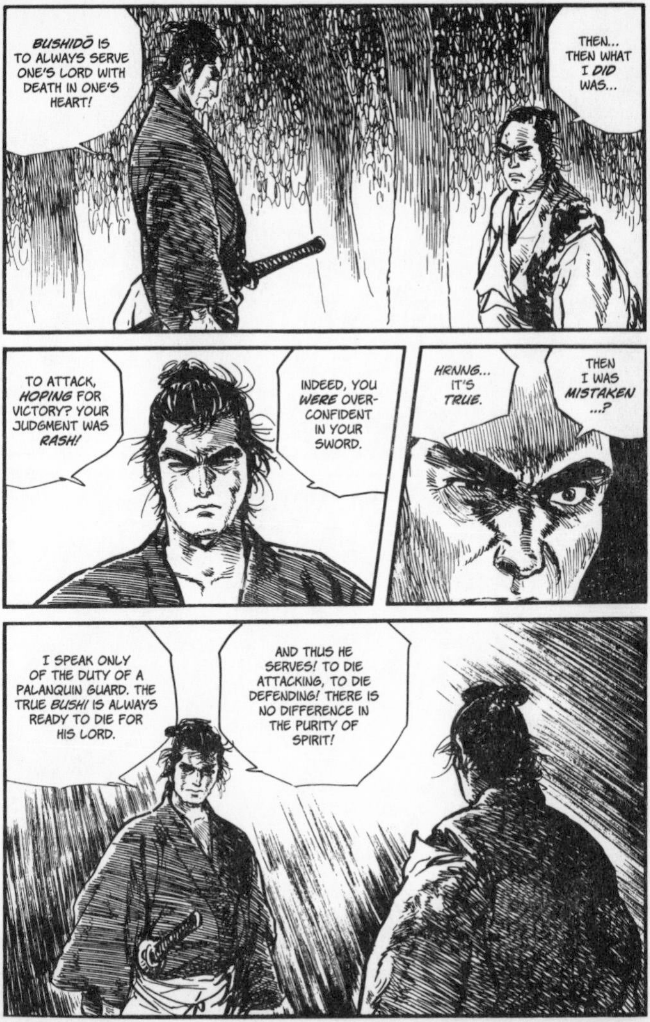
BUSHIDŌ IS TO ALWAYS SERVE ONE'S LORD WITH DEATH IN ONE'S HEART!
THEN... THEN WHAT I DID WAS...
TO ATTACK, HOPING FOR VICTORY? YOUR JUDGMENT WAS RASH!
INDEED, YOU WERE OVER-CONFIDENT IN YOUR SWORD.
HRNNG... IT'S TRUE.
THEN I WAS MISTAKEN ...?
I SPEAK ONLY OF THE DUTY OF A PALANQUIN GUARD. THE TRUE BUSHI IS ALWAYS READY TO DIE FOR HIS LORD.
AND THUS HE SERVES! TO DIE ATTACKING, TO DIE DEFENDING! THERE IS NO DIFFERENCE IN THE PURITY OF SPIRIT!

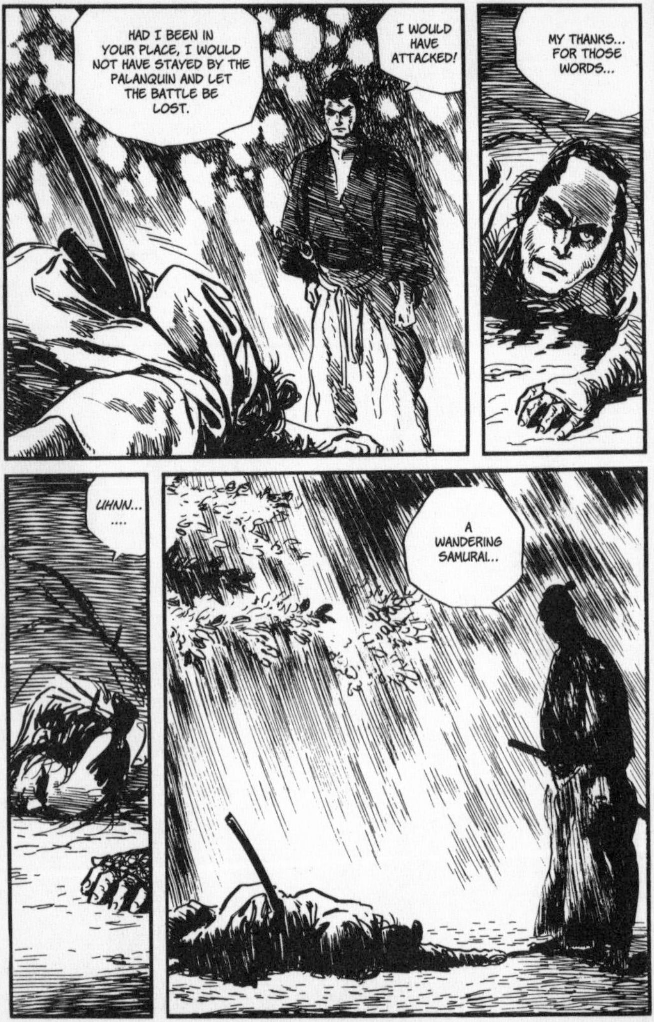
HAD I BEEN IN YOUR PLACE, I WOULD NOT HAVE STAYED BY THE PALANQUIN AND LET THE BATTLE BE LOST.
I WOULD HAVE ATTACKED!
MY THANKS... FOR THOSE WORDS...
UHNN... ....
A WANDERING SAMURAI...

the forty-seventh

Echo of the Assassin

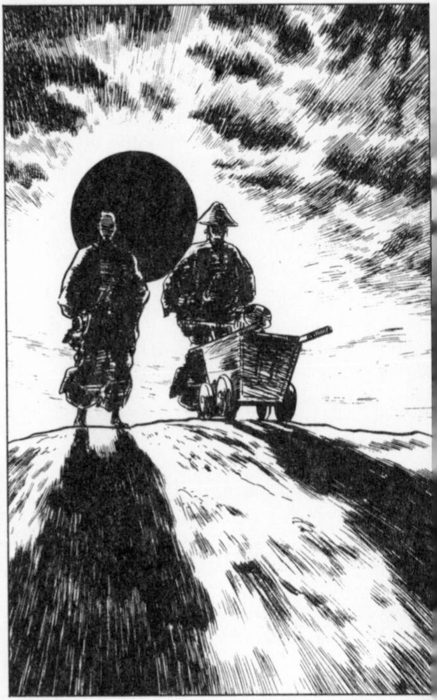

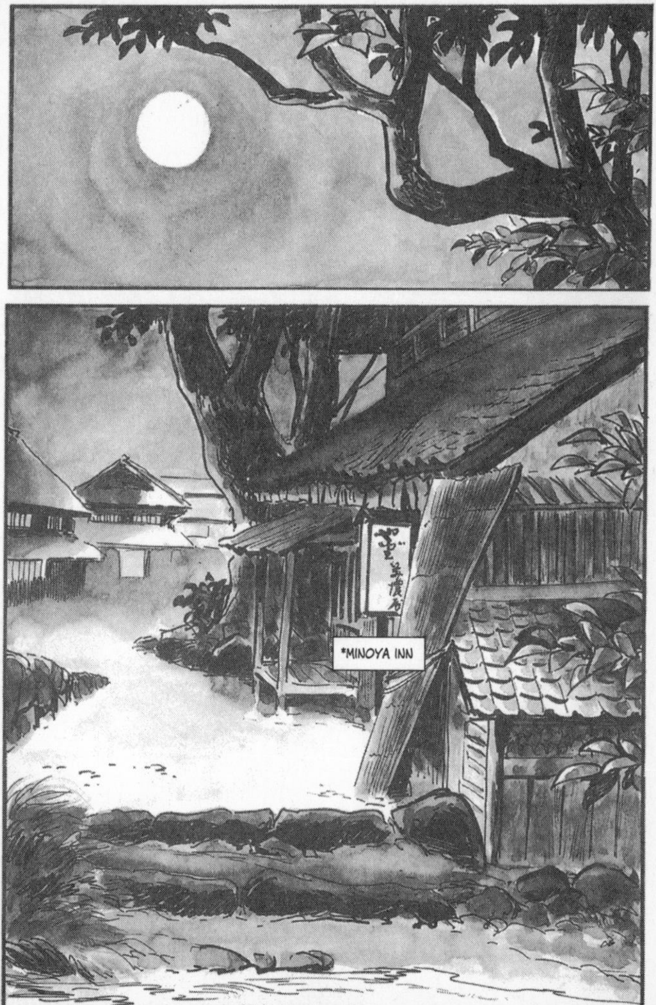
*MINOYA INN

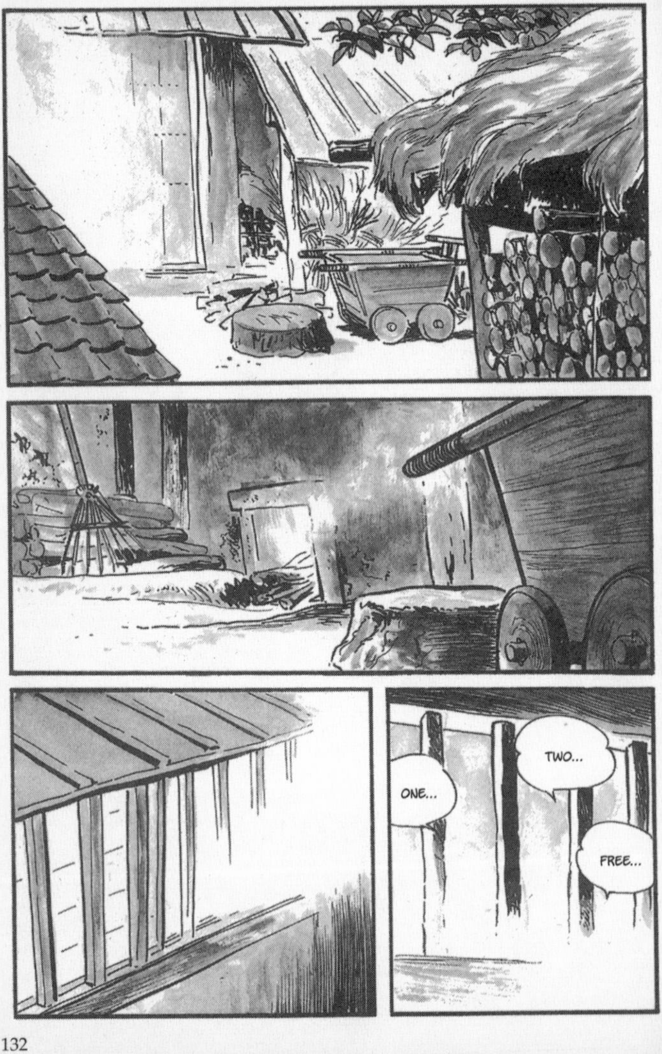
ONE...
TWO...
FREE...

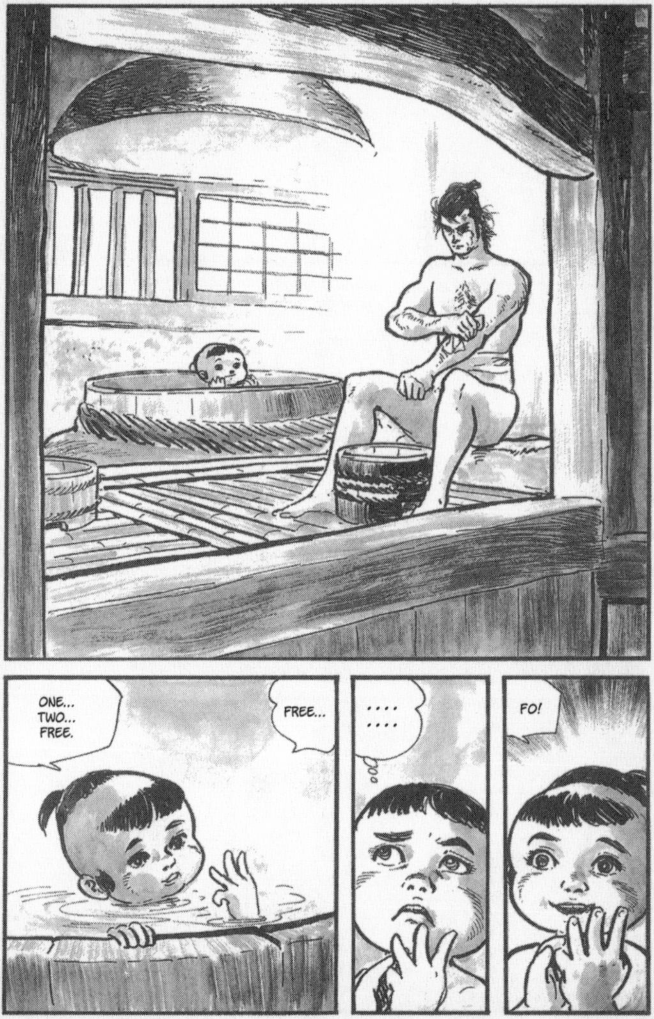
ONE... TWO... FREE.
FREE...
....
....
FO!

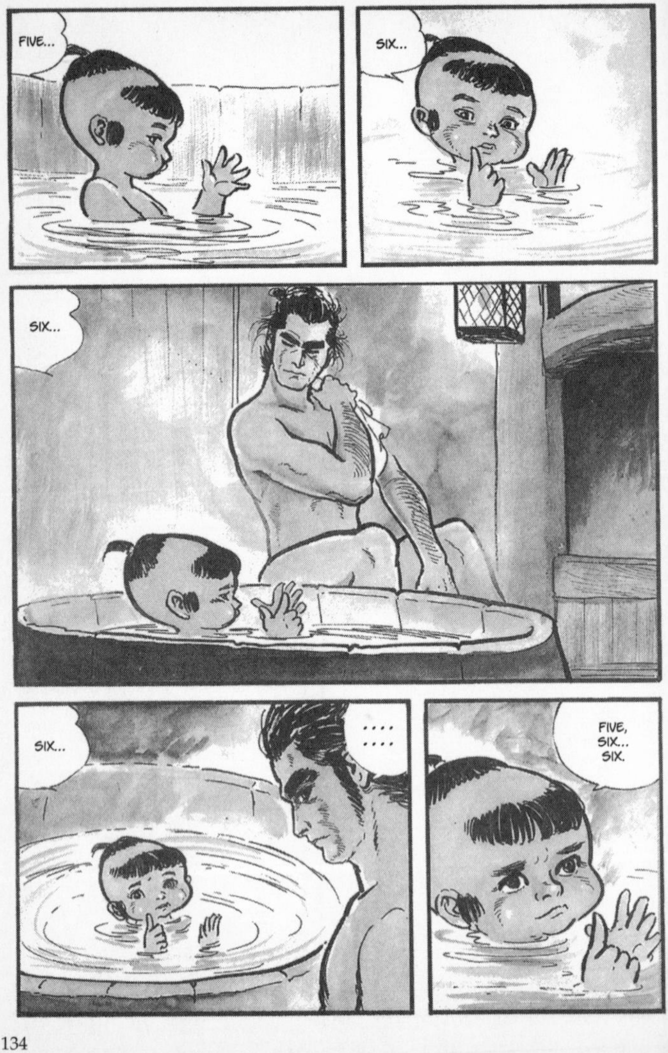
FIVE...
SIX...
SIX...
SIX...
....
....
FIVE, SIX... SIX.

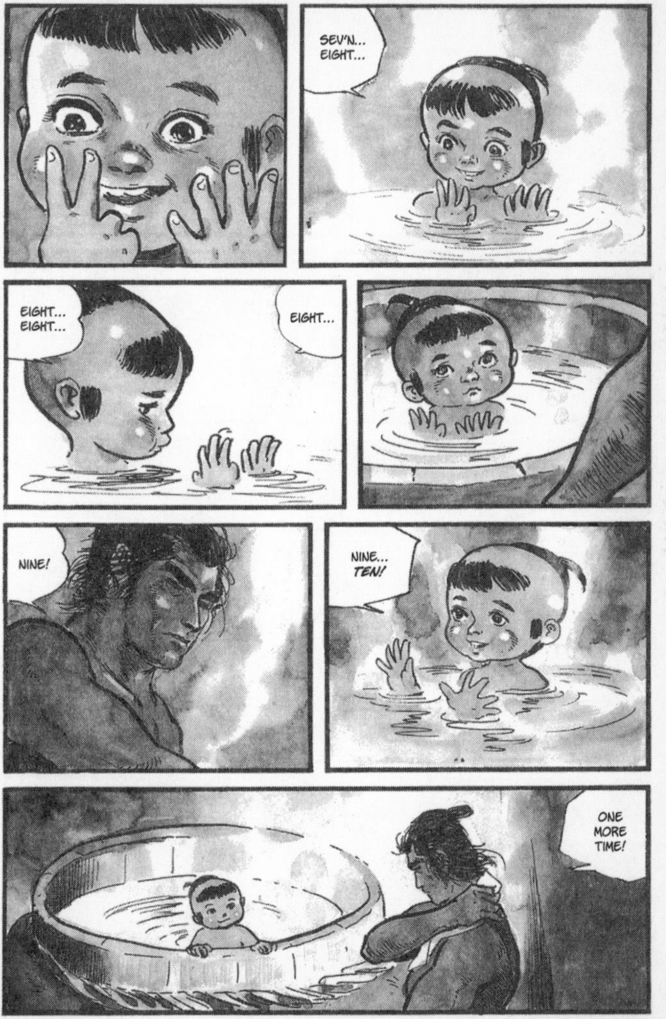
SEV'N... EIGHT...
EIGHT... EIGHT...
EIGHT...
NINE!
NINE... *TEN!*
ONE MORE TIME!

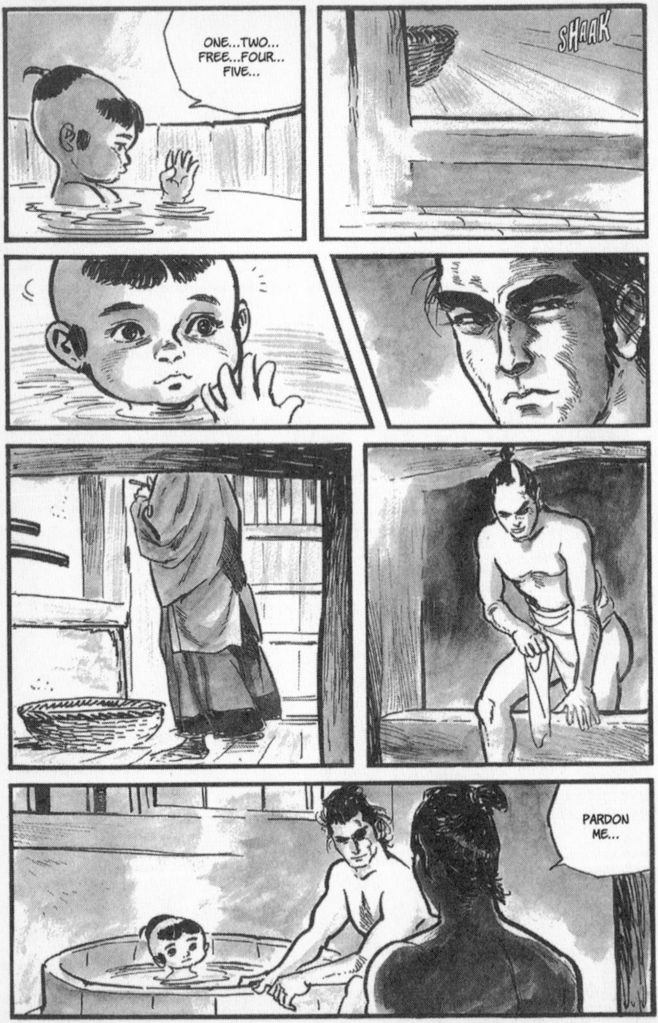
ONE...TWO...
FREE...FOUR...
FIVE...
SHAAK
PARDON
ME...

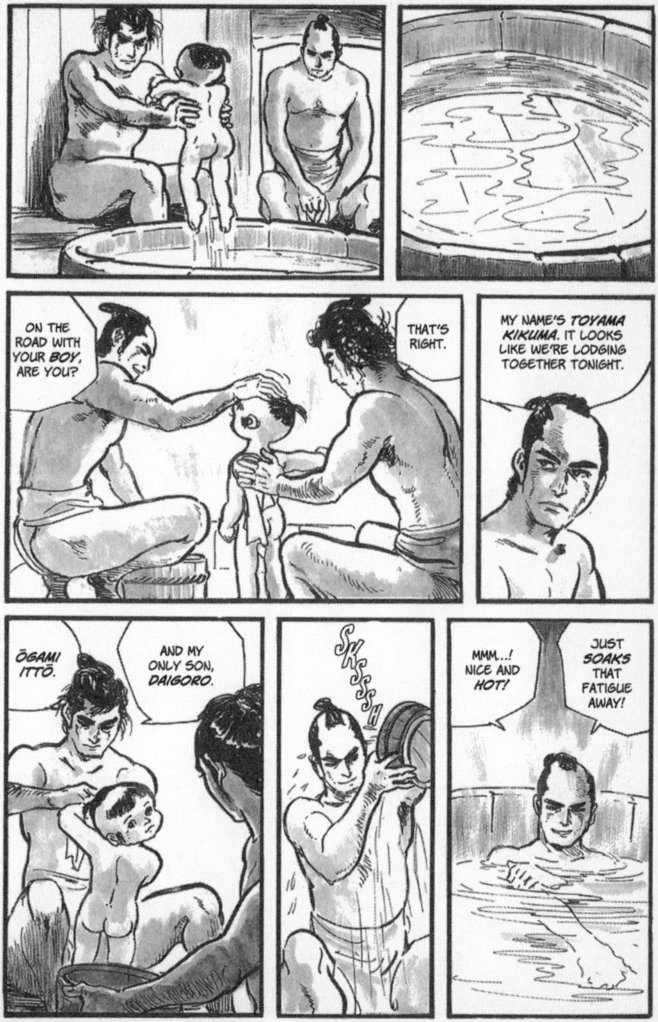
ON THE ROAD WITH YOUR *BOY*, ARE YOU?
THAT'S RIGHT.
MY NAME'S *TOYAMA KIKUMA*. IT LOOKS LIKE WE'RE LODGING TOGETHER TONIGHT.
ŌGAMI ITTŌ.
AND MY ONLY SON, *DAIGORO*.
SKSSSH
MMM...! NICE AND *HOT!*
JUST *SOAKS* THAT FATIGUE AWAY!

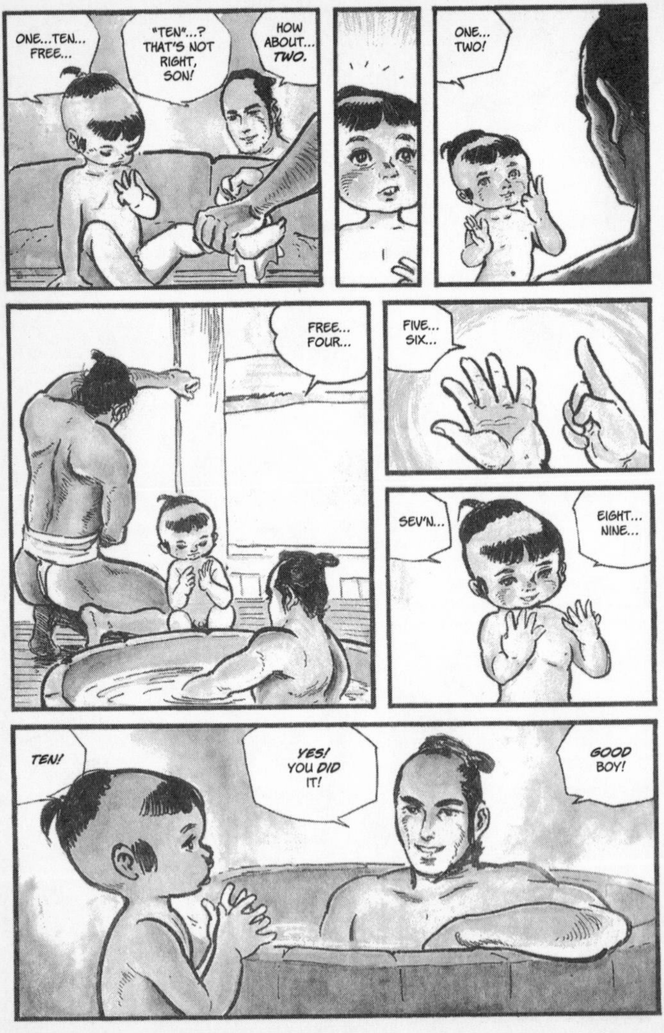
ONE...TEN...
FREE...
"TEN"...? THAT'S NOT RIGHT, SON!
HOW ABOUT... TWO.
ONE... TWO!
FREE... FOUR...
FIVE... SIX...
SEV'N...
EIGHT... NINE...
TEN!
YES! YOU DID IT!
GOOD BOY!

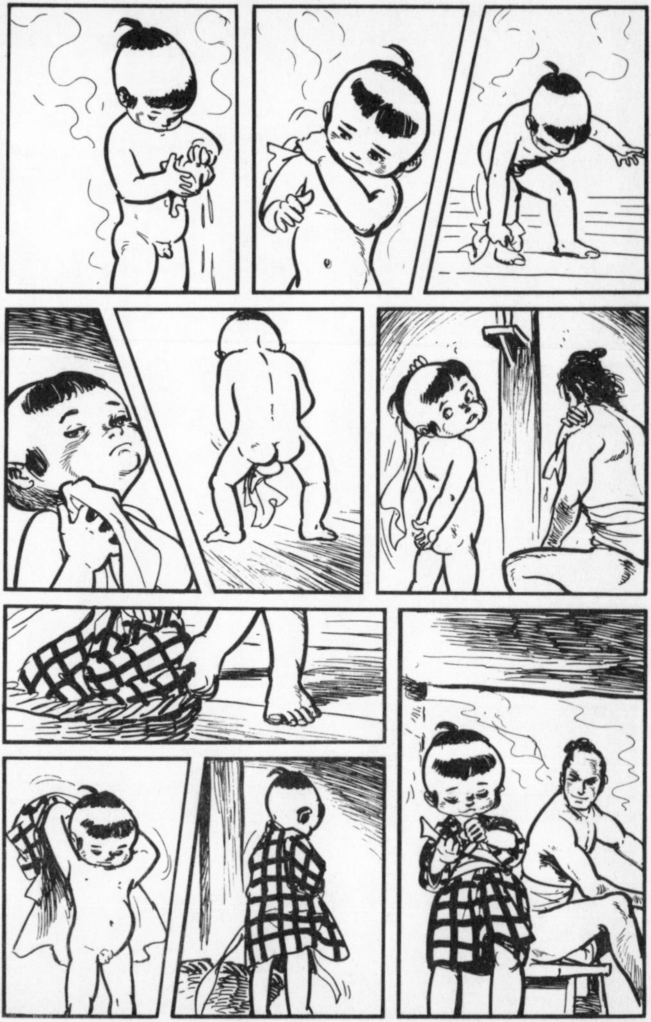

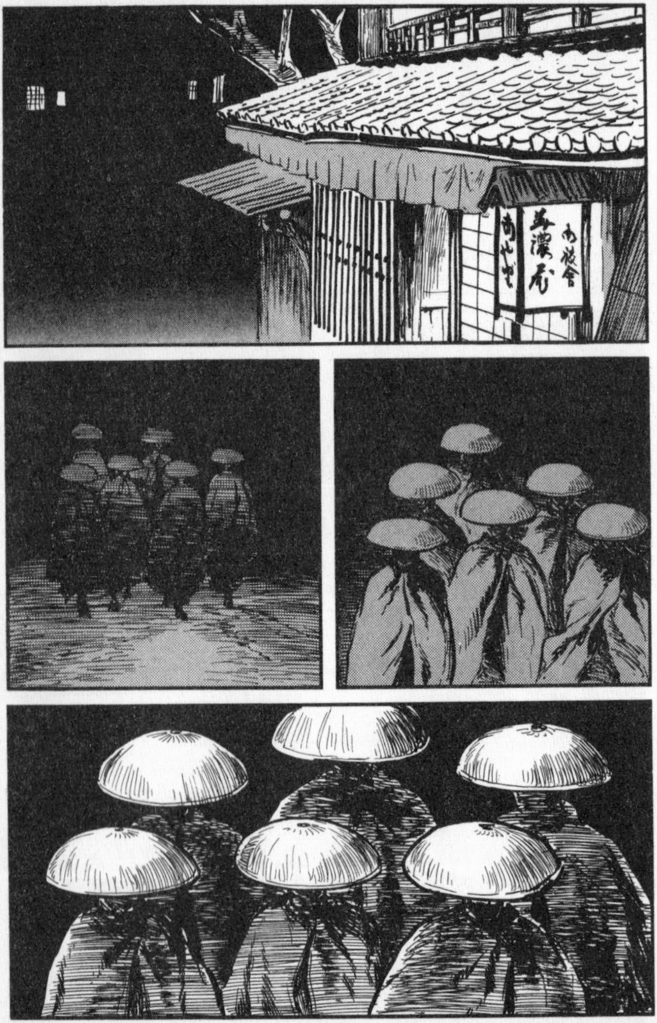

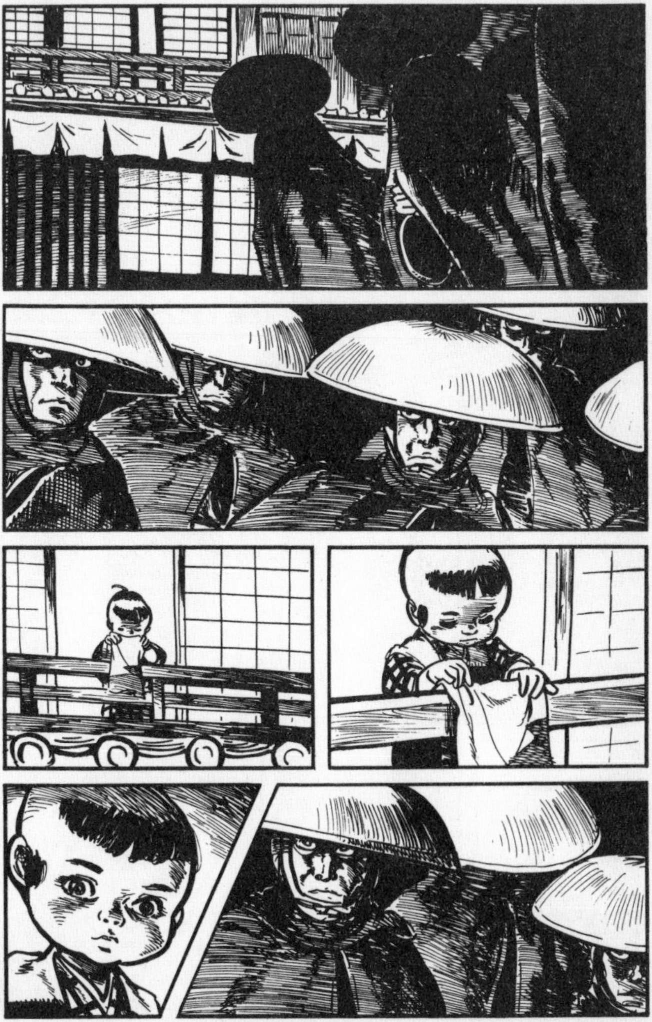

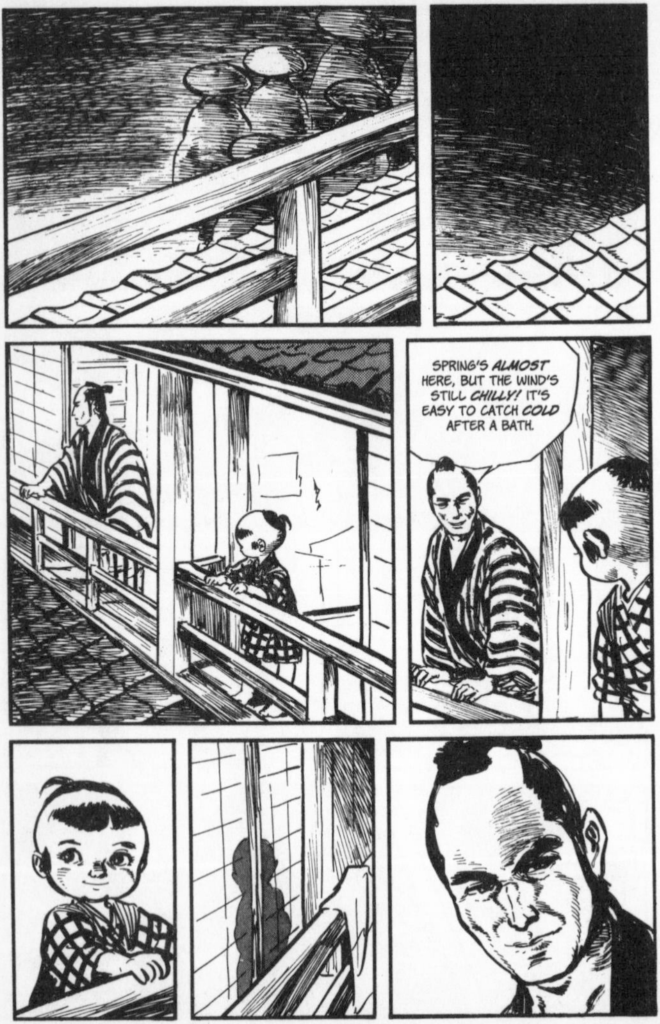
SPRING'S ALMOST HERE, BUT THE WIND'S STILL CHILLY! IT'S EASY TO CATCH COLD AFTER A BATH.

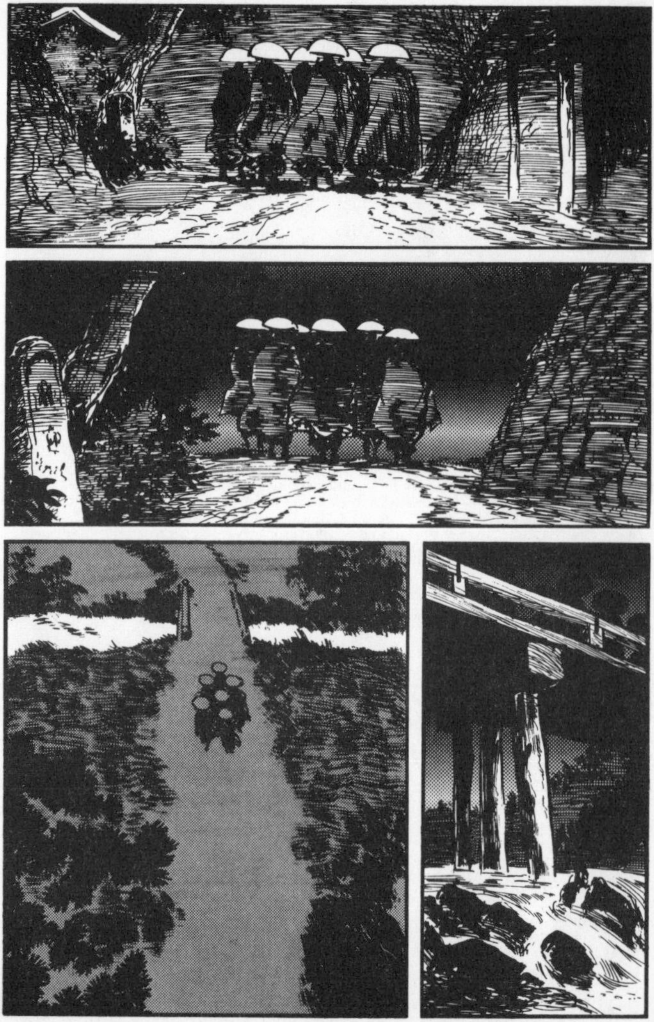

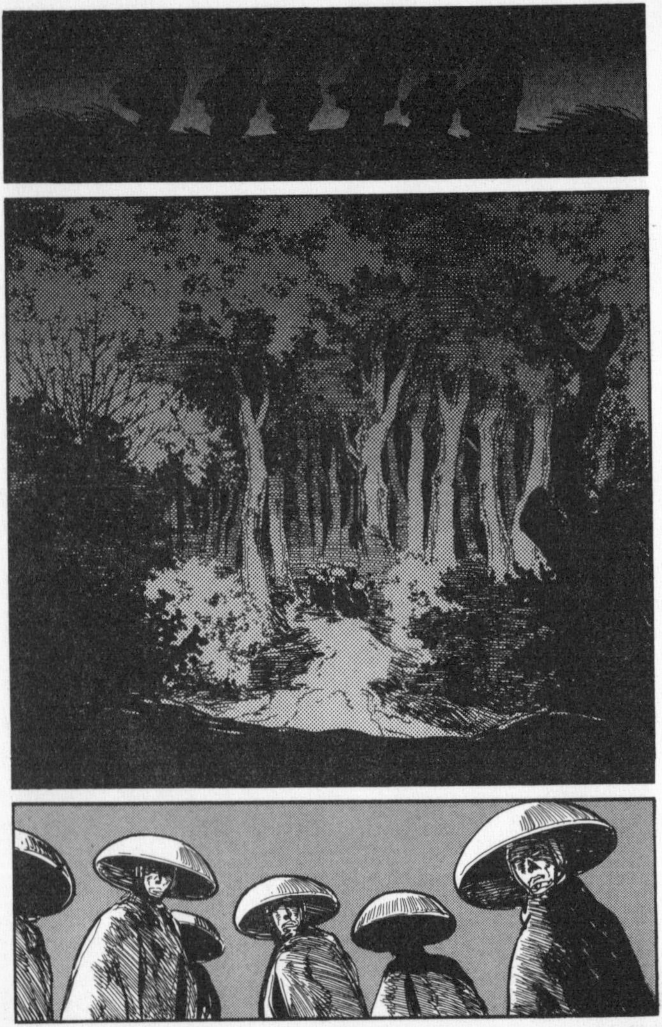

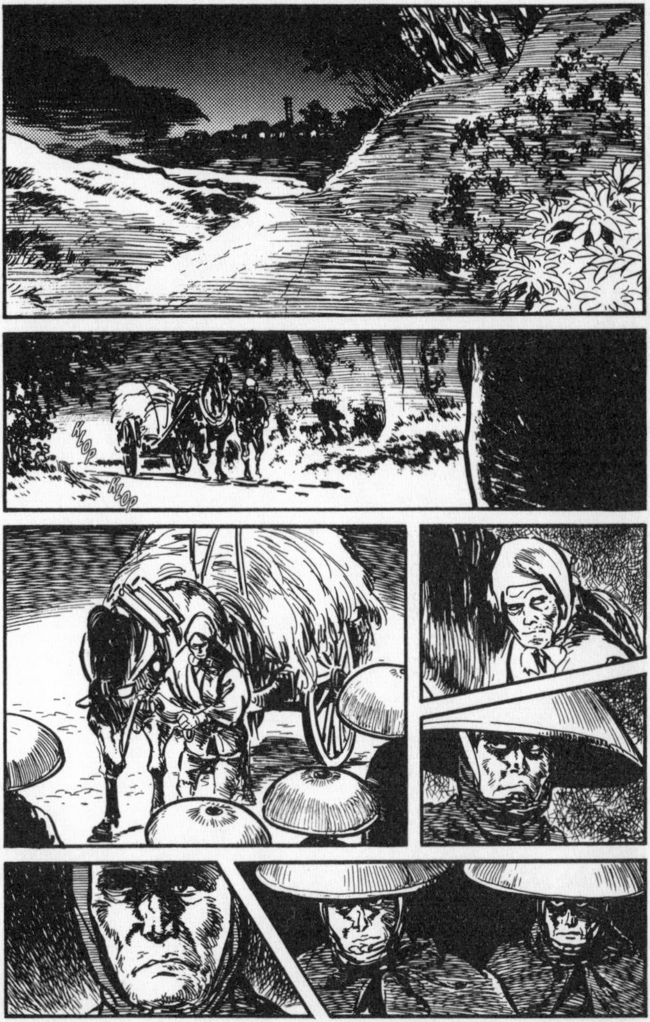
KLOP
KLOP

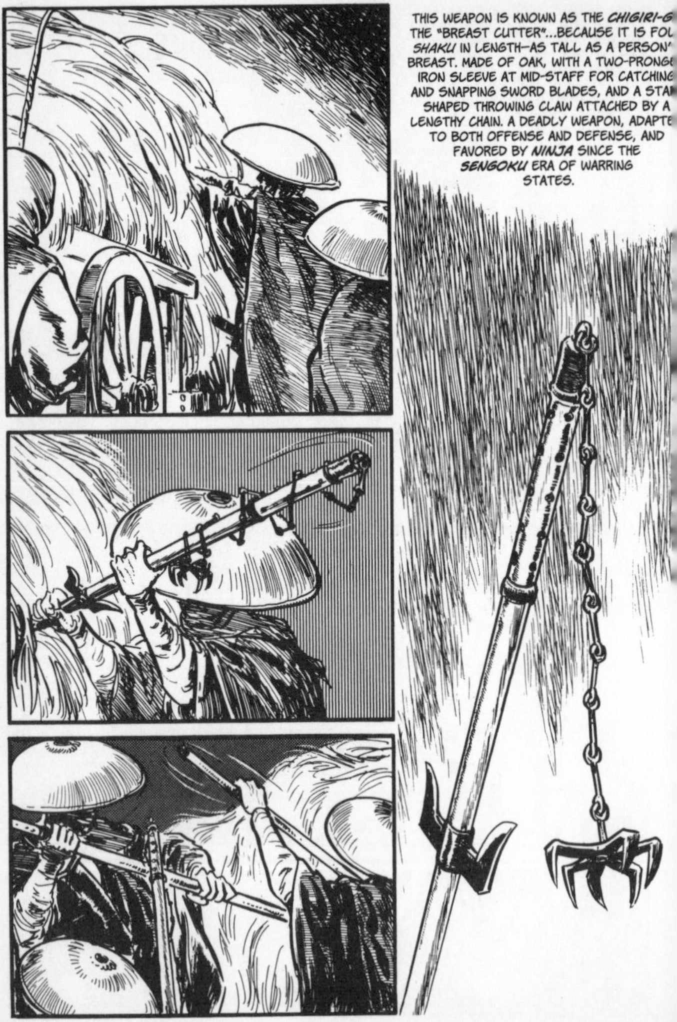
THIS WEAPON IS KNOWN AS THE CHIGIRI-G
THE "BREAST CUTTER"...BECAUSE IT IS FOU
SHAKU IN LENGTH—AS TALL AS A PERSON'
BREAST. MADE OF OAK, WITH A TWO-PRONG
IRON SLEEVE AT MID-STAFF FOR CATCHING
AND SNAPPING SWORD BLADES, AND A STA
SHAPED THROWING CLAW ATTACHED BY A
LENGTHY CHAIN. A DEADLY WEAPON, ADAPTE
TO BOTH OFFENSE AND DEFENSE, AND
FAVORED BY NINJA SINCE THE
SENGOKU ERA OF WARRING
STATES.

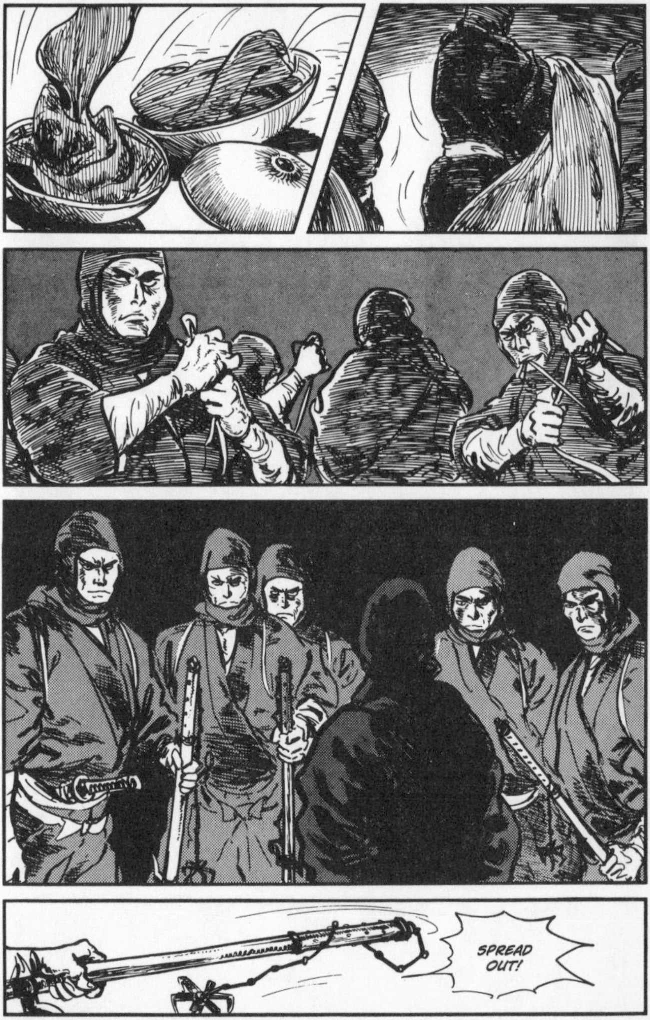
SPREAD OUT!

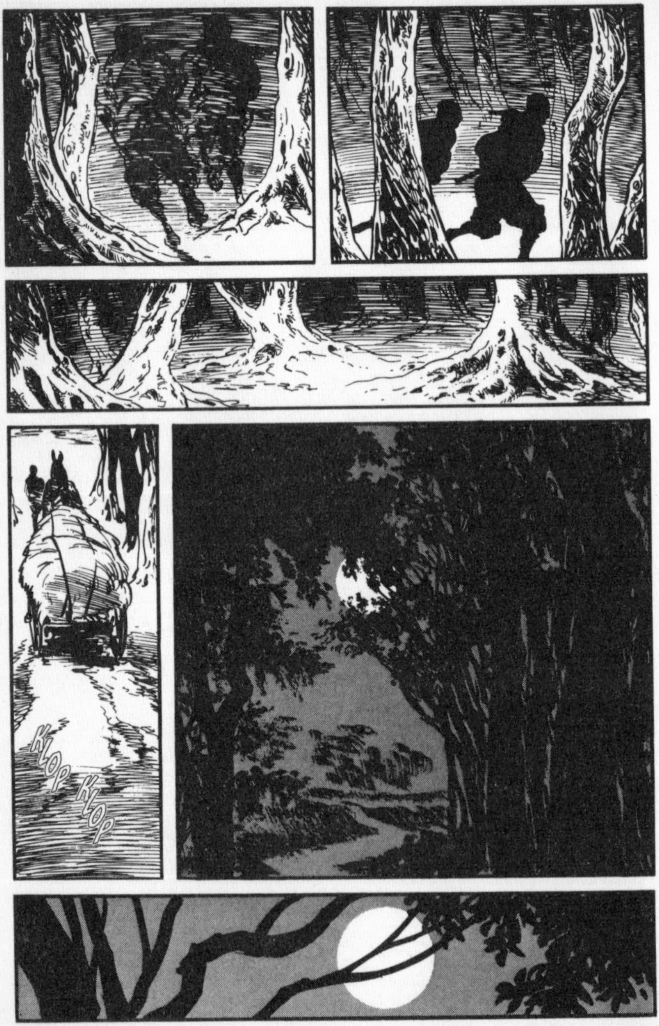
KLOP KLOP

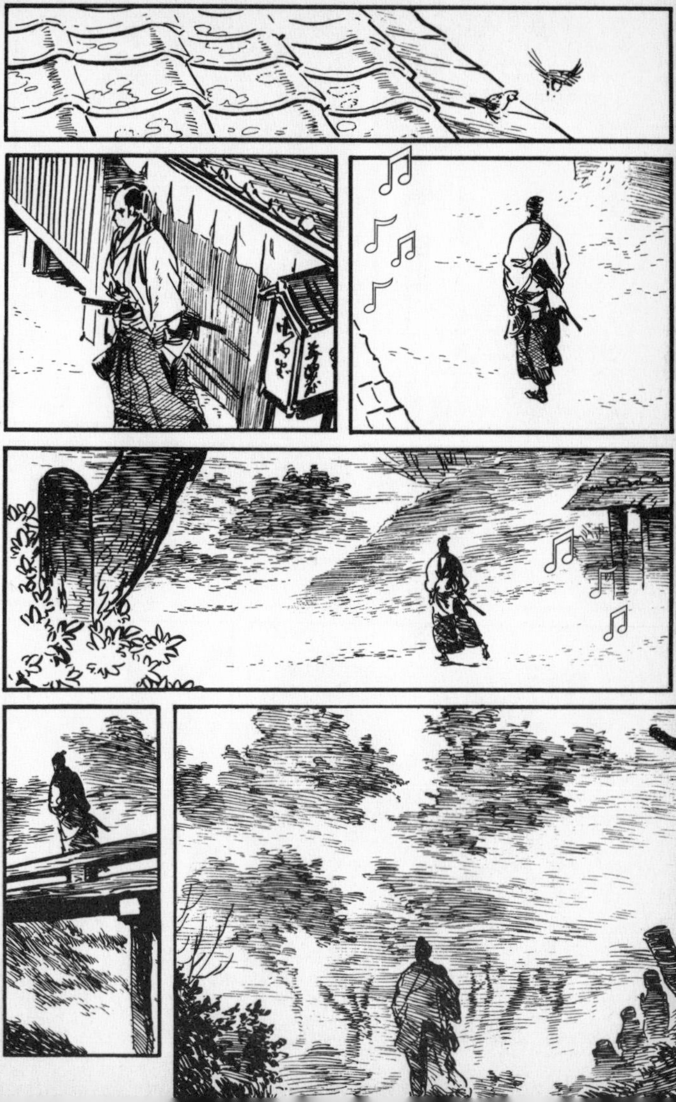

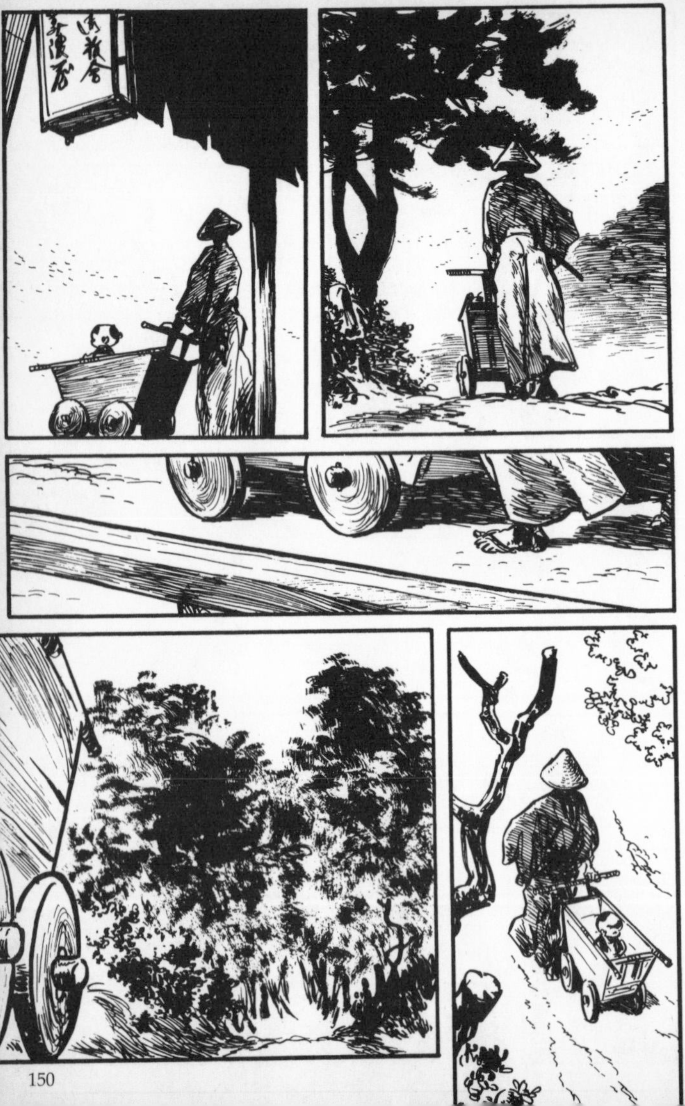

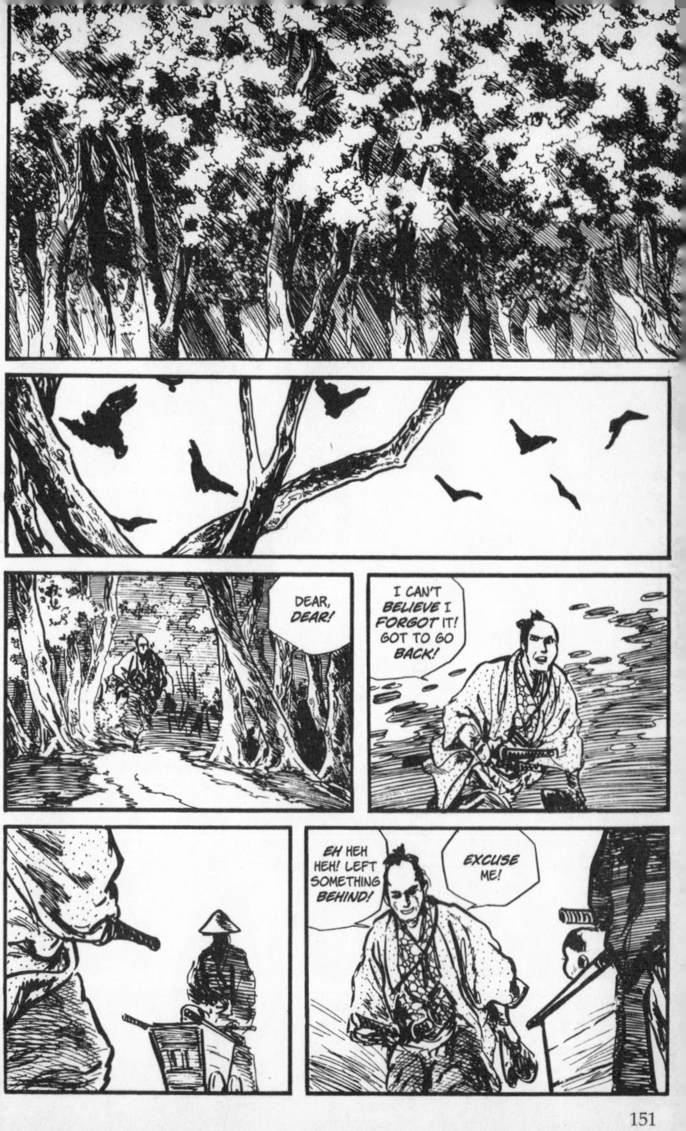
DEAR, DEAR!
I CAN'T BELIEVE I FORGOT IT! GOT TO GO BACK!
EH HEH HEH! LEFT SOMETHING BEHIND!
EXCUSE ME!

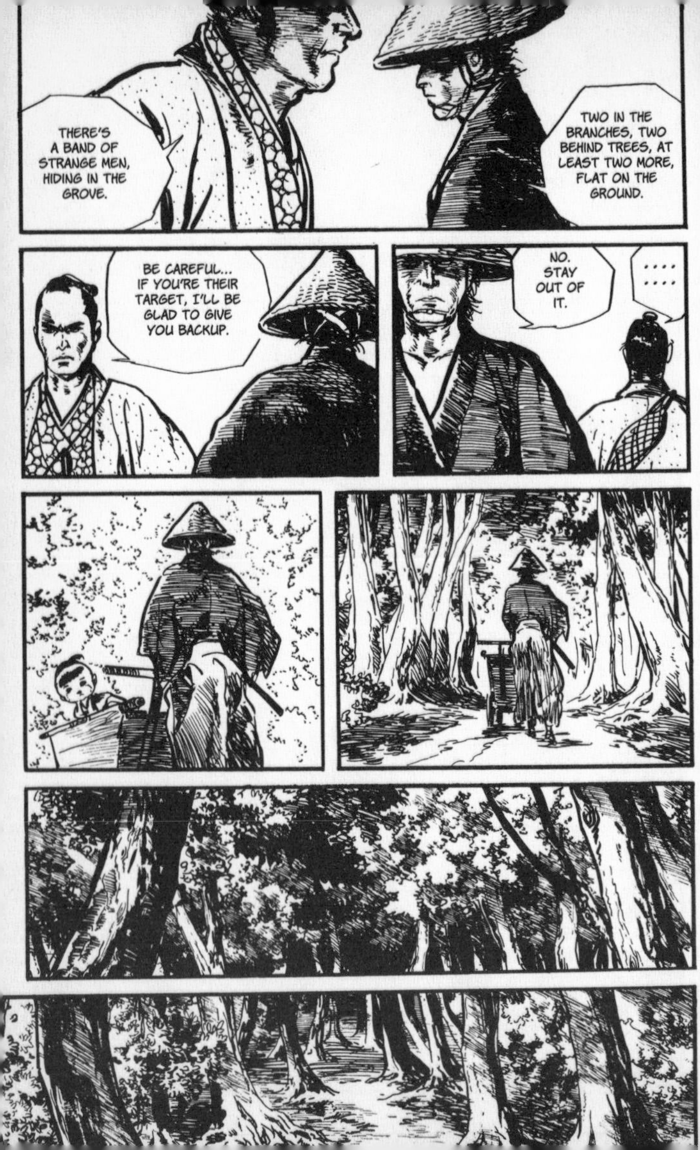
THERE'S A BAND OF STRANGE MEN, HIDING IN THE GROVE.
TWO IN THE BRANCHES, TWO BEHIND TREES, AT LEAST TWO MORE, FLAT ON THE GROUND.
BE CAREFUL... IF YOU'RE THEIR TARGET, I'LL BE GLAD TO GIVE YOU BACKUP.
NO. STAY OUT OF IT.
....
....

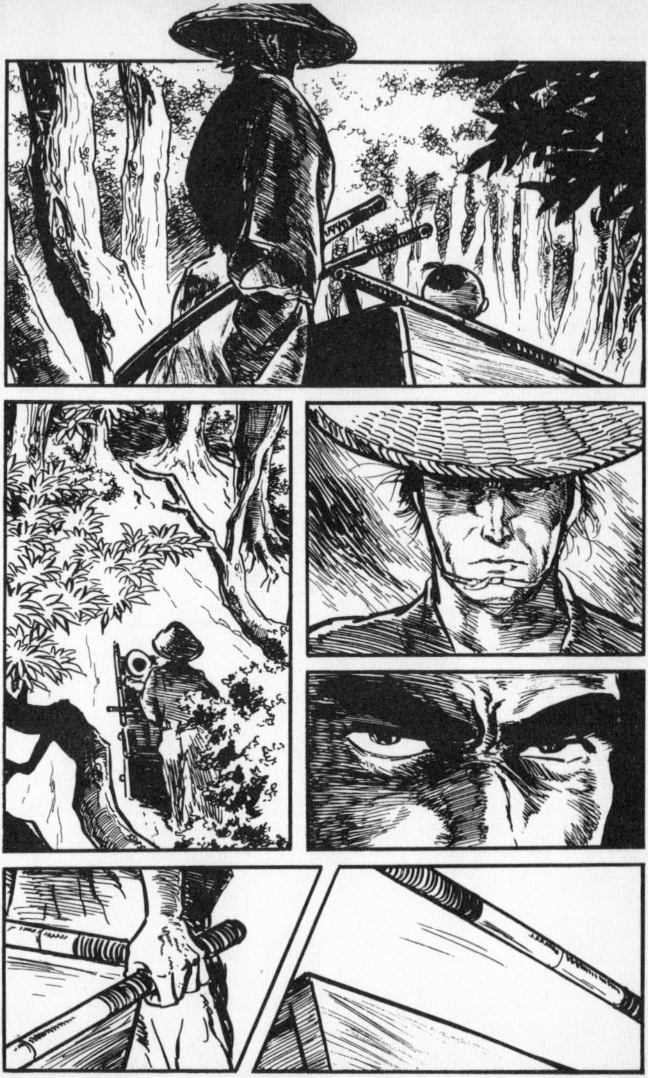

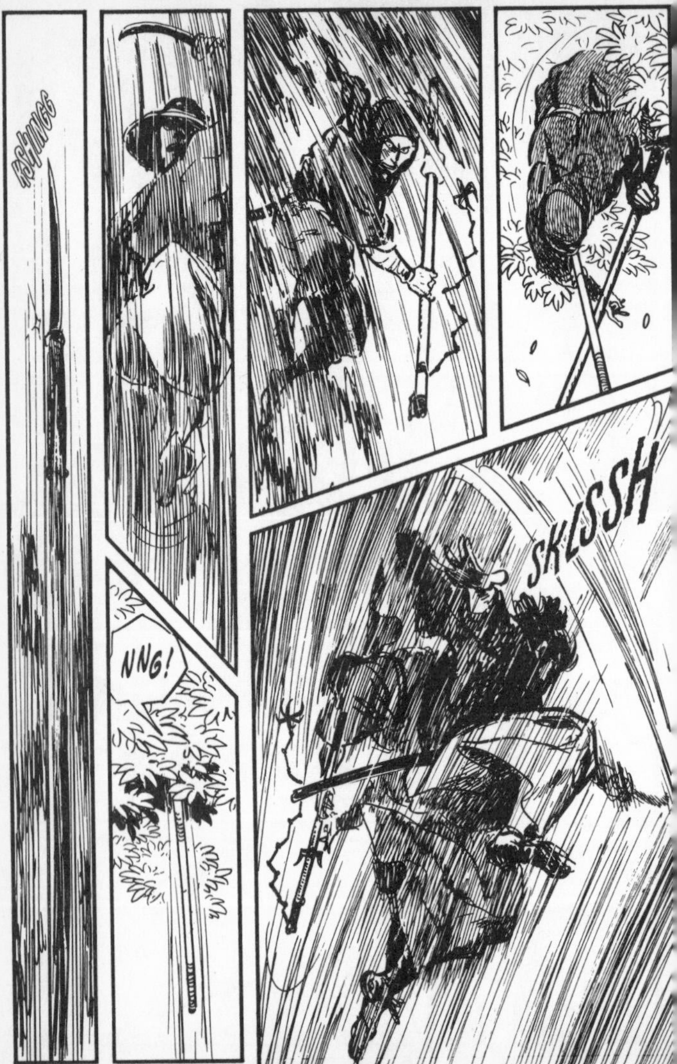
KSHINGG
NNG!
SKLSSH

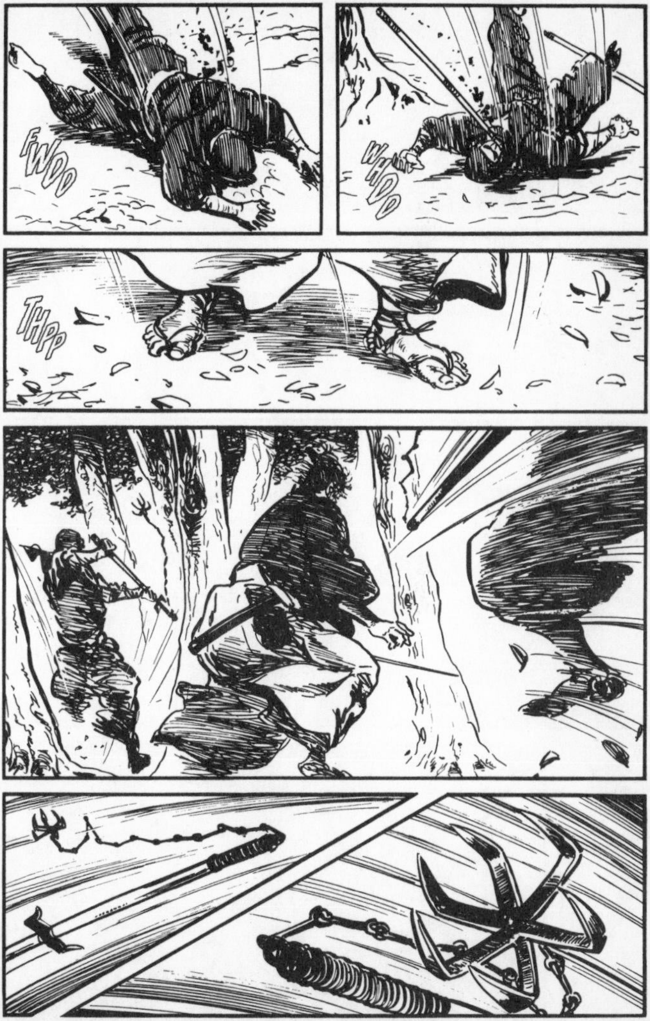
FWOO
WHOO
THPP

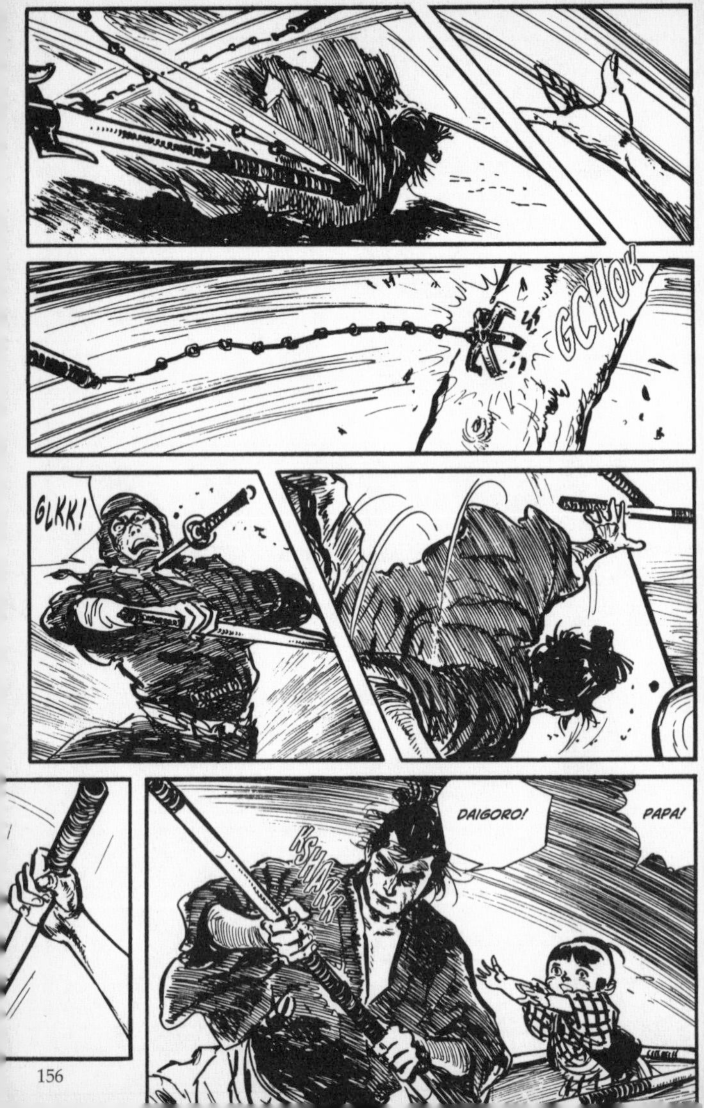
GCHOK
GLKK!
DAIGORO!
KSHAKK
PAPA!

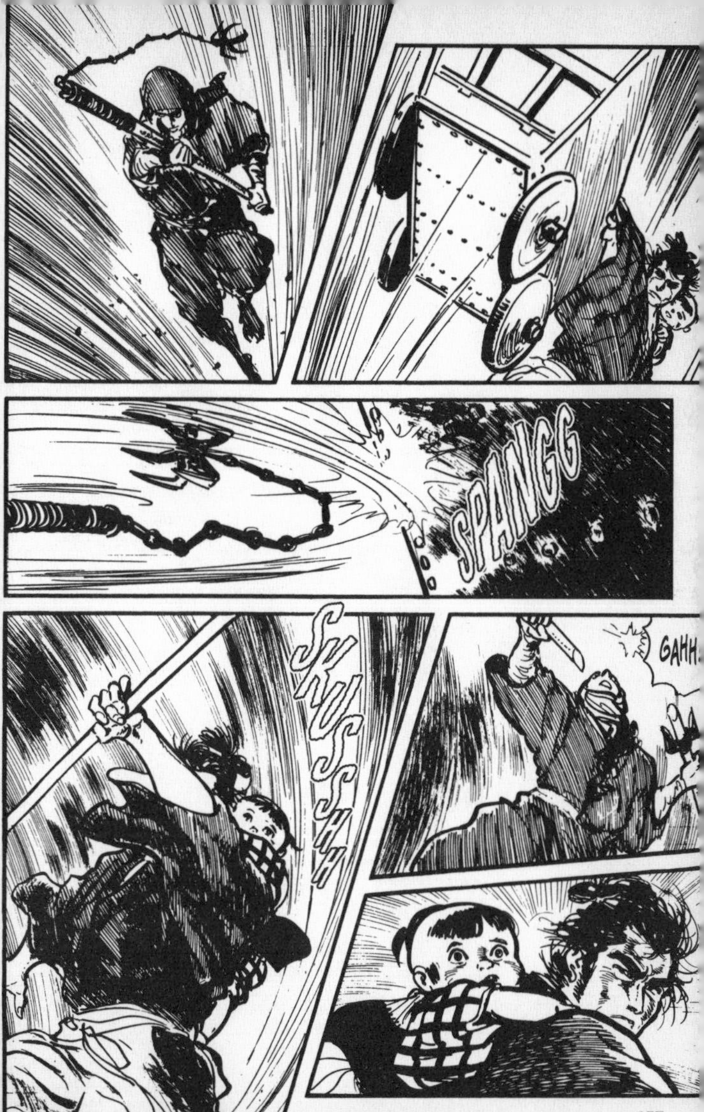
SPANGG
SKUSSSHH
GAHH..

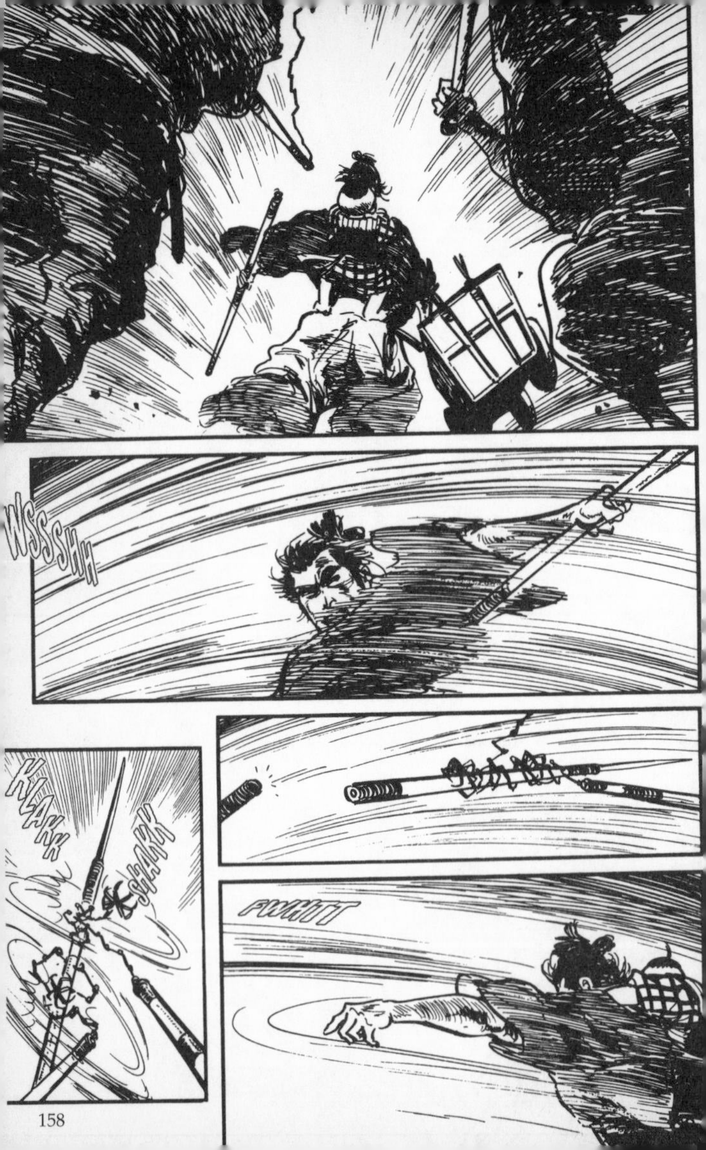
WSSSHH
KLAKK
SHAKK
FWHTT

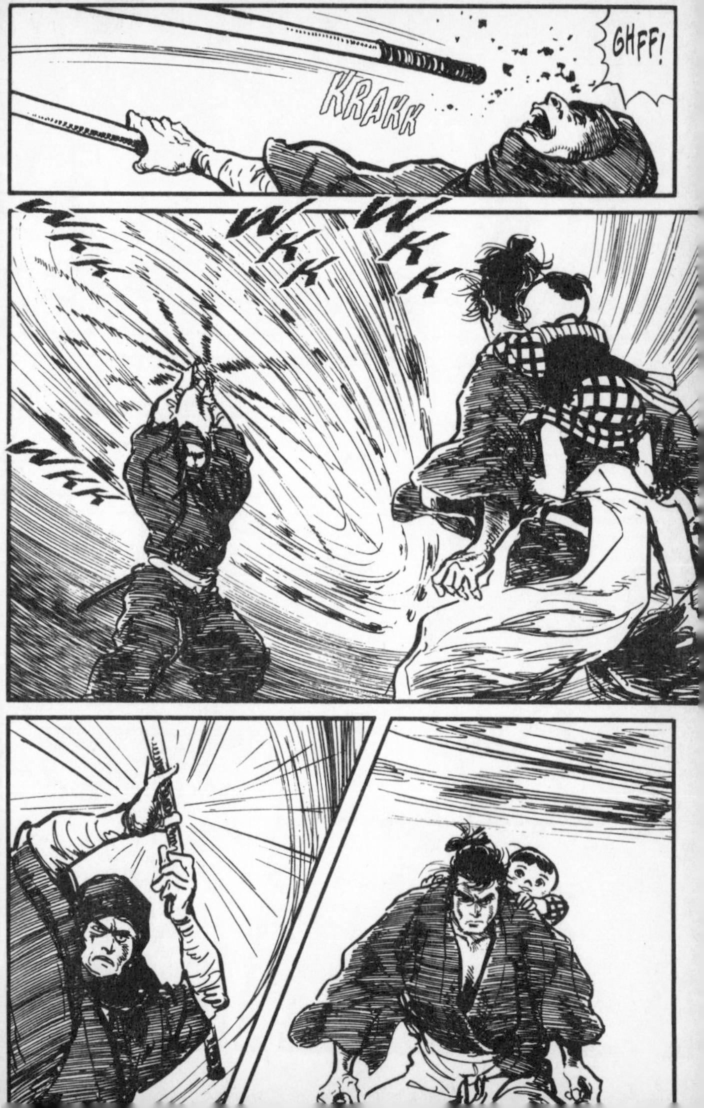
KRAKK
GHFF!
WKKK
WKKK
WKKK
WKKK

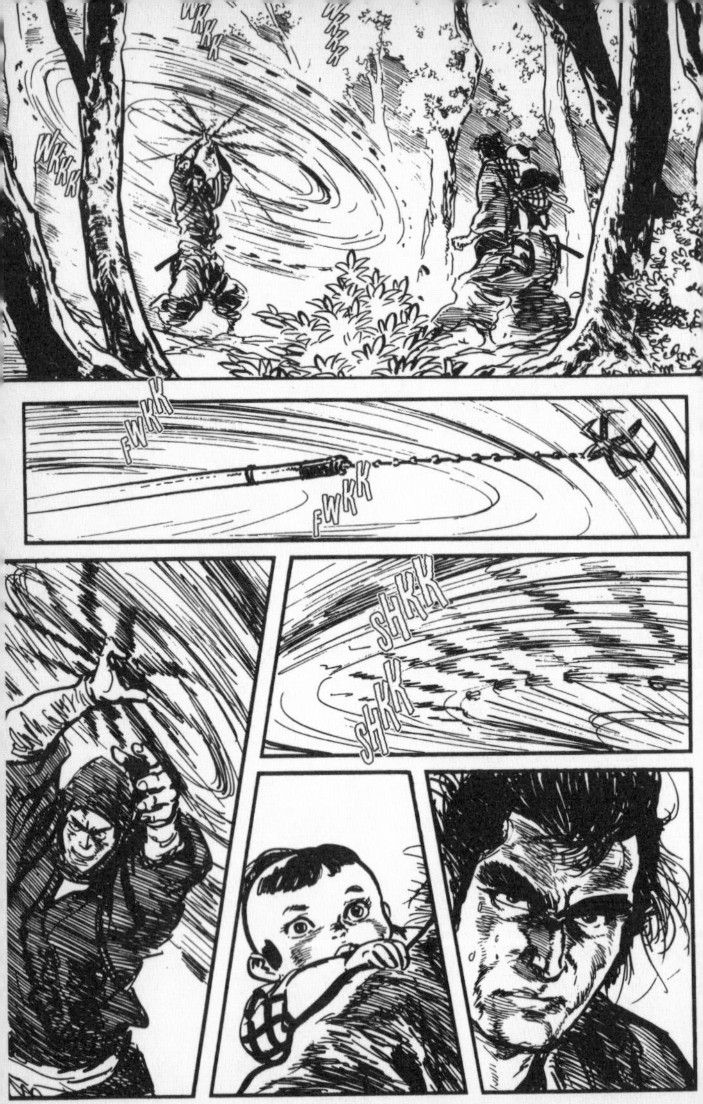
WRKK
WRKK
WRKK
FWKK
FWKK
SHKK
SHKK

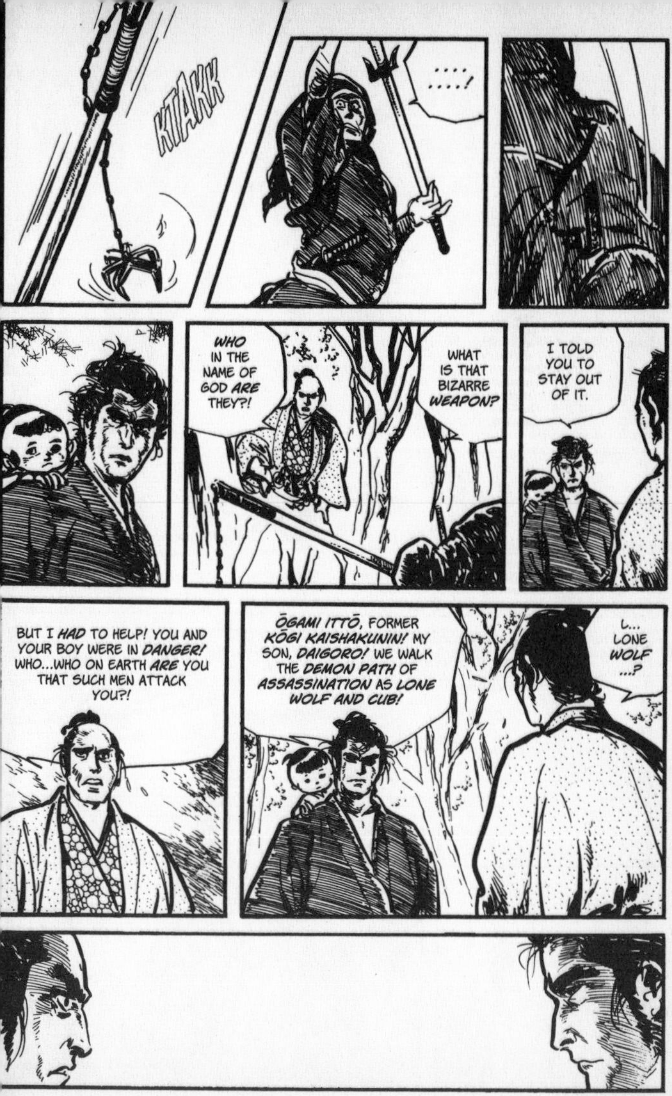
KTAKK
.....
.....!
WHO IN THE NAME OF GOD ARE THEY?!
WHAT IS THAT BIZARRE WEAPON?
I TOLD YOU TO STAY OUT OF IT.
BUT I HAD TO HELP! YOU AND YOUR BOY WERE IN DANGER! WHO...WHO ON EARTH ARE YOU THAT SUCH MEN ATTACK YOU?!
ŌGAMI ITTŌ, FORMER KŌGI KAISHAKUNIN! MY SON, DAIGORO! WE WALK THE DEMON PATH OF ASSASSINATION AS LONE WOLF AND CUB!
L... LONE WOLF ...?

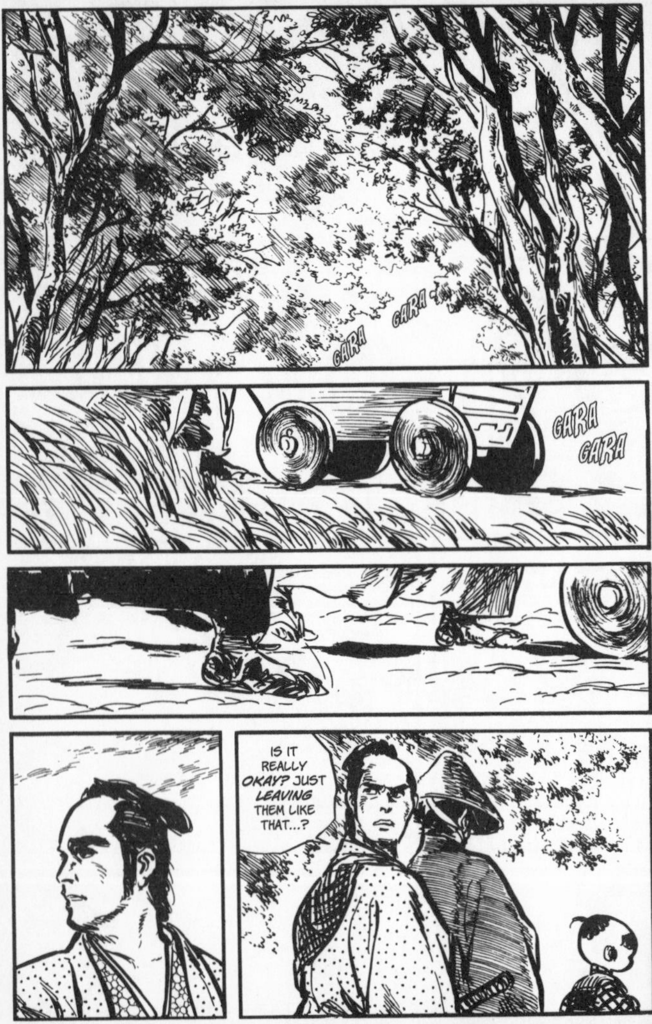
GARA
GARA
GARA
GARA
IS IT REALLY OKAY? JUST LEAVING THEM LIKE THAT...?

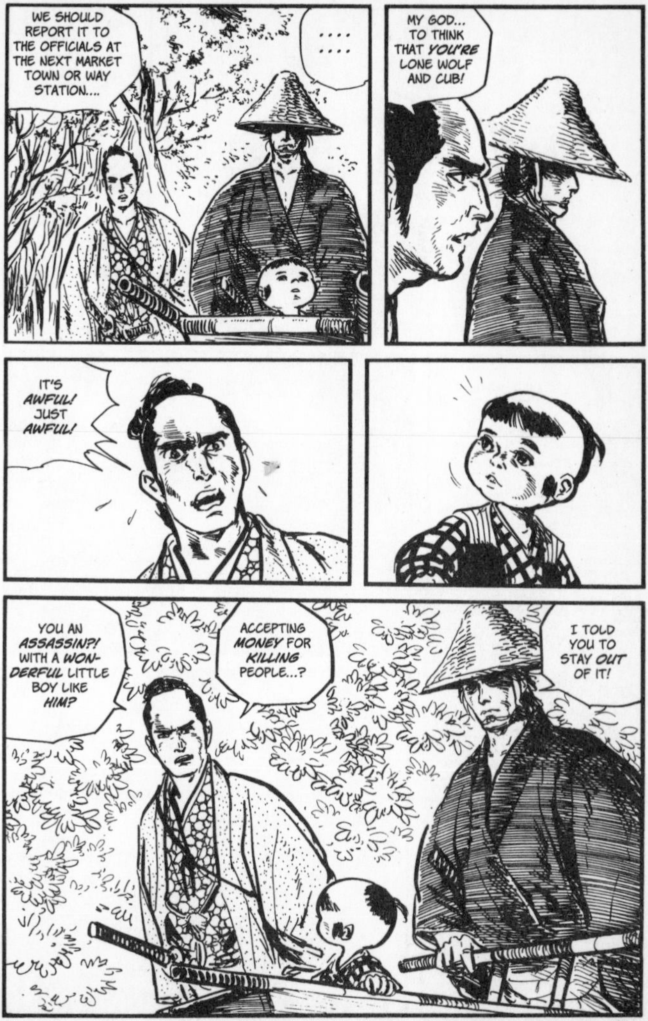
WE SHOULD REPORT IT TO THE OFFICIALS AT THE NEXT MARKET TOWN OR WAY STATION....
....
....
MY GOD... TO THINK THAT YOU'RE LONE WOLF AND CUB!
IT'S AWFUL! JUST AWFUL!
YOU AN ASSASSIN?! WITH A WONDERFUL LITTLE BOY LIKE HIM?
ACCEPTING MONEY FOR KILLING PEOPLE...?
I TOLD YOU TO STAY OUT OF IT!

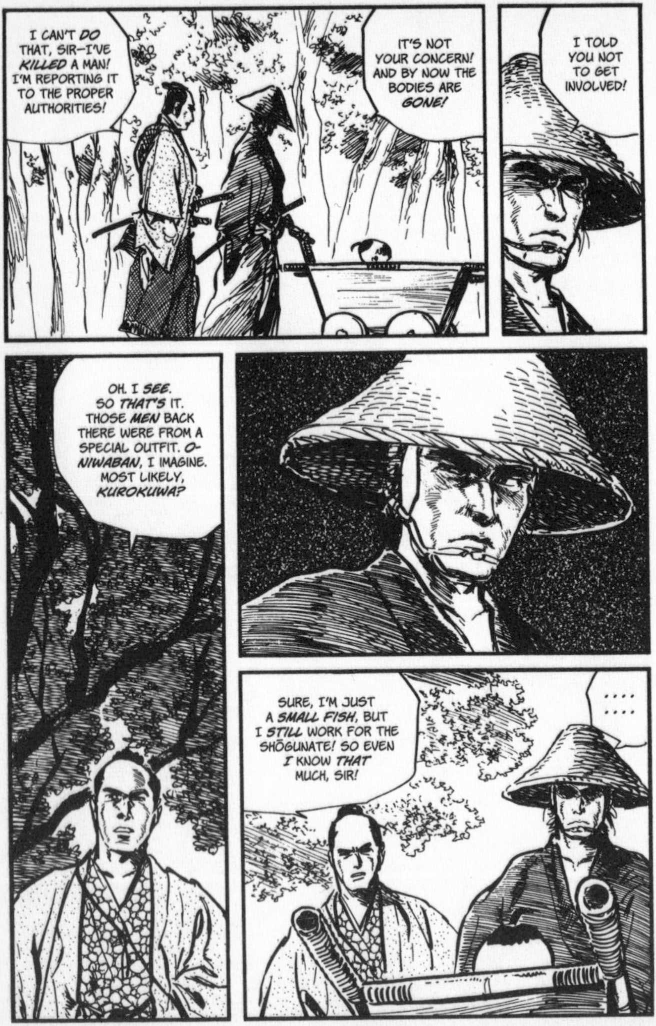
I CAN'T DO THAT, SIR—I'VE KILLED A MAN! I'M REPORTING IT TO THE PROPER AUTHORITIES!
IT'S NOT YOUR CONCERN! AND BY NOW THE BODIES ARE GONE!
I TOLD YOU NOT TO GET INVOLVED!
OH. I SEE. SO THAT'S IT. THOSE MEN BACK THERE WERE FROM A SPECIAL OUTFIT. O-NIWABAN, I IMAGINE. MOST LIKELY, KUROKUWA?
SURE, I'M JUST A SMALL FISH, BUT I STILL WORK FOR THE SHŌGUNATE! SO EVEN I KNOW THAT MUCH, SIR!
....

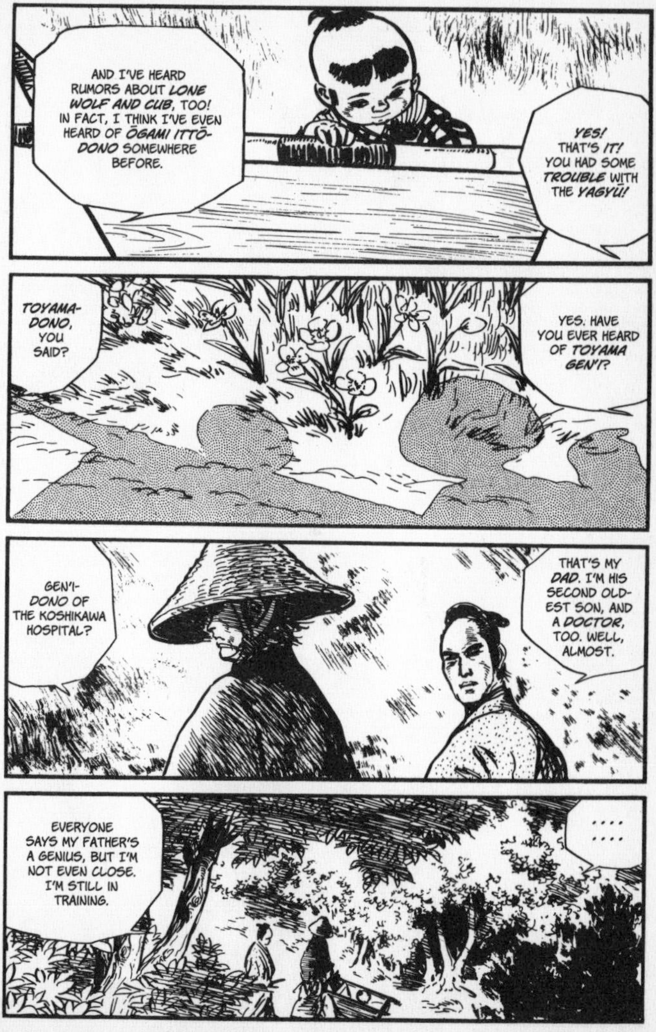
AND I'VE HEARD RUMORS ABOUT LONE WOLF AND CUB, TOO! IN FACT, I THINK I'VE EVEN HEARD OF ŌGAMI ITTŌ-DONO SOMEWHERE BEFORE.
YES! THAT'S IT! YOU HAD SOME TROUBLE WITH THE YAGYŪ!
TOYAMA-DONO, YOU SAID?
YES. HAVE YOU EVER HEARD OF TOYAMA GEN'I?
GEN'I-DONO OF THE KOSHIKAWA HOSPITAL?
THAT'S MY DAD. I'M HIS SECOND OLDEST SON, AND A DOCTOR, TOO. WELL, ALMOST.
EVERYONE SAYS MY FATHER'S A GENIUS, BUT I'M NOT EVEN CLOSE. I'M STILL IN TRAINING.
....
....

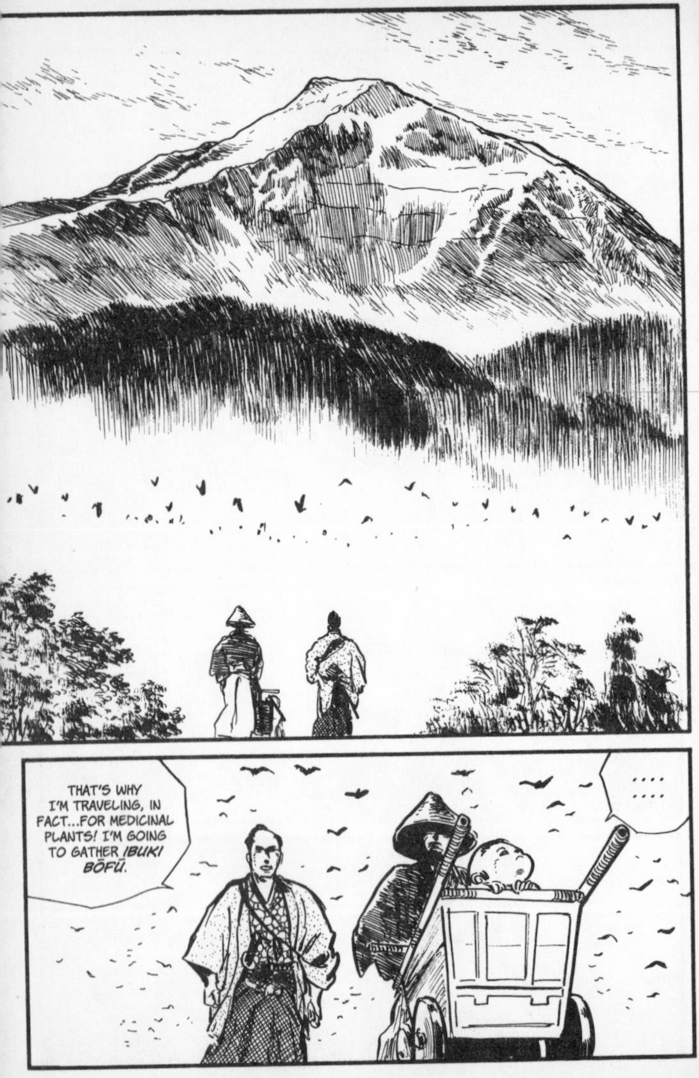
THAT'S WHY I'M TRAVELING, IN FACT...FOR MEDICINAL PLANTS! I'M GOING TO GATHER *IBUKI BŌFŪ*.
....
....

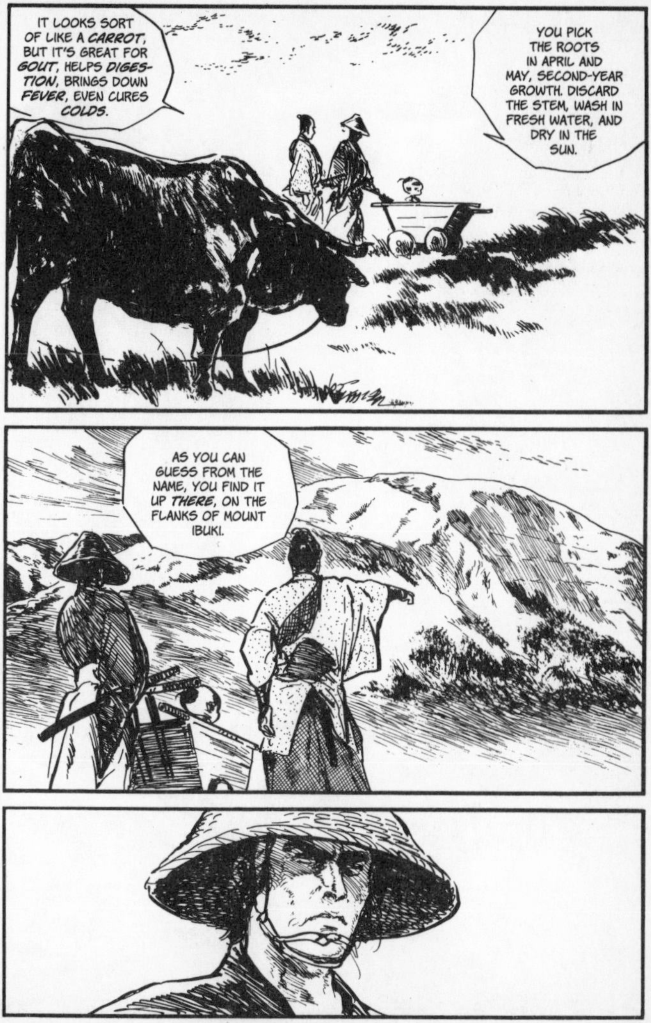
IT LOOKS SORT OF LIKE A CARROT, BUT IT'S GREAT FOR GOUT, HELPS DIGESTION, BRINGS DOWN FEVER, EVEN CURES COLDS.
YOU PICK THE ROOTS IN APRIL AND MAY, SECOND-YEAR GROWTH. DISCARD THE STEM, WASH IN FRESH WATER, AND DRY IN THE SUN.
AS YOU CAN GUESS FROM THE NAME, YOU FIND IT UP THERE, ON THE FLANKS OF MOUNT IBUKI.

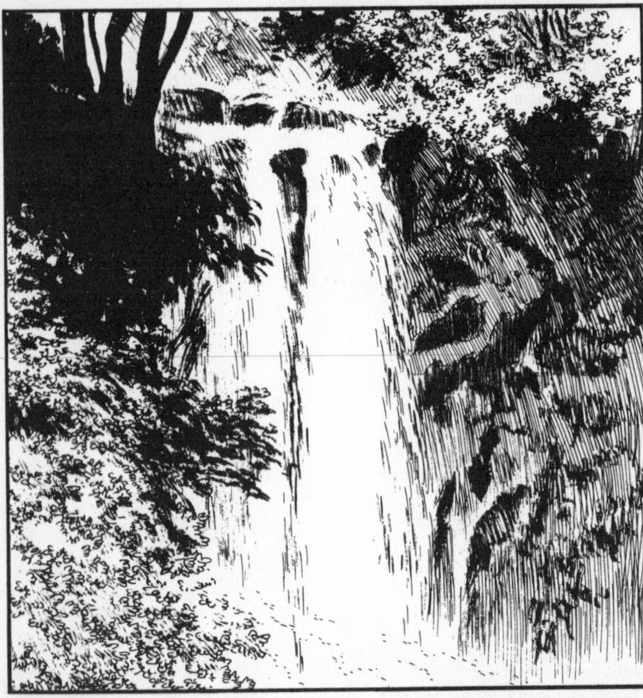

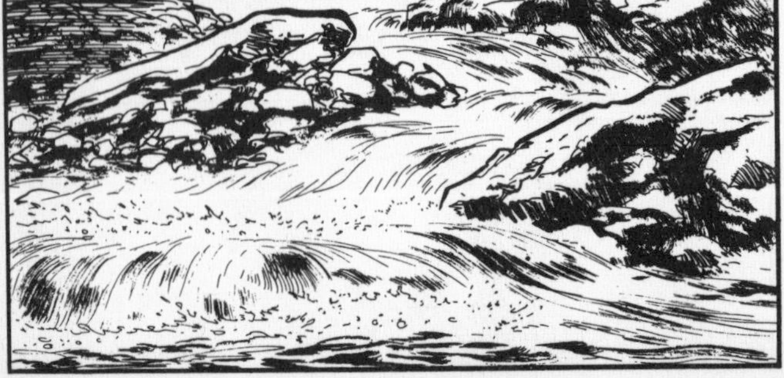

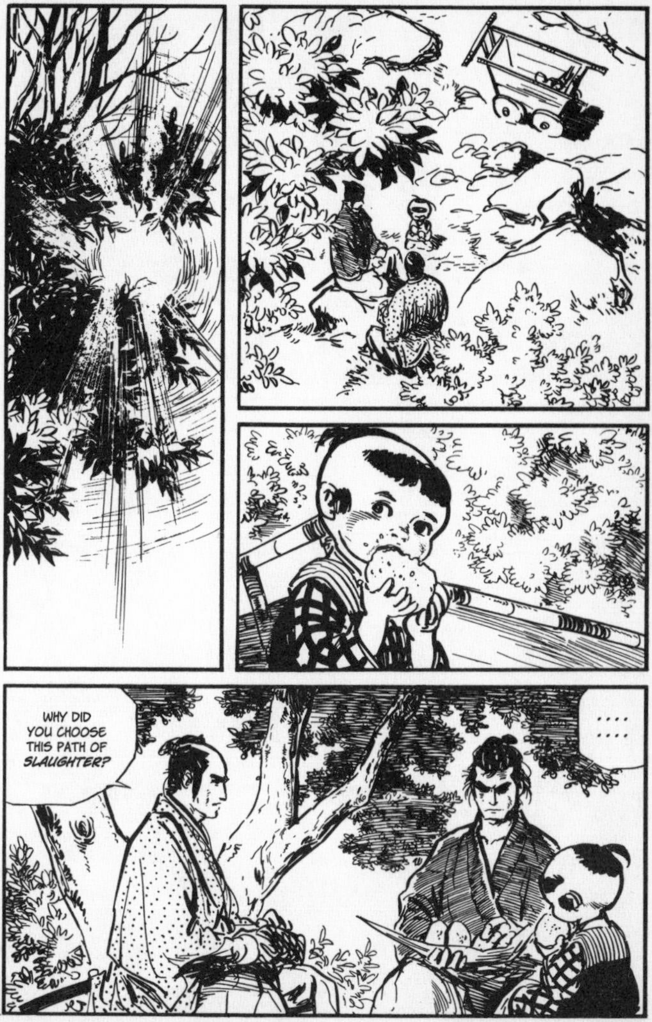

WHY DID YOU CHOOSE THIS PATH OF *SLAUGHTER?*
....
....

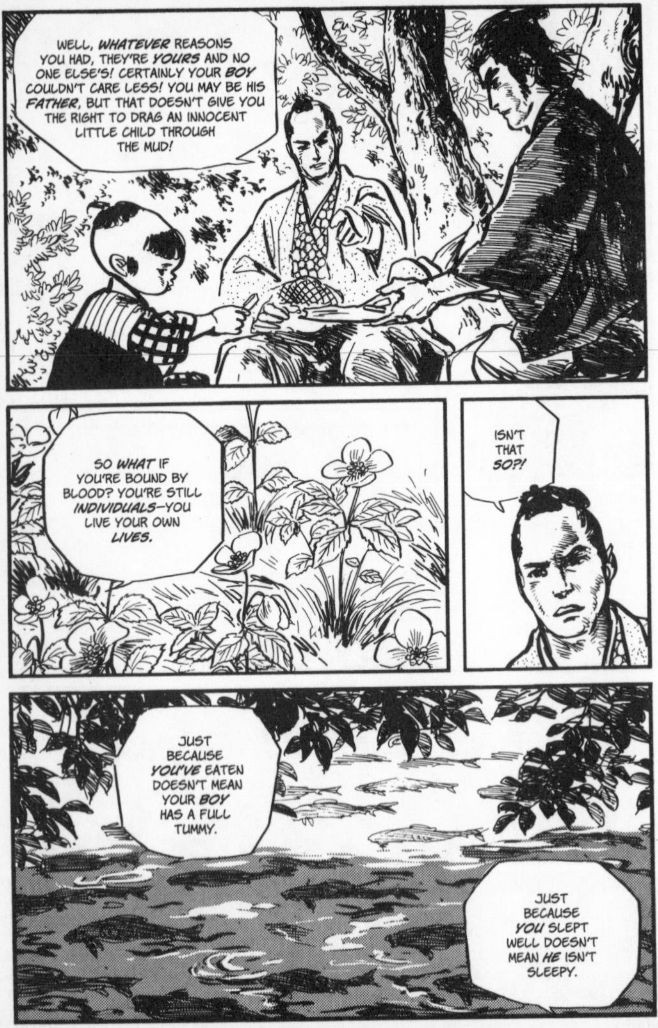
WELL, WHATEVER REASONS YOU HAD, THEY'RE YOURS AND NO ONE ELSE'S! CERTAINLY YOUR BOY COULDN'T CARE LESS! YOU MAY BE HIS FATHER, BUT THAT DOESN'T GIVE YOU THE RIGHT TO DRAG AN INNOCENT LITTLE CHILD THROUGH THE MUD!
SO WHAT IF YOU'RE BOUND BY BLOOD? YOU'RE STILL INDIVIDUALS—YOU LIVE YOUR OWN LIVES.
ISN'T THAT SO?!
JUST BECAUSE YOU'VE EATEN DOESN'T MEAN YOUR BOY HAS A FULL TUMMY.
JUST BECAUSE YOU SLEPT WELL DOESN'T MEAN HE ISN'T SLEEPY.

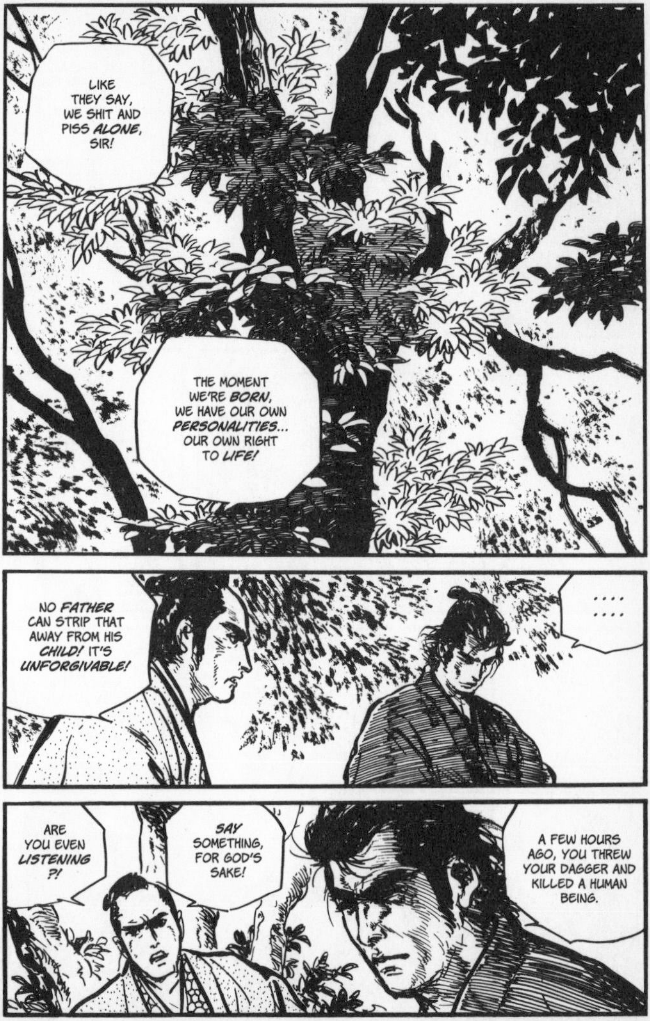
LIKE THEY SAY, WE SHIT AND PISS ALONE, SIR!
THE MOMENT WE'RE BORN, WE HAVE OUR OWN PERSONALITIES... OUR OWN RIGHT TO LIFE!
NO FATHER CAN STRIP THAT AWAY FROM HIS CHILD! IT'S UNFORGIVABLE!
....
ARE YOU EVEN LISTENING ?!
SAY SOMETHING, FOR GOD'S SAKE!
A FEW HOURS AGO, YOU THREW YOUR DAGGER AND KILLED A HUMAN BEING.

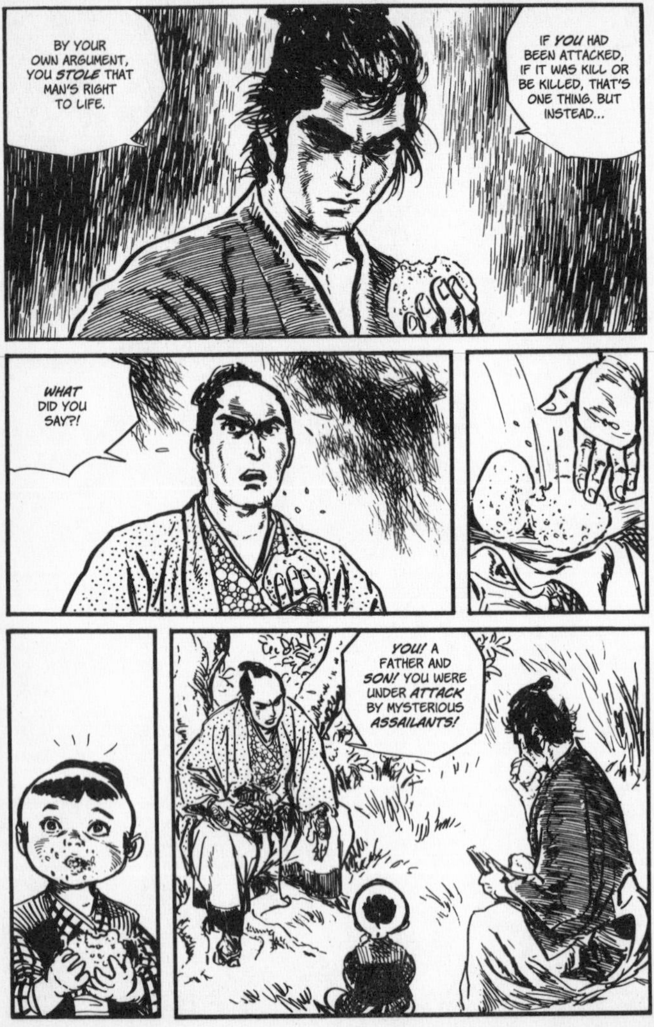
BY YOUR OWN ARGUMENT, YOU STOLE THAT MAN'S RIGHT TO LIFE.
IF YOU HAD BEEN ATTACKED, IF IT WAS KILL OR BE KILLED, THAT'S ONE THING. BUT INSTEAD...
WHAT DID YOU SAY?!
YOU! A FATHER AND SON! YOU WERE UNDER ATTACK BY MYSTERIOUS ASSAILANTS!

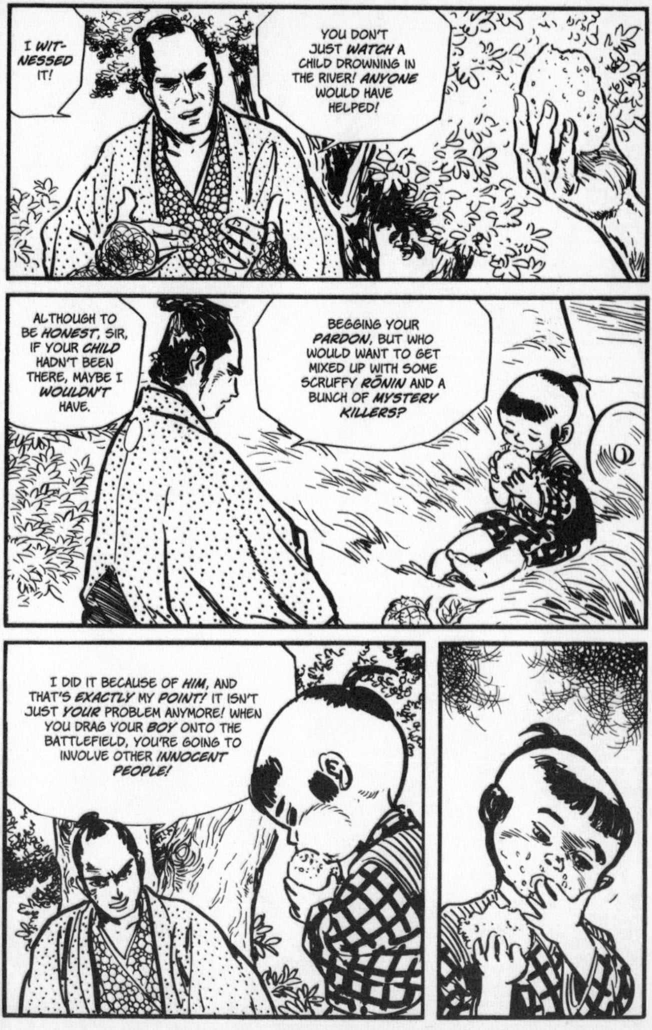
I WIT-NESSED IT!
YOU DON'T JUST WATCH A CHILD DROWNING IN THE RIVER! ANYONE WOULD HAVE HELPED!
ALTHOUGH TO BE HONEST, SIR, IF YOUR CHILD HADN'T BEEN THERE, MAYBE I WOULDN'T HAVE.
BEGGING YOUR PARDON, BUT WHO WOULD WANT TO GET MIXED UP WITH SOME SCRUFFY RŌNIN AND A BUNCH OF MYSTERY KILLERS?
I DID IT BECAUSE OF HIM, AND THAT'S EXACTLY MY POINT! IT ISN'T JUST YOUR PROBLEM ANYMORE! WHEN YOU DRAG YOUR BOY ONTO THE BATTLEFIELD, YOU'RE GOING TO INVOLVE OTHER INNOCENT PEOPLE!

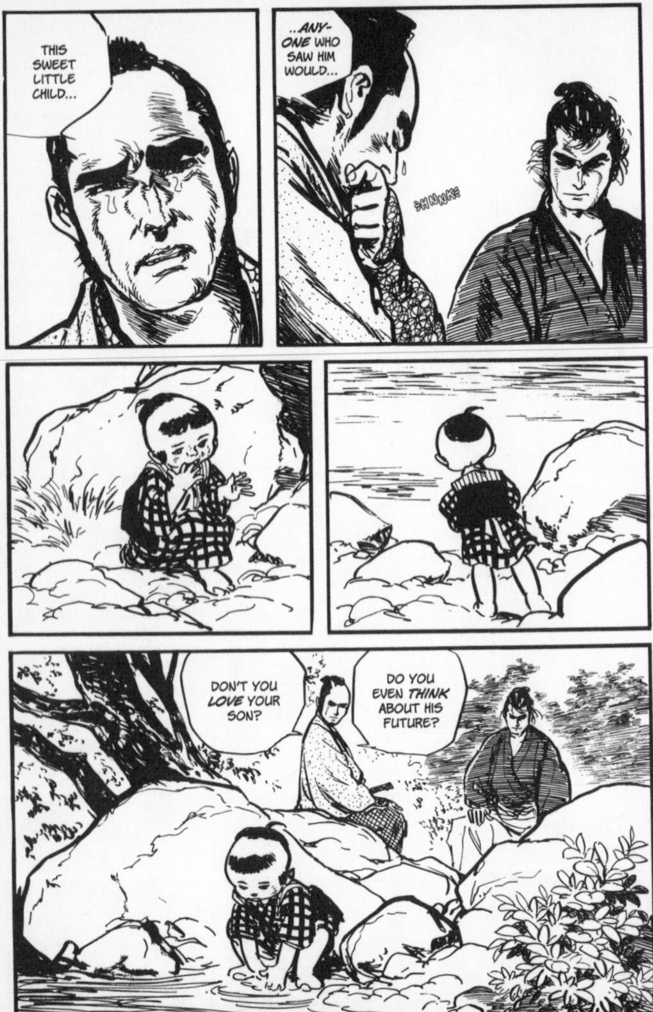
THIS SWEET LITTLE CHILD...
..ANY-ONE WHO SAW HIM WOULD...
SHNNK
DON'T YOU LOVE YOUR SON?
DO YOU EVEN THINK ABOUT HIS FUTURE?

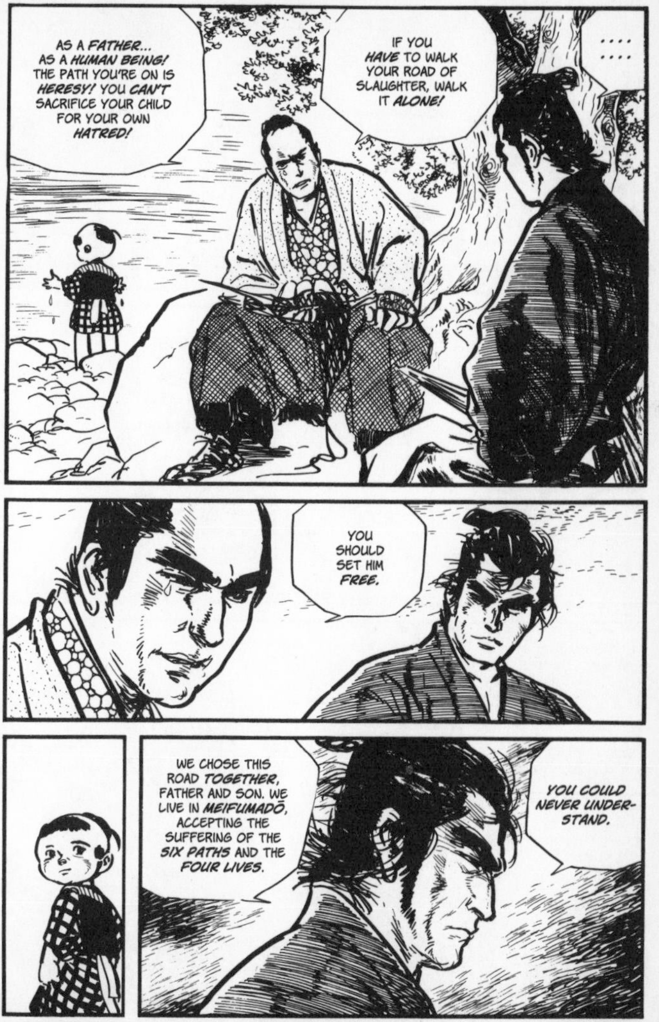
AS A *FATHER*... AS A *HUMAN BEING!* THE PATH YOU'RE ON IS *HERESY!* YOU *CAN'T* SACRIFICE YOUR CHILD FOR YOUR OWN *HATRED!*
IF YOU *HAVE* TO WALK YOUR ROAD OF SLAUGHTER, WALK IT *ALONE!*
....
YOU SHOULD SET HIM *FREE.*
WE CHOSE THIS ROAD *TOGETHER*, FATHER AND SON. WE LIVE IN *MEIFUMADŌ*, ACCEPTING THE SUFFERING OF THE *SIX PATHS* AND THE *FOUR LIVES*.
YOU COULD NEVER UNDERSTAND.

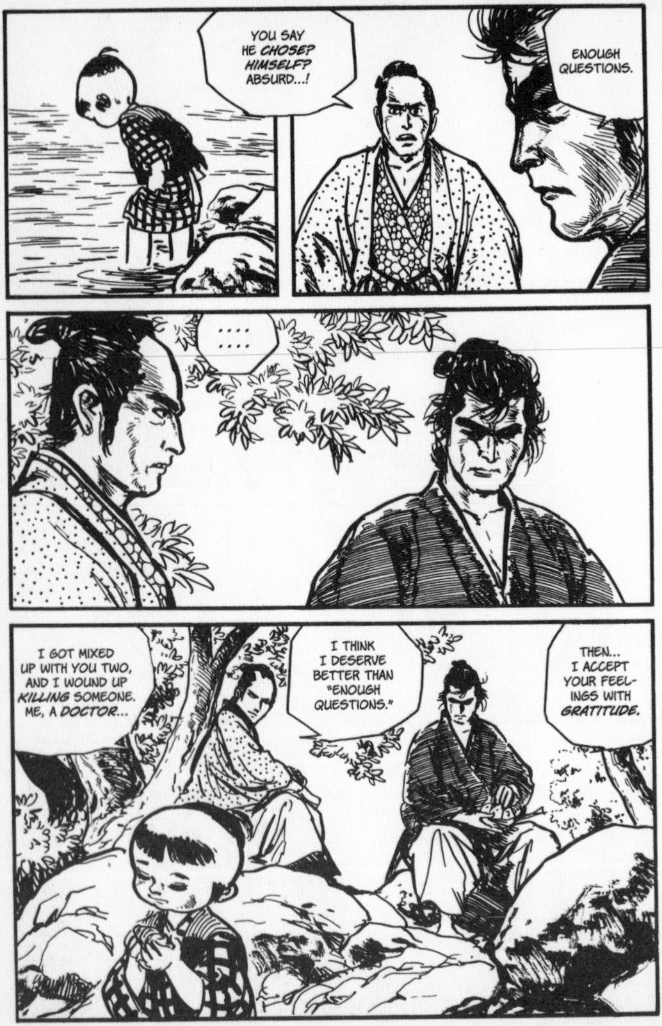

YOU SAY HE *CHOSE?* *HIMSELF?* ABSURD...!
ENOUGH QUESTIONS.
....
....
I GOT MIXED UP WITH YOU TWO, AND I WOUND UP *KILLING* SOMEONE. ME, A *DOCTOR*...
I THINK I DESERVE BETTER THAN "ENOUGH QUESTIONS."
THEN... I ACCEPT YOUR FEEL-INGS WITH *GRATITUDE.*

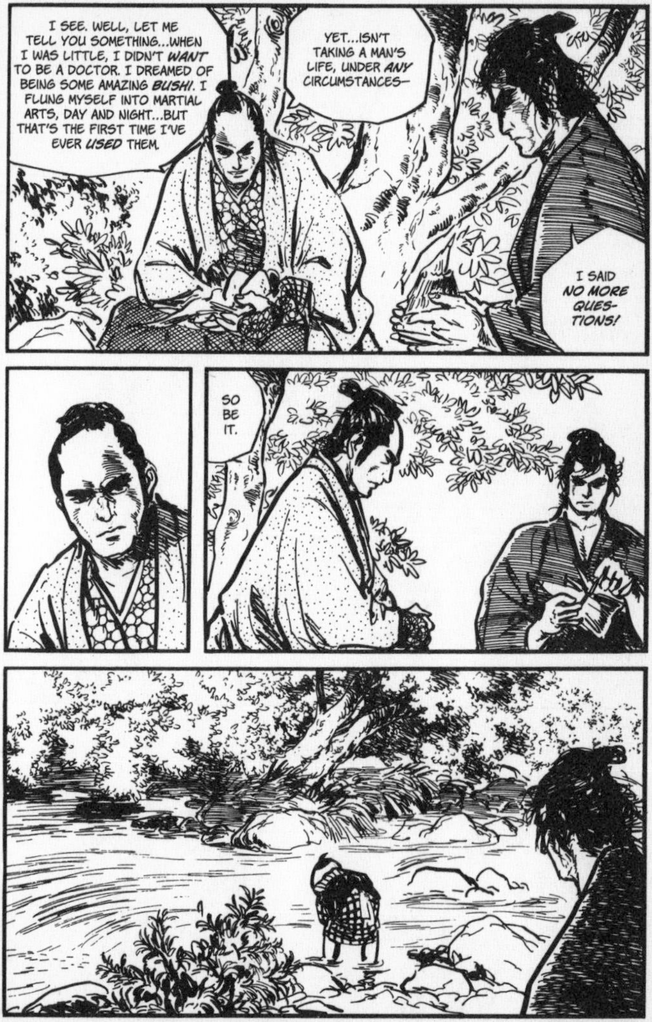
I SEE. WELL, LET ME TELL YOU SOMETHING...WHEN I WAS LITTLE, I DIDN'T *WANT* TO BE A DOCTOR. I DREAMED OF BEING SOME AMAZING *BUSHI*. I FLUNG MYSELF INTO MARTIAL ARTS, DAY AND NIGHT...BUT THAT'S THE FIRST TIME I'VE EVER *USED* THEM.
YET...ISN'T TAKING A MAN'S LIFE, UNDER *ANY* CIRCUMSTANCES—
I SAID *NO MORE QUES-TIONS!*
SO BE IT.

BUT AT LEAST REMEMBER *THIS*.

MAYBE I'M STILL INTERFERING, BUT...

THERE'S A PERENNIAL CALLED *KAKIDŌSHI*—ITS MEDICAL NAME IS *RENSEN-SŌ*.

THIS TIME OF YEAR IT PUTS OUT PALE PURPLE FLOWERS.

PERHAPS AROUND HERE...

AH—THERE'S ONE!

178

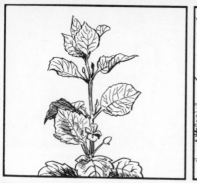

THIS IS *EXCELLENT* WHEN CHILDREN GET COLICKY.

DRY IT IN A SHADED PLACE, WITH A GOOD BREEZE, AND GRIND IT FINE. THE POWDER WILL KEEP ITS HEALING POWERS FOR MANY YEARS.

AND LET ME TELL YOU ABOUT AN EXCELLENT COAGULANT.

IT'S A PALE WHITE MUSHROOM CALLED *ONIFUSUBE.*

IF YOU SPOT ONE, *POUNCE* ON IT. THERE'S *NOTHING* BETTER FOR STAUNCHING BLEEDING.

I'M NOT TELLING YOU THESE THINGS FOR *YOUR* BENEFIT. IT'S FOR THE *BOY.*

. . . . .

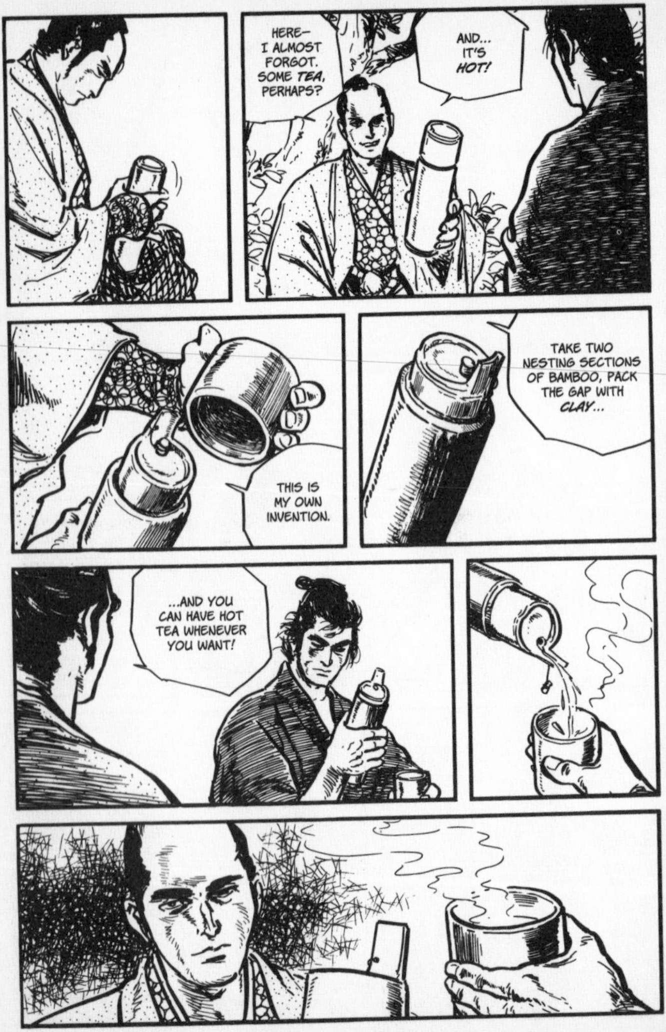
HERE— I ALMOST FORGOT. SOME TEA, PERHAPS?
AND... IT'S HOT!
THIS IS MY OWN INVENTION.
TAKE TWO NESTING SECTIONS OF BAMBOO, PACK THE GAP WITH CLAY...
...AND YOU CAN HAVE HOT TEA WHENEVER YOU WANT!

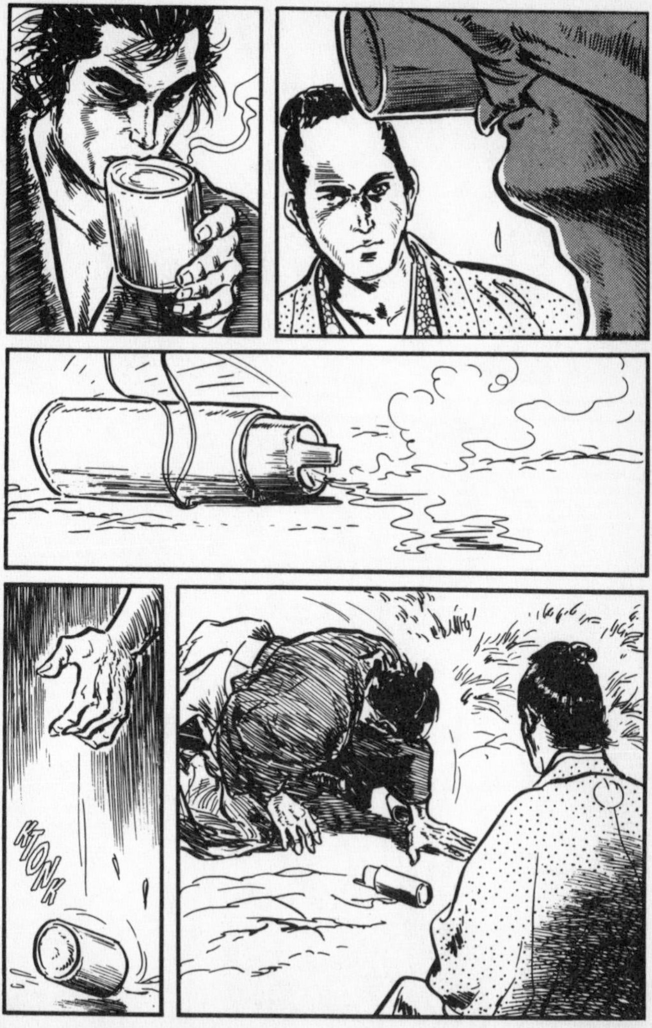
KTONK

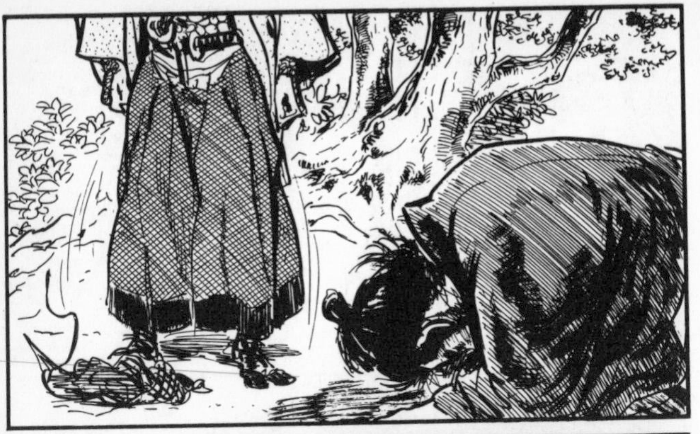

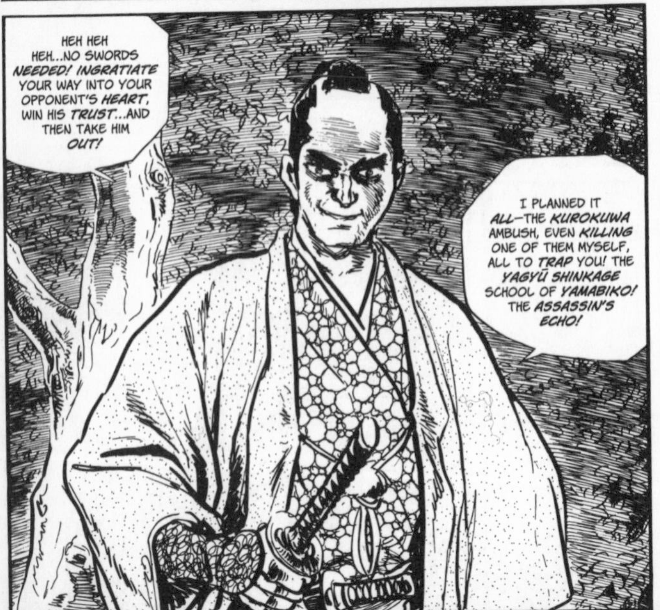
HEH HEH HEH...NO SWORDS NEEDED! INGRATIATE YOUR WAY INTO YOUR OPPONENT'S HEART, WIN HIS TRUST...AND THEN TAKE HIM OUT!
I PLANNED IT ALL—THE KUROKUWA AMBUSH, EVEN KILLING ONE OF THEM MYSELF, ALL TO TRAP YOU! THE YAGYŪ SHINKAGE SCHOOL OF YAMABIKO! THE ASSASSIN'S ECHO!

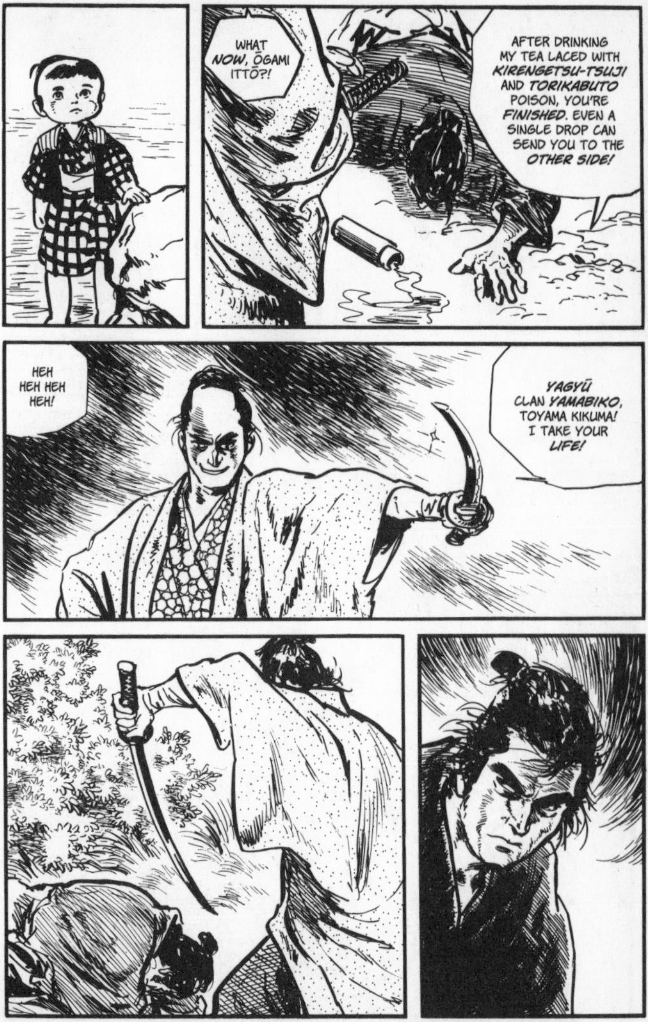
WHAT NOW, ŌGAMI ITTŌ?!
AFTER DRINKING MY TEA LACED WITH KIRENGETSU-TSUJI AND TORIKABUTO POISON, YOU'RE FINISHED. EVEN A SINGLE DROP CAN SEND YOU TO THE OTHER SIDE!
HEH HEH HEH HEH!
YAGYŪ CLAN YAMABIKO, TOYAMA KIKUMA! I TAKE YOUR LIFE!

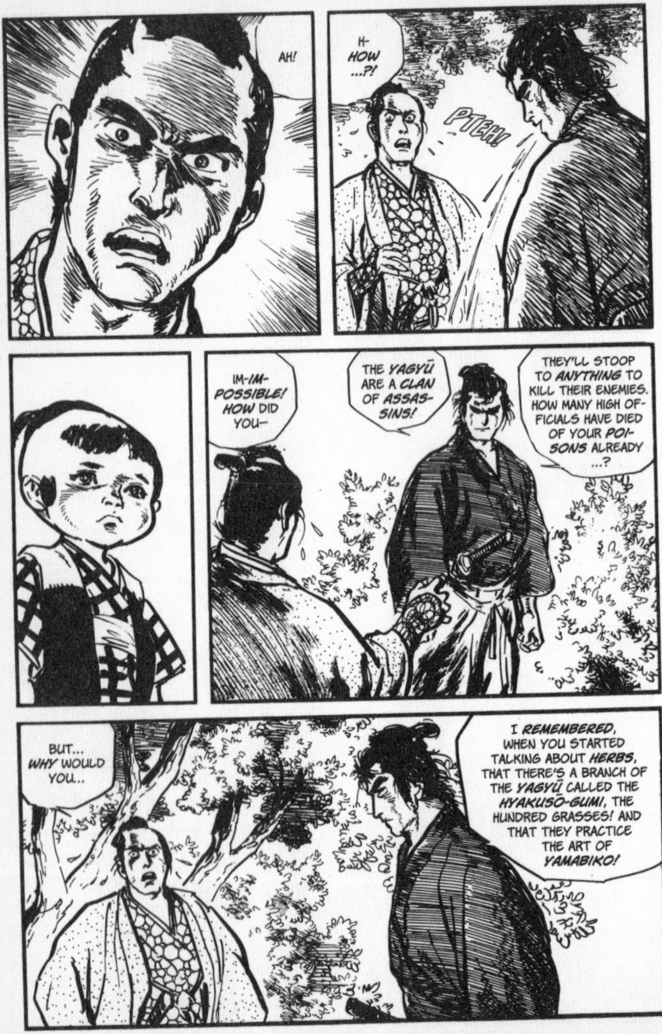
AH!
H-
HOW
...?!
PTEH!
IM-*IM-*
POSSIBLE! HOW DID
YOU–
THE *YAGYŪ* ARE A *CLAN* OF *ASSAS-*
SINS!
THEY'LL STOOP TO *ANYTHING* TO KILL THEIR ENEMIES. HOW MANY HIGH OF- FICIALS HAVE DIED OF YOUR *POI-* *SONS* ALREADY ...?
BUT... *WHY* WOULD YOU...
I *REMEMBERED*, WHEN YOU STARTED TALKING ABOUT *HERBS*, THAT THERE'S A BRANCH OF THE *YAGYŪ* CALLED THE *HYAKUSŌ-GUMI*, THE HUNDRED GRASSES! AND THAT THEY PRACTICE THE ART OF *YAMABIKO!*

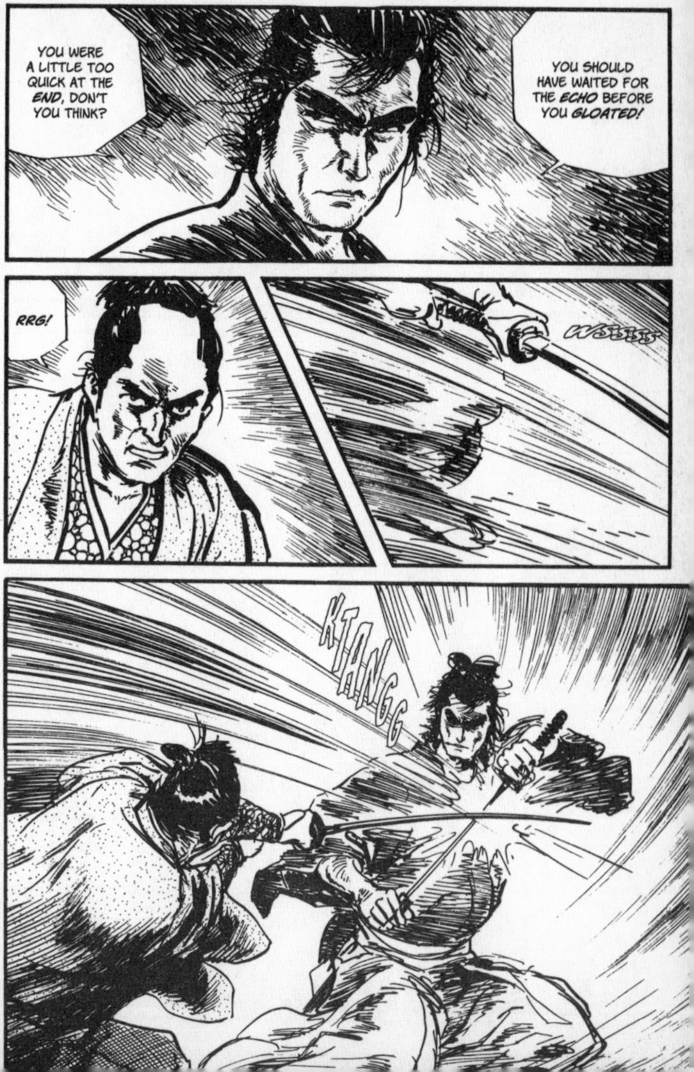
YOU WERE A LITTLE TOO QUICK AT THE END, DON'T YOU THINK?
YOU SHOULD HAVE WAITED FOR THE ECHO BEFORE YOU GLOATED!
RRG!
WSSSSS
KTANGG

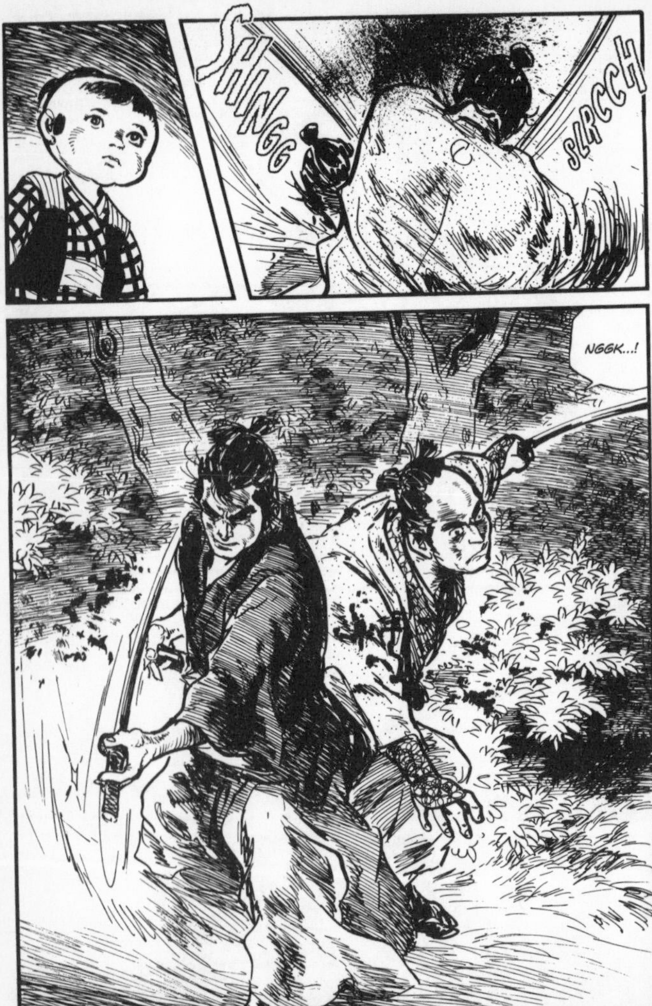
SHINGG
SLRCCH
NGGK...!

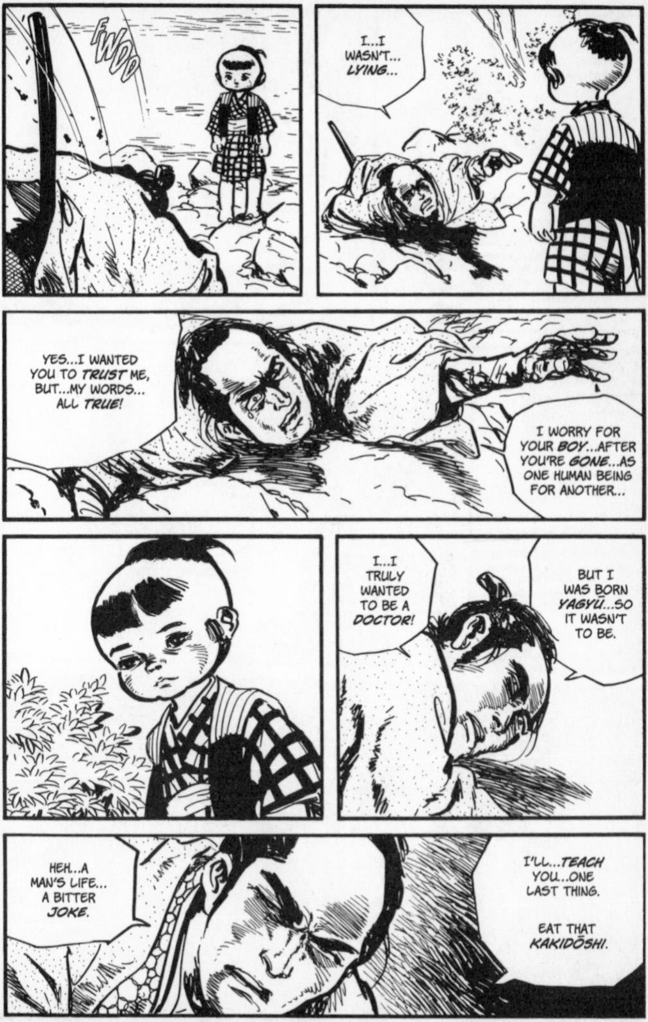
FWOO
I...I WASN'T... LYING...
YES...I WANTED YOU TO TRUST ME, BUT...MY WORDS... ALL TRUE!
I WORRY FOR YOUR BOY...AFTER YOU'RE GONE...AS ONE HUMAN BEING FOR ANOTHER...
I...I TRULY WANTED TO BE A DOCTOR!
BUT I WAS BORN YAGYŪ...SO IT WASN'T TO BE.
HEH...A MAN'S LIFE... A BITTER JOKE.
I'LL...TEACH YOU...ONE LAST THING.
EAT THAT KAKIDŌSHI.

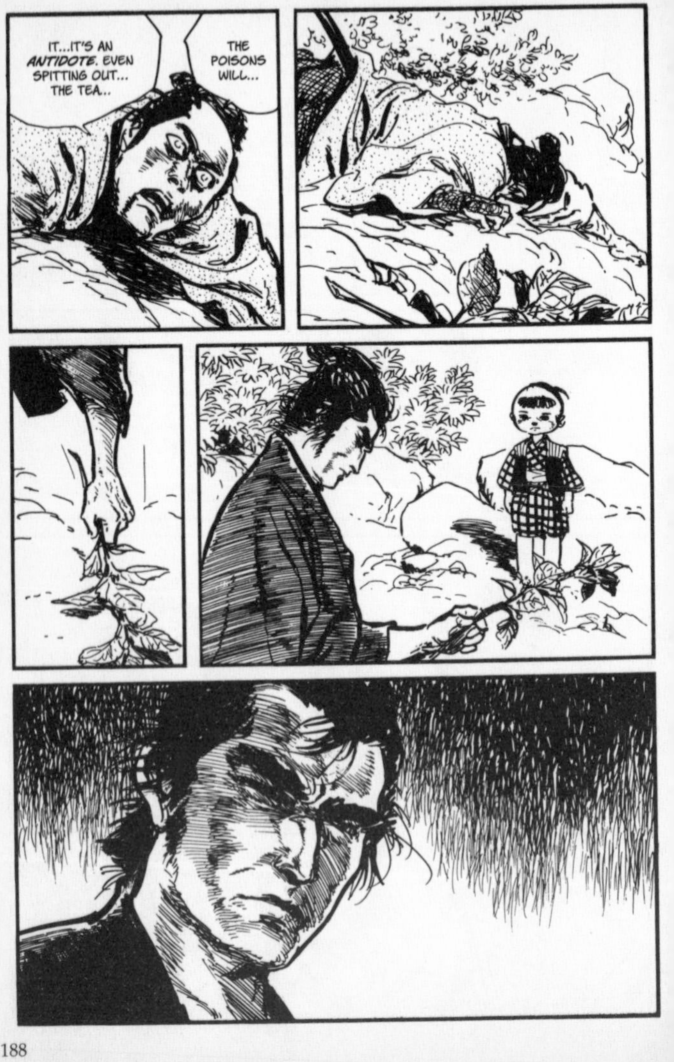
IT...IT'S AN ANTIDOTE. EVEN SPITTING OUT... THE TEA...
THE POISONS WILL...

the forty-eighth

Naked Worms

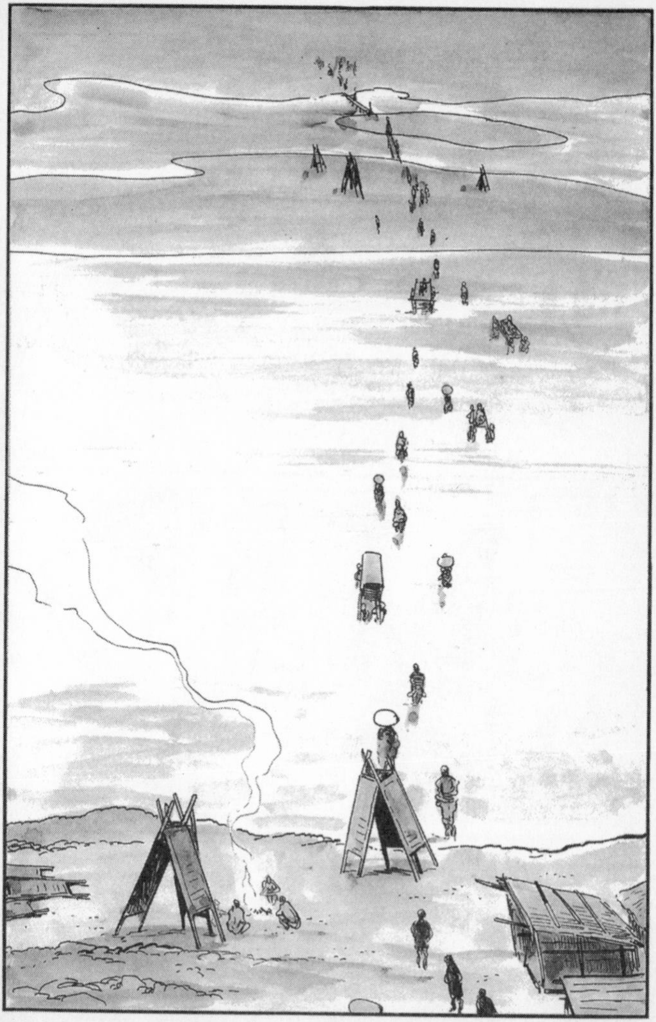

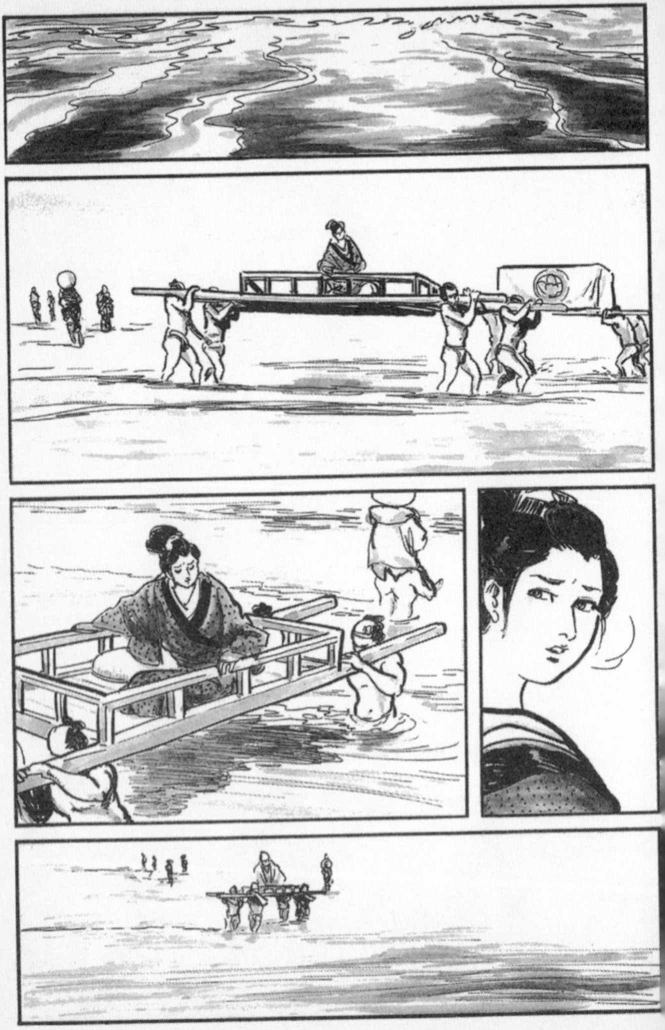

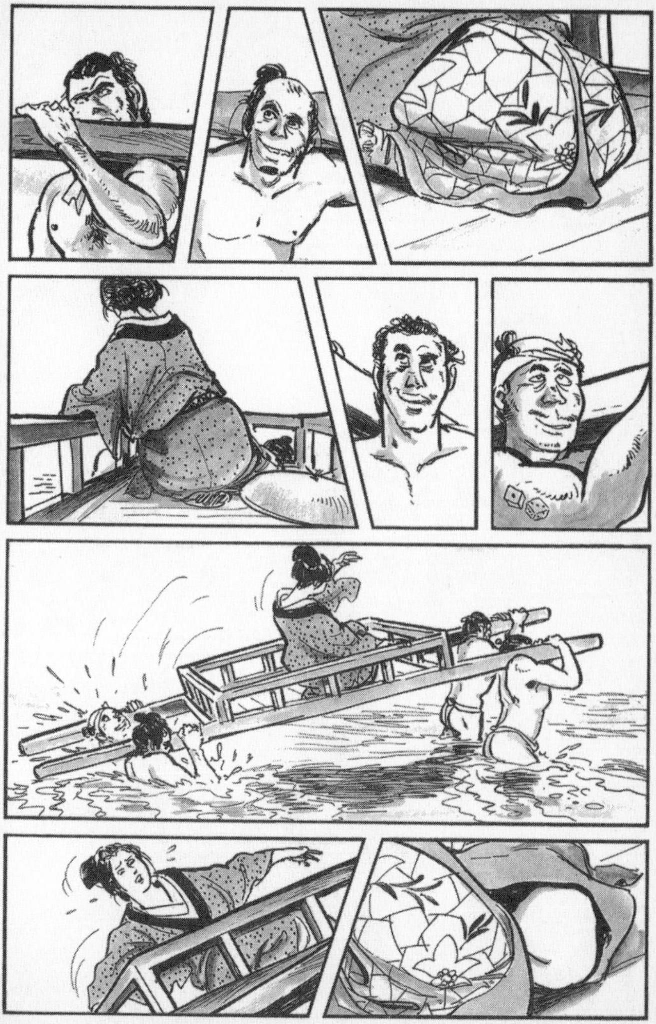

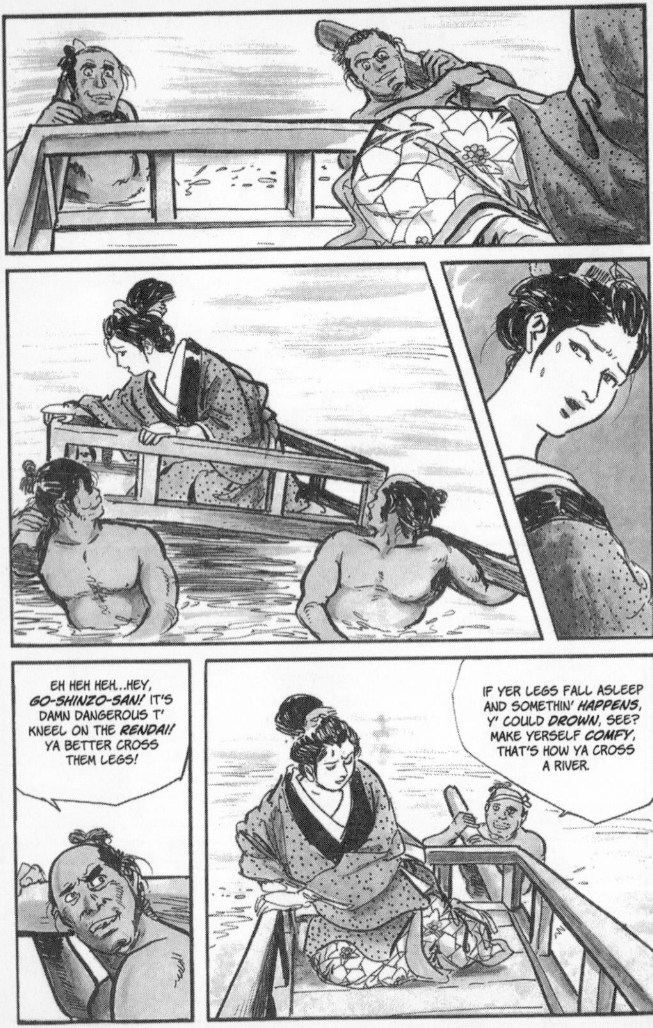
EH HEH HEH...HEY, GO-SHINZO-SAN! IT'S DAMN DANGEROUS T' KNEEL ON THE RENDAI! YA BETTER CROSS THEM LEGS!
IF YER LEGS FALL ASLEEP AND SOMETHIN' HAPPENS, Y' COULD DROWN, SEE? MAKE YERSELF COMFY, THAT'S HOW YA CROSS A RIVER.

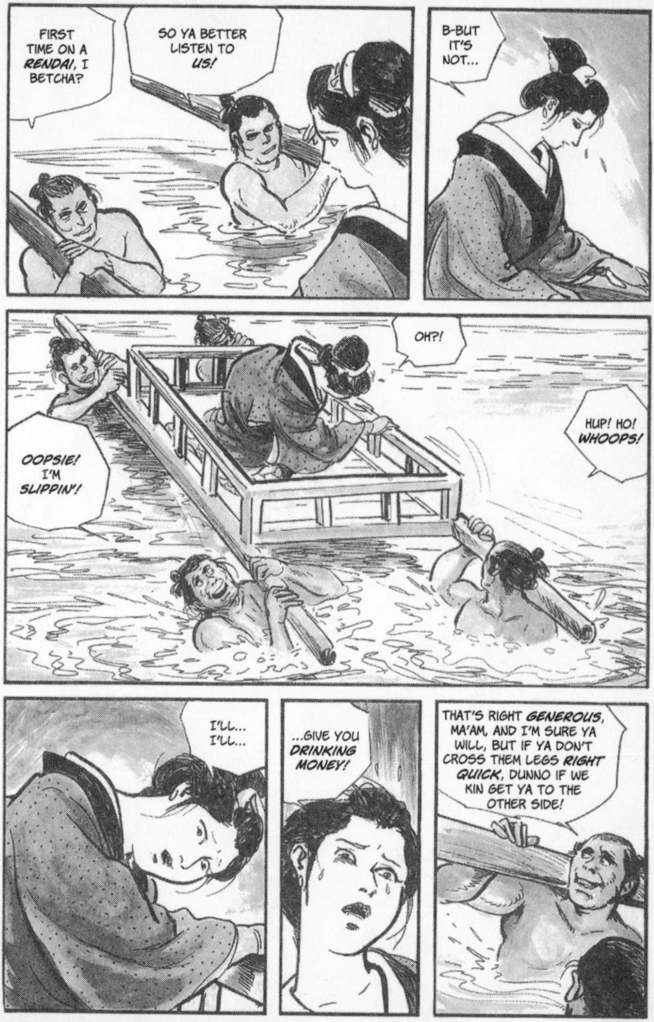
FIRST TIME ON A *RENDAI*, I BETCHA?
SO YA BETTER LISTEN TO *US!*
B-BUT IT'S NOT...
OH?!
HUP! HO! *WHOOPS!*
OOPSIE! I'M *SLIPPIN'!*
I'LL... I'LL...
...GIVE YOU *DRINKING MONEY!*
THAT'S RIGHT *GENEROUS*, MA'AM, AND I'M SURE YA WILL, BUT IF YA DON'T CROSS THEM LEGS *RIGHT QUICK*, DUNNO IF WE KIN GET YA TO THE OTHER SIDE!

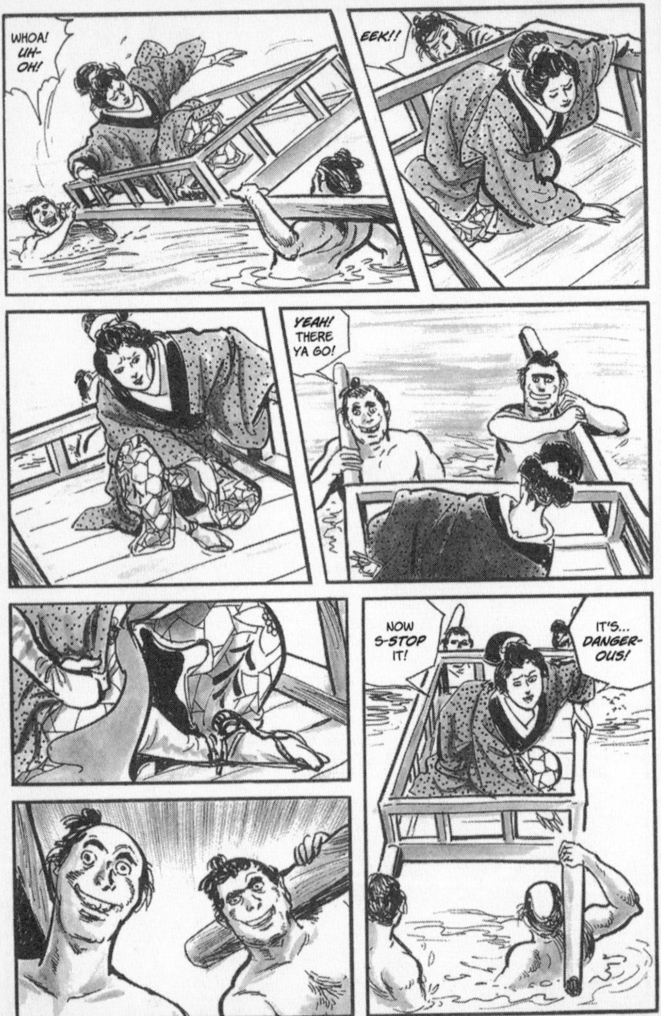
WHOA! UH-OH!
EEK!!
YEAH! THERE YA GO!
NOW S-STOP IT!
IT'S... DANGER-OUS!

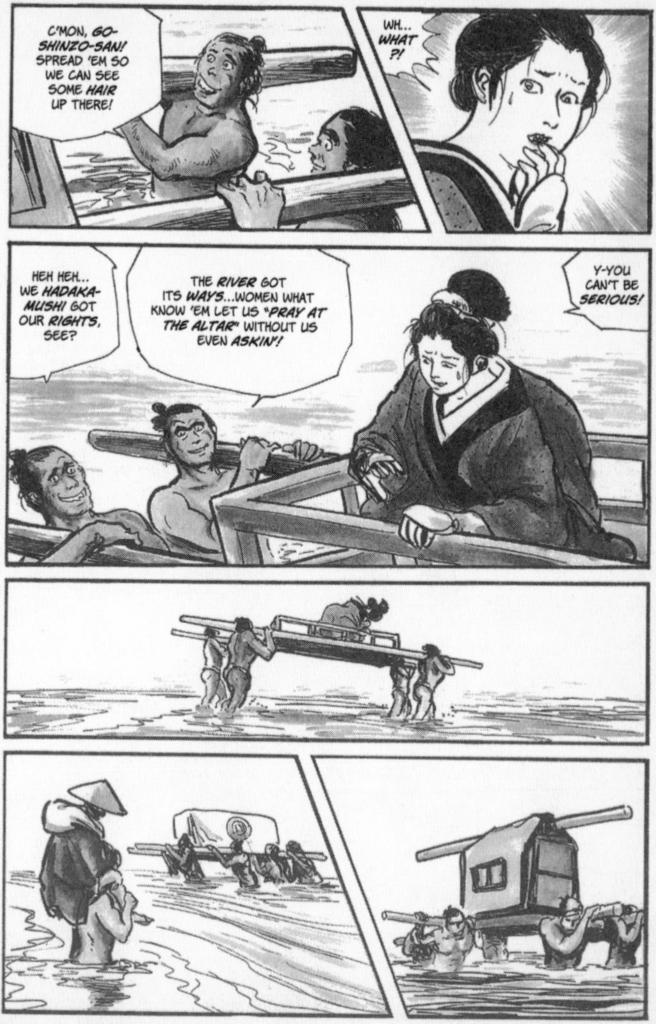

C'MON, GO-SHINZO-SAN! SPREAD 'EM SO WE CAN SEE SOME HAIR UP THERE!
WH... WHAT ?!
HEH HEH... WE HADAKA-MUSHI GOT OUR RIGHTS, SEE?
THE RIVER GOT ITS WAYS...WOMEN WHAT KNOW 'EM LET US "PRAY AT THE ALTAR" WITHOUT US EVEN ASKIN'!
Y-YOU CAN'T BE SERIOUS!

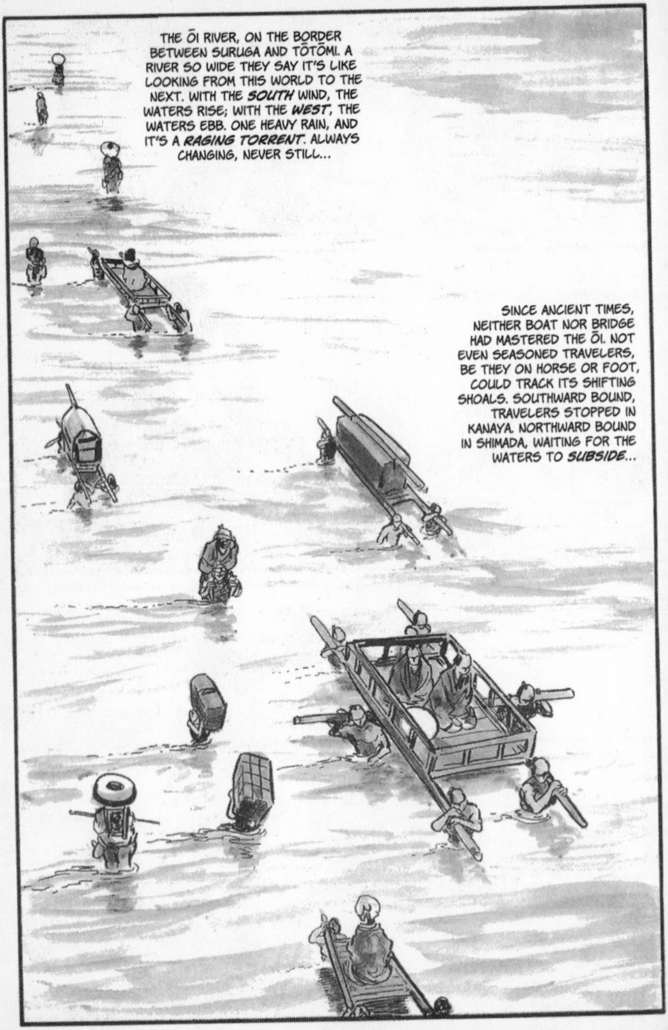
THE ŌI RIVER, ON THE BORDER BETWEEN SURUGA AND TŌTŌMI. A RIVER SO WIDE THEY SAY IT'S LIKE LOOKING FROM THIS WORLD TO THE NEXT. WITH THE *SOUTH* WIND, THE WATERS RISE; WITH THE *WEST*, THE WATERS EBB. ONE HEAVY RAIN, AND IT'S A *RAGING TORRENT*. ALWAYS CHANGING, NEVER STILL...
SINCE ANCIENT TIMES, NEITHER BOAT NOR BRIDGE HAD MASTERED THE ŌI. NOT EVEN SEASONED TRAVELERS, BE THEY ON HORSE OR FOOT, COULD TRACK ITS SHIFTING SHOALS. SOUTHWARD BOUND, TRAVELERS STOPPED IN KANAYA. NORTHWARD BOUND IN SHIMADA, WAITING FOR THE WATERS TO *SUBSIDE*...

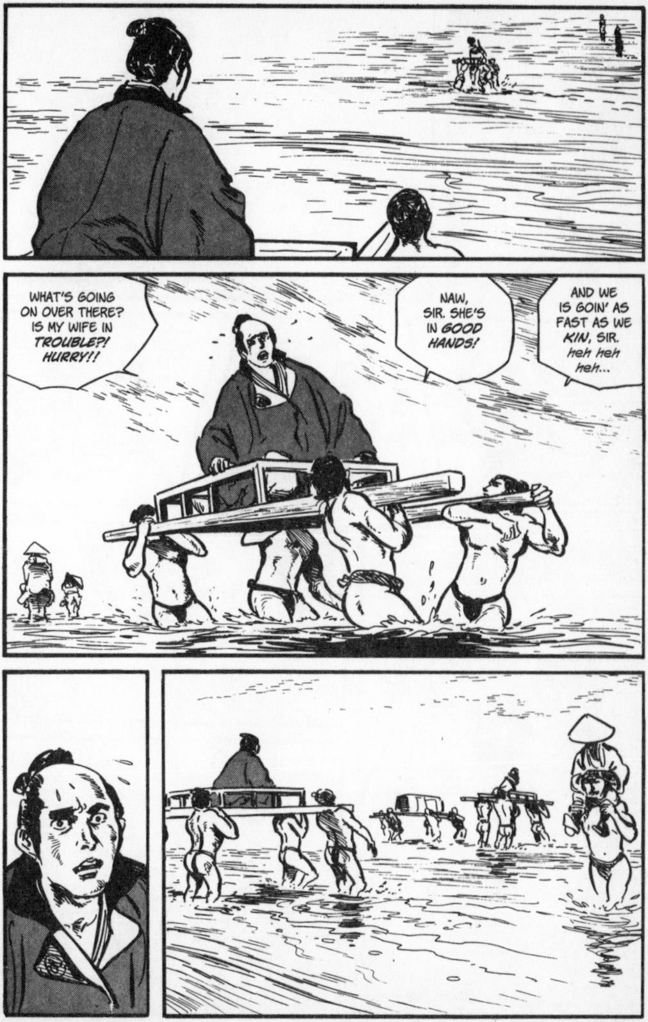
WHAT'S GOING ON OVER THERE? IS MY WIFE IN *TROUBLE?!* *HURRY!!*
NAW, SIR. SHE'S IN *GOOD HANDS!*
AND WE IS GOIN' AS FAST AS WE *KIN*, SIR. *heh heh heh...*

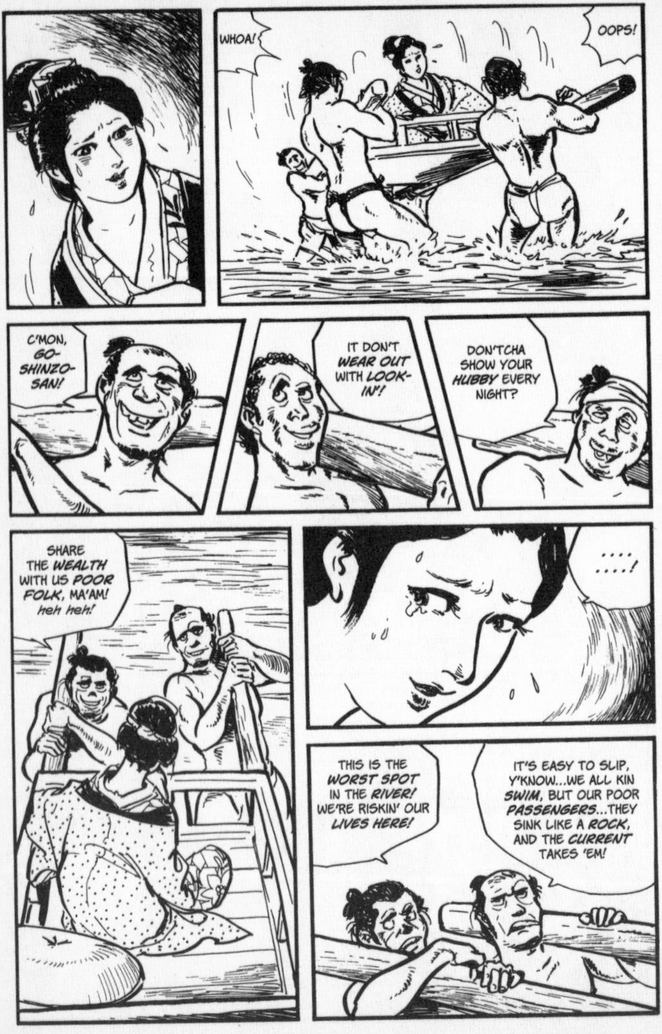
WHOA!
OOPS!
C'MON, GO-SHINZO-SAN!
IT DON'T WEAR OUT WITH LOOKIN'!
DON'TCHA SHOW YOUR HUBBY EVERY NIGHT?
SHARE THE WEALTH WITH US POOR FOLK, MA'AM! heh heh!
....
....!
THIS IS THE WORST SPOT IN THE RIVER! WE'RE RISKIN' OUR LIVES HERE!
IT'S EASY TO SLIP, Y'KNOW...WE ALL KIN SWIM, BUT OUR POOR PASSENGERS...THEY SINK LIKE A ROCK, AND THE CURRENT TAKES 'EM!

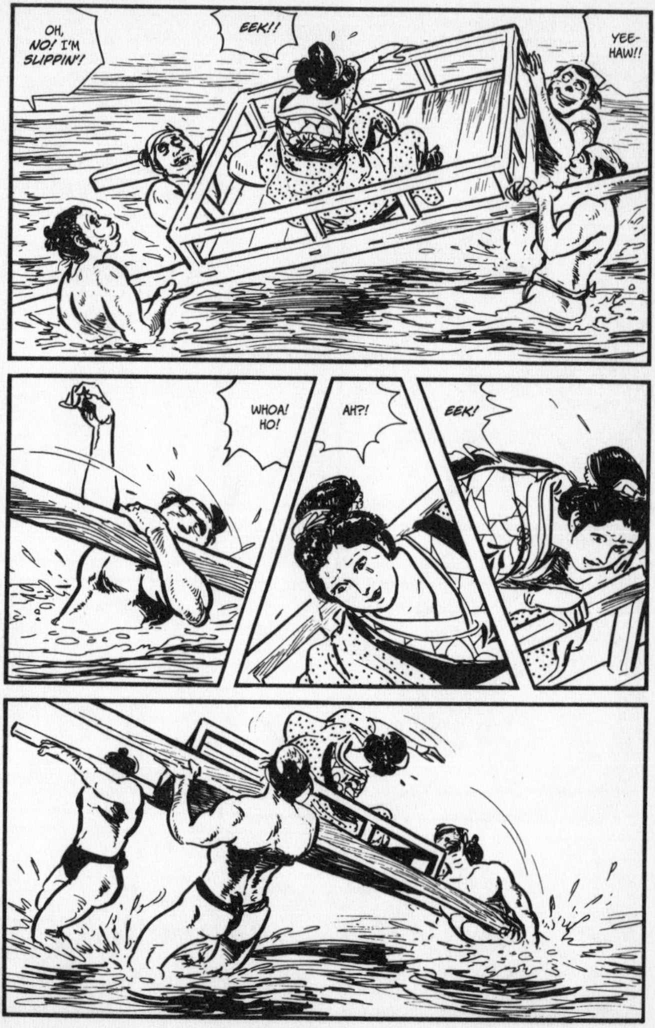
OH, NO! I'M SLIPPIN'!
EEK!!
YEE-HAW!!
WHOA! HO!
AH?!
EEK!

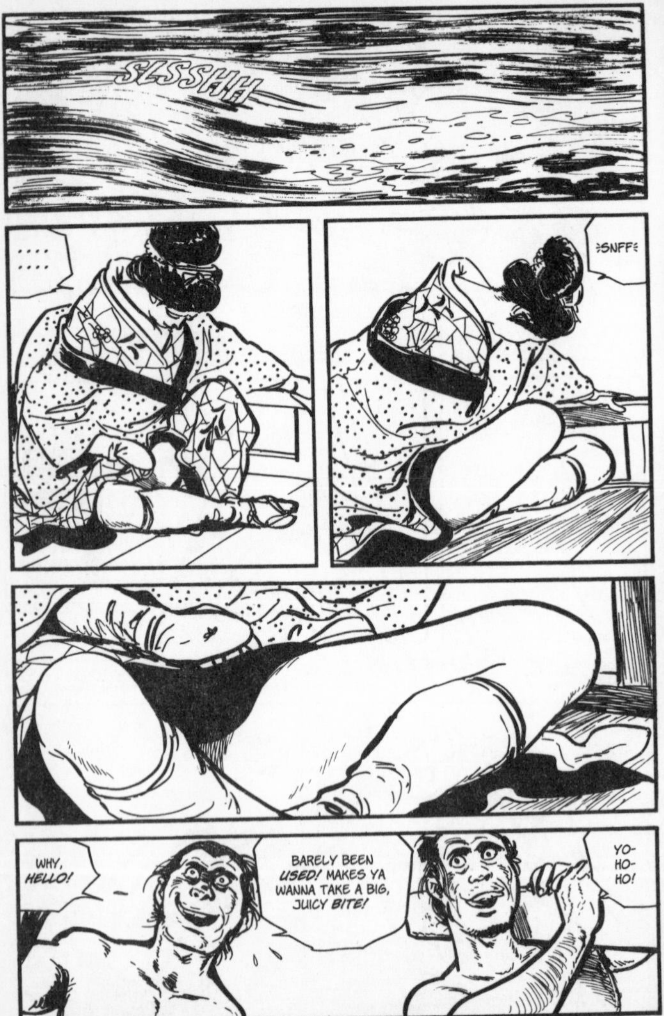
SLSSHH
....
....
SNFF
WHY, HELLO!
BARELY BEEN USED! MAKES YA WANNA TAKE A BIG, JUICY BITE!
YO-HO-HO!

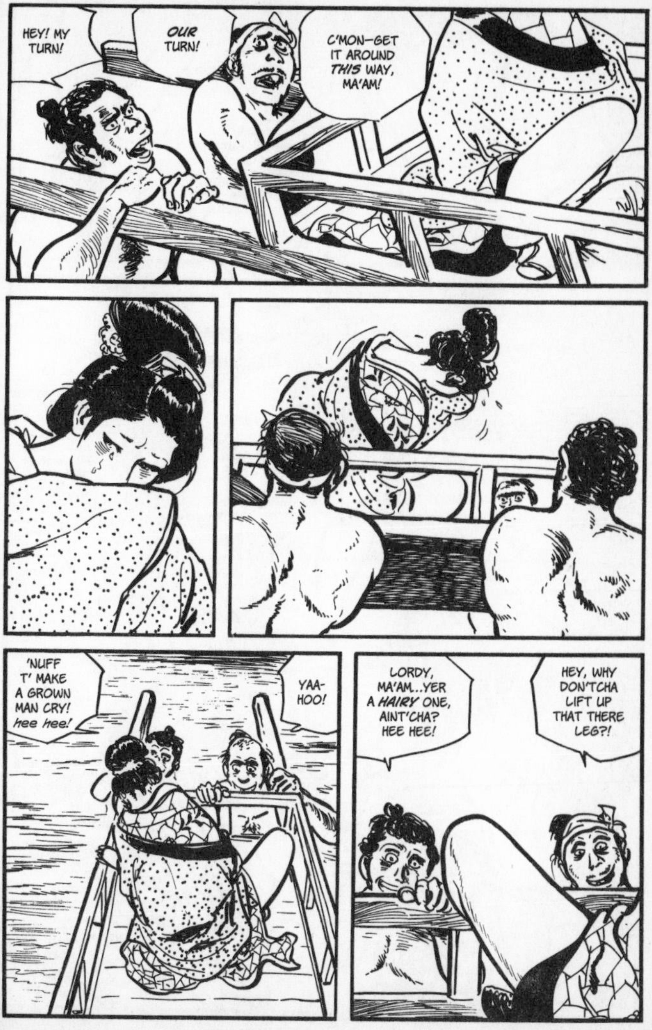
HEY! MY TURN!
OUR TURN!
C'MON—GET IT AROUND *THIS* WAY, MA'AM!
'NUFF T' MAKE A GROWN MAN CRY! *hee hee!*
YAA-HOO!
LORDY, MA'AM...YER A *HAIRY* ONE, AINT'CHA? HEE HEE!
HEY, WHY DON'TCHA LIFT UP THAT THERE LEG?!

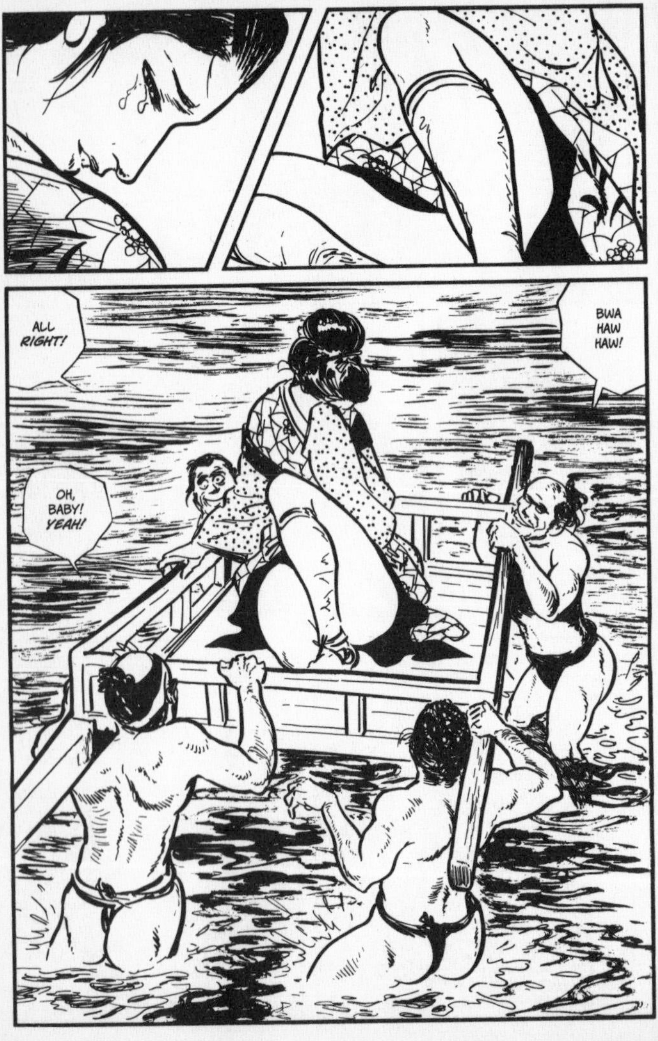
ALL RIGHT!
BWA HAW HAW!
OH, BABY! YEAH!

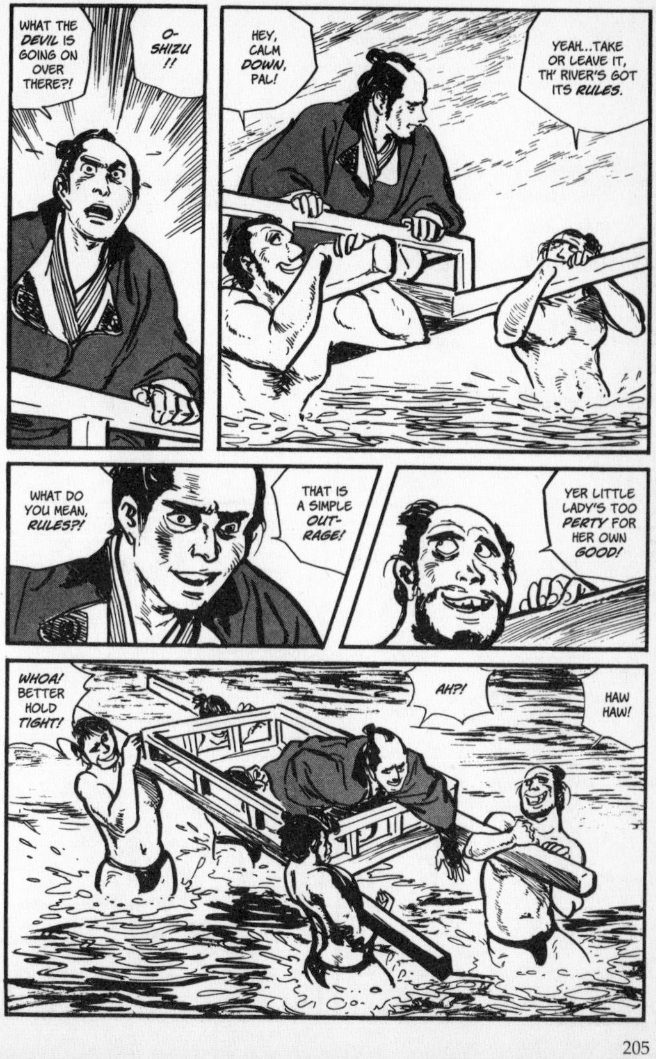
WHAT THE DEVIL IS GOING ON OVER THERE?!
O-SHIZU !!
HEY, CALM DOWN, PAL!
YEAH...TAKE OR LEAVE IT, TH' RIVER'S GOT ITS RULES.
WHAT DO YOU MEAN, RULES?!
THAT IS A SIMPLE OUT-RAGE!
YER LITTLE LADY'S TOO PERTY FOR HER OWN GOOD!
WHOA! BETTER HOLD TIGHT!
AH?!
HAW HAW!

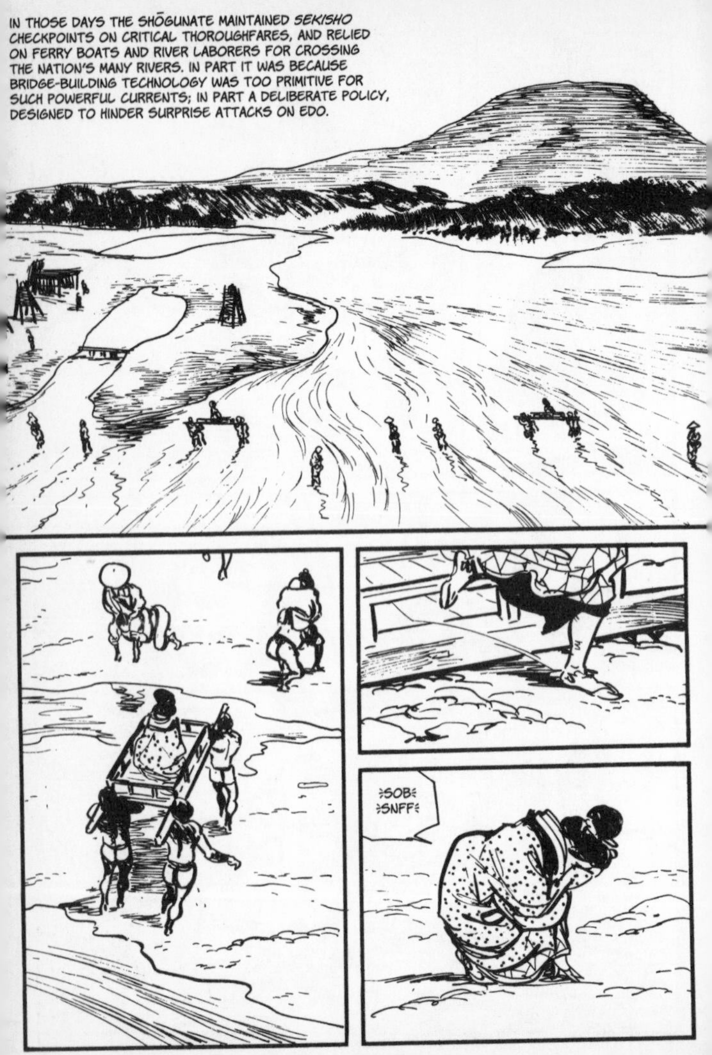
IN THOSE DAYS THE SHŌGUNATE MAINTAINED *SEKISHO* CHECKPOINTS ON CRITICAL THOROUGHFARES, AND RELIED ON FERRY BOATS AND RIVER LABORERS FOR CROSSING THE NATION'S MANY RIVERS. IN PART IT WAS BECAUSE BRIDGE-BUILDING TECHNOLOGY WAS TOO PRIMITIVE FOR SUCH POWERFUL CURRENTS; IN PART A DELIBERATE POLICY, DESIGNED TO HINDER SURPRISE ATTACKS ON EDO.
SOB
SNFF

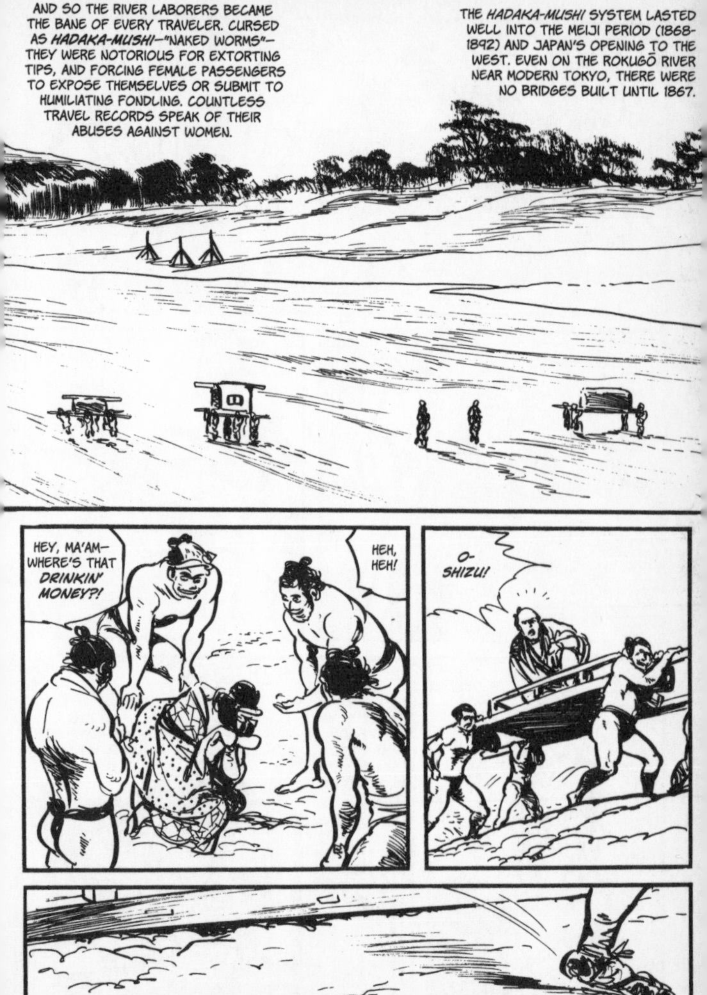
AND SO THE RIVER LABORERS BECAME THE BANE OF EVERY TRAVELER. CURSED AS *HADAKA-MUSHI*—"NAKED WORMS"—THEY WERE NOTORIOUS FOR EXTORTING TIPS, AND FORCING FEMALE PASSENGERS TO EXPOSE THEMSELVES OR SUBMIT TO HUMILIATING FONDLING. COUNTLESS TRAVEL RECORDS SPEAK OF THEIR ABUSES AGAINST WOMEN.
THE *HADAKA-MUSHI* SYSTEM LASTED WELL INTO THE MEIJI PERIOD (1868-1892) AND JAPAN'S OPENING TO THE WEST. EVEN ON THE ROKUGŌ RIVER NEAR MODERN TOKYO, THERE WERE NO BRIDGES BUILT UNTIL 1867.
HEY, MA'AM—WHERE'S THAT *DRINKIN' MONEY?!*
HEH, HEH!
O-SHIZU!

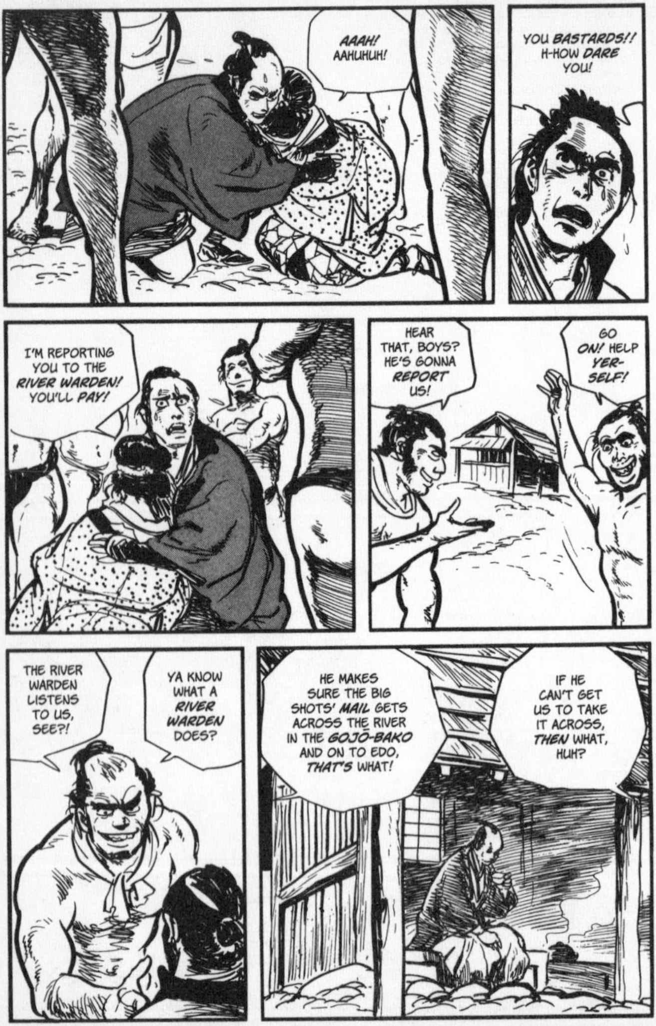
AAAH! AAHUHUH!
YOU BASTARDS!! H-HOW DARE YOU!
I'M REPORTING YOU TO THE RIVER WARDEN! YOU'LL PAY!
HEAR THAT, BOYS? HE'S GONNA REPORT US!
GO ON! HELP YER-SELF!
THE RIVER WARDEN LISTENS TO US, SEE?!
YA KNOW WHAT A RIVER WARDEN DOES?
HE MAKES SURE THE BIG SHOTS' MAIL GETS ACROSS THE RIVER IN THE GOJŌ-BAKO AND ON TO EDO, THAT'S WHAT!
IF HE CAN'T GET US TO TAKE IT ACROSS, THEN WHAT, HUH?

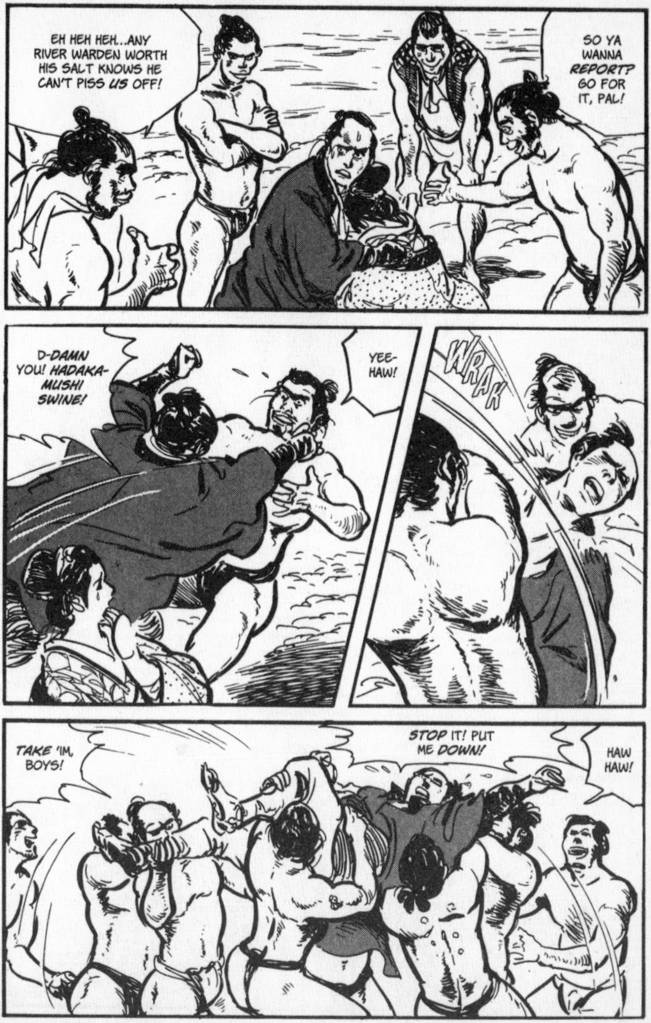
EH HEH HEH...ANY RIVER WARDEN WORTH HIS SALT KNOWS HE CAN'T PISS *US* OFF!
SO YA WANNA *REPORT?* GO FOR IT, PAL!
D-*DAMN* YOU! *HADAKA-MUSHI SWINE!*
YEE-HAW!
WRAK
TAKE 'IM, BOYS!
STOP IT! PUT ME *DOWN!*
HAW HAW!

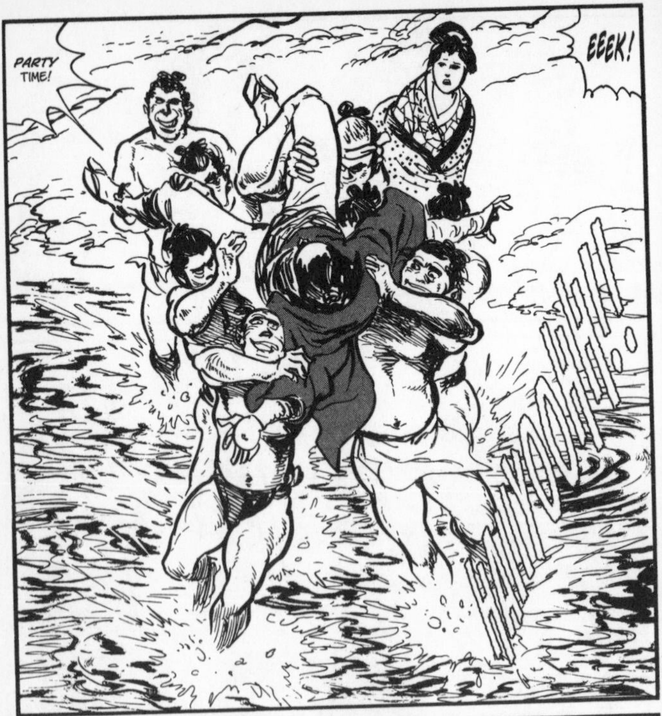
EEEK!
PARTY TIME!
HAYOHHH!!

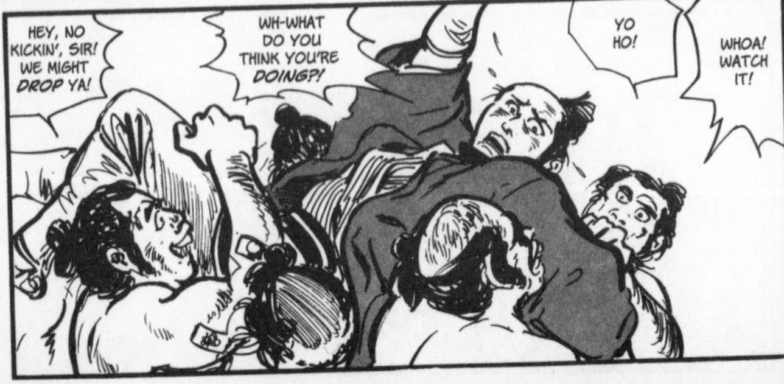
WHOA! WATCH IT!
YO HO!
WH-WHAT DO YOU THINK YOU'RE DOING?!
HEY, NO KICKIN', SIR! WE MIGHT DROP YA!

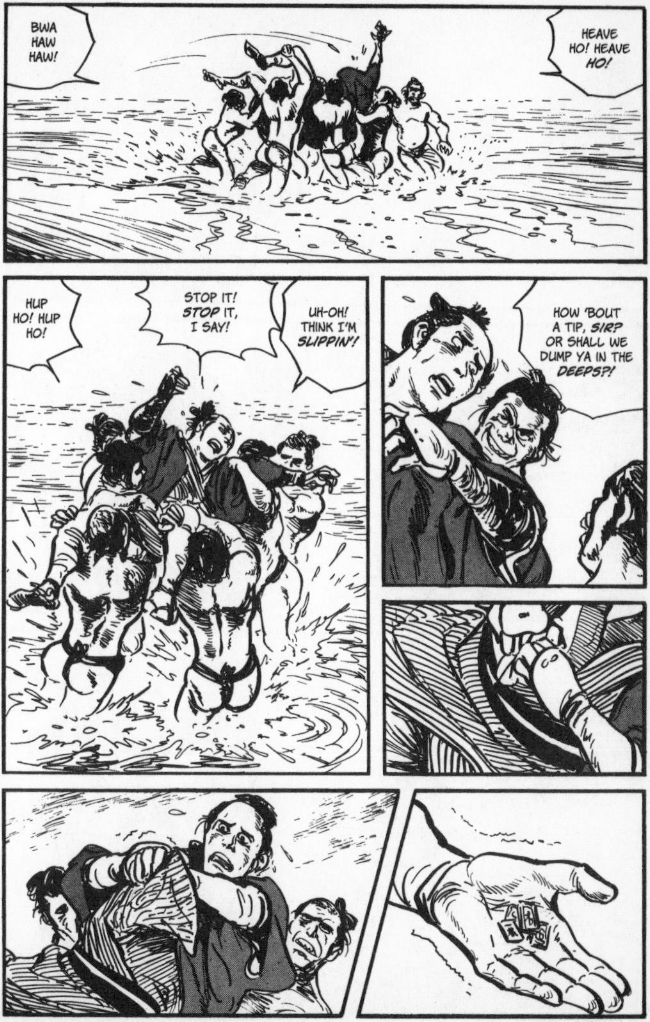
BWA HAW HAW!
HEAVE HO! HEAVE HO!
HUP HO! HUP HO!
STOP IT! STOP IT, I SAY!
UH-OH! THINK I'M SLIPPIN'!
HOW 'BOUT A TIP, SIR? OR SHALL WE DUMP YA IN THE DEEPS?!

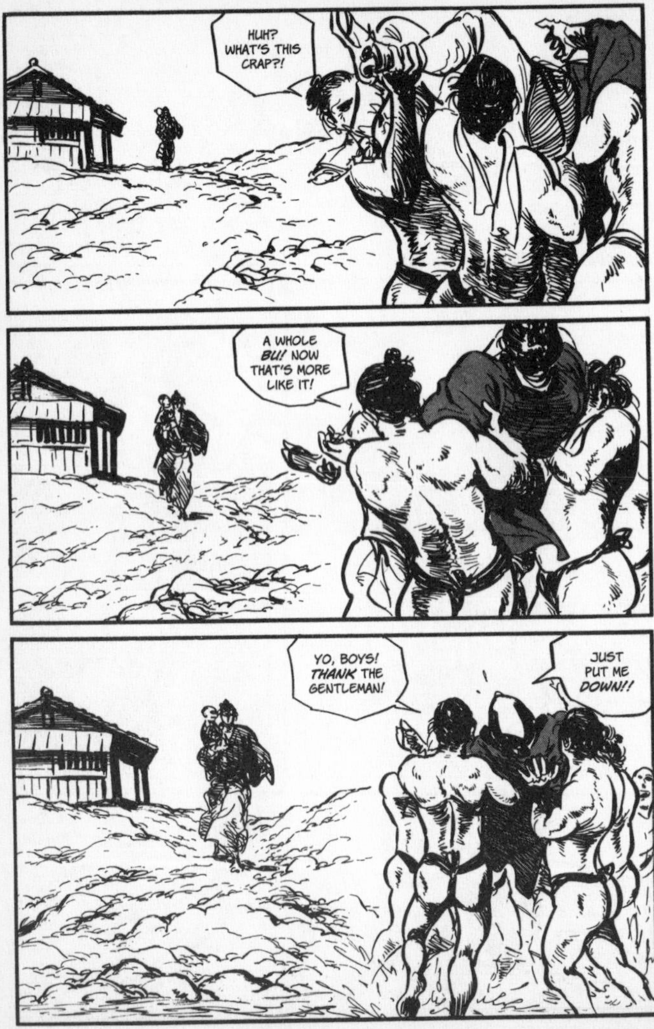
HUH? WHAT'S THIS CRAP?!
A WHOLE *BU!* NOW THAT'S MORE LIKE IT!
YO, BOYS! ***THANK*** THE GENTLEMAN!
JUST PUT ME ***DOWN!!***

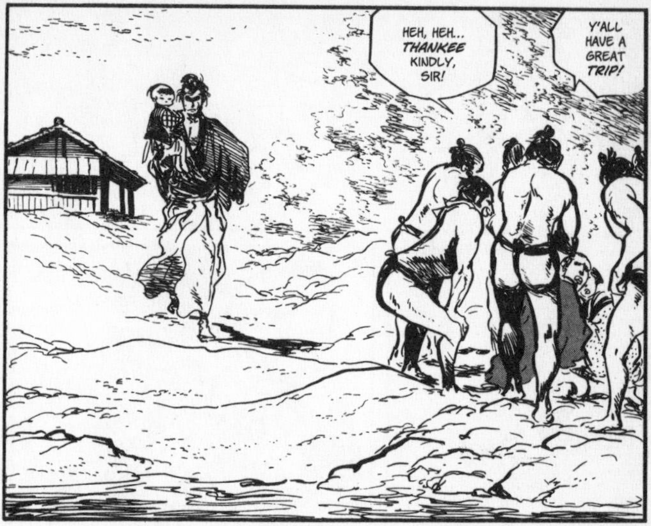
HEH, HEH... THANKEE KINDLY, SIR!
Y'ALL HAVE A GREAT TRIP!

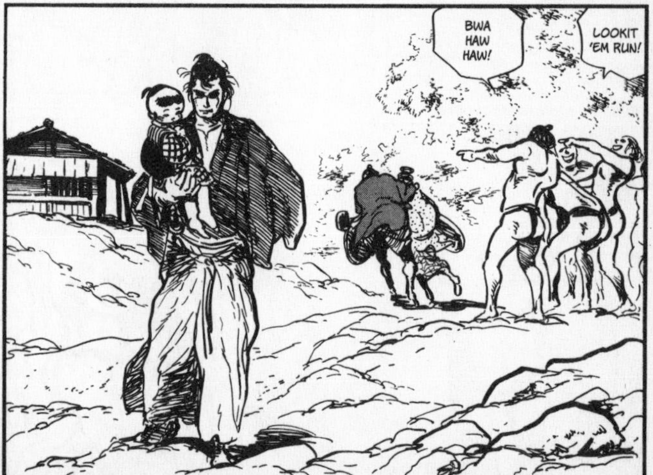
BWA HAW HAW!
LOOKIT 'EM RUN!

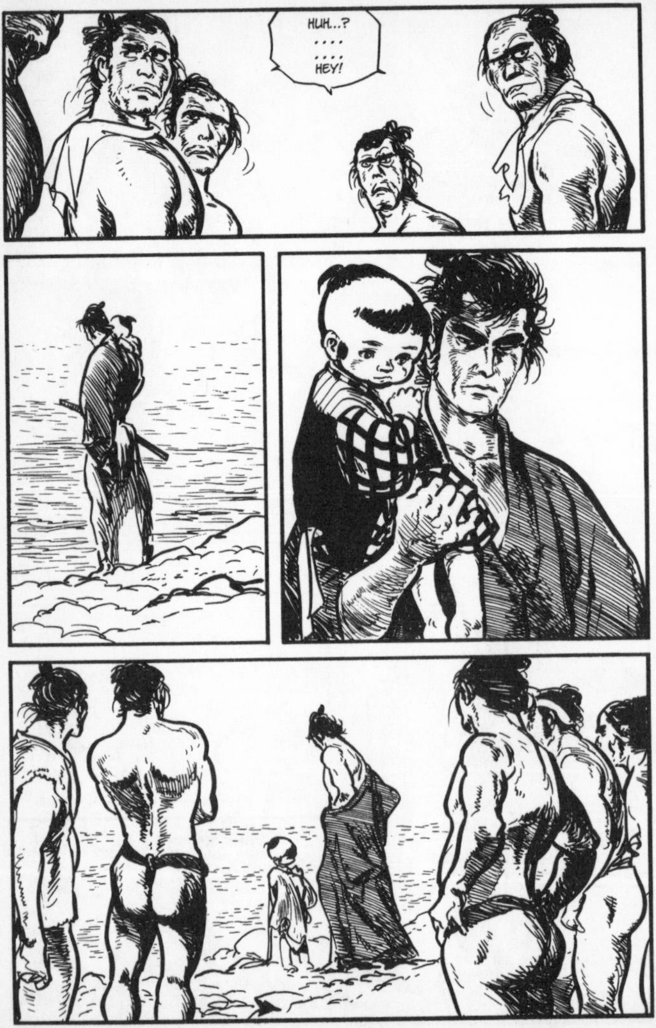
HUH...? .... HEY!

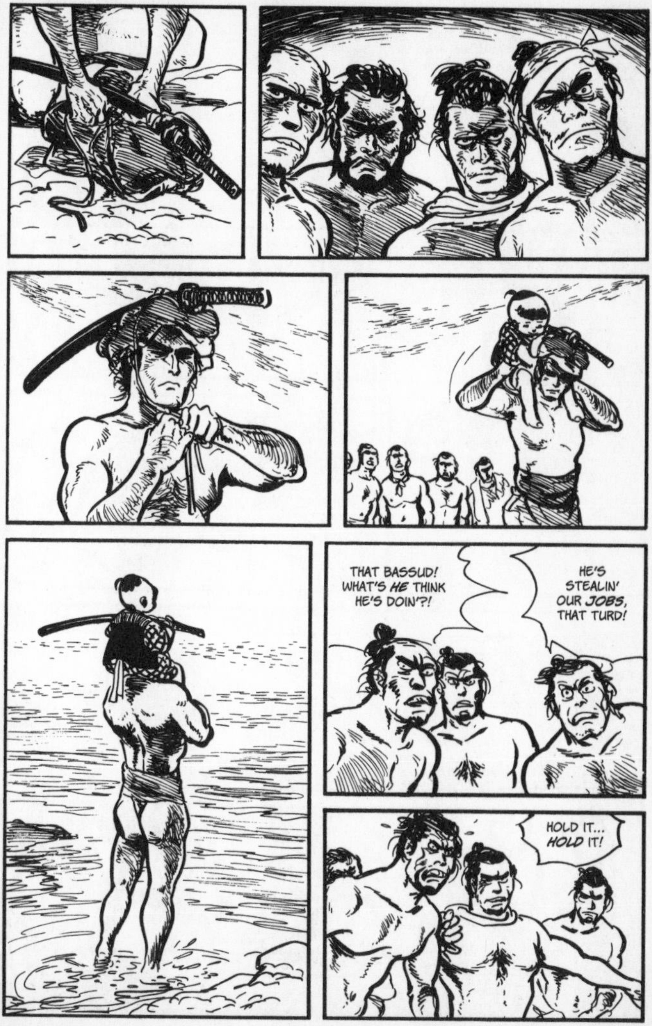
THAT BASSUD! WHAT'S *HE* THINK HE'S DOIN'?!
HE'S STEALIN' OUR *JOBS*, THAT TURD!
HOLD IT... *HOLD* IT!

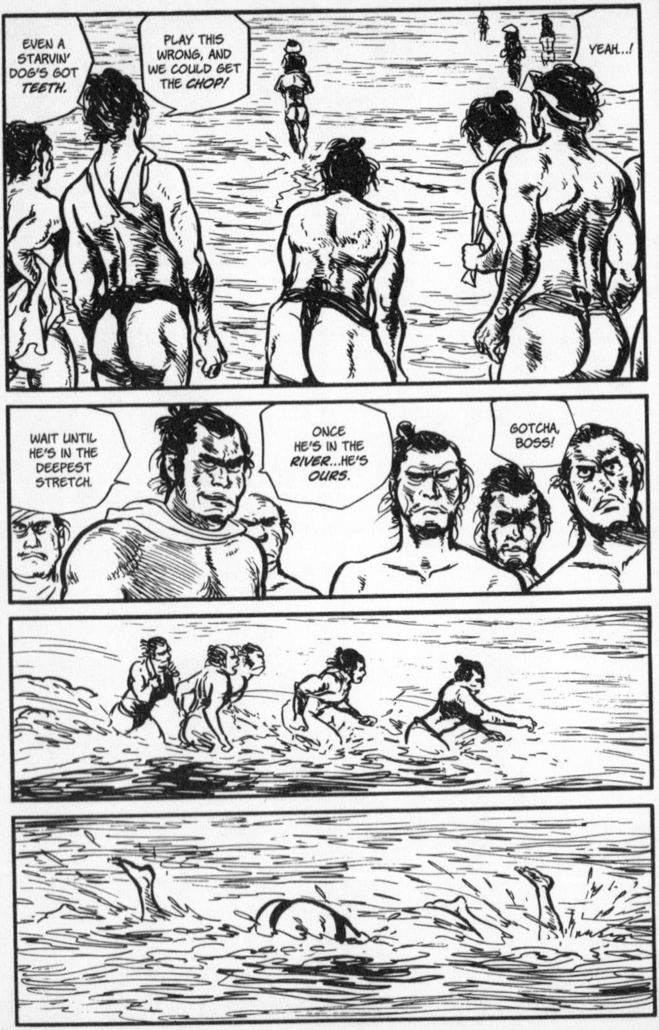
EVEN A STARVIN' DOG'S GOT TEETH.
PLAY THIS WRONG, AND WE COULD GET THE CHOP!
YEAH...!
WAIT UNTIL HE'S IN THE DEEPEST STRETCH.
ONCE HE'S IN THE RIVER...HE'S OURS.
GOTCHA, BOSS!

SLOSH
SLOSH

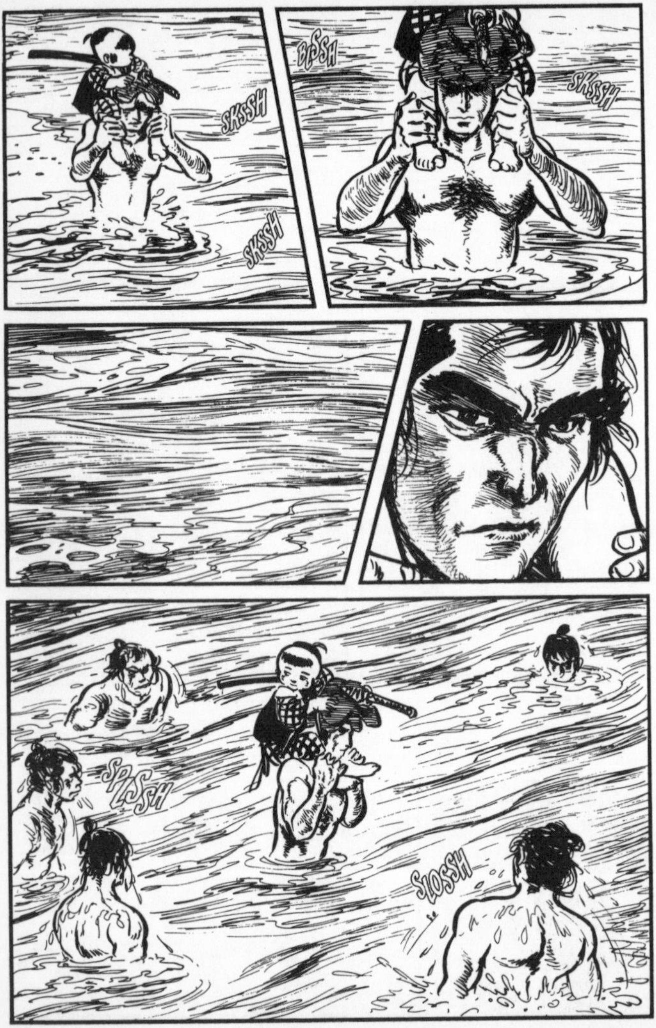
SKSSH
SKSSH
BLSSH
SKSSH
SPLSSH
SLOSSH

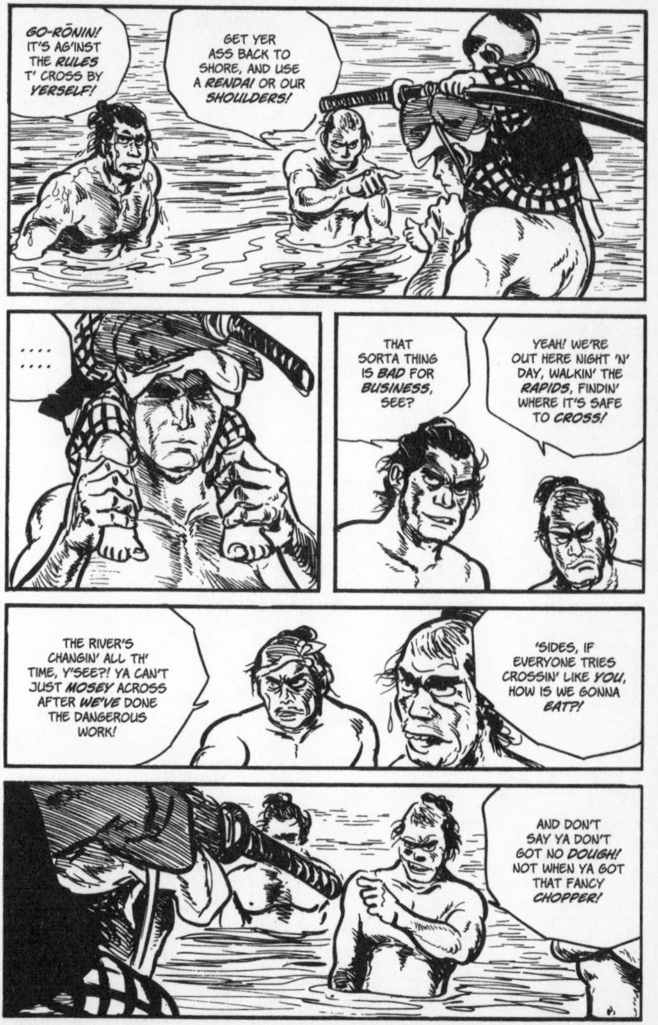
GO-RŌNIN! IT'S AG'INST THE RULES T' CROSS BY YERSELF!
GET YER ASS BACK TO SHORE, AND USE A RENDAI OR OUR SHOULDERS!
....
....
THAT SORTA THING IS BAD FOR BUSINESS, SEE?
YEAH! WE'RE OUT HERE NIGHT 'N' DAY, WALKIN' THE RAPIDS, FINDIN' WHERE IT'S SAFE TO CROSS!
THE RIVER'S CHANGIN' ALL TH' TIME, Y'SEE?! YA CAN'T JUST MOSEY ACROSS AFTER WE'VE DONE THE DANGEROUS WORK!
'SIDES, IF EVERYONE TRIES CROSSIN' LIKE YOU, HOW IS WE GONNA EAT?!
AND DON'T SAY YA DON'T GOT NO DOUGH! NOT WHEN YA GOT THAT FANCY CHOPPER!

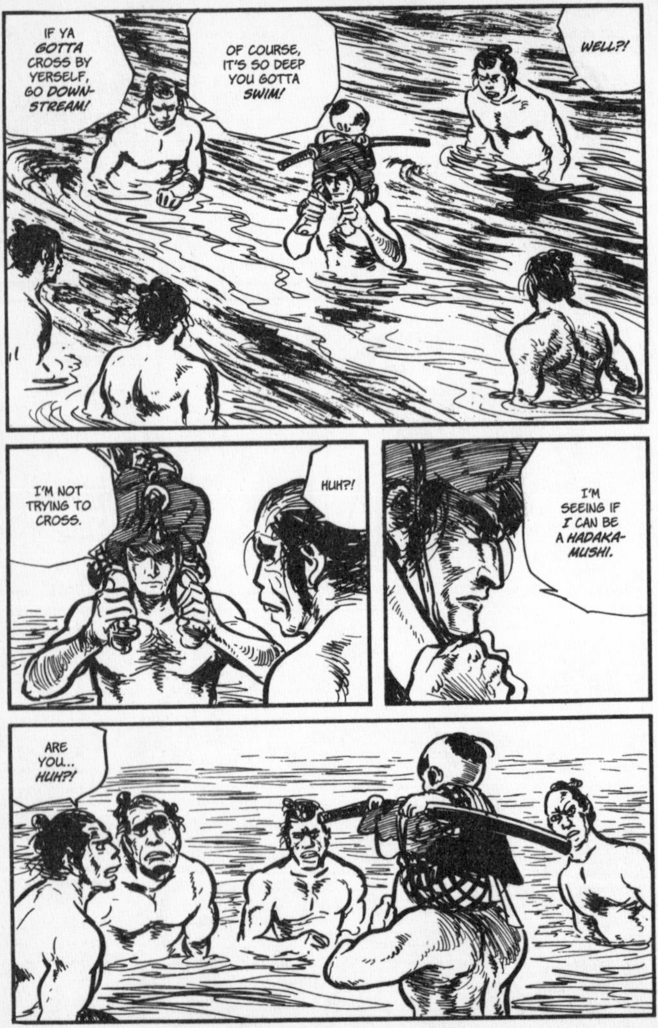
IF YA GOTTA CROSS BY YERSELF, GO DOWN-STREAM!
OF COURSE, IT'S SO DEEP YOU GOTTA SWIM!
WELL?!
I'M NOT TRYING TO CROSS.
HUH?!
I'M SEEING IF I CAN BE A HADAKA-MUSHI.
ARE YOU.. HUH?!

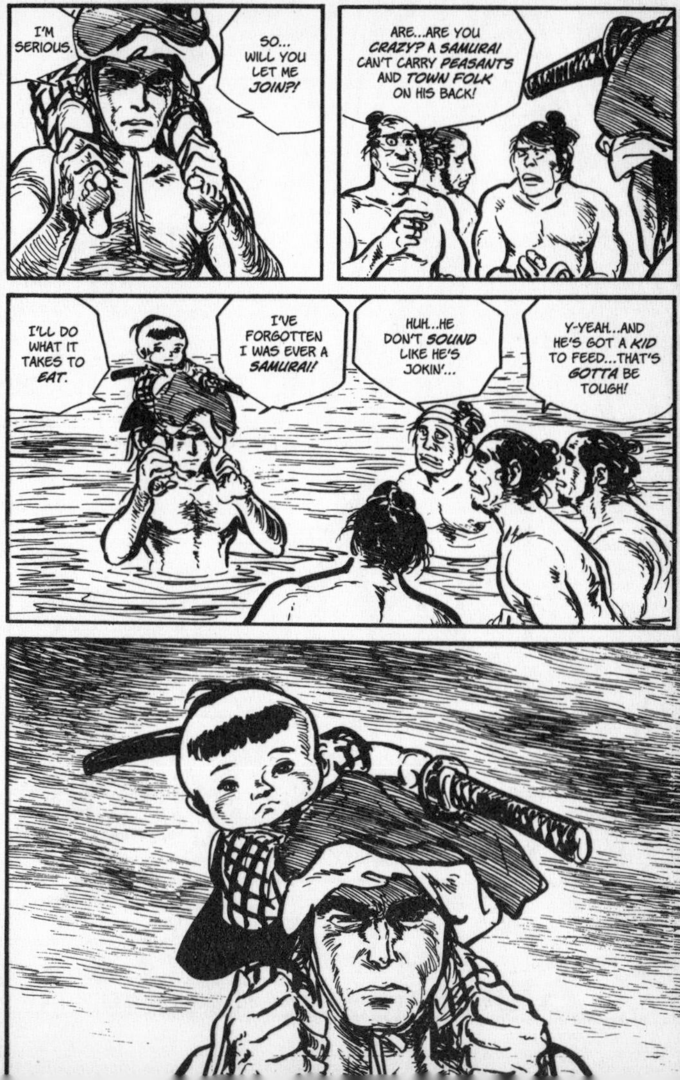
I'M SERIOUS.
SO... WILL YOU LET ME JOIN?!
ARE...ARE YOU CRAZY? A SAMURAI CAN'T CARRY PEASANTS AND TOWN FOLK ON HIS BACK!
I'LL DO WHAT IT TAKES TO EAT.
I'VE FORGOTTEN I WAS EVER A SAMURAI!
HUH...HE DON'T SOUND LIKE HE'S JOKIN'...
Y-YEAH...AND HE'S GOT A KID TO FEED...THAT'S GOTTA BE TOUGH!

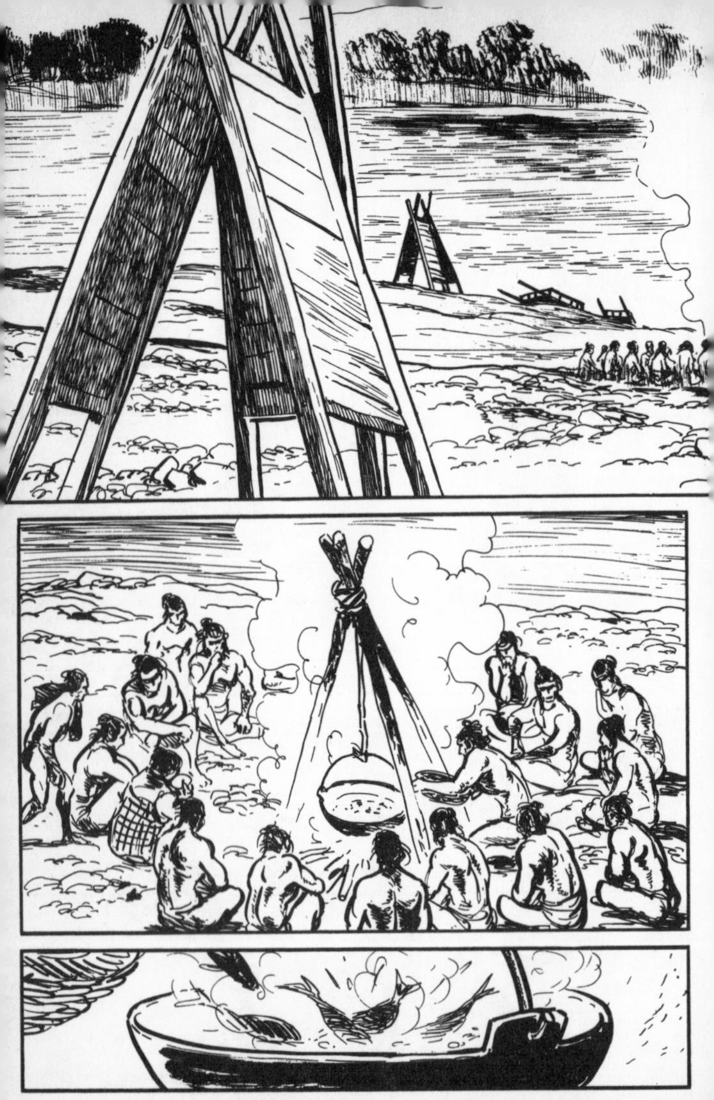

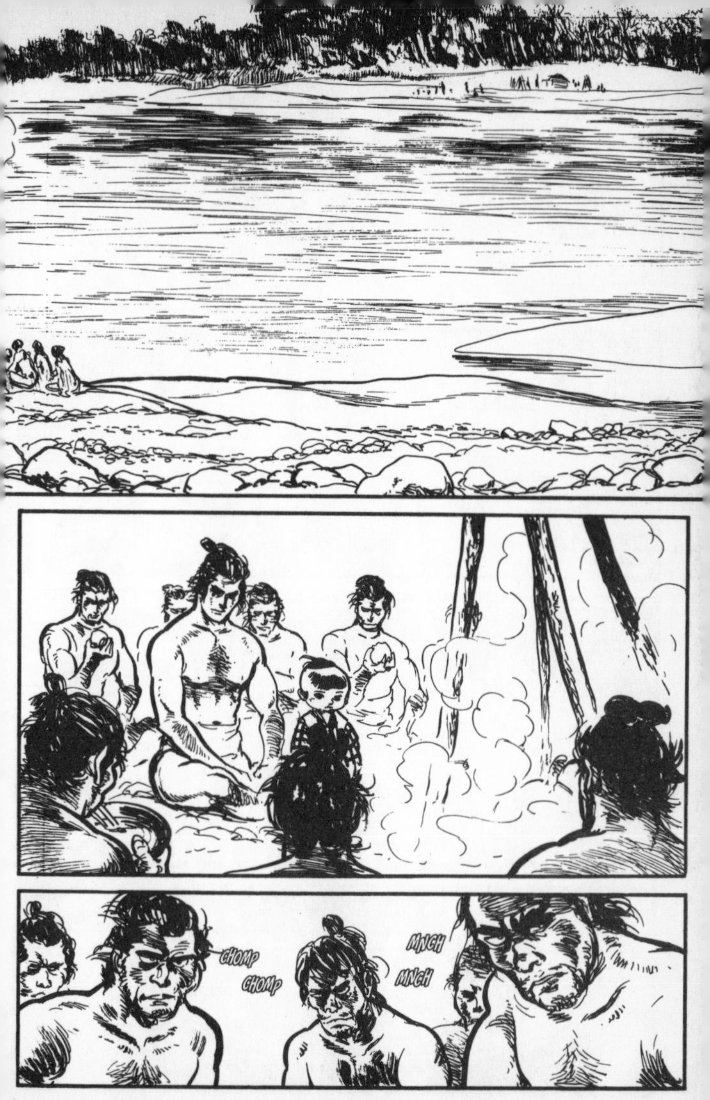
CHOMP
CHOMP
MNCH
MNCH

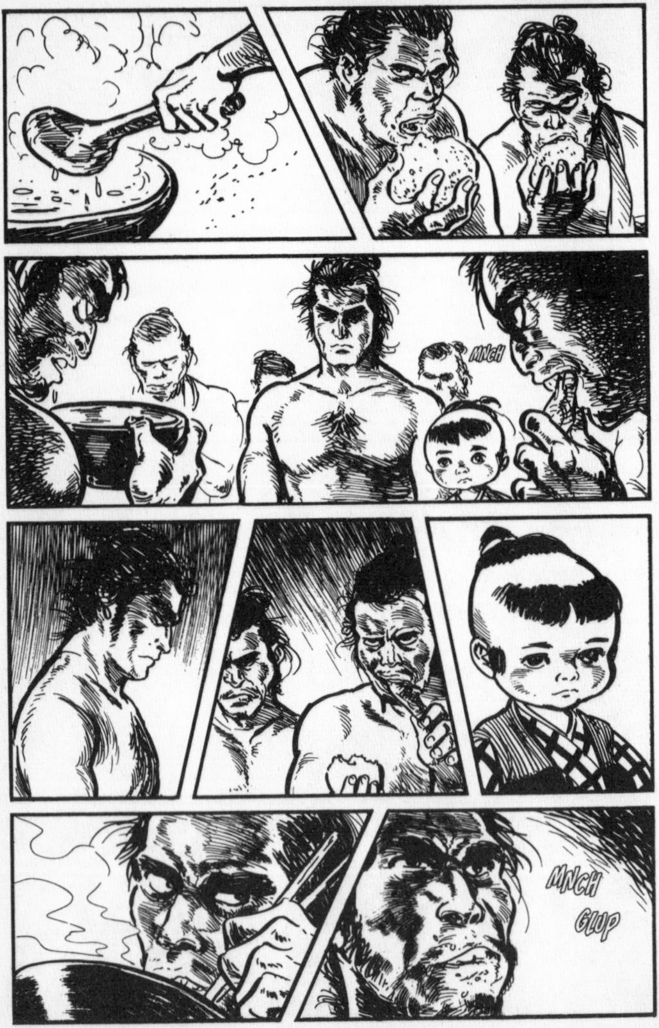
MNCH
MNCH
GLUP

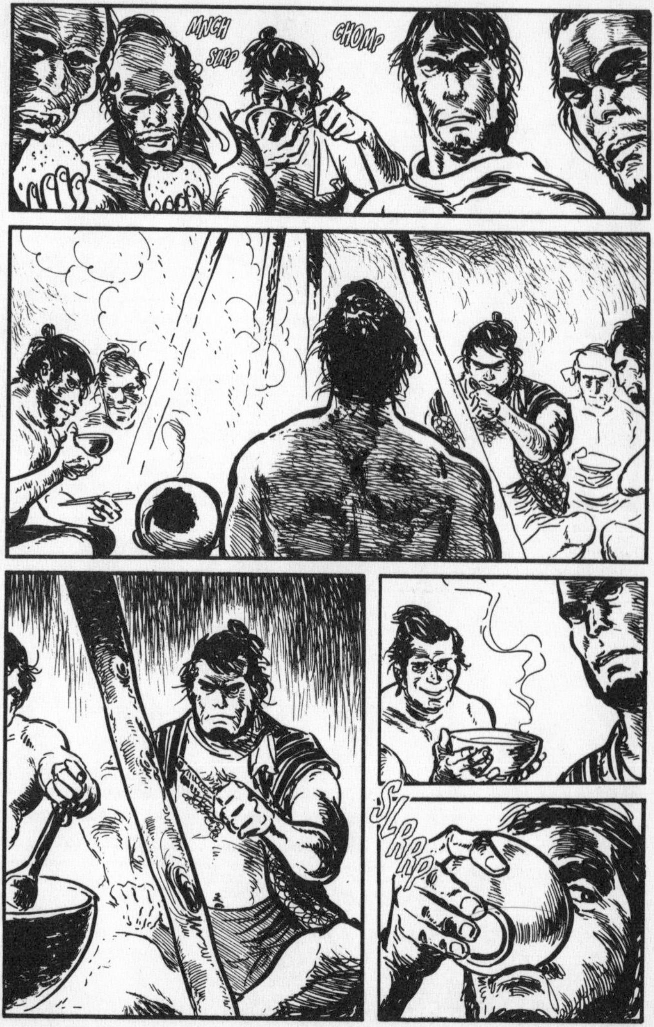
MNCH
SLRP
CHOMP
SLRRP

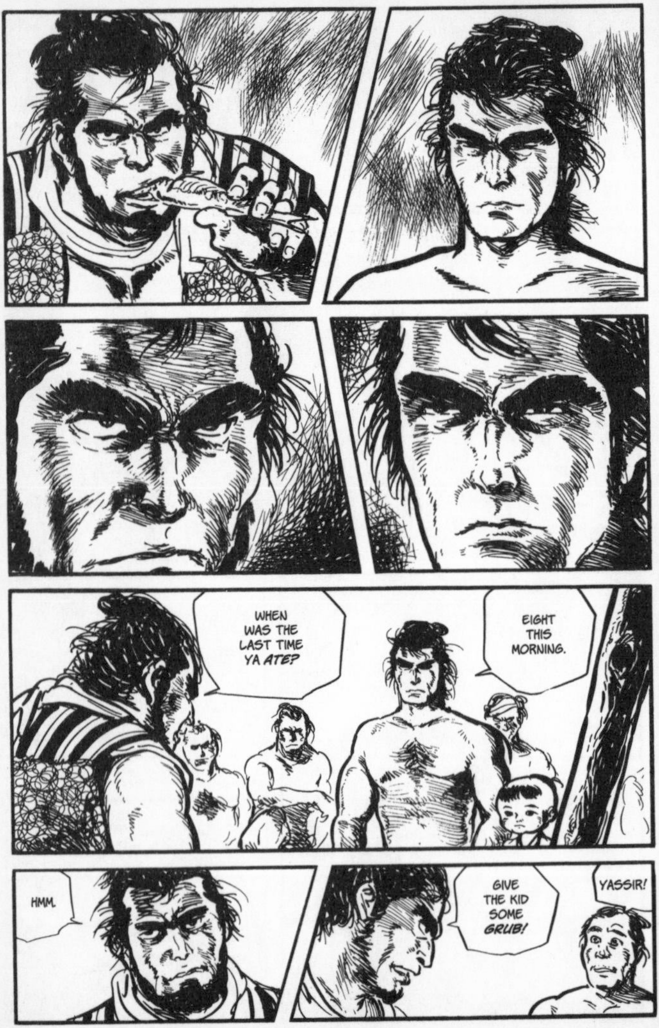
WHEN WAS THE LAST TIME YA *ATE?*
EIGHT THIS MORNING.
HMM.
GIVE THE KID SOME *GRUB!*
YASSIR!

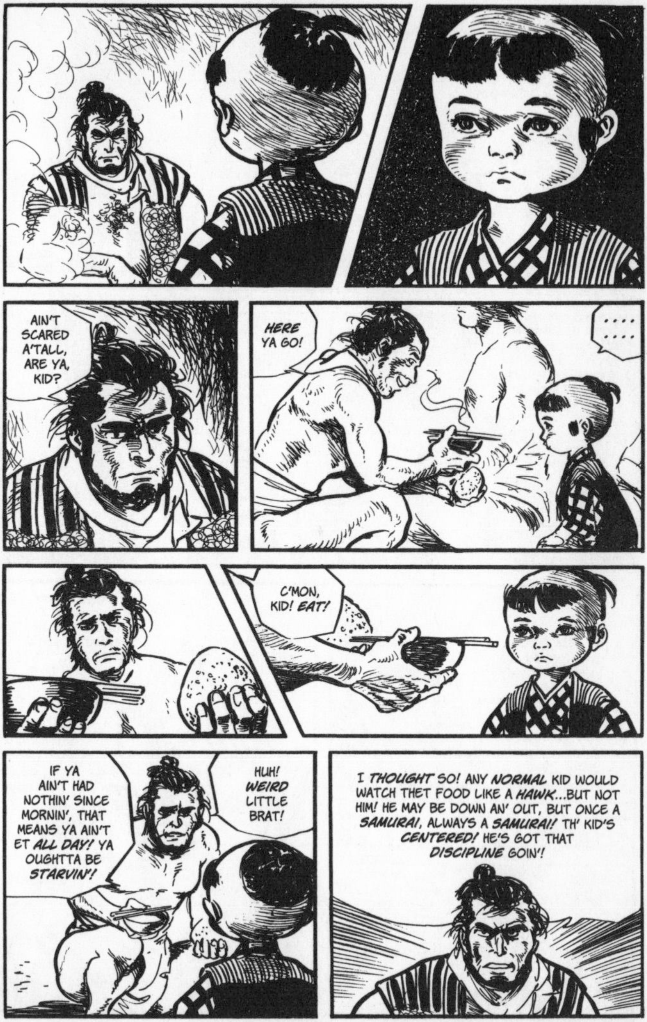
AIN'T SCARED A'TALL, ARE YA, KID?
HERE YA GO!
....
....
C'MON, KID! EAT!
IF YA AIN'T HAD NOTHIN' SINCE MORNIN', THAT MEANS YA AIN'T ET ALL DAY! YA OUGHTTA BE STARVIN'!
HUH! WEIRD LITTLE BRAT!
I THOUGHT SO! ANY NORMAL KID WOULD WATCH THET FOOD LIKE A HAWK...BUT NOT HIM! HE MAY BE DOWN AN' OUT, BUT ONCE A SAMURAI, ALWAYS A SAMURAI! TH' KID'S CENTERED! HE'S GOT THAT DISCIPLINE GOIN'!

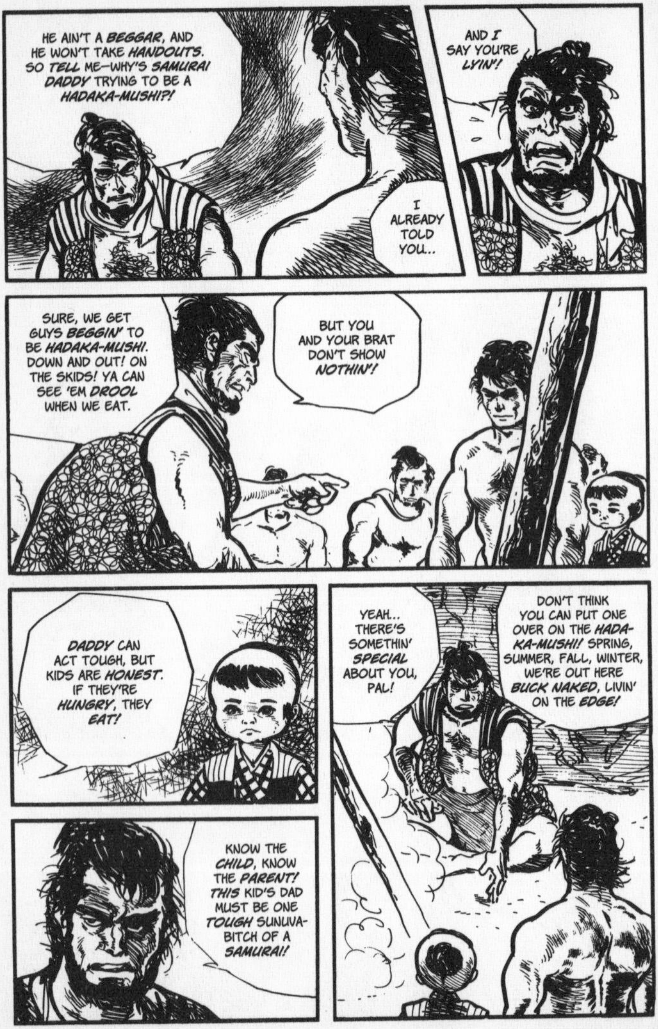
HE AIN'T A BEGGAR, AND HE WON'T TAKE HANDOUTS. SO TELL ME—WHY'S SAMURAI DADDY TRYING TO BE A HADAKA-MUSHI?!
I ALREADY TOLD YOU...
AND I SAY YOU'RE LYIN'!
SURE, WE GET GUYS BEGGIN' TO BE HADAKA-MUSHI. DOWN AND OUT! ON THE SKIDS! YA CAN SEE 'EM DROOL WHEN WE EAT.
BUT YOU AND YOUR BRAT DON'T SHOW NOTHIN'!
DADDY CAN ACT TOUGH, BUT KIDS ARE HONEST. IF THEY'RE HUNGRY, THEY EAT!
KNOW THE CHILD, KNOW THE PARENT! THIS KID'S DAD MUST BE ONE TOUGH SUNUVA-BITCH OF A SAMURAI!
YEAH... THERE'S SOMETHIN' SPECIAL ABOUT YOU, PAL!
DON'T THINK YOU CAN PUT ONE OVER ON THE HADA-KA-MUSHI! SPRING, SUMMER, FALL, WINTER, WE'RE OUT HERE BUCK NAKED, LIVIN' ON THE EDGE!

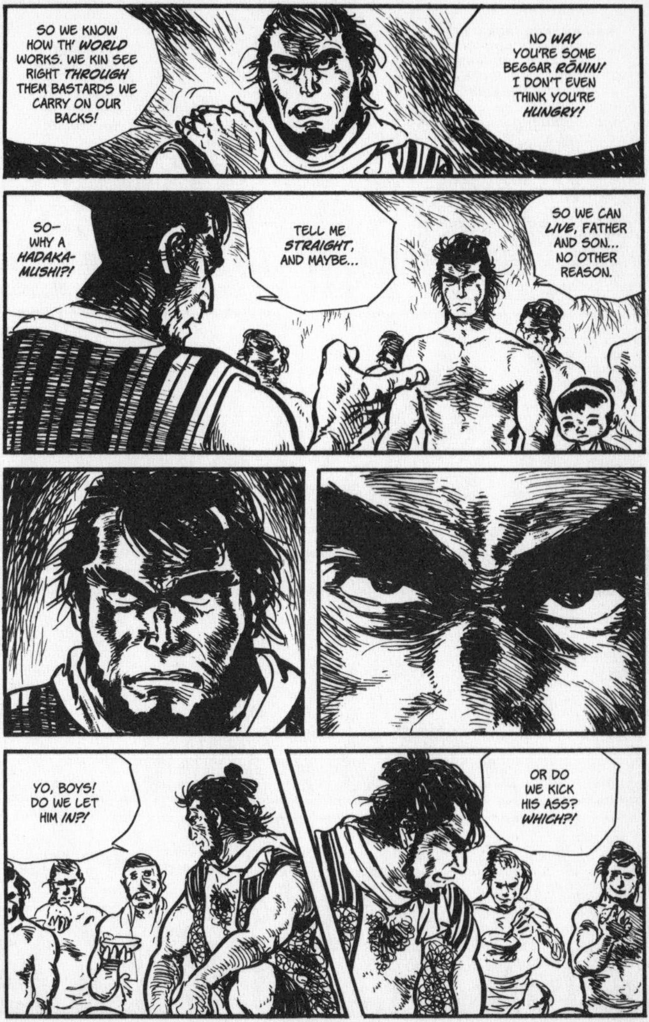
SO WE KNOW HOW TH' WORLD WORKS. WE KIN SEE RIGHT THROUGH THEM BASTARDS WE CARRY ON OUR BACKS!
NO WAY YOU'RE SOME BEGGAR RŌNIN! I DON'T EVEN THINK YOU'RE HUNGRY!
SO— WHY A HADAKA-MUSHI?!
TELL ME STRAIGHT, AND MAYBE...
SO WE CAN LIVE, FATHER AND SON... NO OTHER REASON.
YO, BOYS! DO WE LET HIM IN?!
OR DO WE KICK HIS ASS? WHICH?!

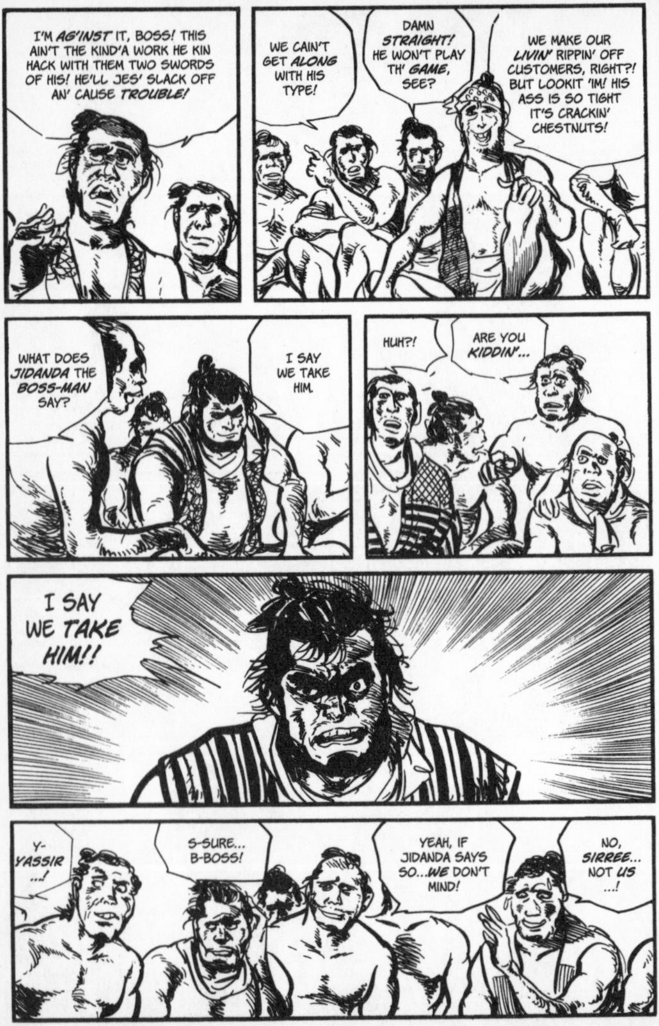
I'M AG'INST IT, BOSS! THIS AIN'T THE KIND'A WORK HE KIN HACK WITH THEM TWO SWORDS OF HIS! HE'LL JES' SLACK OFF AN' CAUSE TROUBLE!
WE CAIN'T GET ALONG WITH HIS TYPE!
DAMN STRAIGHT! HE WON'T PLAY TH' GAME, SEE?
WE MAKE OUR LIVIN' RIPPIN' OFF CUSTOMERS, RIGHT?! BUT LOOKIT 'IM! HIS ASS IS SO TIGHT IT'S CRACKIN' CHESTNUTS!
WHAT DOES JIDANDA THE BOSS-MAN SAY?
I SAY WE TAKE HIM.
HUH?!
ARE YOU KIDDIN'...
I SAY WE TAKE HIM!!
Y-YASSIR ...!
S-SURE... B-BOSS!
YEAH, IF JIDANDA SAYS SO...WE DON'T MIND!
NO, SIRREE... NOT US ...!

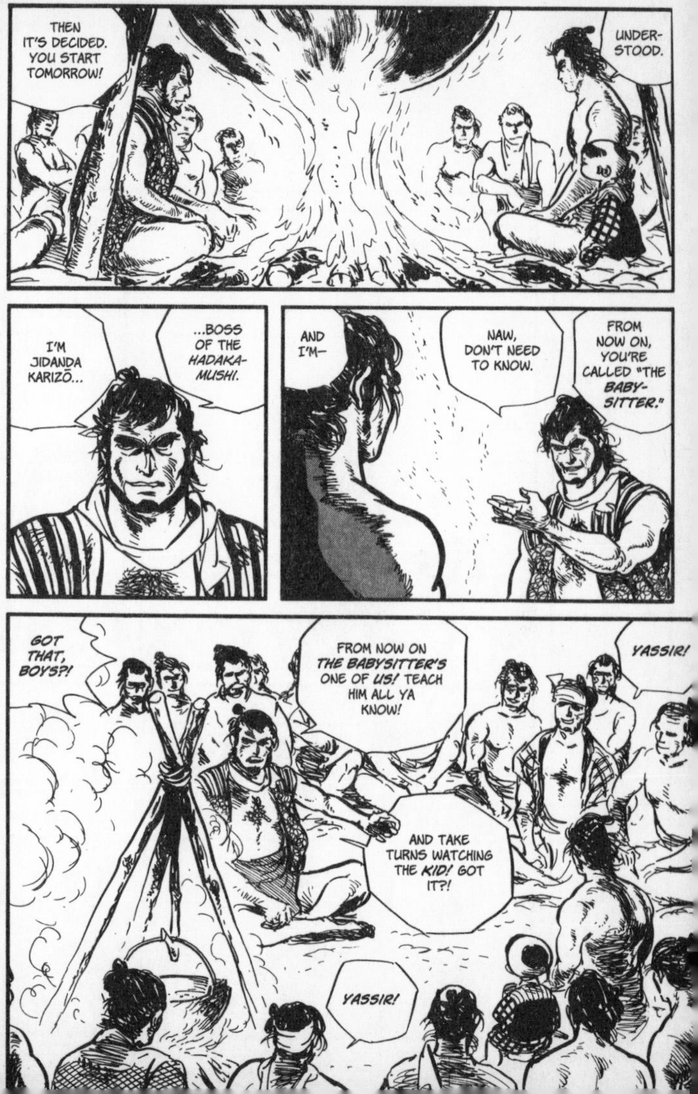
THEN IT'S DECIDED. YOU START TOMORROW!
UNDER-STOOD.
I'M JIDANDA KARIZŌ...
...BOSS OF THE *HADAKA-MUSHI.*
AND I'M—
NAW, DON'T NEED TO KNOW.
FROM NOW ON, YOU'RE CALLED "THE *BABY-SITTER.*"
GOT THAT, BOYS?!
FROM NOW ON *THE BABYSITTER'S* ONE OF *US!* TEACH HIM ALL YA KNOW!
YASSIR!
AND TAKE TURNS WATCHING THE *KID!* GOT IT?!
YASSIR!

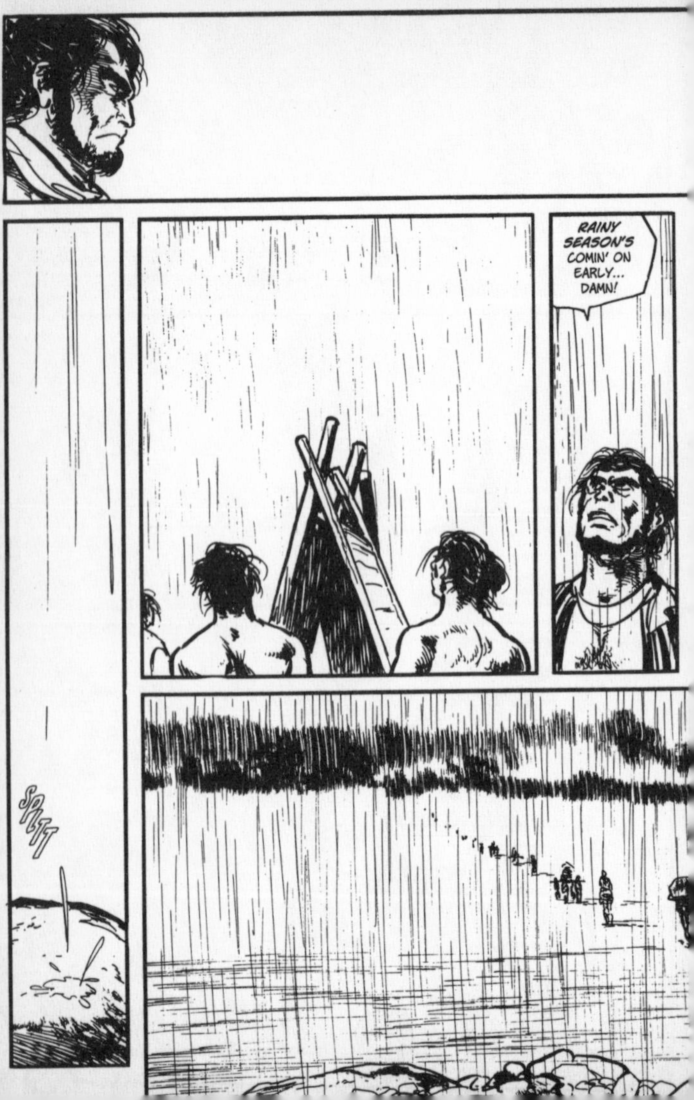
RAINY SEASON'S COMIN' ON EARLY... DAMN!
SPLTT

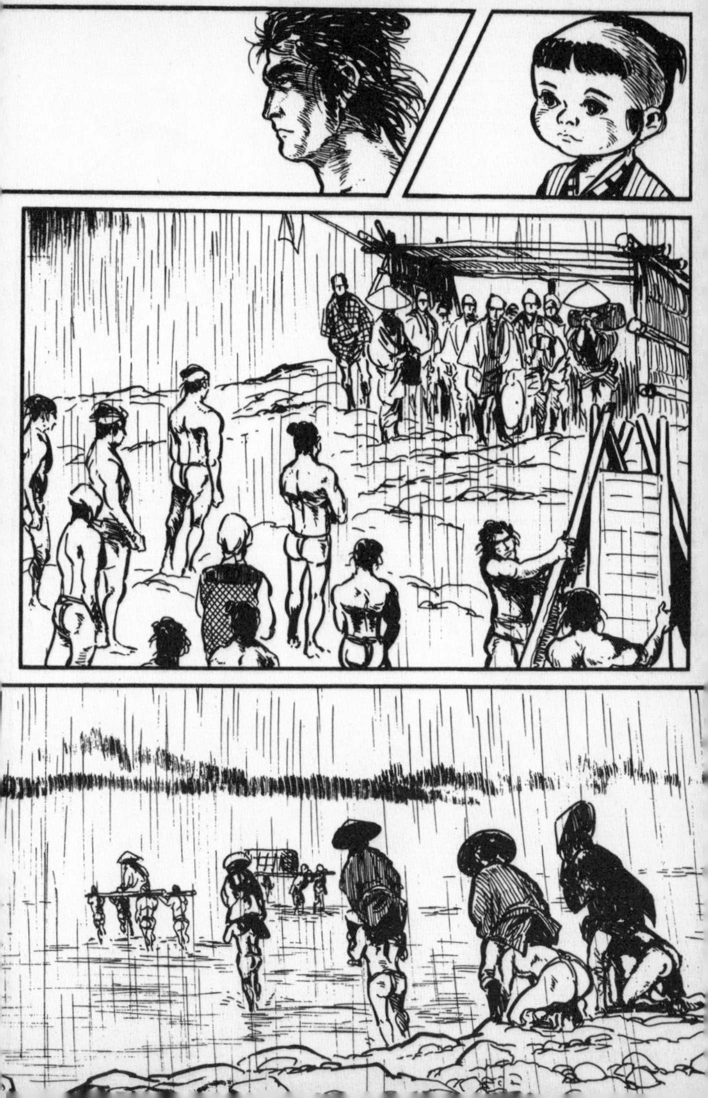

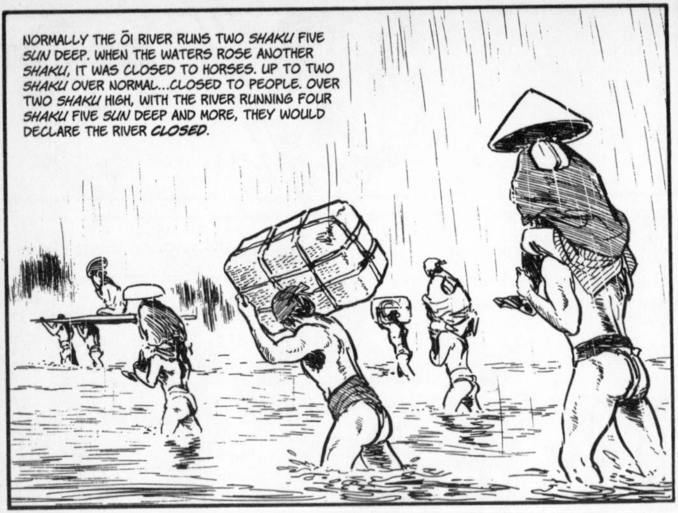
NORMALLY THE ŌI RIVER RUNS TWO *SHAKU* FIVE *SUN* DEEP. WHEN THE WATERS ROSE ANOTHER *SHAKU*, IT WAS CLOSED TO HORSES. UP TO TWO *SHAKU* OVER NORMAL...CLOSED TO PEOPLE. OVER TWO *SHAKU* HIGH, WITH THE RIVER RUNNING FOUR *SHAKU* FIVE *SUN* DEEP AND MORE, THEY WOULD DECLARE THE RIVER ***CLOSED***.

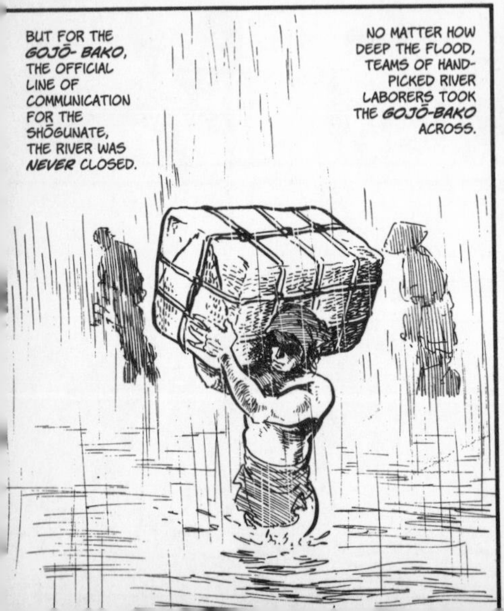
BUT FOR THE *GOJŌ- BAKO*, THE OFFICIAL LINE OF COMMUNICATION FOR THE SHŌGUNATE, THE RIVER WAS ***NEVER*** CLOSED.
NO MATTER HOW DEEP THE FLOOD, TEAMS OF HAND-PICKED RIVER LABORERS TOOK THE *GOJŌ-BAKO* ACROSS.

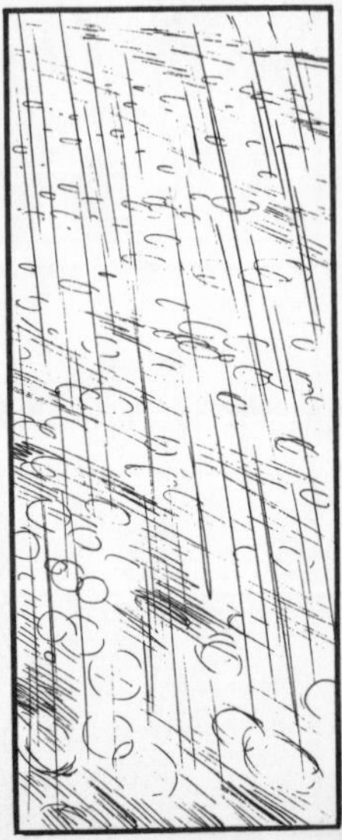

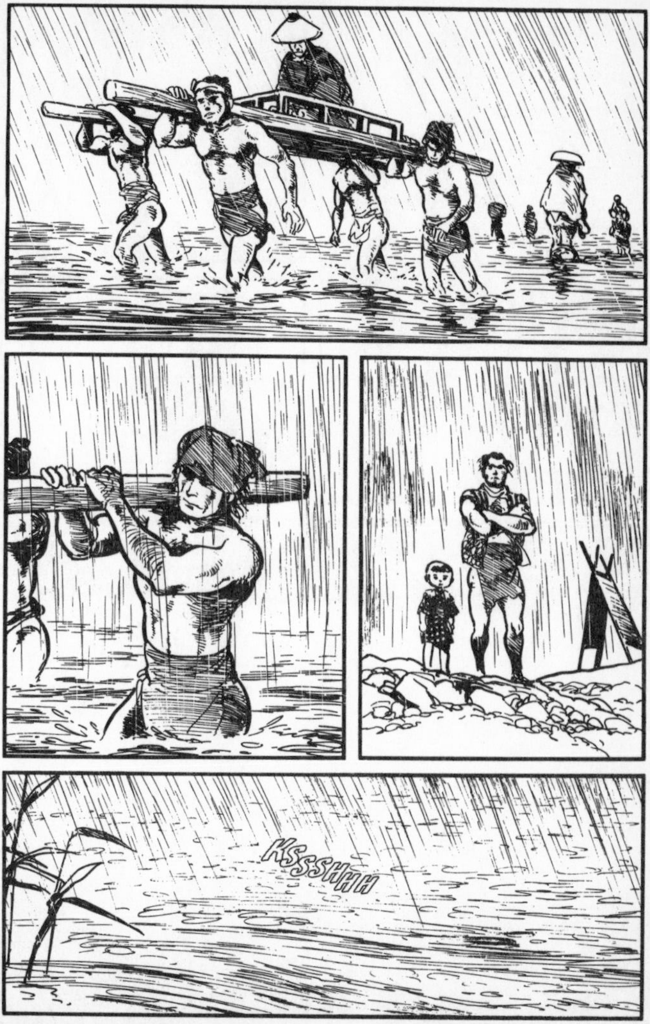
KSSSHHH

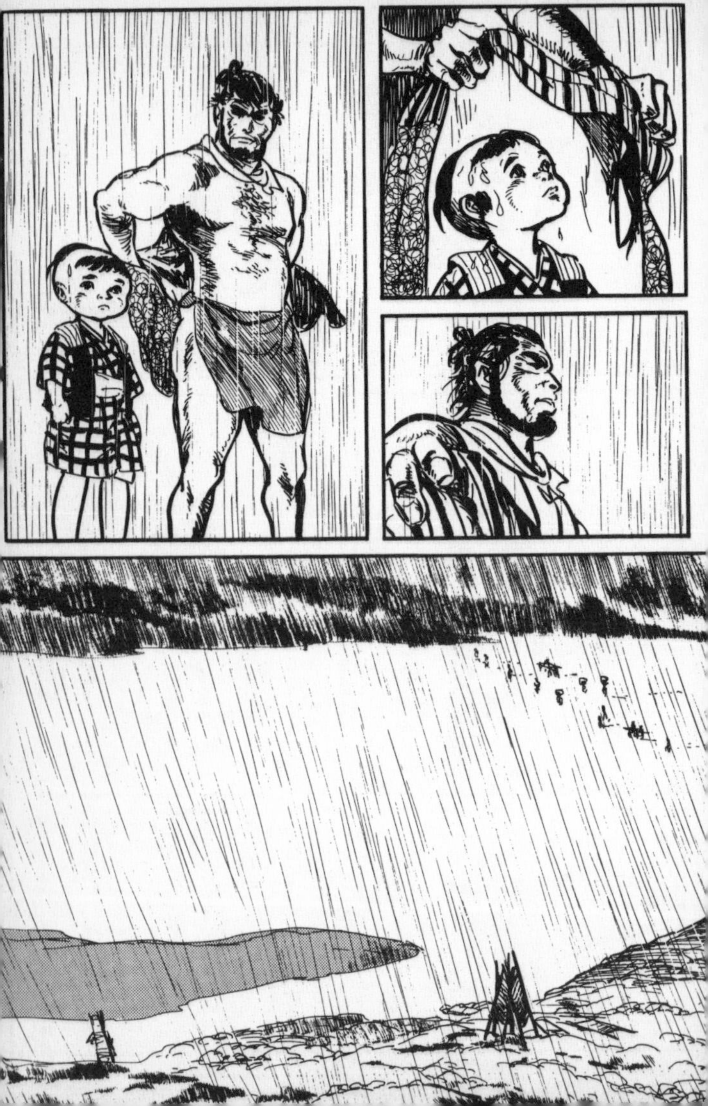

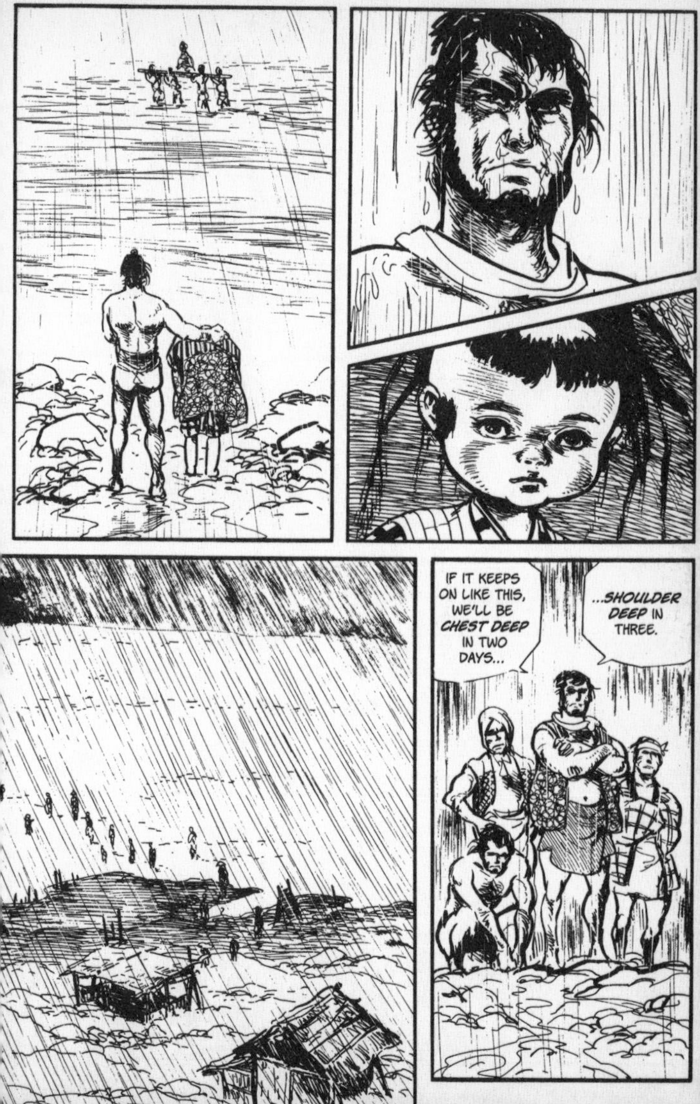
IF IT KEEPS ON LIKE THIS, WE'LL BE CHEST DEEP IN TWO DAYS...
...SHOULDER DEEP IN THREE.

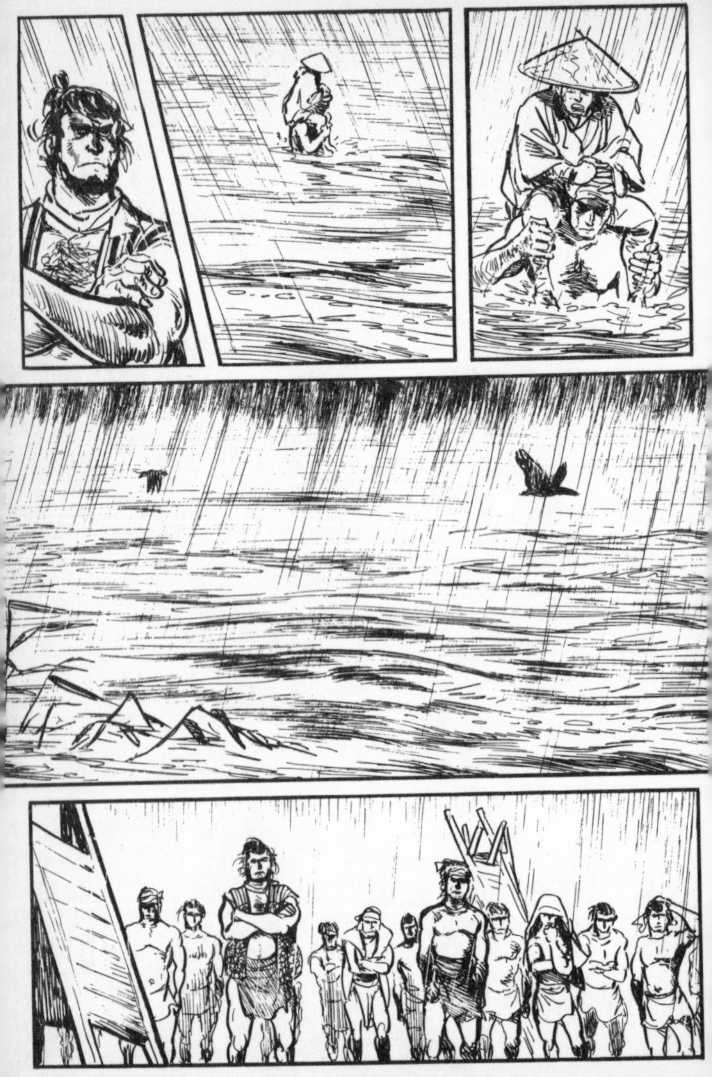

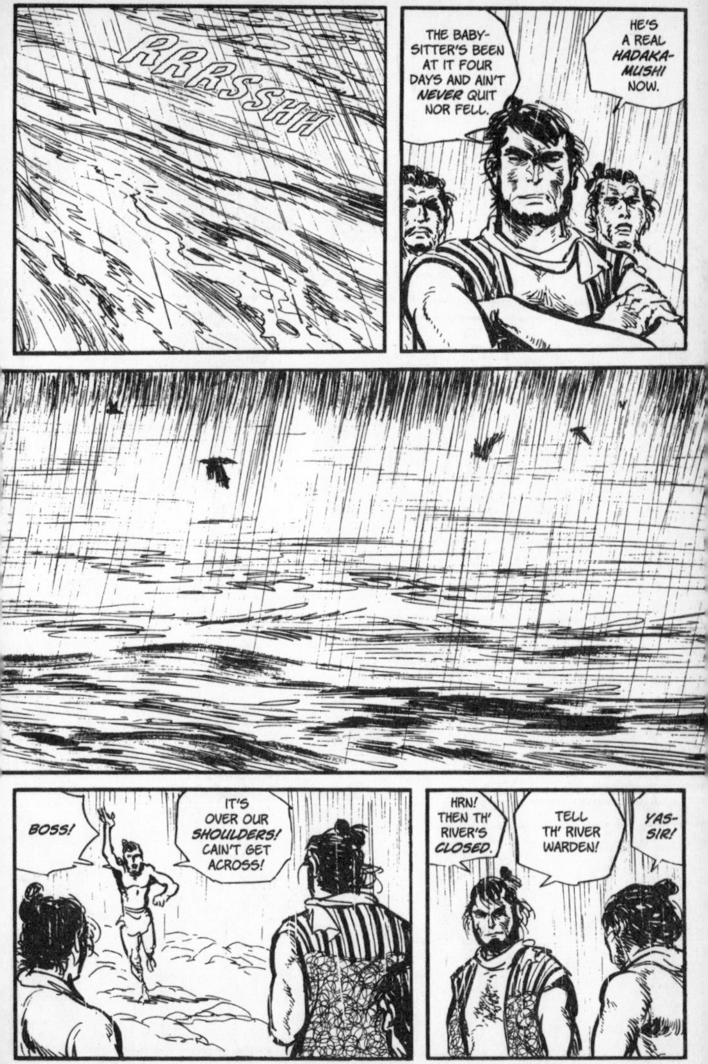
RRRSSHH
THE BABY-SITTER'S BEEN AT IT FOUR DAYS AND AIN'T NEVER QUIT NOR FELL.
HE'S A REAL HADAKA-MUSHI NOW.
BOSS!
IT'S OVER OUR SHOULDERS! CAIN'T GET ACROSS!
HRN! THEN TH' RIVER'S CLOSED.
TELL TH' RIVER WARDEN!
YAS-SIR!

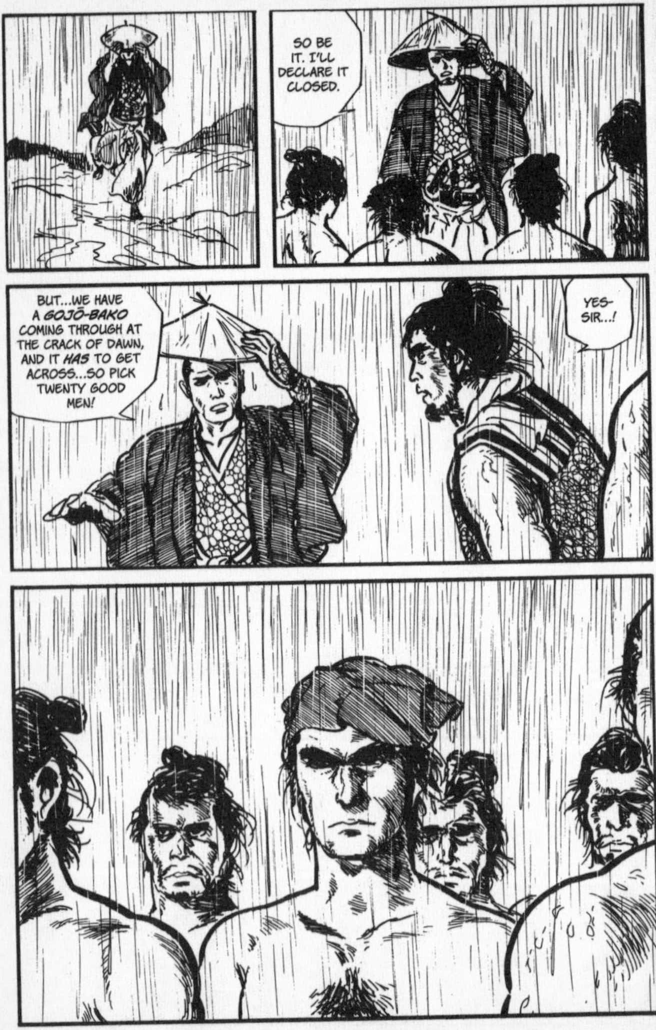
SO BE IT. I'LL DECLARE IT CLOSED.
BUT...WE HAVE A *GOJŌ-BAKO* COMING THROUGH AT THE CRACK OF DAWN, AND IT *HAS* TO GET ACROSS...SO PICK TWENTY GOOD MEN!
YES-SIR...!

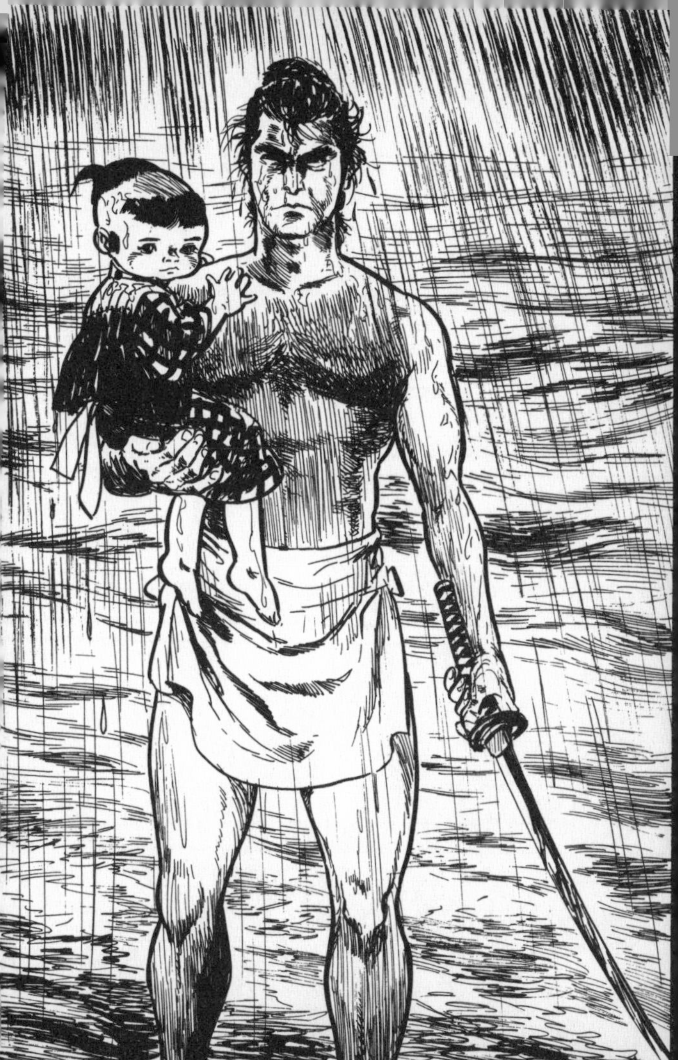

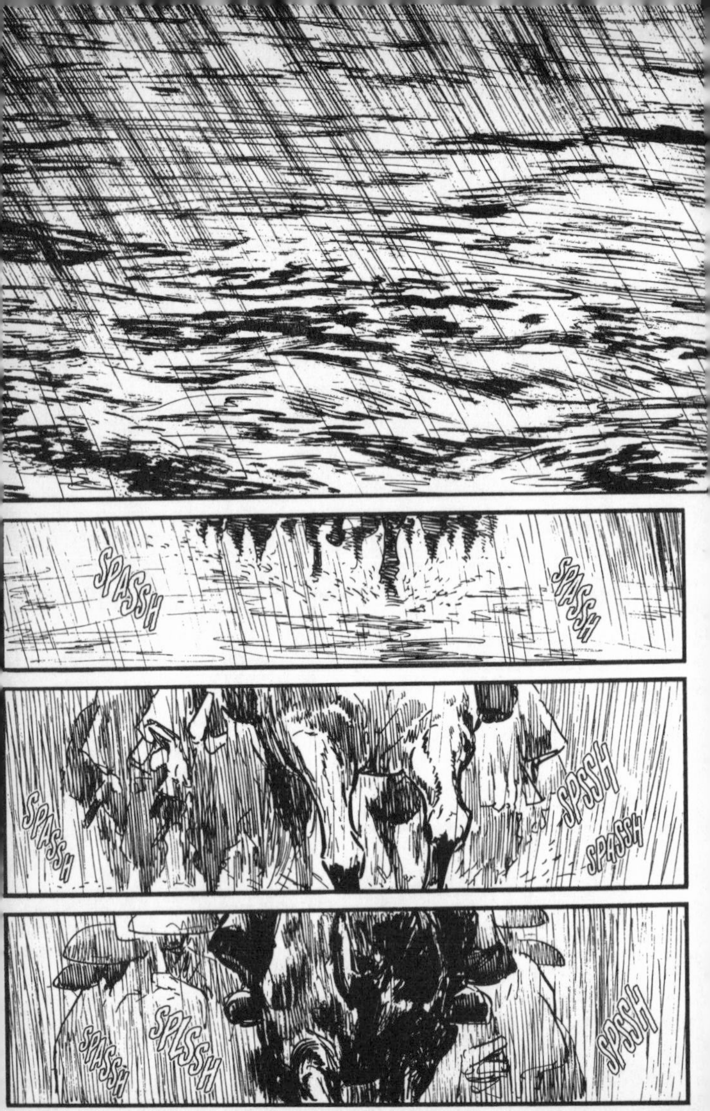
SPASSH
SPASSH
SPASSH
SPSSH
SPASSH
SPASSH
SPLSSH
SPSSH

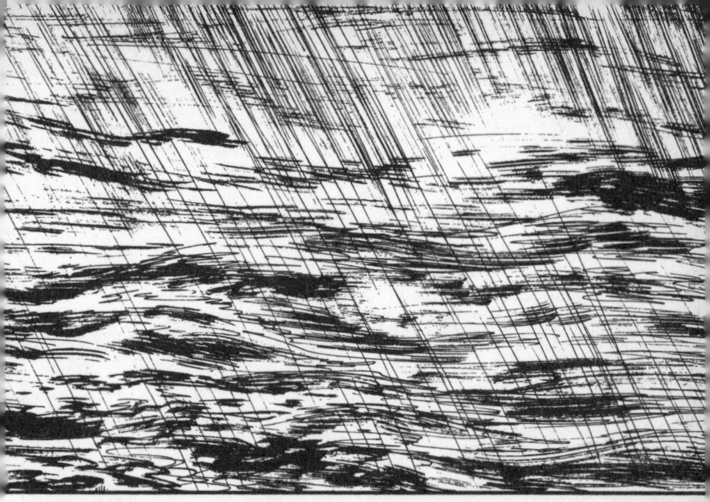

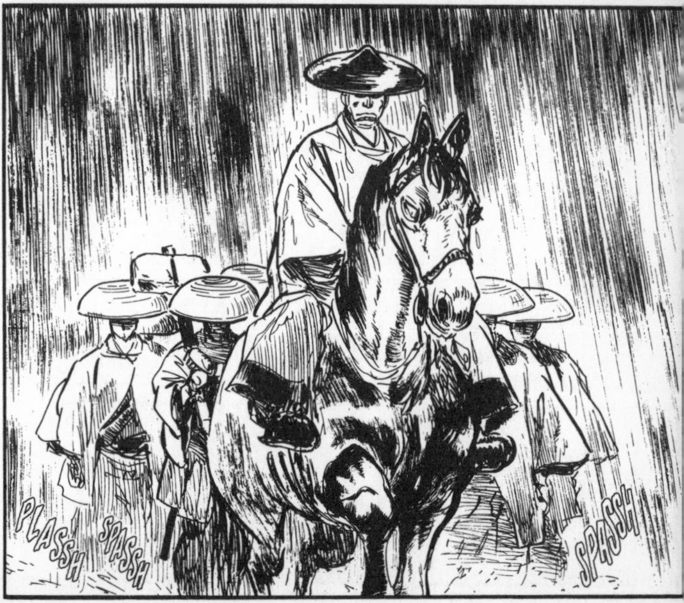
PLASSH
SPASSH
SPASSH

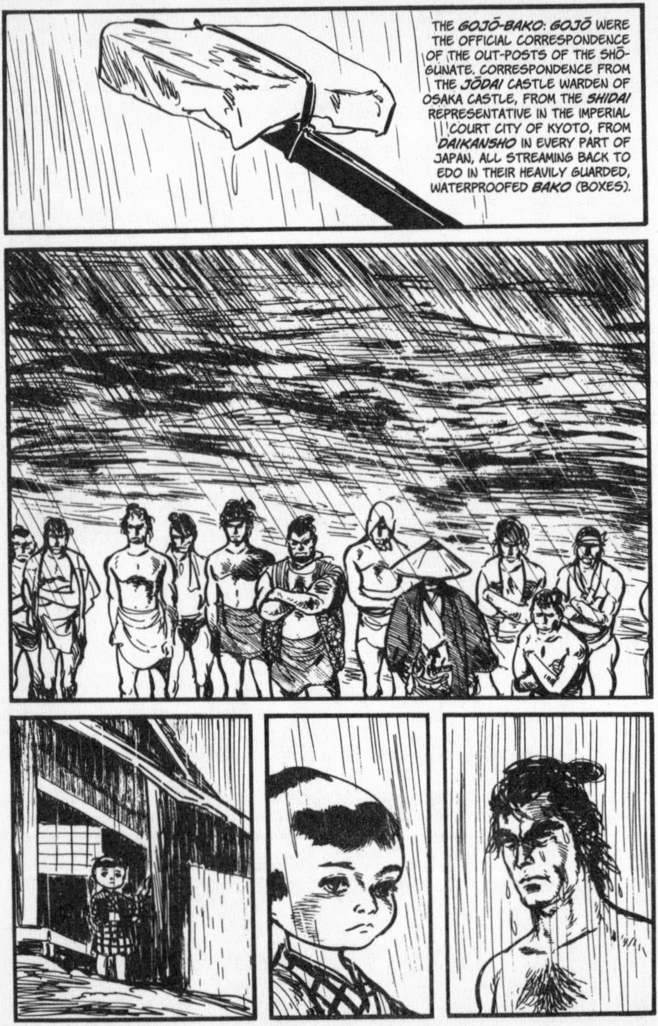
THE *GOJŌ-BAKO*: *GOJŌ* WERE THE OFFICIAL CORRESPONDENCE OF THE OUT-POSTS OF THE SHŌGUNATE. CORRESPONDENCE FROM THE *JŌDAI* CASTLE WARDEN OF OSAKA CASTLE, FROM THE *SHIDAI* REPRESENTATIVE IN THE IMPERIAL COURT CITY OF KYOTO, FROM *DAIKANSHO* IN EVERY PART OF JAPAN, ALL STREAMING BACK TO EDO IN THEIR HEAVILY GUARDED, WATERPROOFED *BAKO* (BOXES).

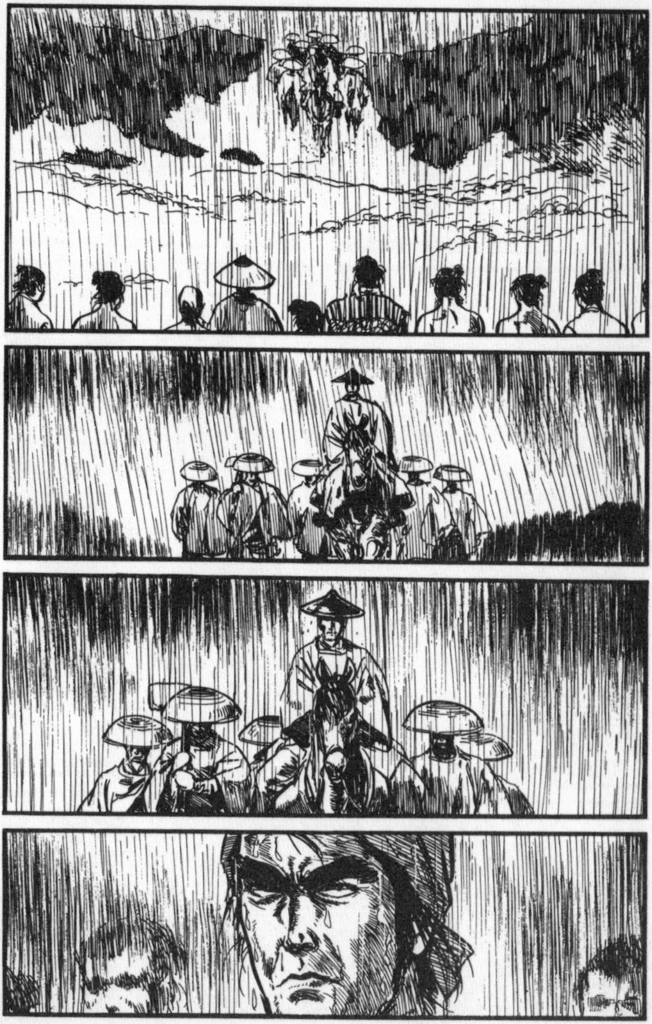

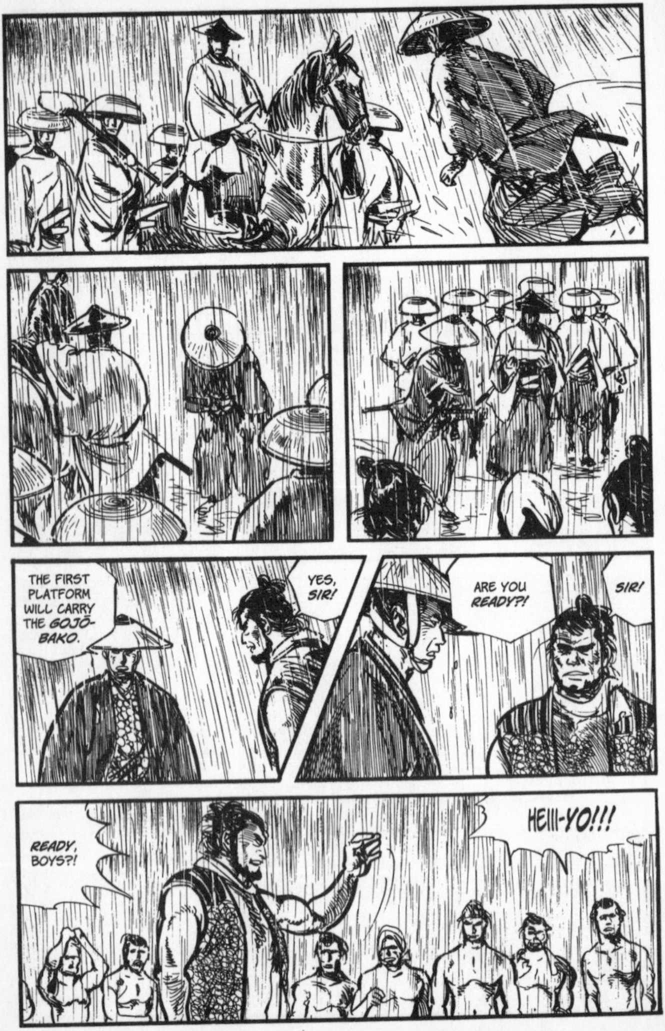
THE FIRST PLATFORM WILL CARRY THE GOJŌ-BAKO.
YES, SIR!
ARE YOU READY?!
SIR!
READY, BOYS?!
HEIII-YO!!!

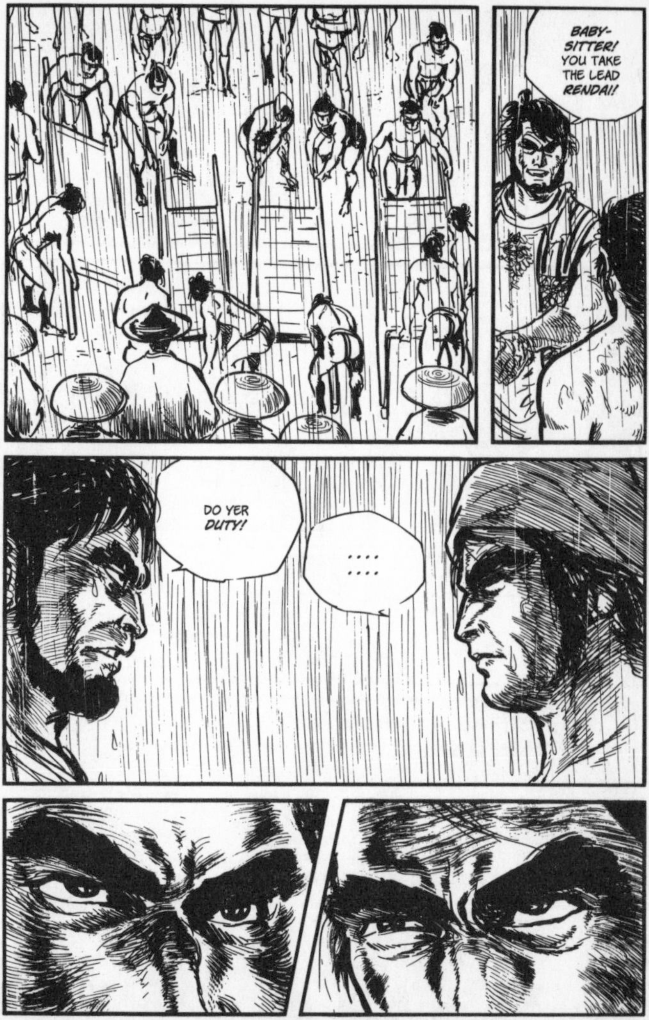
BABY-SITTER! YOU TAKE THE LEAD RENDAI!!
DO YER DUTY!
....
....

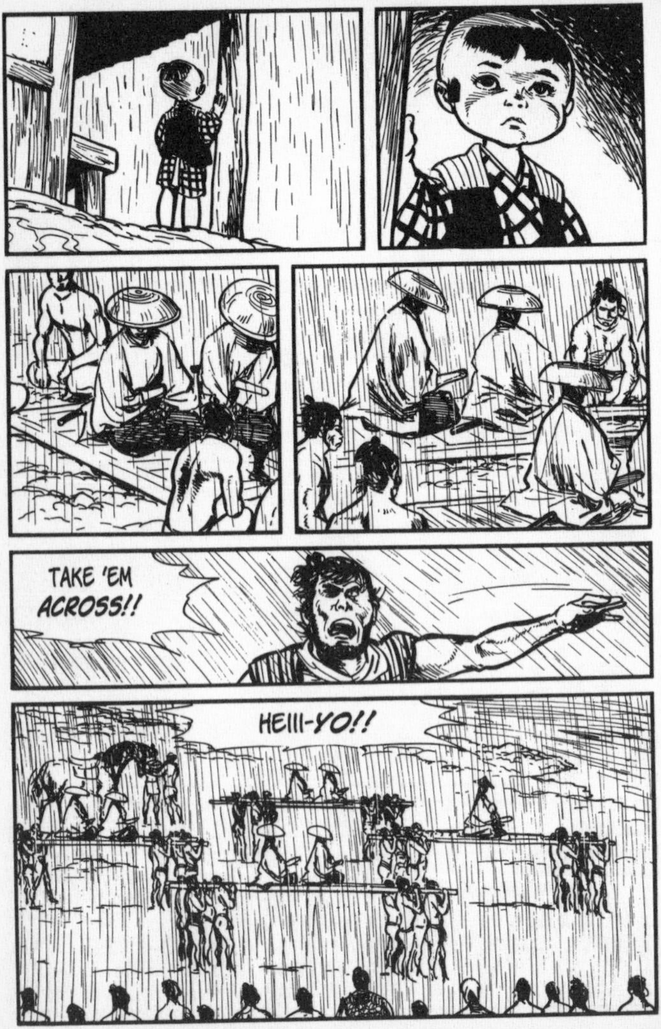
TAKE 'EM ACROSS!!
HEIII-YO!!

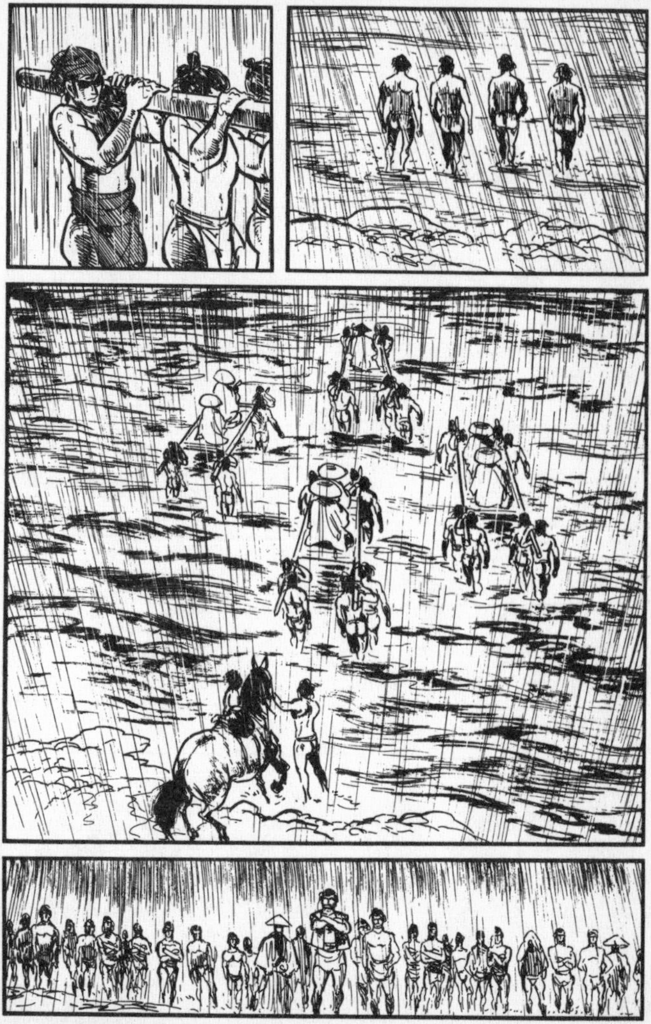

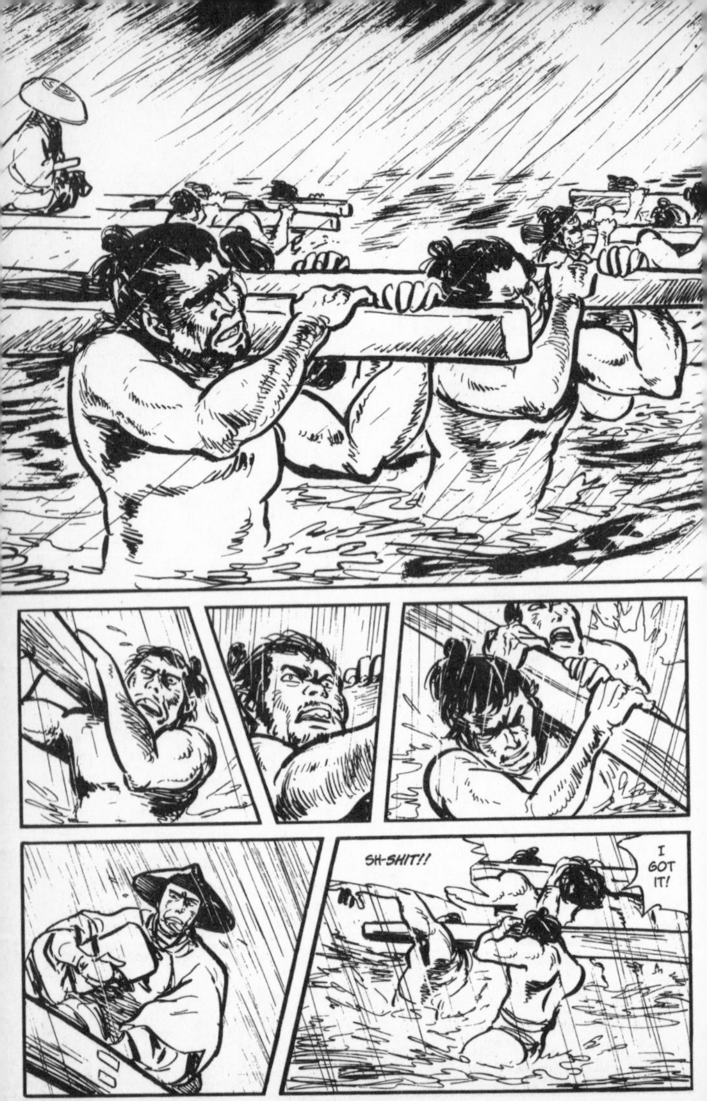
SH-SHIT!!
I GOT IT!

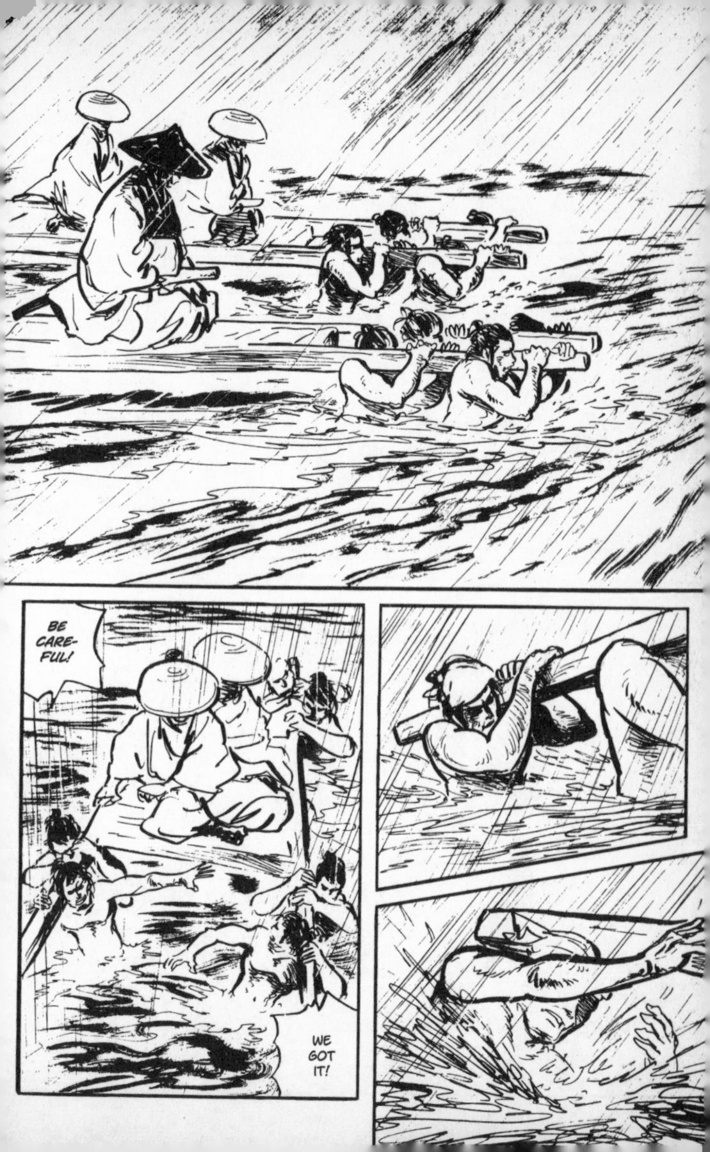
BE CARE-FUL!
WE GOT IT!

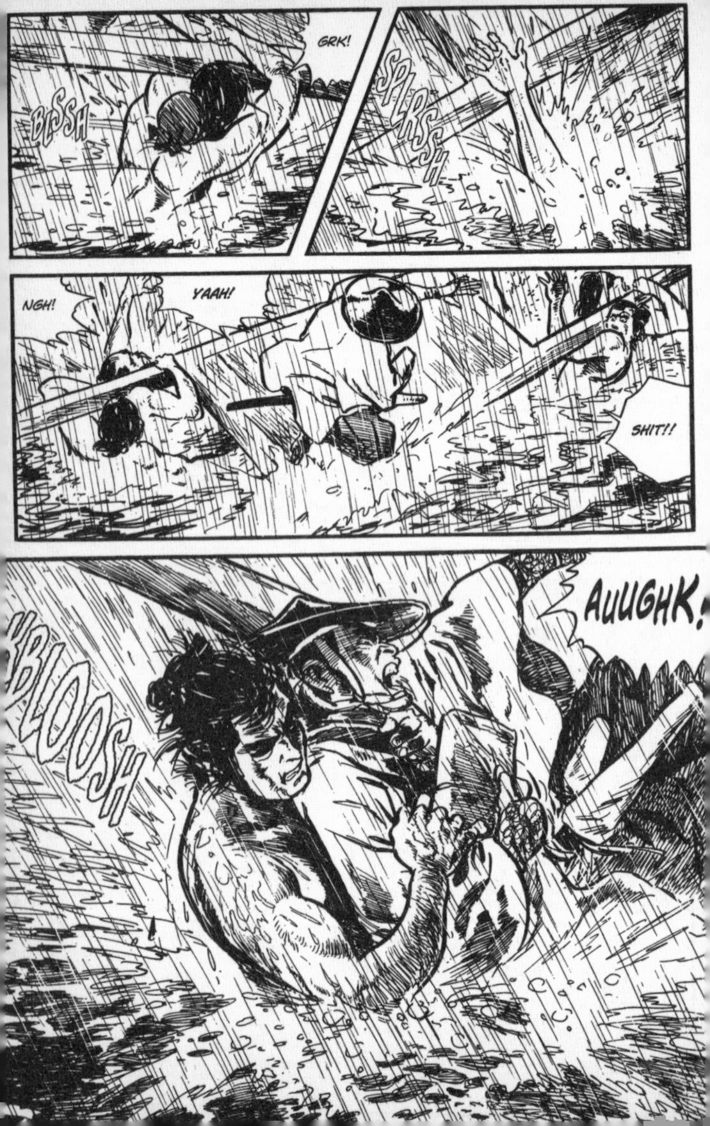
GRK!
BLSSH
SPLRSSH
NGH!
YAAH!
SHIT!!
AUUGHK!
BLOOSH

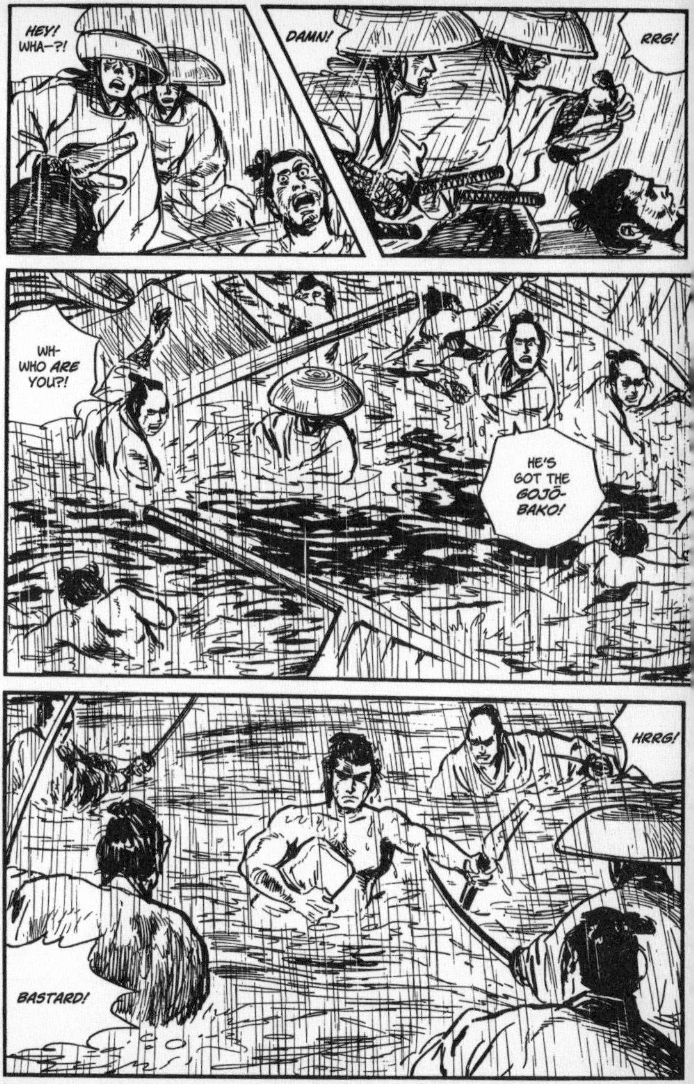
HEY! WHA–?!
DAMN!
RRG!
WH- WHO *ARE* YOU?!
HE'S GOT THE *GOJŌ-BAKO!*
HRRG!
BASTARD!

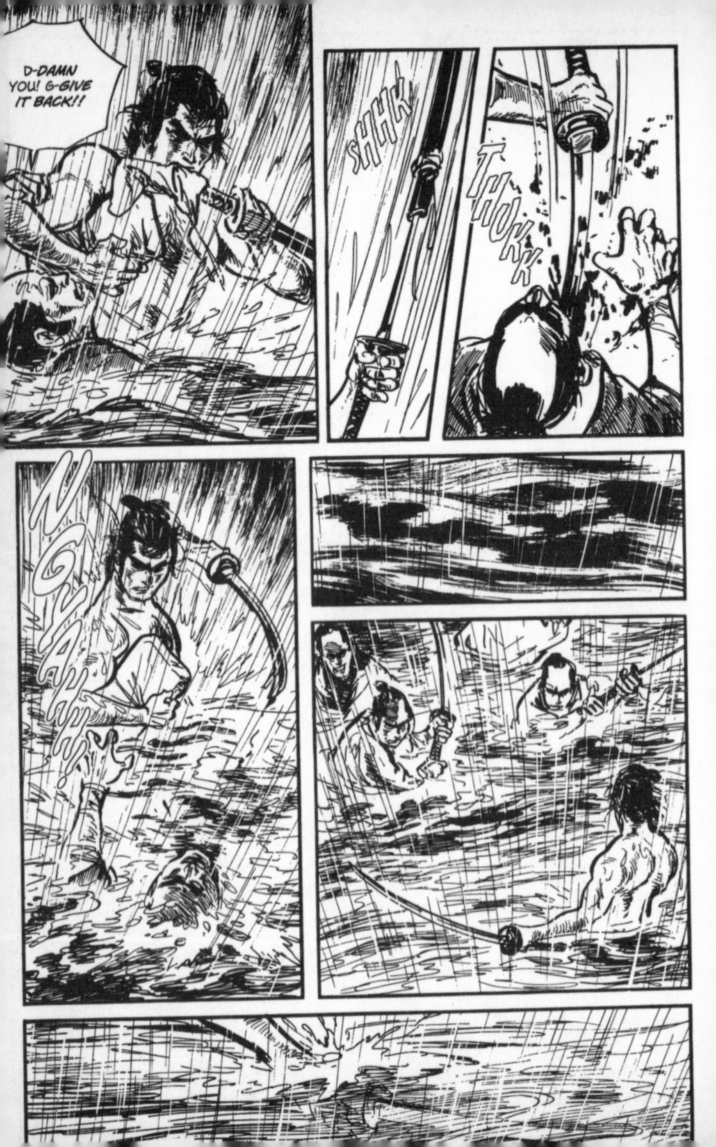

D-DAMN YOU! G-GIVE IT BACK!!
SHHK
THUNK

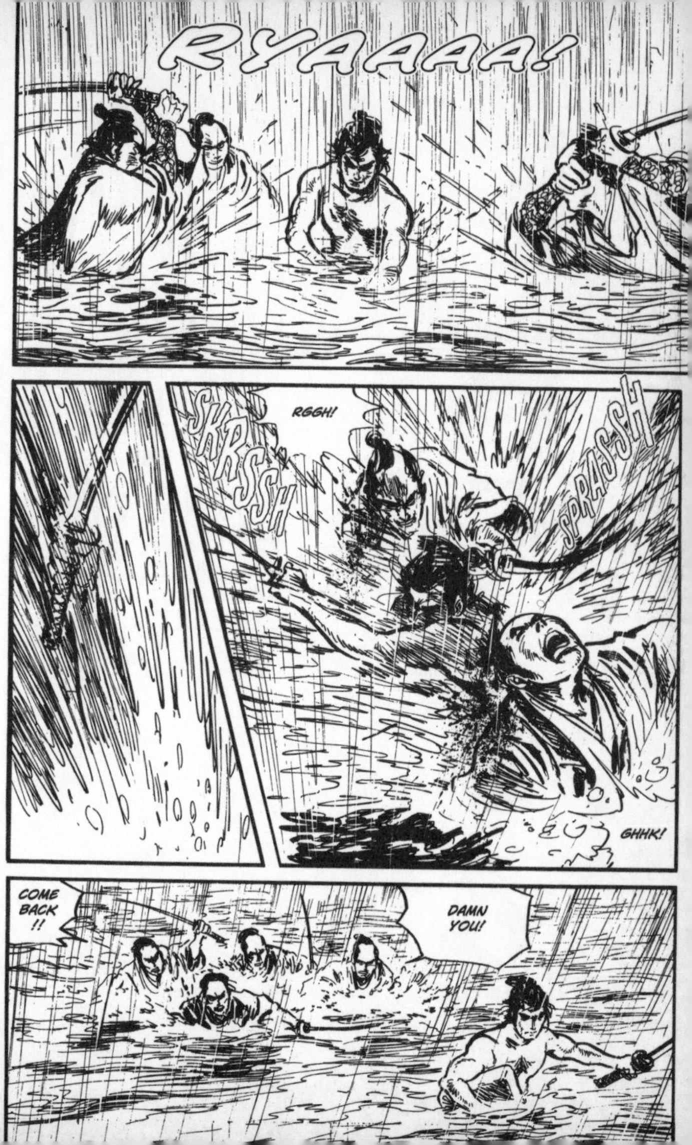
RYAAAA!
SKRSSH
RGGH!
SPRASSH
GHHK!
COME BACK !!
DAMN YOU!

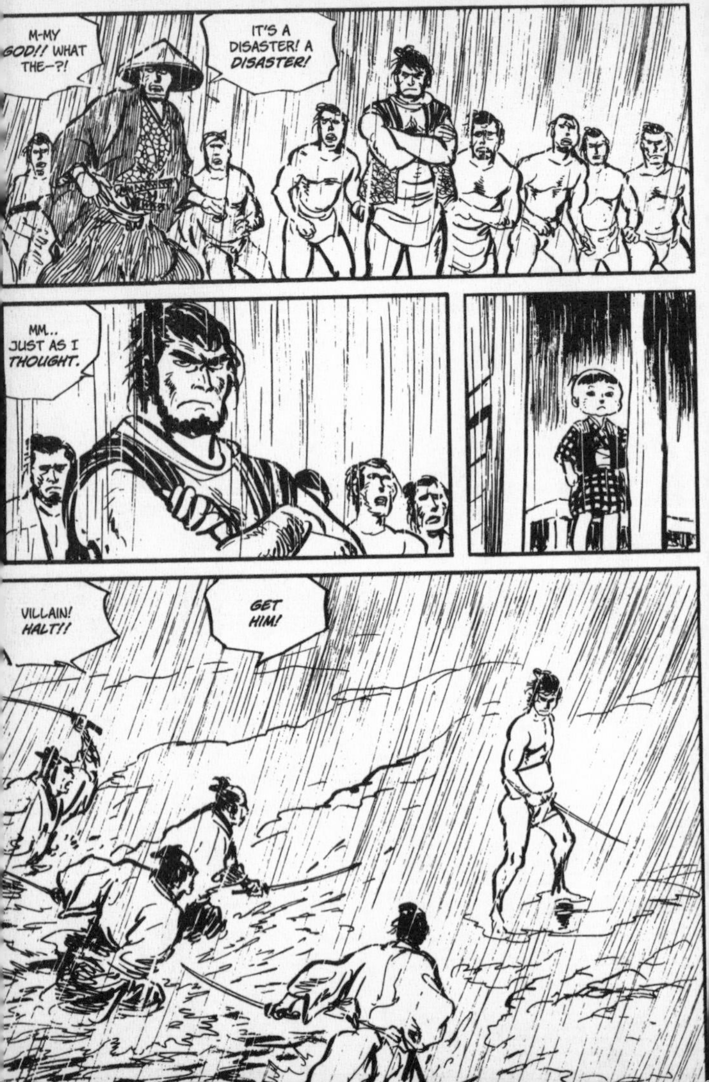
M-MY GOD!! WHAT THE-?!
IT'S A DISASTER! A DISASTER!
MM.. JUST AS I THOUGHT.
VILLAIN! HALT!!
GET HIM!

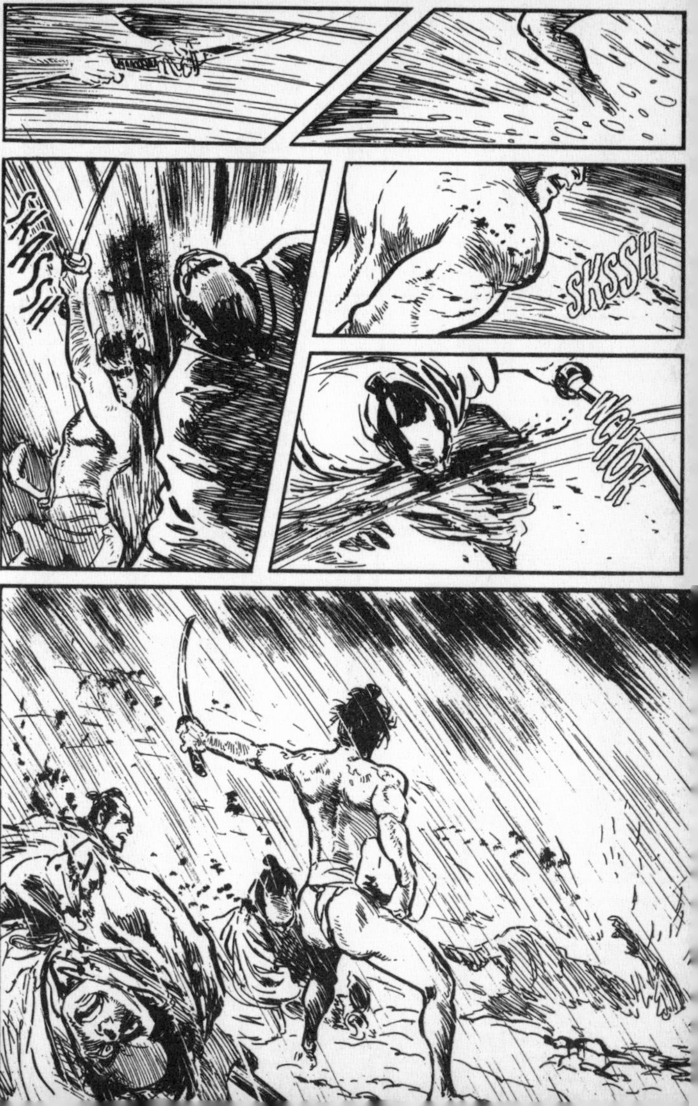
SKASSH
SKSSH
NCHOK

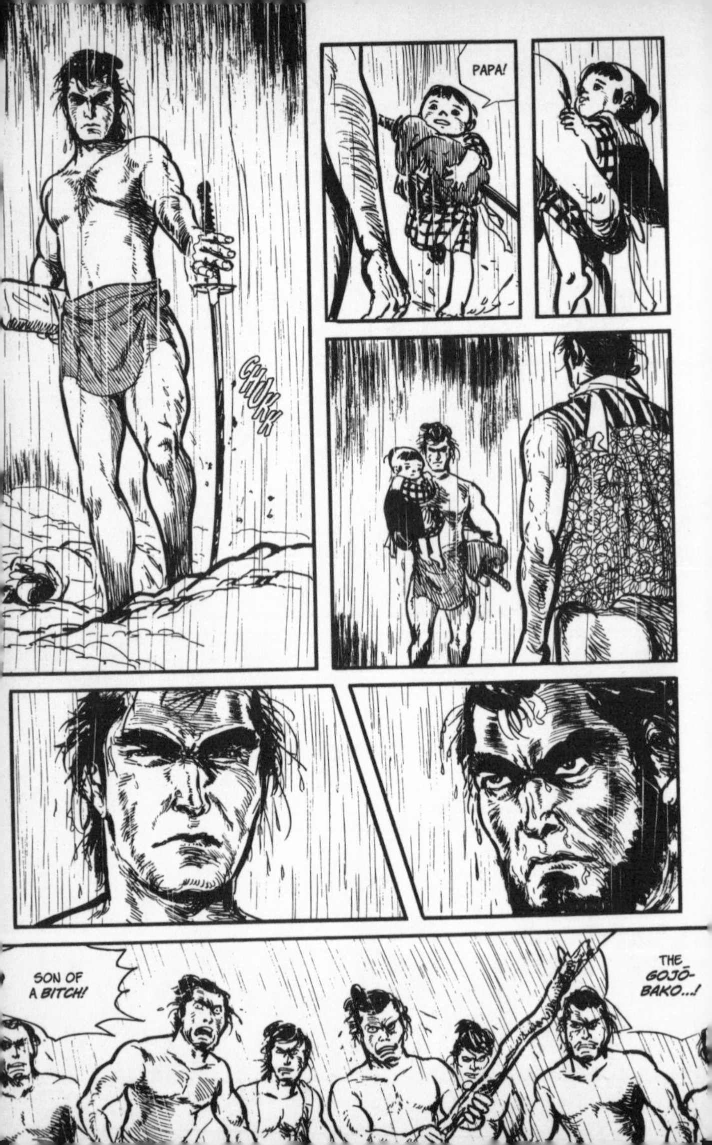
CHOKK
PAPA!
SON OF A BITCH!
THE GOJŌ-BAKO...!

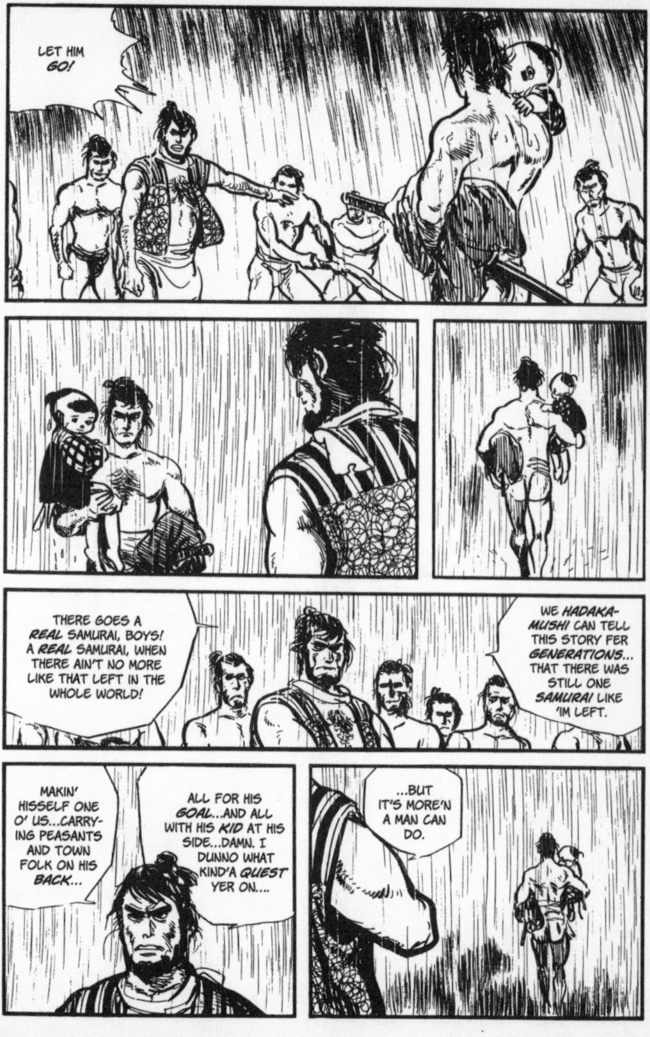
LET HIM GO!
THERE GOES A REAL SAMURAI, BOYS! A REAL SAMURAI, WHEN THERE AIN'T NO MORE LIKE THAT LEFT IN THE WHOLE WORLD!
WE HADAKA-MUSHI CAN TELL THIS STORY FER GENERATIONS... THAT THERE WAS STILL ONE SAMURAI LIKE 'IM LEFT.
MAKIN' HISSELF ONE O' US...CARRY-ING PEASANTS AND TOWN FOLK ON HIS BACK...
ALL FOR HIS GOAL...AND ALL WITH HIS KID AT HIS SIDE...DAMN. I DUNNO WHAT KIND'A QUEST YER ON....
...BUT IT'S MORE'N A MAN CAN DO.

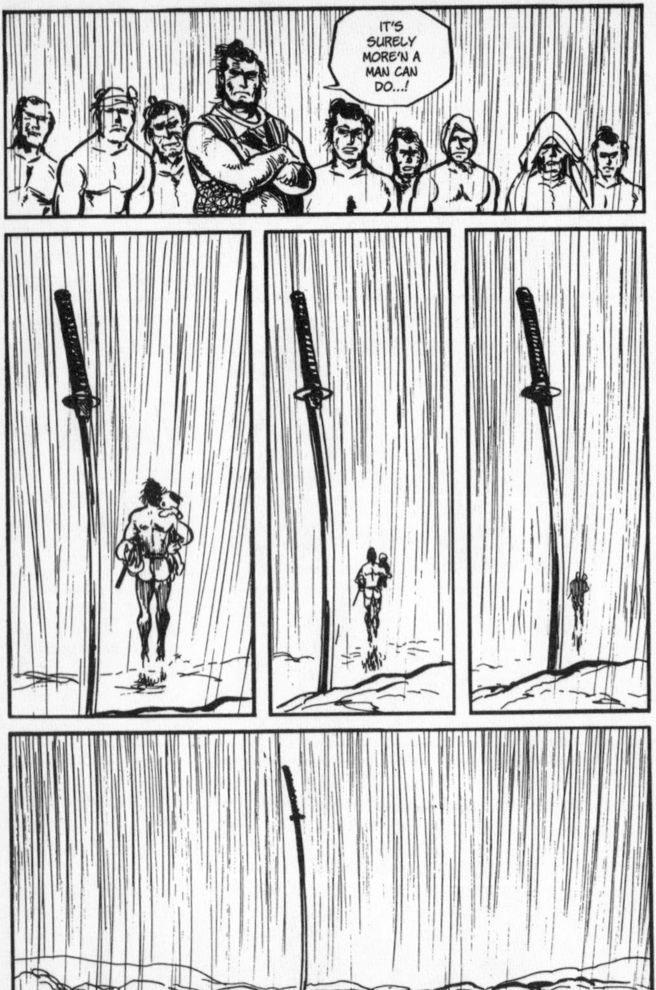
IT'S SURELY MORE'N A MAN CAN DO...!

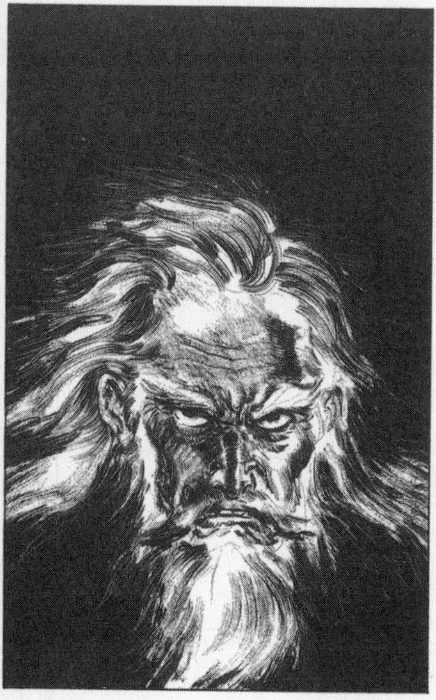

the forty-ninth

The Yagyū Letter: Prologue

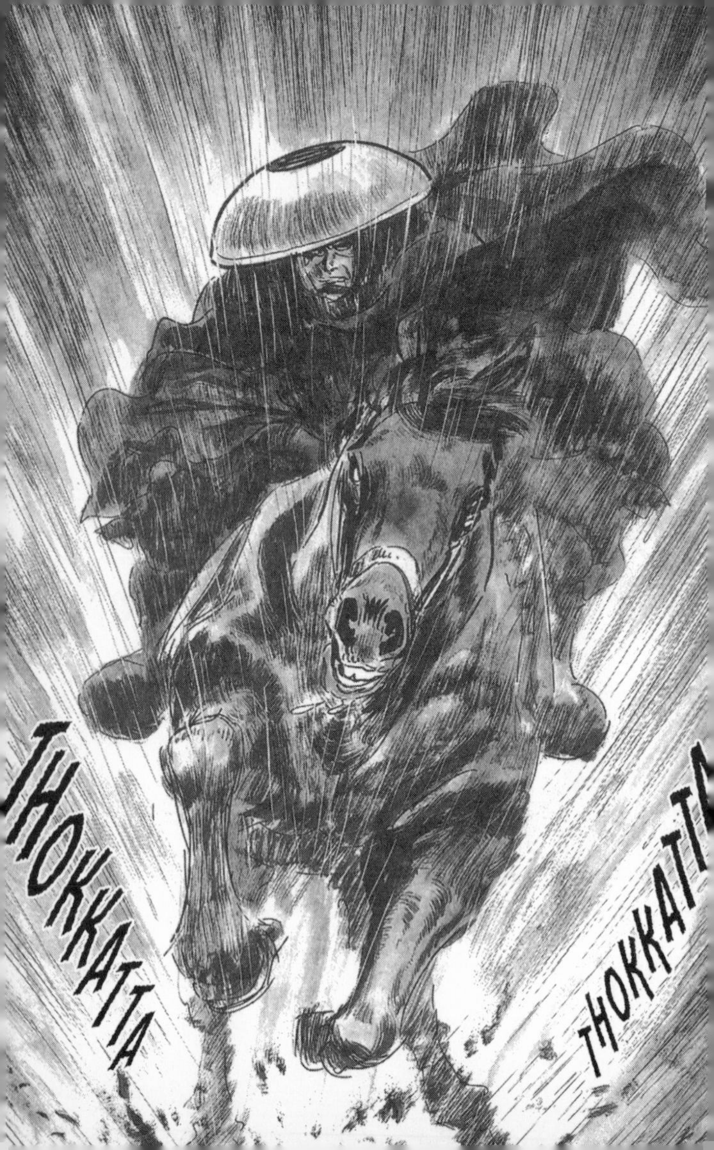
THOKKATTA
THOKKATT

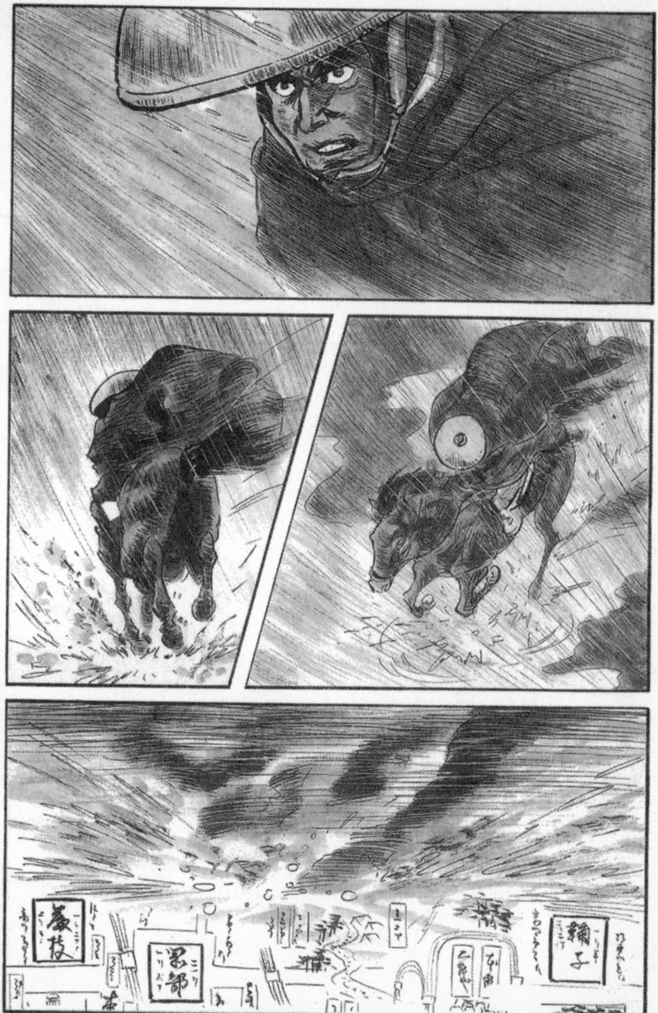

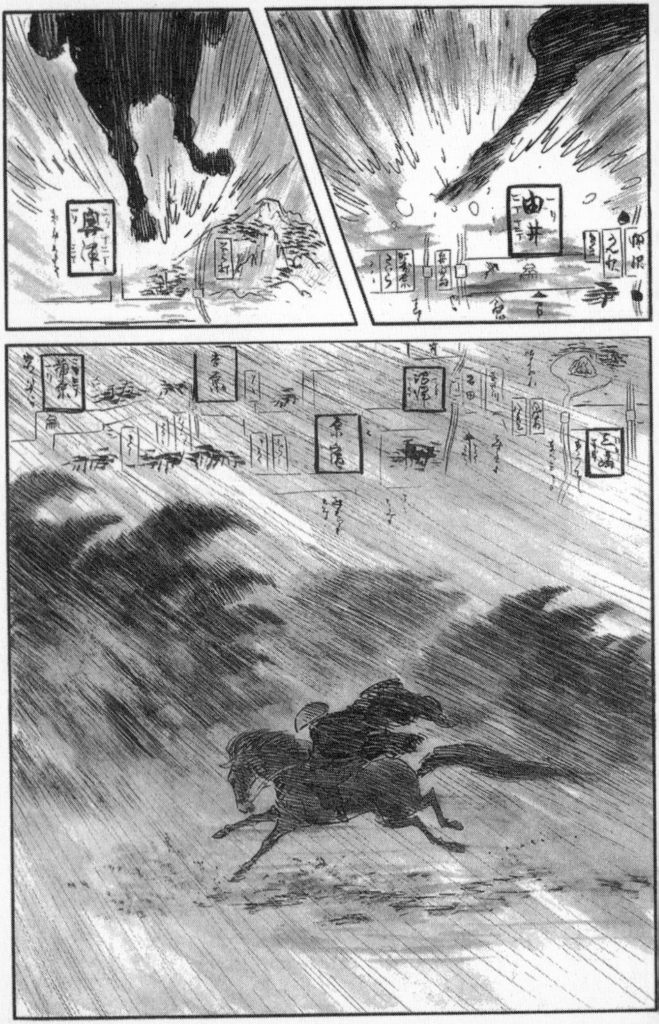
興津
由井
蒲原
吉原
沼津
三嶋

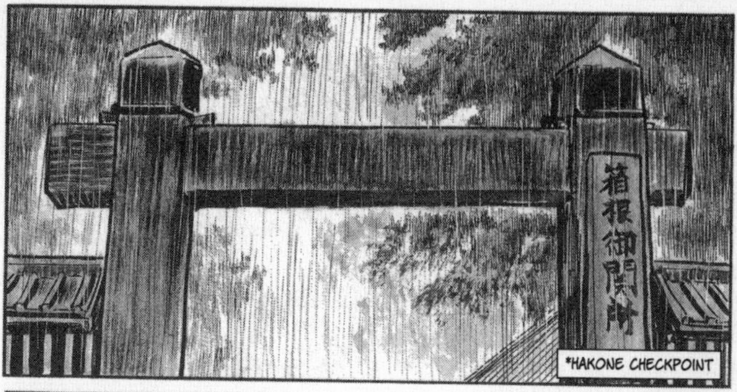
箱根御関所
*HAKONE CHECKPOINT

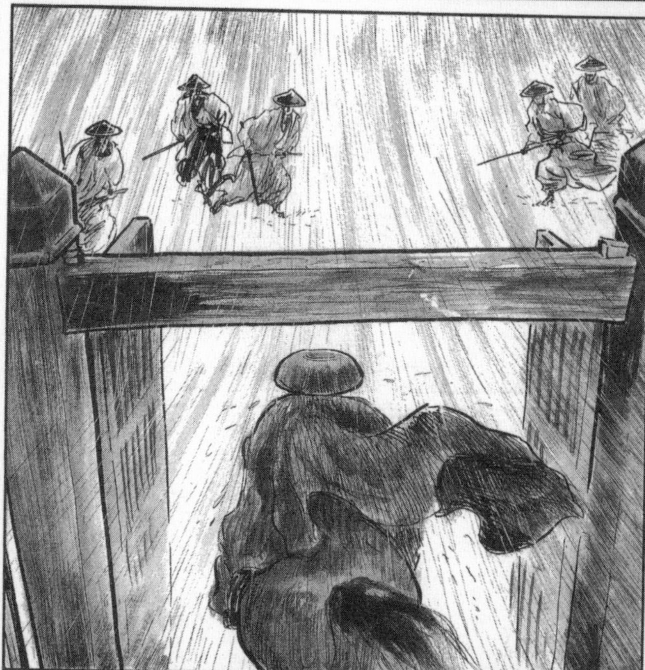

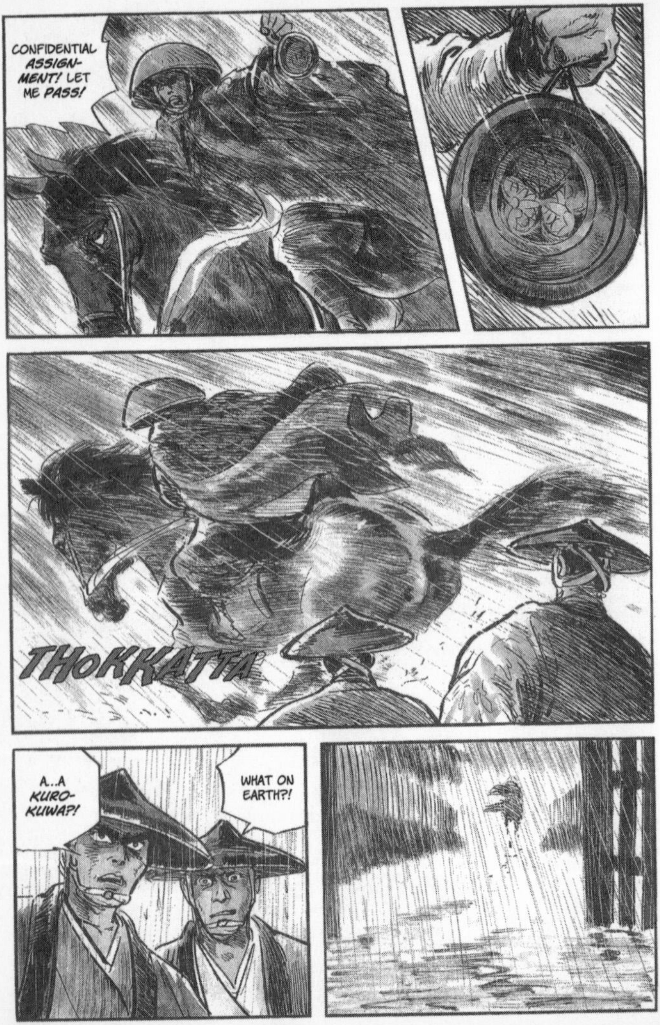
CONFIDENTIAL ASSIGN-MENT! LET ME PASS!
THOKKATTA
A..A KURO-KUWA?!
WHAT ON EARTH?!

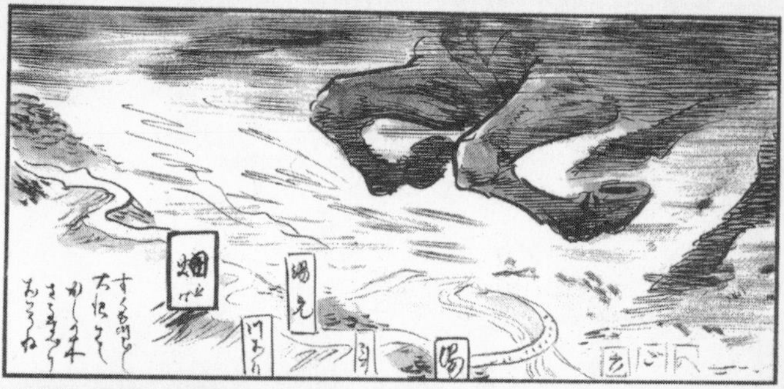
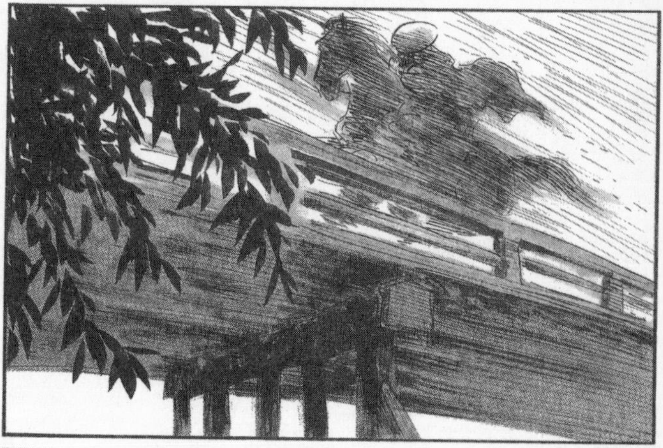
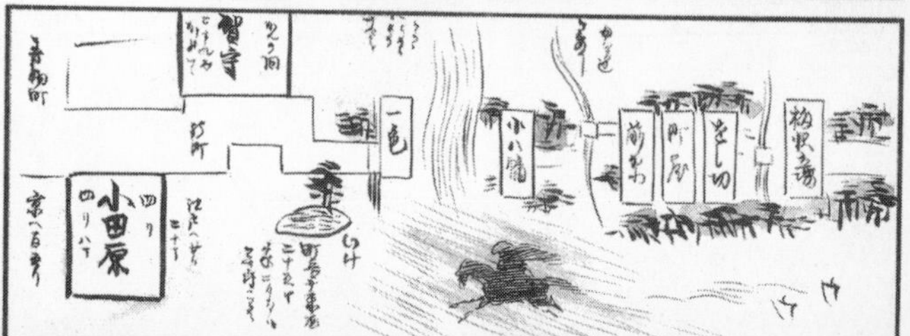
小田原
一色
小八幡

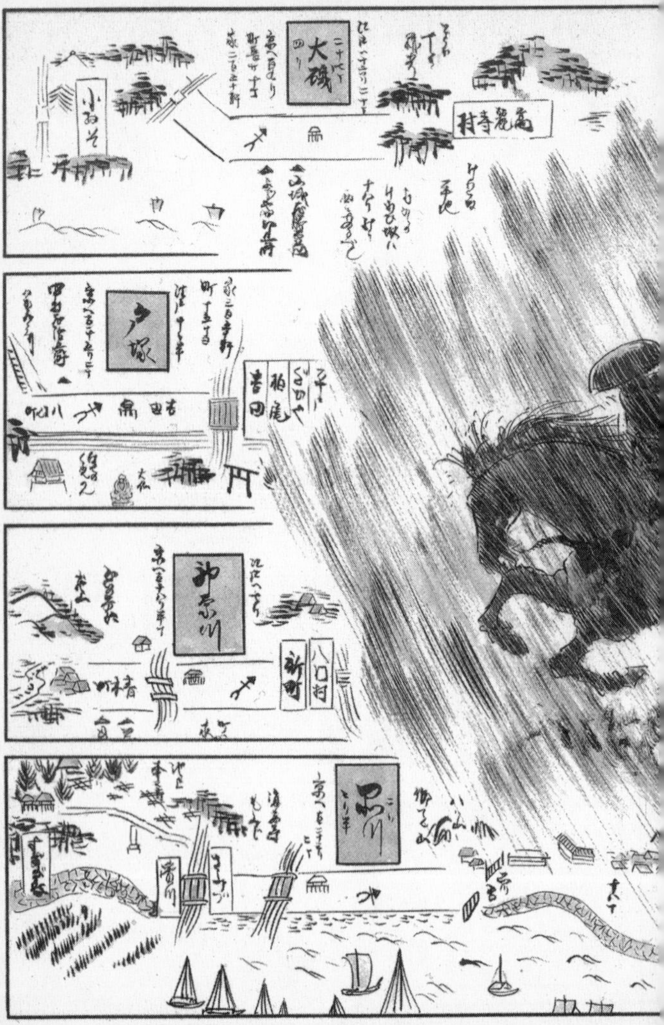
大磯
高麗寺村
戸塚
吉田
柏尾
神奈川
新町
品川

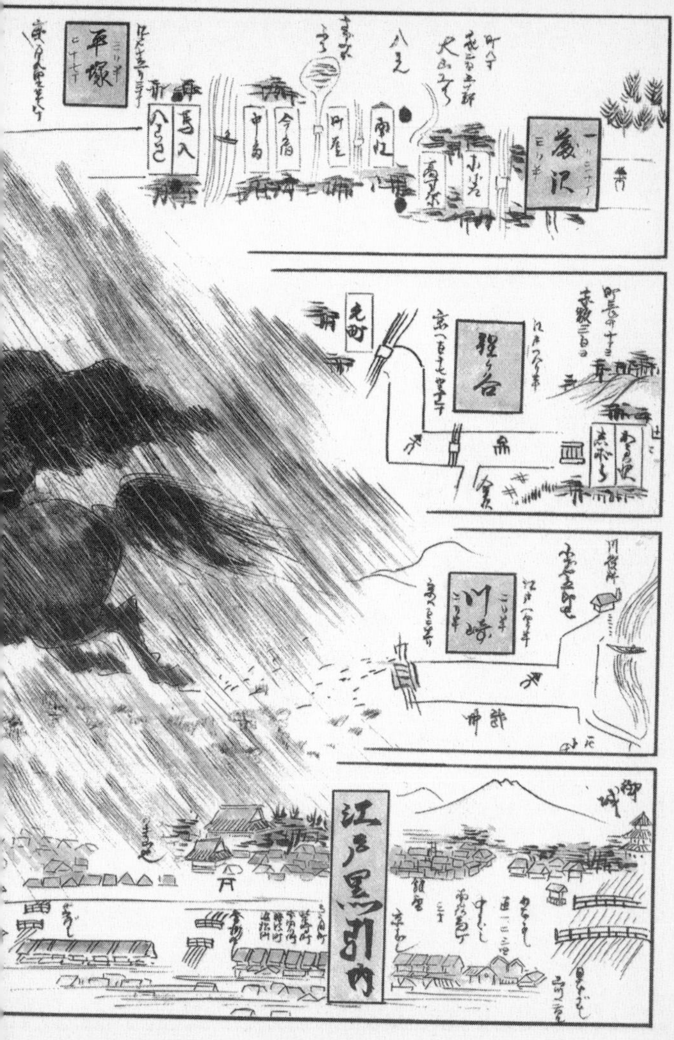

平塚
藤沢
程ヶ谷
川崎

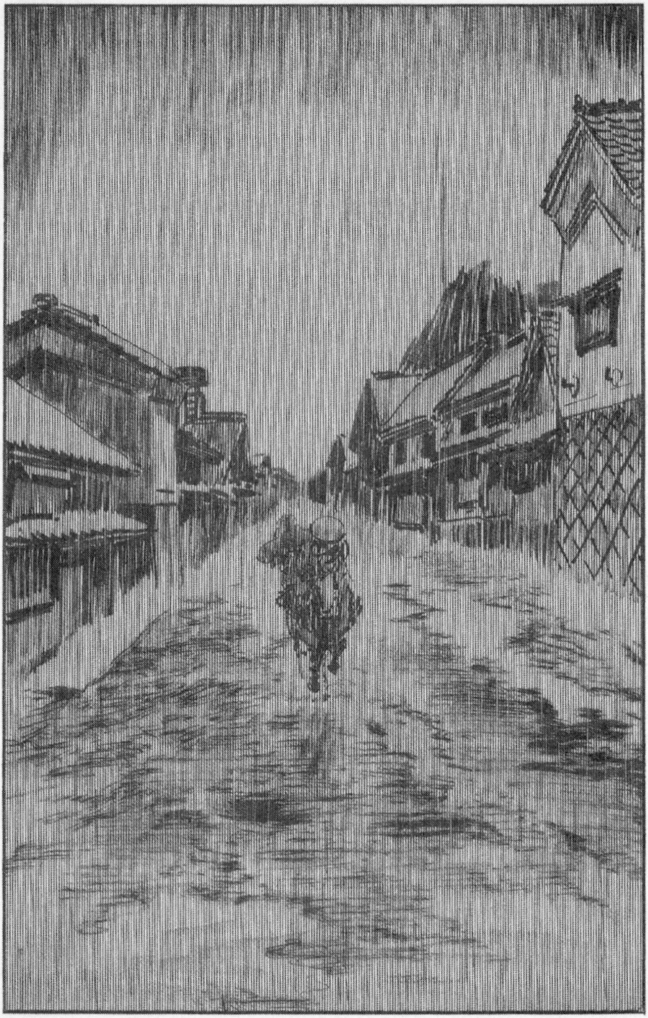

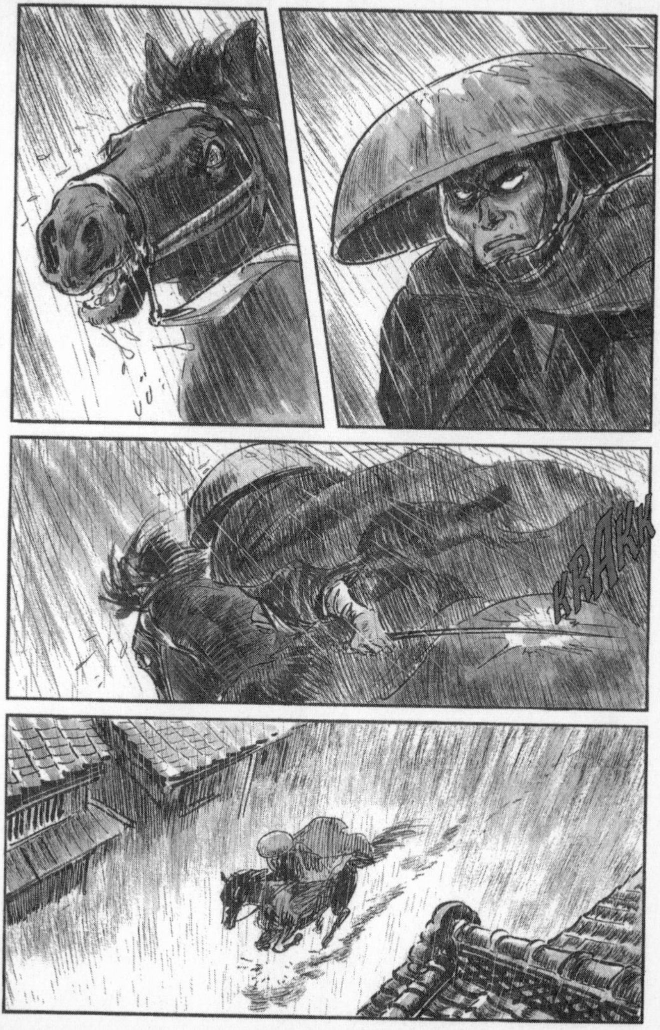
KRAKK

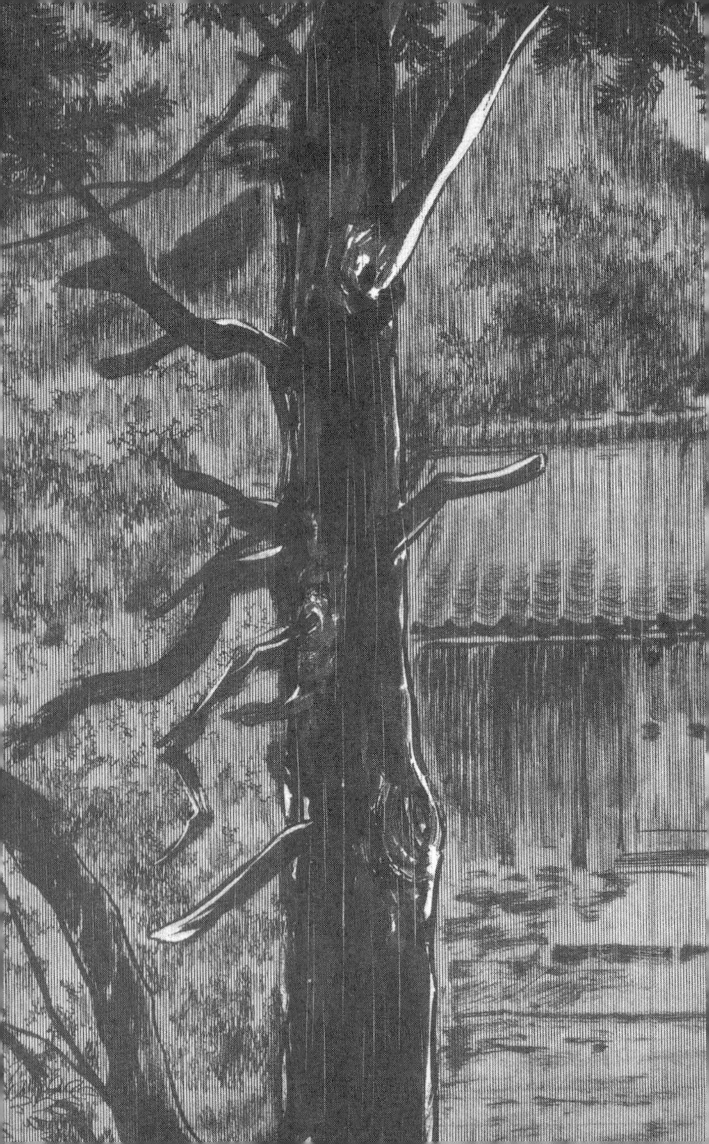

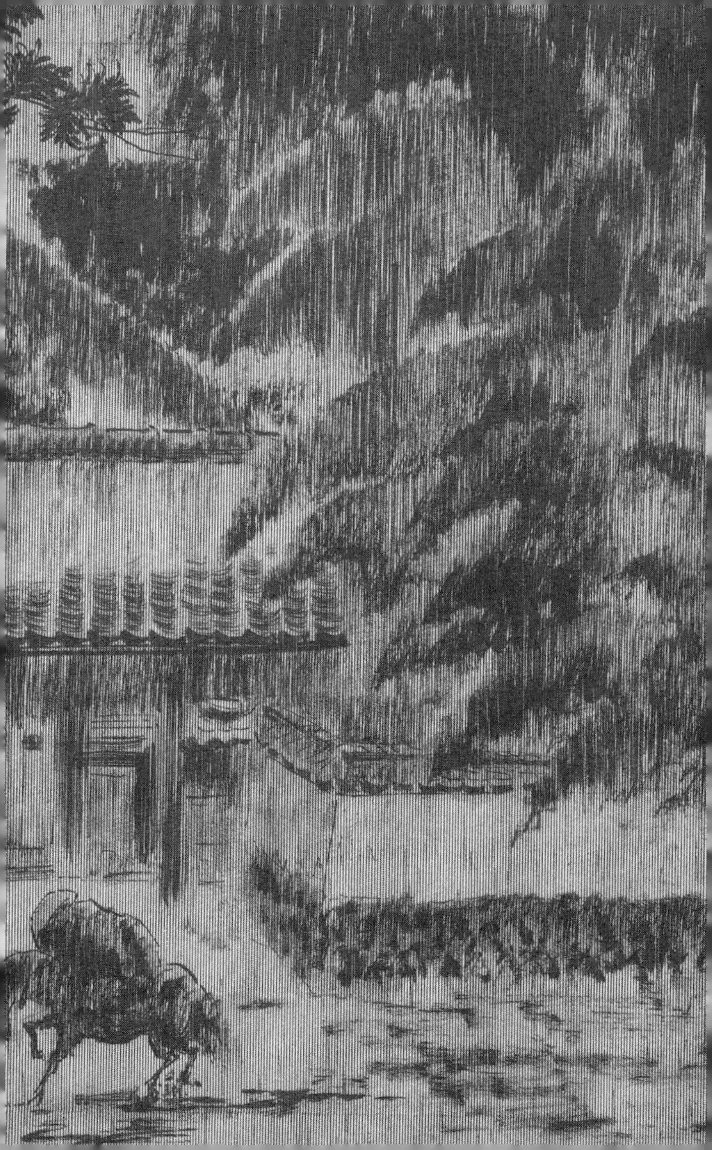

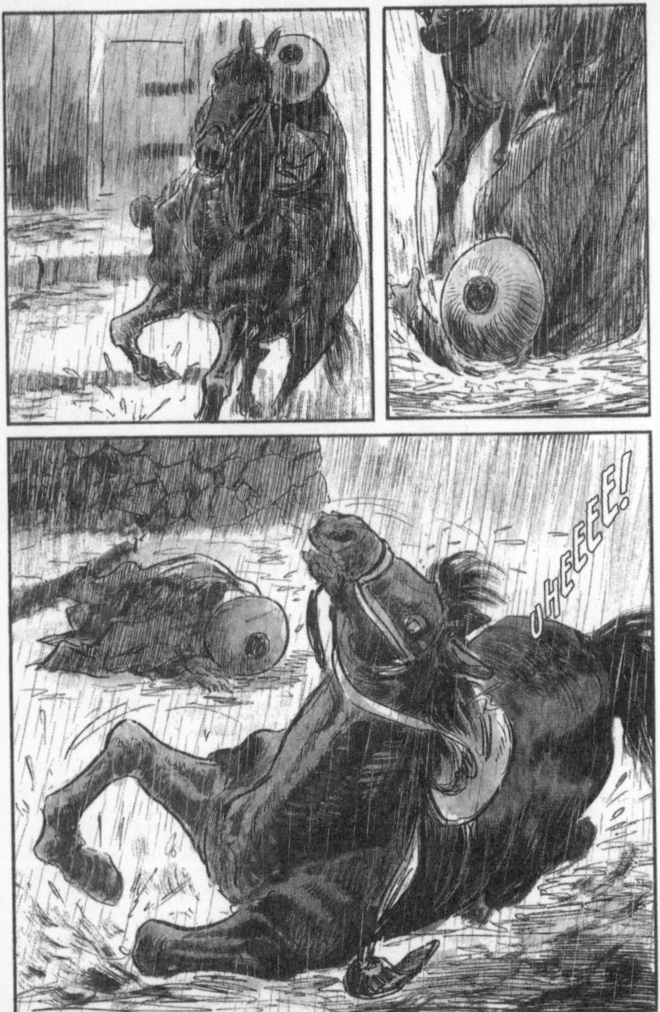
UHEEEE!

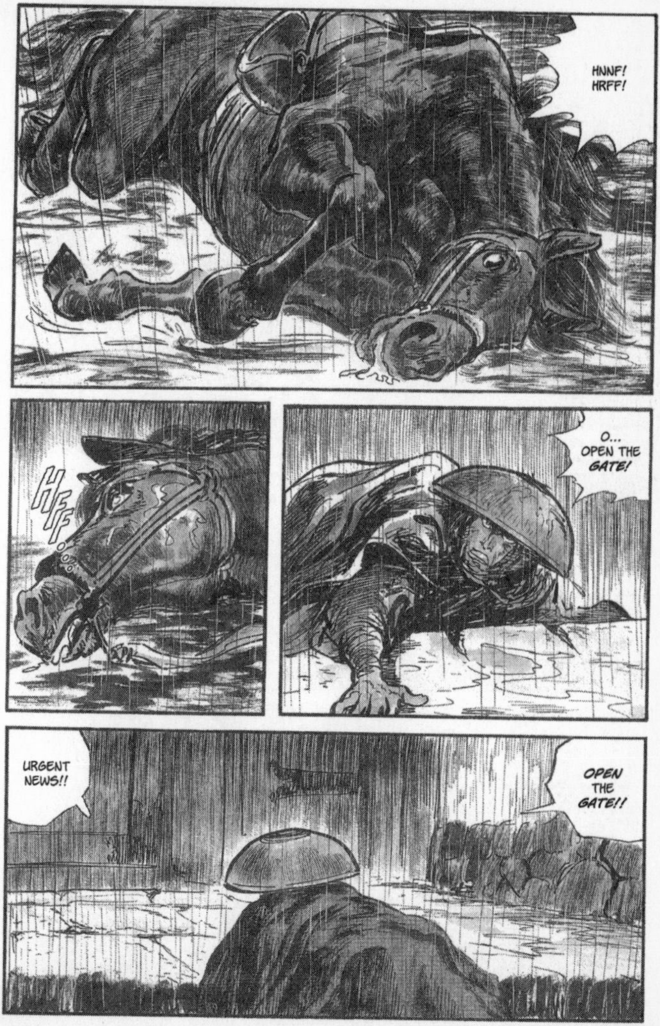
HNNF!
HRFF!
HFF
O...
OPEN THE
GATE!
URGENT
NEWS!!
OPEN
THE
GATE!!

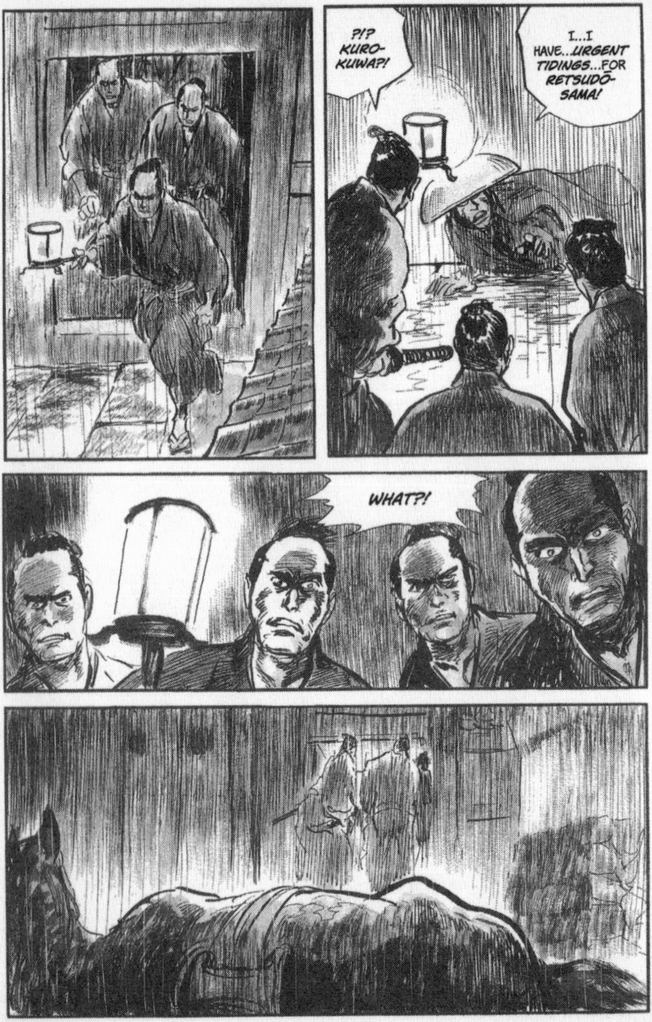
?!? KURO-KUWA?!
I...I HAVE...URGENT TIDINGS...FOR RETSUDŌ-SAMA!
WHAT?!

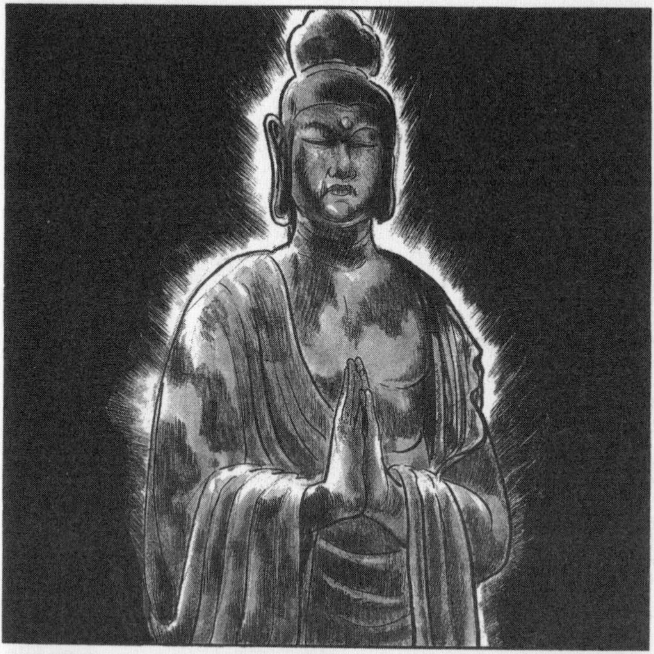

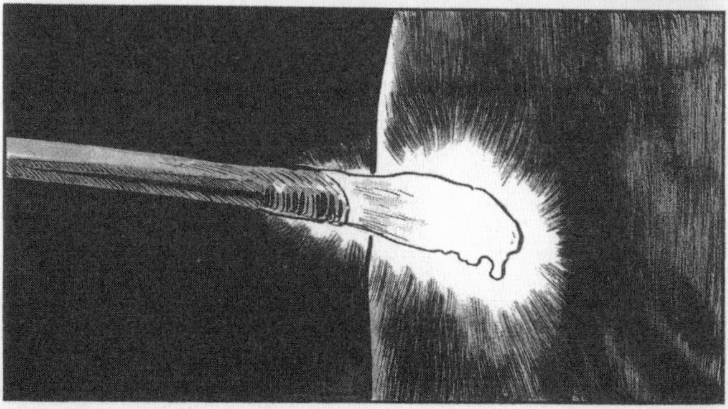

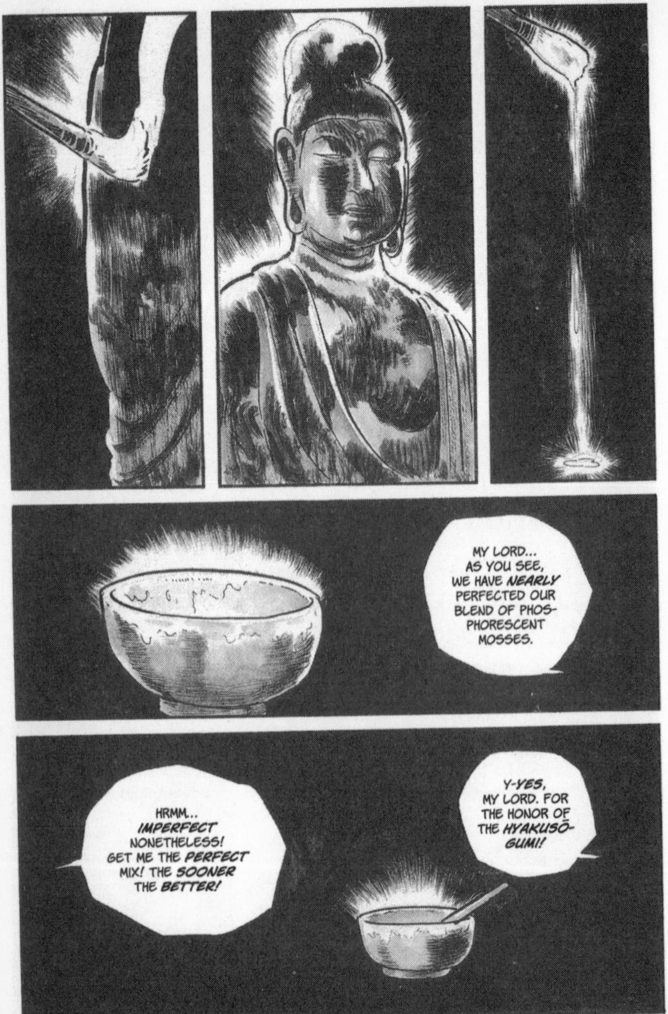
MY LORD... AS YOU SEE, WE HAVE NEARLY PERFECTED OUR BLEND OF PHOS-PHORESCENT MOSSES.
HRMM... IMPERFECT NONETHELESS! GET ME THE PERFECT MIX! THE SOONER THE BETTER!
Y-YES, MY LORD. FOR THE HONOR OF THE HYAKUSŌ-GUMI!

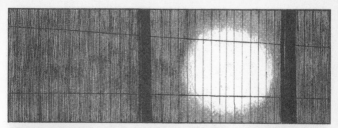

MY *LORD!*
A *KUROKUWA*
RIDER AT THE GATES!
HE SAYS HE BEARS
URGENT NEWS...

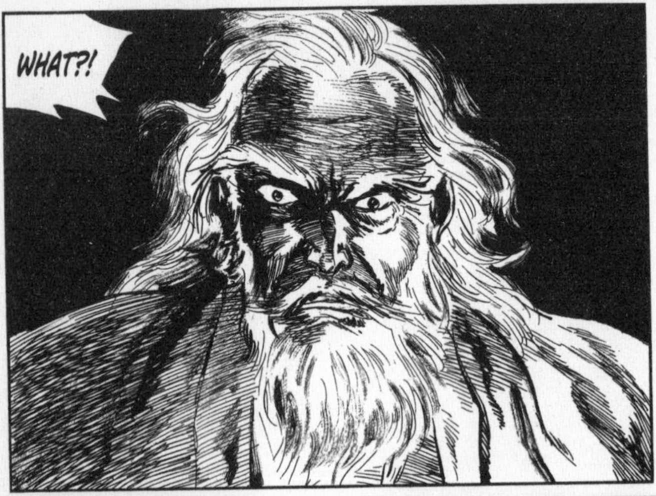
WHAT?!

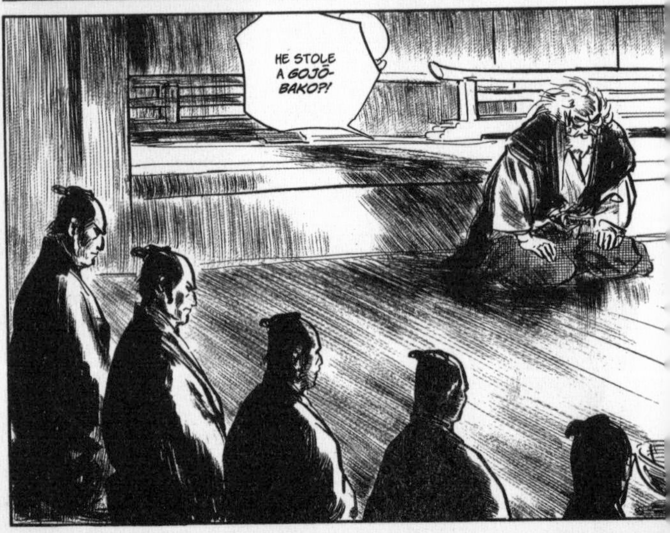
HE STOLE A GOJŌ-BAKO?!

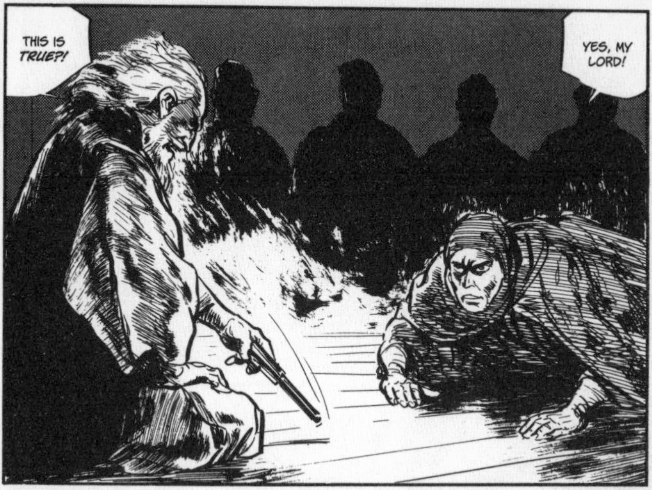
THIS IS *TRUE?!*
YES, MY LORD!
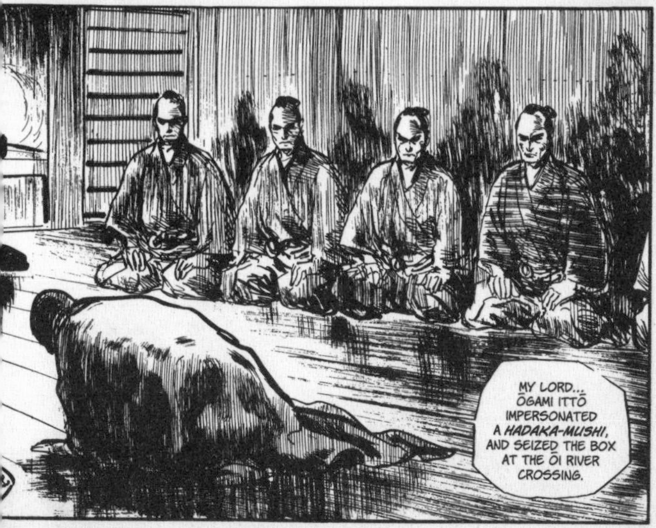
MY LORD... ŌGAMI ITTŌ IMPERSONATED A *HADAKA-MUSHI*, AND SEIZED THE BOX AT THE ŌI RIVER CROSSING.

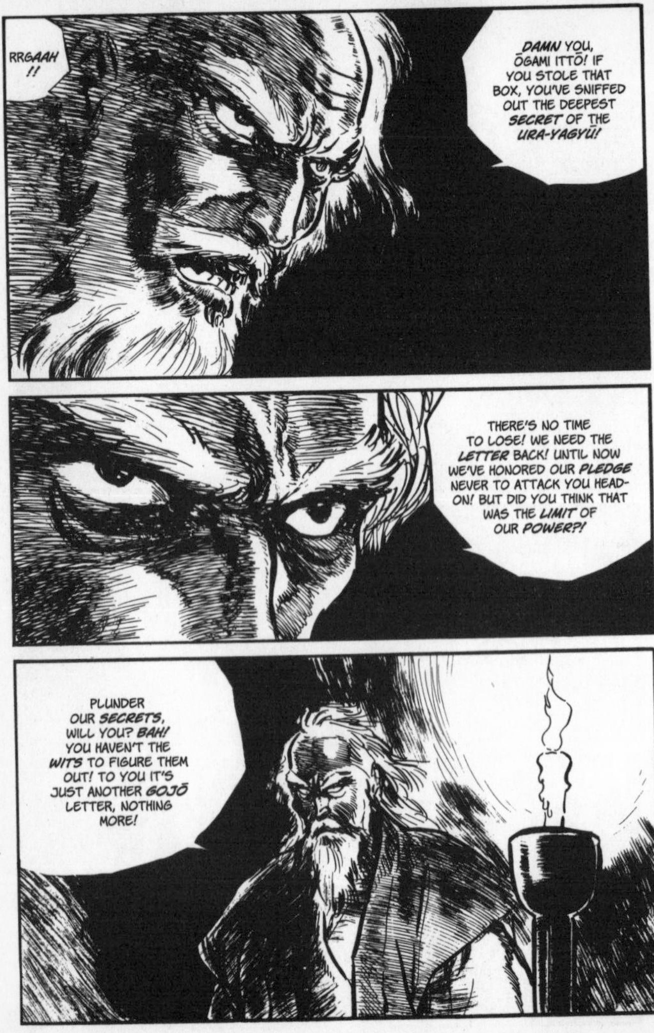
RRGAAH !!
DAMN YOU, ŌGAMI ITTŌ! IF YOU STOLE THAT BOX, YOU'VE SNIFFED OUT THE DEEPEST SECRET OF THE URA-YAGYŪ!
THERE'S NO TIME TO LOSE! WE NEED THE LETTER BACK! UNTIL NOW WE'VE HONORED OUR PLEDGE NEVER TO ATTACK YOU HEAD-ON! BUT DID YOU THINK THAT WAS THE LIMIT OF OUR POWER?!
PLUNDER OUR SECRETS, WILL YOU? BAH! YOU HAVEN'T THE WITS TO FIGURE THEM OUT! TO YOU IT'S JUST ANOTHER GOJŌ LETTER, NOTHING MORE!

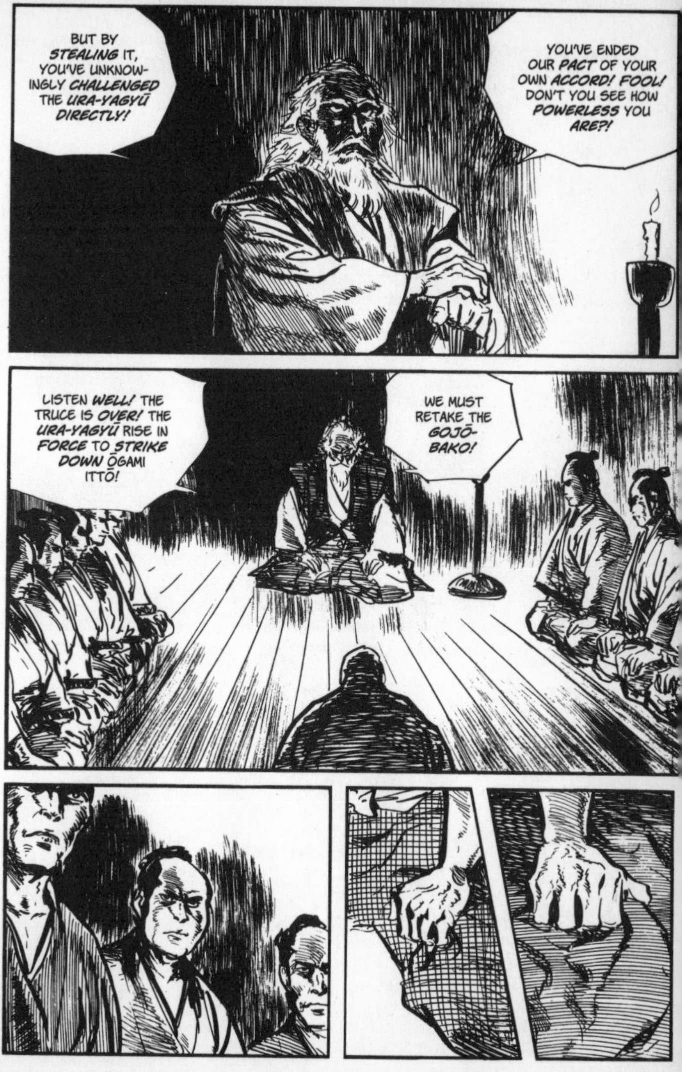
BUT BY STEALING IT, YOU'VE UNKNOWINGLY CHALLENGED THE URA-YAGYŪ DIRECTLY!
YOU'VE ENDED OUR PACT OF YOUR OWN ACCORD! FOOL! DON'T YOU SEE HOW POWERLESS YOU ARE?!
LISTEN WELL! THE TRUCE IS OVER! THE URA-YAGYŪ RISE IN FORCE TO STRIKE DOWN ŌGAMI ITTŌ!
WE MUST RETAKE THE GOJŌ-BAKO!

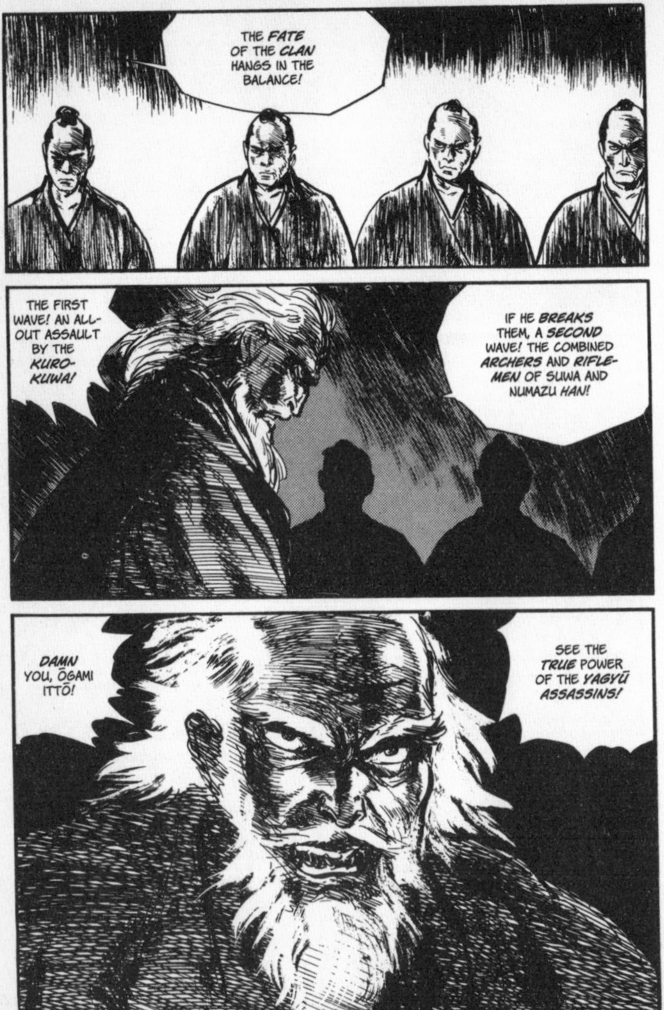
THE *FATE* OF THE *CLAN* HANGS IN THE BALANCE!
THE FIRST WAVE! AN ALL-OUT ASSAULT BY THE *KURO-KUWA!*
IF HE *BREAKS* THEM, A *SECOND* WAVE! THE COMBINED *ARCHERS* AND *RIFLE-MEN* OF SUWA AND NUMAZU *HAN!*
DAMN YOU, ŌGAMI ITTŌ!
SEE THE *TRUE* POWER OF THE *YAGYŪ ASSASSINS!*

LONE WOLF AND CUB BOOK NINE: THE END
TO BE CONTINUED

GLOSSARY

ashigara
A lightly armed foot soldier, one of the lowest ranks of the samurai caste.

bu
A small coin, worth 1/4th of a *ryō*.

buke
A samurai household.

bushi
A samurai. A member of the warrior class.

bushidō
The way of the warrior.

daikansho
The office of the *daikan*, the primary local representative of the shōgunate in territories outside of Edo. The *daikan* and his staff collected taxes owed to Edo and oversaw public works, agriculture, and other projects administered by the central government.

daimyō
A feudal lord.

Edo
The capital of medieval Japan and the seat of the shōgunate. The site of modern-day Tokyo.

han
A feudal domain.

hanshi
Samurai in the service of a *han*.

honorifics
Japan is a class and status society, and proper forms of address are critical. Common markers of respect are the prefixes *o* and *go*, and a wide range of suffixes. Some of the suffixes you will encounter in *Lone Wolf and Cub*:
chan – for children, young women, and close friends
dono – archaic; used for higher-ranked or highly respected figures
sama – used for superiors
san – the most common, used among equals and near-equals
sensei – used for teachers, masters, respected entertainers, and politicians

jōdai
Castle warden. The ranking *han* official in charge of a *daimyō*'s castle when the *daimyō* was spending his obligatory years in Edo.

kōgi kaishakunin
The shōgun's own second, who performed executions ordered by the shōgun.

koku
A bale of rice. The traditional measure of a *han*'s wealth, a measure of its agricultural land and productivity.

meifumadō
The Buddhist Hell. The way of demons and damnation.

o-niwaban
A ninja. Literally, "one in the garden." Ninja had their heyday in the time of

warring states before the rise of the Tokugawa clan. Originally mercenaries serving different warlords, by the Edo period they were in the service of the central government. The most famous were the ninja of Iga and Kaga, north of Kyoto. The Kurokuwa that appear in *Lone Wolf and Cub* were officially the laborers and manual workers in Edo Castle. Whether they truly served as a secret spy corps is lost in history.

rendai

Platforms used for carrying travelers across rivers. Named for their resemblance to the *rendai* (lotus platform) altar in Buddhist temples.

rōjū

Senior councilors. The inner circle of councilors directly advising the shōgun. The *rōjū* were the ultimate advisory body to the Tokugawa shōgunate's national government.

rōnin

A masterless samurai. Literally, "one adrift on the waves." Members of the samurai caste who have lost their masters through the dissolution of *han*, expulsion for misbehavior, or other reasons. Prohibited from working as farmers or merchants under the strict Confucian caste system imposed by the Tokugawa shōgunate, many impoverished *rōnin* became "hired guns" for whom the code of the samurai was nothing but empty words.

ryū

Often translated as "school." The many variations of swordsmanship and other martial arts were passed down from generation to generation to the offspring of the originator of the technique or set of techniques, and to any *deshi* students that sought to learn from the master.

The largest schools had their own *dōjō* training centers and scores of students. An effective swordsman had to study the different techniques of the various schools to know how to block them in combat. Many *ryū* also had a set of special, secret techniques that were only taught to school initiates.

sankin kōtai

The Tokugawa required that all *daimyō* spend every other year in Edo, with family members remaining behind when they returned to their *han*. This practice increased Edo's control over the *daimyō*, both political and fiscal, since the cost of maintaining two separate households and traveling to and from the capital placed a huge strain on *han* finances.

sengoku

Warring states. For two centuries between the old central rule in Kyoto and the rise of Oda Nobunaga (1534-1582), the first unifier of Japan, the country was in a state of anarchy, riven by constant civil war between rival warlords.

shaku

10 *sun*, approximately 30 centimeters.

shinzo

The young wife of another man.

sun

Approximately 3 centimeters.

yakuza

Japan's criminal syndicates. In the Edo period, *yakuza* were a common part of the landscape, running houses of gambling and prostitution. As long as they did not overstep their bounds, they were tolerated by the authorities, a tradition little changed in modern Japan.